ENGLISH CHANNEL

P9-BAT-391

CALAIS
BOULOGNE

AMIENS

ROUEN
CAEN
PARIS
RHEIMS
NORMANDY
FALAISE
VEXIN

BRITTANY
RENNES
MAINE
LE MANS
SENS
ORLEANS

NANTES
ANJOU
TOURS
ANGERS
TOURAINE
BLOIS

POITIERS
BOURGES

POITOU
FRANCE
NEVER

LA MARCHE
LIMOGES
AUVERGNE

AQUITAINE
PERIGORD

BORDEAUX

GASCONY

TOULOUSE

NAVARRE

HARTM'N

ARAGON

MY LIFE FOR MY SHEEP

Also by Alfred Duggan

KNIGHT WITH ARMOUR

CONSCIENCE OF THE KING

THE LITTLE EMPERORS

THE LADY FOR RANSOM

LEOPARDS AND LILIES

MY LIFE
FOR MY SHEEP

BY ALFRED DUGGAN

*As the Father knoweth me and I know the Father;
and I lay down my life for my sheep.* —JOHN 10

Coward-McCann, Inc. New York

COPYRIGHT © 1955 BY ALFRED DUGGAN

All rights reserved. This book, or parts thereof, must
not be reproduced in any form without permission.

Library of Congress Catalog Card
Number: 55-10305

MANUFACTURED IN THE UNITED STATES OF AMERICA

Contents

Contents

Note on the Succession to the Crown of England

IN THE Middle Ages the succession to the English crown was neither hereditary nor elective; conquest, descent, and the assent of the magnates, or feudal lords, were all elements in the royal title. For a century before this story opens the crown had usually been seized by armed force, as follows:

In 1041 the Danish dynasty was overthrown and Edward the Confessor was proclaimed King. He was a son of the Saxon King Ethelred the Unready, who had been overthrown by the Danish King Canute.

In 1066 King Edward died childless, bequeathing the crown to his great-nephew William, Duke of Normandy. Earl Harold, King Edward's brother-in-law, seized the throne and defeated a Danish claimant; but in the same year Duke William killed him in battle. William wanted to rule as King Edward's heir, but the Saxon nobility constantly rebelled, and by the end of his reign they had been replaced by a Norman aristocracy.

In 1087 William I was succeeded by his second son, William Rufus, though his eldest son, Robert, Duke of Normandy, fought unsuccessfully for the crown.

In 1100 the childless William II was succeeded by his younger brother Henry. Robert of Normandy again fought for his inheritance, was beaten, and imprisoned for life.

In 1135 Henry I died, leaving no son; but his magnates had promised to crown his daughter Matilda, widow of the Emperor Henry and wife of the Count of Anjou. The magnates, unwilling to be ruled by a woman, broke their oath and crowned Stephen, Count of Blois, son of a daughter of William I. For years Matilda fought for her rights, without success.

In 1154 Stephen died. Though he left a son the magnates offered the crown to Henry, Count of Anjou, son of Matilda by her second marriage. As grandson of Henry I he had an hereditary claim, though the claim of his mother must be better while she lived. Nevertheless, Henry II thought of himself as an hereditary king, and tried to introduce an hereditary succession by crowning his eldest son in his own lifetime. Henry the Young King died before his father, and in 1189 Henry II was succeeded by his eldest surviving son, Richard, the first rightful heir to succeed to the crown of England.

Yet when Richard I died in 1199 he was succeeded, not by the rightful heir Arthur of Brittany, son of his next brother, but by John, his youngest brother.

The crown of England continued to descend in this haphazard fashion until the eighteenth century, when the Act of Settlement fixed the succession in its present regular form.

MY LIFE FOR MY SHEEP

CHAPTER I

Off to School

ON SUCH a day everything should have looked different. It was disappointing that the whole of London seemed absorbed in its own affairs, though of course Cheapside was the busiest street in the city, and September was the busiest season of the year. In September everyone felt rich, with all that food stored for the winter; it was impossible to imagine the short fare of spring, or the real hunger which might follow a bad season. There was plenty to eat, and the men of Middlesex were eager to spend their wealth in the booths of Cheapside. Luckily a number of them wanted sound oxhide, which was good for the family prosperity. But those preoccupied buyers crowding into the shop might have spared a glance for young Thomas peering out of the gable window of the chamber above.

Young Thomas was alone in the little chamber, which in itself marked the day as something special; for the whole family lived in the hall, and only climbed to the chamber for sleeping.

3

To be alone was even more extraordinary than to be in the sleeping quarters after sunrise. Thomas tried to recall the last time he had been indoors and alone; but he could not.

The remarkable solitude must not be wasted. Here was a crisis in his life, and he was lucky to have this chance to think undisturbed. To begin with, he must renew his good resolutions. He would mind his book and give value for his father's money, spent so freely to get him a good education. That seemed in prospect rather a depressing plan, but when it came to the point it would probably turn out pleasantly enough; the alphabet had lately begun to make sense, and even reading long words could not be too difficult; the priest at St. Mary Colechurch opposite, who had baptized him and taught him his catechism, managed to blurt out some very long and unfamiliar words at the altar, after peering at his Missal and muttering to himself; and the whole of Cheapside said that the vicar of St. Mary Colechurch was the most foolish clerk in London.

But he must be more than merely a diligent scholar. Among the other boys at the priory school of Merton he must bear himself worthily, for the honor of the family would be in his hands; he must always behave as a freeborn Norman. That was important. The foreigners of Surrey were inclined to take it for granted that a Londoner must be English; already, sixty years after the Conquest, men forgot that the conquering army had contained decent middle-class spearmen and archers as well as proud knights. He had learned from his father the family legend: that his great-grandfather had fought at Hastings among the Duke's own foot soldiers. He got nothing from the victory save a silver buckle from the belt of a dead Englishman, and presently went home to help with the plowing. Yet that was why, when Grandfather died and Uncle Robert took over the family holding, his father had come to England to seek his fortune, instead of journeying south to Italy where any Norman could so easily win wealth. There was already a family tradition that England owed them a living in return for the exertions of their ancestor.

Thus he had a position to uphold. The family was not noble; yet they were pure Norman, of the stock of the conquerors. In a sense he, Thomas, was nearer to the great lords whom he saw riding to the crown-wearings at Westminster than to young Edward Godricson next door, who wore leather shoes summer and winter and rode a special pony of his own, with other extravagant signs of wealth; but who rattled off his Hail Marys in throaty English, and could barely understand a dozen words of French.

Above all, when he got to school he must keep his temper. That would be the most difficult task. He was tall and strong, and had never been beaten by a boy of his own age; but he himself was frightened of the red rage which curtained his eyes when someone hit him hard enough to hurt. There was that day a year ago when a street urchin spat at him; he had picked up a cobblestone and if his mother had not intervened he might have battered the little brute to death. Once the red curtain was down he could not halt his attack; the only remedy was to stifle his anger before it had mastered his mind. *He must keep his temper,* or he would perpetrate some assault that would get him dismissed with ignominy from the monastery. He made up his mind firmly, at the same time asking Our Lady to help him in keeping his resolution; this last he did almost without conscious thought, because he had already formed the habit of asking Our Lady for anything he desired.

In the hall below Goodman Gilbert looked round for his saddlebag. It hung on a peg, already packed with his nightgear, as though for one of the familiar journeys he undertook to buy hides for his drysalting. But this was a special journey, and he seemed to be taking it too much as a matter of course. He ought to prove that he was treating the occasion with the importance it deserved, by discussing it once more with his wife.

"The horse is ready, Rose," he called into the gloom of the inner end of the hall. "Help me to bar the main door. You had better shut the shop while I am away, though if anyone comes with a good offer of course you may use your own judgment. Is that clear? I shall be back tomorrow night."

He spoke in the pure French of Normandy, without a trace of English accent, and Rose answered in the same tongue.

"I shan't deal with strangers. If I hear of a good bargain I shall consult Goodman Osbert. Mind you see the children's dormitory at the Priory, and if you get a chance put your head in the kitchen. Men without women are always untidy, so don't bother if it looks a mess; but it must smell sweet. And don't leave without talking to the schoolmaster."

"That I won't, I promise you. Our Thomas needs a bit of explaining. I've thought it out carefully, and this is what I'll say. First I'll tell them how quick he is, and how hard he works. That's true, and they'll be pleased to hear it. Then I'll warn them of his pride, for he's pigheaded enough to mope to death if they insult him. And I'll tell them to beware of his rage, though I don't see how he can get into a fight in a well-ordered Priory. They won't like that so much, but they must be used to dealing with human wickedness. Even the children of the cloister, vowed to God as soon as they are born, must come into the community with their ordinary share of sin."

"That's all right as far as it goes, but you have forgotten half the things we agreed on. Make them understand that he has outgrown his strength, and that he feels the cold more than most. They must give him plenty to eat; proper nourishing food, not their messes of cabbage and beans. Try to arrange extra blankets for his bed, and leave a little money to buy him extra wine and meat if he looks peaky. But the great thing is to make them realize that he doesn't want to be a monk, and that we

don't want him to be one either. That won't be easy to explain
without seeming rude, but you must do it. He's a good boy,
who says his prayers and tries to keep the Commandments; but
he is not cut out for the life of religion. One day he'll make an
honest merchant, or perhaps a clever lawyer. Let him take
vows, and he'll kill himself trying to keep them, fighting against
his inclination. He is so stubborn that he must never undertake
anything too hard for him."

"You have it all planned, my darling Rose. Do you think we
are planning too thoroughly? It's not too late to keep him at
home and train him to take over the drysalting when I am
gone."

"We have had this out, dear," said Rose, with the appealing
but perfunctory smile of a loving and well-loved wife who
knows she can get her way in all important matters. She had
been a pretty girl, and was still very pleasant to look at, though
her pink cheeks were beginning to wrinkle; about her was the
comfortable and completely nonsexual charm of the busy
housewife who divides her time between the kitchen and the
church. "We've had this out before, and we agreed that there
is something special about our Thomas. For one thing it's a
miracle that he's in this world at all. He would be dead if Our
Lady had not listened to my prayers."

"Yes, yes, of course," Gilbert muttered roughly. He was a
decent regular churchgoer, but his wife's habit of mentioning
religion on weekdays embarrassed him. "You had a very bad
time, and perhaps when it was over I lost my head. If I had
known he was going to live I would not have run across to St.
Mary's to see him christened at once; and if the vicar had not
been so flustered by my fright he would have been spared that
eccentric name. I hope his schoolfellows don't make fun of it."

"Why should they? It's all bound up with the miracle of his
survival. It was St. Thomas's feast day, and when you were stuck
for a name there was the Missal open on the altar, with Thomas

painted in red and gold. The patron of our son was a great Apostle and Martyr."

"So long as St. Thomas doesn't make him a martyr I suppose it's all right. Yet our Thomas must have something special about him, when you think of his birth. The girls were no trouble at all."

As he came down the ladder from the chamber young Thomas overheard this last speech. The realization that there was something special about his very existence fortified him for the coming adventure, as it had fortified him in other crises of his short life; he had known the exciting story of his difficult birth and hurried baptism since he was old enough to talk. By all human probability he should have been dead, in the painless but unecstatic Limbo of unbaptized infants; from that fate Our Lady and St. Thomas had saved him, and he must thank them every time he said his prayers. It was natural for him to think he had survived because some great destiny was in store for him.

At last the great moment arrived. Thomas crossed the yard to the kitchen to kiss his two baby sisters. Then his mother caught him up and hugged him. His eyes filled with tears, but he kept his mouth steady; he was feeling so well that her anxious reminders about eating good food and wrapping up warmly seemed unnecessary, and surely in a priory they would make him say his prayers even if he forgot to do it of his own accord.

Soon regrets were banished in the novel excitement of riding pillion. Hitherto when he had gone farther than his baby legs could carry him he had been placed on the saddlebow, like a piece of baggage. Grown ladies and invalids rode pillion, and it was the next best thing to having Snowball all to himself. He was well away from the rasping mane and hard neck which had sometimes made his nose bleed, and though his father's broad back blocked the view in front he could see the bustle of the streets beside him.

Cheapside and London Bridge were familiar, though it was delightful to wave to old friends from such an eminence. But once through the ramparts at Southwark they were in open country, and there was much to interest a little Cockney. The road was busy with single travelers, and father and son rode without companions; for this was September 1126, the Twenty-sixth year of King Henry the Lion of Justice, and never had England enjoyed such firm peace.

They dined by the roadside and came to Merton in time for supper. When the Prior received them in the strangers' parlor Thomas sat quietly in a corner, hearing himself discussed as though in his absence; but an only son is used to that.

He heard his father rehearsing the instructions about his health that his mother had commanded; they were so familiar that he hardly listened. But when the Prior answered he was all attention. The Prior was a kindly old man, with a tired but patient expression.

"Very well, Goodman Gilbert," he said with finality, as one used to cutting short the explanations of loving parents, "we shall teach your son reading and writing, and the simple rules of numbers. We shall not teach him Divinity beyond the catechism that every Christian should know, and we shall not influence him to choose the life of the cloister. Though if you don't want him to be a monk you run some risk in sending him here at all. The life of religion, seen at close quarters, is more attractive than you laymen understand."

"We won't stand in the way of a real vocation, Father Prior. But my wife and I want our only son to be a clever merchant or a learned lawyer, living in the world. That's why I was so careful to explain that he is not a child of the cloister, vowed to God from his birth."

"Quite so. You have been generous with your money, and we shall carry out our side of the bargain. We shall not make a monk of him. I suppose you won't mind if he wears the cowl while he is here? That is the custom in English monasteries, as you may know, and it does not commit him for the future. It solves the problem of what clothes are fitting to wear in the cloister. Some parents have very bizarre ideas on that subject."

As Gilbert nodded assent the Prior produced a sheet of parchment from his bosom. "There is one other thing. In case of emergency would a messenger who inquired in London for Goodman Gilbert the drysalter find you easily?"

"Well, no, perhaps not. These English are apt to think every Norman is called either William or Robert, and if they know my name half of them pronounce it Willibrod. I am not grand enough to be Gilbert of London or even Gilbert of Cheapside, and people have forgotten that once I was Gilbert of Rouen. I have a nickname, Gilbert Becket. That was my name back at Thierceville in Normandy, because my father's holding lay beside the brook. Becket of Cheapside would be known even to Englishmen who cannot say Gilbert."

The Prior listened with some amusement. He guessed that this burgess dearly longed to be known as Gilbert of London, and felt ashamed of the plebeian nickname which implied that the only notable thing about him was that once he had lived beside a brook.

"Then you will go down on my list as Goodman Gilbert Becket of London. I hope we never need to send you a message, or if we do that it is only good news. That is all. Your son may go home for a few days at Christmas and Easter, and the long holiday comes at harvest time. Now I shall leave you to say good-bye in private. Then Thomas must go to the boys' dormitory to be fitted for his cowl."

Thomas took an affectionate and respectful leave of his father. His education had been arranged for him, without inquiry into his own wishes; perhaps he would have preferred to be a monk, in a not too strict community where there was plenty of time for reading. If his opinion had been asked he might have suggested it; but as it had not been asked he did what was expected of him.

He found Merton a pleasant place. The Priory was not really a monastery, though that was what everyone called it; it was a house of Augustinian canons, specializing in the education of children who would live in the world; for Augustinians, though they are very nearly monks, like to have some secular purpose besides prayer and contemplation.

In themselves, the lessons were utterly dull; endless learning by heart of conjugations and declensions, or painstaking rendering word by word of snippets of Latin into French. The boys were there to learn Latin grammar, and no one ever taught them anything else. Strictly speaking, even their Latin was not taught to them; each evening they were given a task to learn by rote, and a canon heard them repeat it in the morning, beating any pupil who was not word-perfect.

But Thomas quickly began to see the rewards of learning. By the end of October he understood some phrases of the Psalms, which he heard endlessly repeated in the daily office. Once he could read Latin all knowledge would be open to him, all history, all philosophy, every tale of travel, satire, or adventure; once he could speak it he might converse with any fellow Christian anywhere, except ignorant peasants and the queer schismatic Greeks, from Jerusalem to Corunna, from Sicily to Norway; if he spoke it well and fluently he might plead in any law court which acknowledged Pope or Emperor. Such a prize was worth a little exertion in the winning.

Discipline was strict and pettifogging. The boys were hardly ever free to amuse themselves, and for the greater part of the day they must keep silence. Of course there were no games.

But Thomas had no difficulty in obeying the strict regulations. He was in the habit of doing as he was told, and after his work he had no energy for play. He was shooting up to a remarkable tallness, at the same time getting thinner and more purple in the hands, feet, and ears; he was always cold, though he wore the thickest cowl he could get hold of. That cowl helped him to behave; dressed as a monk he felt that he ought to act as a monk, and he always did what was expected of him.

Sometimes his thoughts turned to his mother and sisters, hardly ever to his father. As a rule he was too busy to be homesick. After he had learned to read easily, a trick that came suddenly when he had been at school a few weeks, his masters praised his diligence; and praise was a spur that would always keep him hard at work. The next art to be mastered was writing, but he found that more difficult. His long bony arms could not control the immense red hands dangling at their ends, and his fingers were usually thickened by chilblains. Prior Robert was disappointed, but obviously it was not the boy's fault; though he could write a private letter he would never be able to compose a beautiful Missal.

Throughout his time at Merton he shared a desk with the same companion, who also slept beside him and sat next to him in chapel. Robert was a self-possessed young Norman from London, sharing his own background; but he looked forward to a very different future. His parents had vowed him to God before he was born, and he himself would take the vows of an Augustinian as soon as he was old enough. He seemed well suited to the monastic life, without any hankering for the world outside; and he was even more studious and law-abiding than Thomas. He showed occasional traces of original thought, which Thomas never did; Robert would advance his own reasons for believing some point of theology, or his own justification for some decision of daily conduct; while Thomas reproduced accurately and exactly what his teachers had told him. They were about the same age, though Robert had been longer in the cloister. They did not exactly love one another, but each was thoroughly at ease when the other was beside him, since each knew every recess in the other's mind.

Yet underneath his scholarly exterior Thomas was perpetually troubled by the hot temper which had made his parents doubt his fitness for the school. When he made a mistake, or did not know the right answer, he accepted correction without resentment; but when he thought he was right, and was told he was wrong, he had to sit still, thinking hard about the gentle kindness of Our Lady, before he could bring himself to acknowledge his fault. Only once did a schoolfellow deliberately quarrel with him, the son of a small rustic freeholder who delighted to sneer at the vulgar money-grubbing burgesses of London. Thomas clenched his fists, standing breast to breast with his tormentor; then he swung away, to pass the rest of the recreation hour kneeling in the chapel. But he had looked so stark that no one tried to quarrel with him again.

For besides Latin grammar one other thing was taught at Merton. Everyone there, from the Prior to the youngest pupil, was continually exercising self-control, in chapel, in the refectory, in the dormitory, at lessons in the cloister; a grave carriage and a friendly but remote smile were formally demanded during every waking hour.

When Thomas came home for Christmas his parents noted the change in him. Their son, once so hot-tempered and quick to change his moods, now sat smiling quietly through any annoyance. Rose knew that within himself he was as quick to anger as he had ever been, and admired his self-possession. Gilbert merely remarked that those canons were quick workers; they had changed the nature of young Thomas in less than half a year.

*   *   *

The following July, when he rode home behind a groom (for his father had guests and could not come to fetch him), he found a greater change awaiting him. The house itself looked different, for the stable was full of horses, and the yard full of swaggering sergeants in leather jacks girt with great swords. Rose ran to greet him, but his father remained in the hall, perched on a stool while he talked to someone who sat in the only chair, which should have been the throne of the master of the house. As his son entered he hardly looked up.

"This is the boy," he said in a deferential tone. "If you think him worthy of the honor he could ride with you tomorrow. Thomas, come here and kneel before the lord Richer de l'Aigle, who has offered to rear you in courteous manners at his castle of Pevensey."

"It was the least I could offer, Goodman Gilbert," the stranger answered graciously. "When I came to deal with those penny-pinching clerks at the Exchequer your advice was invaluable."

"It was nothing, my lord," Gilbert went on, in a subservient whine which Thomas thought unpleasant. "If I didn't know my way about the Exchequer I should soon owe the King more than I possess. Besides," and Thomas was pleased to see his back straighten, "in this strange land we Normans must stick together."

Thomas knelt before the lord Richer, as he had been taught to kneel before the Prior of Merton. "Welcome to my father's hall," he said carefully and distinctly, for he genuinely enjoyed ceremonious behavior. "If my father desires me to serve you I shall serve you loyally—and I have never been inside a great castle."

"You are not to serve me," Richer answered. "It would be poor repayment for your father's kindness to make his only son my vassal. No, the arrangement is quite different. If it pleases you, you shall come with me to Pevensey for the summer, until it is time for you to return to Merton. You shall learn to ride, and fly a hawk, and play chess, and carve at table, with the sons of my neighbors who are learning these things in my castle."

Thomas's heart gave a bound. He had been aware of social distinctions since he was old enough to go out into the crowded streets of London. The son of a burgess, he was being offered the training of a gentleman. He rose to his feet and bowed low, bending from the waist at right angles as when he served Mass at Merton.

"You approve, I see," said the lord Richer with a smile. "We may as well begin at once, with your bow. Don't bob at me as though I were the Crucifix on the High Altar. Tuck in your stomach, bend your backbone, and bring forward your shoulders so that I see the top of your head. Like this." Rising, he bowed gracefully and deferentially to young Thomas. As he resumed his seat he spoke once more to Gilbert.

"The boy speaks the French of Normandy, so the rest should come easily. If his tongue had been the horrible half-English jargon you hear in Cheapside my work would have been impossible. It is amazing to see how our language has altered in a mere sixty years."

"We are true Normans," said Gilbert proudly. "My children were born here in London; but my wife is from Caen, and I myself was born in Thierceville and reared in Rouen. Thomas has no taint of the conquered English. He is Norman through and through."

Thomas meanwhile was inspecting his new lord, and approving what he saw. The lord Richer was young, not more than twenty-five; in figure he was tall and spare, with the broad shoulders and slim waist of a warrior; his eyes and hair were dark, and he had inherited the fierce hooked nose which had given his family its surname. But he had a merry smile, and the wrinkles round his eyes, which spoke of much staring into the sun, formed an encouraging pattern. His clothes were such as a great man should wear on an unimportant occasion: a tunic and hood of excellent blue cloth over a fine linen shirt; hose in the natural gray of the wool, cross-gartered in scarlet leather to match scarlet leather shoes bearing burnished spurs. His mantle, also of plain blue cloth, was fastened on the right shoulder with a ruby brooch, and his scarlet leather belt ended in a buckle of scarlet enamel. His knightly broadsword, in its red leather scabbard fastened to a red leather baldric, was at present propped against the chair.

Noting the boy's curious gaze on his dress, Richer took up the subject. "At Merton I suppose you wear the cowl. That outfit must be what you took there a year ago. It's too small for you, and not quite what you should wear in a castle. Under my roof you may wear my livery; in fact you should, if you are to serve as a page. No, Gilbert, I insist. Let me do the thing handsomely. We shall open the bales after supper, and your mother shall choose something that fits you."

After supper Rose and the lord Richer's steward conferred together for what seemed like hours, while he stood like a lay figure before them, clad only in his shirt. At Pevensey there were several pages, so the Michaelmas livery included plenty of clothes to fit a boy in his ninth year. He was given a tunic of fine thin cloth for great occasions, thicker tunics for riding, thin hose and padded riding-hose, soft shoes covering the instep lest the stirrup chafe him, a belt and cross-garters of untanned leather; finally the steward handed him a plain steel dagger, its bone hilt carved into the eagle head of the de l'Aigles. Rose did not want him to take it, protesting that a clerk should not carry arms; but Thomas was thrilled. He had never before worn steel. His only regret was that since the hilt had no guard it was impossible to see the knife as a miniature of the cross-hilted knightly sword.

As soon as the bundles were refastened the pack train and

escort set out for Sussex. They would travel through the night to reach Pevensey after one halt. But the lord Richer and his personal following would start in the morning; the journey was only sixty miles, and warriors could accomplish it in one day.

Thomas might no longer sleep in the chamber with his parents and sisters; he had grown too old, and a part of his childhood was gone forever. There was a pallet for him at the back of the hall, where also slept the lord Richer and his companions. But since Thomas went to bed while his elders still sat over their wine Rose took this rare opportunity for a private talk with him.

"I am sure you are disappointed not to spend your holiday with us," she began, "but your father could not miss this lucky chance. We have been useful to the lord Richer in his dealings with the Exchequer. He's a good honest man, for all that he's a great lord, and I could see that he was looking for some way to repay us. He is too courteous to offer money to his host, and he can't put much business in our way. I made him think of this plan, by talking of your return and lamenting the lack of room in this house. Don't waste the opportunity. When you leave Merton you will be a learned clerk, able to make your own way in the world. There is no position too high for you, if you use the wits God gave you. But often one thing holds back the cleverest clerks. Do you know what it is?"

"Do you mean that they don't know how to fight? Is that what I shall learn from the lord Richer?"

"No, my darling. Clever clerks need not fight, and I hope fighting never comes your way. But some learned men never get the advancement they deserve because they don't know how to behave in the company of the great. The lord Richer will teach you how knights live in castles, and how to be courteous to noble ladies. He will also teach you to ride a war horse and to joust, and I see that is what you wish to learn from him. But it is more important that you learn how to carve meat for the high table, how to pass the wine cup, how to eat neatly and quietly, using only two fingers and never splashing the gravy. Learn chess also, if you find someone willing to teach you without betting on the game. Listen attentively to troubadours; don't bother to learn the words of their poems, but you ought to know the stories, about Roland, and Ogier the Dane, and King Arthur who once reigned in this land (though when I was a girl no one had heard of him; if you ask me he is just a modern invention). If you know the stories you can mention them in conversation, and that's one of the marks of a gentleman. Any scullion can quote snippets from the poems, but only the well-born know the whole stories. Then there is hunting, and all the host of queer words the gentry have invented to prove that chasing a deer is more noble than chasing our cat Tib. If the lord Richer offers to take you hunting of course you must jump at it; but even if he doesn't you can pick up a lot by talking with huntsmen and grooms. If you learn all you can, and notice how the people round you behave in their private affairs, your manners will be good enough for any company in the land. And if you ever feel shy and unworthy of your noble companions, remember that you are a true Norman. You had an ancestor at Hastings, which is as much as the greatest of them can boast."

She kissed him good night and left him. In the morning there was such a bustle that he had no chance of further talk with her before he set out.

The ride to Pevensey showed him that he had a lot to learn. When his father visited Merton, only eighteen miles from London, he stayed the night and returned the next day. The lord Richer and his train thought sixty miles a fair day's ride, which showed they were accustomed to a different breed of horse. Thomas was mounted on a quiet hobby, normally the war horse of a hobilar or light-armed sergeant. He could sit on it and control it well enough, chiefly because it had no wish to leave its companions. But he was not accustomed to long hours at a hand-gallop, and before he had gone twenty miles the saddle had chafed him raw.

In the afternoon, as they slowed to a walk, threading one of the muddy tracks of the Weald, the lord Richer called him up to ask a few civil questions about what he was learning at Merton. To Thomas it was the typical conversation of a grown-up man; they always asked you how far you had got in your Latin and whether writing was really as difficult as it looked; and you knew very well that they scarcely listened to your careful answers.

But in fact it was not a random conversation. Richer de l'Aigle had been wondering how to treat this little merchant's brat; on a sudden impulse of kindness he had offered to train him as a gentleman, but the boy might be a clod, incapable of improvement. In that case he would feed him well and give him the run of the mews and the stables; he would enjoy country life and return to his family none the worse. But the child might have more in him than the calculating blood of a dry-salter; any Norman could make a good warrior. If he showed promise it would be interesting to teach him the management of arms, until he had the skill of a knight as well as the learning of a clerk. An educated knight, or a clerk who could use a sword, would be something of a rarity in England.

The lord Richer had noticed his discomfort; his tender knees had been rubbed by the saddle and the jolting gallop had upset his stomach. He was not afraid of his hobby, nor of the big war horses which splashed beside him, and that was all to the good; but he might be so unused to discomfort, and so sorry for himself, that he could not answer politely. Then there would be no point in going further, for the first lesson a warrior must learn is to disregard fatigue and pain.

When he sent the boy back to his place in the little column

the lord Richer had made up his mind. This lad was something out of the ordinary. You could see him pulling himself together, and that was not quite as it should be; for a good knight always looked composed, no matter what strain might be distressing him. But he *had* pulled himself together, and answered the banal questions carefully; he had even managed a smile, when he was not far from being sick in the saddle. He had more than self-control; he had unusual determination. Within him was a warrior; it would be an absorbing task to bring out his latent qualities.

Therefore during the first weeks at Pevensey Thomas was constantly in the company of his lord, and of the two young sons of noblemen whom he was "nourishing." There were three other pages, but they were sons of Richer's vassals, there to make themselves useful in return for board and wages; not to be trained in the art of courteous living, which was the real object of "nourishing" the son of a friend. Thomas had been quick to see the niche into which he was expected to fit, in the elaborate hierarchy of the great castle. He knew that he had won approval, and that the best was open to him; he determined to deserve it.

His elders were impressed by his self-control, though some thought it too marked to be a wholly admirable quality. In the evening after he had spent his first day in the mews Richer discussed him with a neighbor, young Reginald de Braoze, who had ridden over from Bramber to hawk in the marsh.

"Did you notice that boy when the peregrine nipped him in the wrist? Of course it was his own fault, for he had the jesses in a tangle; but he went on hooding the bird without squeezing her any harder. Most lads of that age would have tried to get their own back on the hawk. He has the making of a falconer."

"I saw him," Reginald agreed. "He's a noticeable type, isn't he? With those gawky hands and feet he stands out in any crowd. By the way, he's passing the jug now, and spilling half of it. But that may be nerves. All the same, I wasn't very taken with him. I saw his face when he was bitten, and it didn't look pleasant. Then he glanced quickly at you, and swallowed his feelings with an effort. He didn't harm the hawk, and that's to his credit. But I could fairly see him thinking he was on his best public behavior, under the eye of his host and lord. Obviously he has a fiendish temper, though at present the desire to please is stronger. One day his temper may win, and then there's no telling what he may do. Even that would be better than calculated self-control, putting up with anything to keep on the right side of a benefactor. He may have the making of a falconer; he also has the making of a self-seeking toady."

"He has his way to make in the world. His father is a merchant of London; he was useful to me, and I repay him by training the son. It's a business arrangement, not a friendly favor. He is right to make full use of his opportunity."

"It's your concern, not mine. When he grows up I wouldn't like him as an enemy, but I wouldn't want him as a vassal either. You say he is of merchant stock? Then, depend on it, he'll serve himself and no other, as these merchants always do."

That settled the personality of Thomas to the satisfaction of the high table.

Pevensey was a very big castle, since the outer walls had once enclosed a fortified camp, in the days when Britain was a province of Rome. The stone keep in a corner provided lodging for the lord Richer and his immediate household, but a large population of sergeants, craftsmen, and retainers lived in wooden huts behind the Roman wall. The hall was always filled with a crowd of many social classes, sharply differentiated. Thomas found much to learn, and he was interested in learning it.

At the top of the pyramid, immediately below the lord Richer himself, came the senior officials—warden, constable, butler, and steward—technically men of gentle birth; their wives and daughters were the senior ladies, for Richer was an unmarried orphan. There were always a few knights putting in the annual forty days of castle-guard which was part of their service as vassals of de l'Aigle. These were the gentry, and though there were wide differences of status between them, to a page they were all on the same level, far above him.

Below them, dining also at the high table but in other ways leading a life apart, came the clerks. Master William, who kept my lord's seal, liked to hear himself called the chancellor, though really no one below the rank of count or bishop should have a chancellor of his own; he was undoubtedly head of a group of nearly a dozen educated men, from the powerful and important clerk of the kitchen to the underpaid vicar who gabbled through Sunday Mass in the parish church. They were set apart not because they were ministers of religion (for some of them had only the lowest orders), but because they were celibate; they did not join in the unending wooing, or teasing, of ladies which was the staple form of conversation at the high table. Although they were educated, they were not particularly intelligent; the service of a private lord was a dead-end career, which only the second-rate would choose. Thomas could not help comparing them to the canons of Merton, the only other group of clerks well known to him; they came very poorly out of the comparison, and he seldom thought about them.

The next class comprised those who dined at the first table in the body of the hall, the table where young Thomas passed the wine; because they did not get the best quality and it did not matter if he spilled some. These were the skilled members of the household who were not gentry; but their skills were very various. First came the petty officers of the garrison, preeminent because their trade was arms; they were mostly quick-tempered and stupid. More interesting were the heads of technical departments, the stud groom, the head falconer, the chief huntsman, the farrier, and the armorer; these had risen in the world from lowly beginnings, outdistancing their fellows because they were intelligent. Their conversation would have been interesting if Thomas could have understood it; but it was so full of technical terms that they might have been speaking a foreign language. Most of them were married, but there were no women at the table; their families lived in huts in the outer courtyard, and the men dined by themselves in hall because dinner at their lord's table was an important part of their wages.

At another table sat the common sergeants, crossbows or spearmen. They were men of little account, but even they lived by the sword; so they were far above ordinary servants and laborers who never went to war. They could not be expected to eat with unarmed riffraff; but they drank beer instead of wine, and needed no page to wait on them.

There were two more tables, for the mere servants, male and female; these spoke English, and did not matter.

This was the whole company who dined in the hall of Pevensey castle, rather less than three hundred in all. Cooks and scullions ate in the kitchen, and pages and serving men after the first sitting had finished. The castle sheltered more than four hundred men, a considerable world for young Thomas to find his way in.

His mornings and afternoons were devoted to the stable and the mews. Here he had no duties; he came as the friend and pupil of the lord Richer. But he was compelled to work very hard, for he had much to learn. It was easy to sit on a well-mannered war horse, and he was not at all afraid; yet at first he nearly despaired, for the lord Richer and his head groom seemed to be asking him to do the impossible. He must keep his legs straight, with the toes well out in front; that only needed thought, though it was not the way he had been taught to ride an ambling hackney. It was the things he had to do with his hands which made it so difficult. On his left arm was a leather shield, holding his wrist almost immovable, so that only the tips of his fingers could reach the reins; he could never shorten these, or gather in the slack, because he was forbidden to use his right hand for anything except the management of his lance, at present represented by a slender stick. At the other end of the reins was a bit, of such savage severity that a light accidental jab brought the war horse to a rearing stop; but he must keep a feel of this bit, or the horse would sprawl in his gallop. Just to make his difficult task quite impossible, they put long prick-spurs on his heels; if his feet moved, the horse began to buck.

Every day he sat in the saddle until the horse was tired (no one noticed his own fatigue). Then, if there was time, he visited the line of hooded hawks standing on perches in the mews. Here he had to begin by learning a completely new language; for the anatomical terms for falcons were unlike ordinary French, but it was very disgusting to use them incorrectly. He must handle the savage birds and do complicated things to their heads and wings, putting on hoods sewn with little bells or mending a damaged pinion. Whatever the hawk did to him he must not annoy or vex her, that was the prime law of falconry; and she would be vexed if she sensed he was nervous. For the whole basis of hawking was really a kind of confidence trick: it was impossible to compel a bird in the air to come back to her master; but she must never find this out.

The gentry thought riding and hawking quite easy, and as Thomas continued his training his respect for them increased.

In September, when it was time for him to go back to Merton, he was pressed to return to Pevensey next year. He had learned much that was quite new to him, and he was anxious to continue his training; it was more remarkable that the lord Richer wanted him. It was impossible to find fault with him, since he did exactly as he was told; nor could anyone reproach him for a milksop, since he had thrown himself into his riding and falconry with a passionate determination which disregarded pain and danger. But he made hard work of what should have been enjoyment. One of the principles of aristocratic life is that skill should never deteriorate into effort; a good horseman must not only ride well, he must ride easily. Thomas tried too hard.

At Merton it was the same. Thomas was approved by his teachers because he gave them no trouble; his schoolfellows did not dislike him, but they did not seek his company.

Young Thomas was well aware of this. He was an only son, who did not mix easily with his English neighbors in Cheapside because of his Norman background; at home he had never found an intimate friend, and now at Merton and Pevensey close friendship was still denied to him. That was regrettable, but it could not be helped. The other boys he knew had such mild and tepid desires that they could not share the raging passions in his breast.

His leading passion was, of course, ambition. He did not yet know in which field he would excel, but excel he must. At Merton he saw himself as a great scholar, rewarded with high office in the Church. In that atmosphere learning seemed obviously the highest good. He liked to dream that one day a lean bookworm, his black gown turning green with age, would tap on the arm another shabby student, saying: "There goes Master Thomas. He's thin and ugly and poorly dressed, but he knows more about . . . than any other clerk in Christendom. They wanted to make him a Cardinal, but he can't spare the time from his books."

The trouble about this dream was that he could not fill in the missing word, the subject of his profound researches. He was fascinated by the idea of the great international Republic of Letters. It was wonderful to think that wise men in France and

Italy and Germany and Greece, and even among the infidels of Spain and Asia, were all pondering the Nature and Attributes of God, pooling their knowledge as soon as a new truth was defined; it was even more wonderful to know that any new discovery must be made known in Latin, so that when he had thoroughly mastered the grammar through which he was now hacking his way he would be able to debate the latest theology with a Hungarian or a Pole. He had the quickest brain in the school, and when anything was explained by a teacher he could always follow the explanation. But he could not think of a subject that needed investigation; though when it had been investigated and he was told the result he saw that it had been an obvious line of inquiry.

Perhaps Prior Robert of Merton was right when he said ruefully that young Thomas had a most accurate mind, which lacked any trace of original thought.

His second daydream was one that would come first in the minds of most boys of his age. He would be the best knight in the West, the scourge of the infidels who menaced the Holy City.

One other subject often filled his mind, though it could not be an object of ambition. He genuinely loved God, and the Mother of God. At Merton he was surrounded by men whose whole lives were devoted to God's service, so that was not very surprising. But his was more than the conventional piety of the catechism-class. The idea that God had come down to earth to share the suffering of mankind had captured his imagination; whenever he was hungry or in pain he thought of God's sufferings on the Cross. And whenever he was unusually happy, and on the whole he was often very happy, he thought with gratitude of the Mother of God, who had brought Salvation into the world. He did not aspire to repay this great debt of gratitude, but there were a few simple rules he must keep or he would not get into Heaven; in his monastic school the chief of these commandments seemed that concerning chastity. Like all his fellows, he had known the machinery of generation since he was old enough to notice the difference between a bull and a cow; before he had felt the first stirrings of puberty he had resolved that he would be chaste until he died.

In his daydreams he never *did* anything. His deeds were already performed, and he was receiving the admiration of the crowd because he behaved as was expected of a scholar or a knight.

For six years he continued his studies at Merton, spending the summer holidays at Pevensey; so that he only visited Cheapside for the short vacations at Christmas and Easter. At each visit he was conscious of changes in his home. Every year his father did less business; not because he was a failure as a drysalter, but because he did not want to make more money; he had enough to live on, in a style suitable to his rank, and he was gradually buying houses in the city with his savings; soon he would be able to retire altogether, to live on the rent of his property. That was not so honorable as holding land by knight-service, but it was better than earning bread by buying and selling, notoriously a way of life tempting to sharp practice.

His sisters were no longer charming babies to be played with and cooed over: the elder, Margaret, was betrothed to the son of a prosperous tanner; Mary, the younger, lodged with the nuns of Barking in Essex, and it had already been decided that she should enter that wealthy and fashionable community as soon as she was old enough to take her vows.

He had never been particularly close to his father, and now his sisters were withdrawn from intimate companionship. That left only his mother. To her he was still baby Thomas, the clever but self-willed child who must be shielded from the consequences of his own quick temper. She loved him dearly, but she could not follow his thoughts. He was, in practice, alone in the world.

One wise man studied him closely, and took an interest in his future. In the summer of 1133, when Thomas was in his fifteenth year, Prior Robert of Merton sent for Goodman Gilbert. In the parlor, when they were alone, he came straight to the point.

"I have been thinking about your son, and I have made up my mind. He must either leave Merton soon or stay for the rest of his life. It is for you, his father, to decide. In body he is almost a man, and his mind also is formed. An original idea has never entered his head, and I don't suppose one ever will; but he is quick and accurate and painstaking, and we have taught him all the secular learning he can find in a convent of canons. I gather you don't want him at home until he is ready to start work. But all the other boys follow his lead. They don't like him, but the force of his character compels them. A layman of such influence is out of place in a monastery. He always obeys a lawful command, and if you order him to take vows he can join our community. He won't be a holy monk, but he will never be scandalous, and his brain will be useful to the house. But bear in mind that he has never expressed a desire for the life of religion. I hate to see a man take vows against his inclination, even if he keeps them afterward. I advise you to take him away. In any case he is too mature, and too forceful, to stay on as a lay scholar."

Gilbert was taken aback by this sudden call for a decision.

"It's too late to apprentice him, Father Prior. I took it for granted that he could stay here until he got some clerk's post in the lord Richer's establishment at Pevensey. They are bound to offer him something one day. It seems a pity to waste his learning, but I suppose he must keep accounts for some rich merchant."

"You need not waste his learning. He's not cut out for religion, but he will make a good clerk, say a lawyer. There are good grammar schools in London; let him live at home and study at one of them for a year or so. Then, if he still shows promise, you could send him to some greater school oversea where he can learn canon law."

"Very well, Father Prior. It shall be as you advise. I won't press him to be a monk against his inclination. Perhaps the priesthood is the career for him."

"I doubt it. He thinks too much of his repute in this world. Subdeacon and lawyer is nearer his mark. But he is intelligent, and his conduct will never disgrace you."

So it was arranged. As usual, Thomas was not consulted; he was merely informed that next September he would be entering the grammar school conducted by the canons of St. Paul's Cathedral; and that this summer would be his last holiday at Pevensey.

He went there fiercely determined to make the most of his last chance of learning the arts of chivalry. He astonished his companions by his daring and energy when they jousted with padded lances in the lists; he could not always stop his horse, but certainly he could urge it to the charge.

He also threw himself into the business of falconry, and that brought him into mortal danger for the first time in his life.

When the lord Richer rode out with falcons and spaniels on the wide expanse of Pevensey Level, Thomas was merely an onlooker in the background, unless he was permitted to make himself useful as a cadger, bearing the wooden cadge on which falcons traveled. But he was allowed a sparrowhawk to tame himself, for those short-winged "birds of the bush" were not nearly so valuable as the graceful "birds of the tower," which mounted into the sky before stooping on a quarry flushed by the spaniels; sparrowhawks chased their prey from behind, and so were less interesting to the watching sportsman.

In one way birds of the bush might afford more excitement. While a falcon could be watched from any open space, even by a dismounted man, Thomas must ride after his hawk. She would follow her chosen prey wherever it flew, and when she killed she would loiter to eat it unless he had kept her in sight. The gallop through thick bush beside a stream could be as exciting as hunting a stag.

On one August afternoon Thomas rode out alone on a spirited hobby, hawk on fist. He considered his bird tamed, and was determined to lure her back from her kill without help from the astringer who had shown him how to educate her. Near the millstream he put up a teal, and cast off his hawk. But he was not quite quick enough, the quarry had a good start, and he settled down to ride in pursuit.

The day was warm, but the bushes were in full leaf, and he pulled forward his hood to protect his face from scratches. He crouched on the neck of his little horse, the reins loose, peeping up to keep his hawk in sight and leaving his mount to pick the way. As he galloped downstream he heard, above the patter of hoofs, the clacking of the mill wheel. The teal heard also, and veered away from the sound; his hawk cut a corner and overtook to kill. Thomas saw her standing on her prey, just below the mill but on the far side of the stream.

There was only one thought in his mind: this was the first time he had flown a hawk by himself, and he must lure her before she was lost. The stream was too wide to jump and too deep to ford, but the millrace was spanned by a little plank bridge. A sportsman won praise by riding over difficult places. In two strides he would be over, before he had time to be frightened. With a wrench at the bit he set his horse straight at the bridge, and again dropped the reins on his neck.

Then things began to happen all at once. Hoofs slipped on the wet planking, and the horse, striving to keep its feet, gave a wriggle of its backbone more disconcerting than any buck. As Thomas shot out of the saddle he was conscious of a single agonizing thought: the hobby had his feet under him again, and would cross the stream safely; he, Thomas, had "dismounted of his own free will," as the grooms said caustically when an unpracticed jouster lay on the ground with his charger standing over him. As a horseman he was disgraced, and at Pevensey horsemanship counted for more than anything else in the world.

A moment later panic displaced shame. He was borne along by the current, unable even to call for help; for his hood, twisted in the water, now completely covered his face. He could hear the clack of the wheel, though he could not see when he would reach it to be flogged to pieces by the great baulks of timber. In a few seconds he would be dead.

When he came to himself he was lying prone over a log, vomiting water. As someone turned him over he groaned. Then he was aware of a rough figure looming over him, rumbling quietly but continually in the English of Sussex. "Eh, master, you were born to be hanged, that I see. Falling into the race with the wheel going, and your mouth stopped by your hood! Water won't drown a skylarking boy, so they say; but you tried your luck very high. Bothering me when I have all that grist to sack and weigh! Boys and hawkers, they're always a nuisance to an honest miller; but a boy with a hawk beats all! Are you feeling better? I'll catch your pony and set you on your way."

Thomas sat up, found himself fainting, and lay back again.

"Ah, you'll have to wait a bit, master," the miller continued. "You're not the first I've fished out of the race, and 'tis a fearful thing. But, come to think of it, you're the first who couldn't cry for help. I just came forth to stop the wheel, with the stones grinding air; and there you were. 'Tis so damned lucky it must mean something. Maybe your doom is a great one, and you must live until it comes to you. Tell me your name, lad, and I'll remember it. I may hear it again."

"I am Thomas fitzGilbert, or Thomas Becket, or Thomas of Cheapside in London. And I thank you for saving my life," Thomas murmured.

"Don't rub it in. Maybe I saved your life, but then, d'ye see, I owe a life to the river. Better say an angel saved your life. So you're a Norman? Well, there may be some good ones. I can't say your father's name, and London is a big place; but Becket I can remember, it's the name we give to that black bird over there. If ever Thomas Becket makes a stir in the world I shall know for sure that this morning's work was a miracle."

Thomas rode gently home by the high road (but the hawk flew away and was never recovered). His talk with the miller had given him something to think over. It was really very extraordinary that the man should have come out to stop his wheel at the exact moment that a drowning boy was being swept to his death, and that the current should have carried him to the feet of his rescuer. He knew the rustic superstition that it is dangerous to cheat a river of its prey; that was why the miller had tried to lay the responsibility on Fate. But the miller might be right, all the same. Perhaps he, Thomas, was reserved for some great destiny.

CHAPTER II

Thomas of Cheapside

AT the age of fifteen he had the freedom of an adult. For the discipline of St. Paul's grammar school seemed as light as silk after the unrelenting rectitude of Merton. At the Priory he could never let himself go; even Recreation was no more than decorous conversation on seemly subjects, and the cowl all wore reminded them that they must behave as Augustinians every waking moment. Now he wore the blue tunic and gray hose that had been his livery at Pevensey, only donning the black gown of a clerk when he was in the classroom. In the evening he was free to wander through the streets of London.

The most fascinating part of the city lay at his own doorstep, Cheapside of the goldsmiths and drapers. Here were the wealth and luxury which had made London famous: silk mantles from the great Christian cities of the eastern Mediterranean, sugar from infidel lands even farther to the eastward, ginger from the realm of Prester John on the far side of the infidels, and parrots and monkeys, fashionable pets for fashionable ladies, from beyond the known world. Just as valuable, though they came from nearer home, were the trinket boxes decorated with enamel from Limoges or Cosmati-work from Rome. Drapers sold heavily embroidered vestments and mantles of ceremony, stiff with gold and silver thread; these were just beginning their long journey, for opus Anglicanum, English embroidery, was the best in the world, sold by merchants in Poland and Constantinople. For these luxuries, which they could get nowhere else in England, great men or their stewards visited Cheapside; the taverns and cookshops catered for the rich, and the merchants standing in their doorways were dressed like great lords. But Goodman Gilbert was grander than the grandest draper. He never stood in his doorway soliciting custom. He lived chiefly by the rent of house-property he had bought, and nowadays when he dealt in hides it was often by letter. His home showed no trace of vulgar commerce, and all through the summer a shield above his door indicated that some lord had accepted the hospitality of a fellow Norman while he settled his affairs in the city.

Eastward on the river lay Billingsgate, and beyond it the tidal stream where moored the ships from overseas. That was the gay quarter, where wine shops full of painted women opened their doors to sailors. It was the favorite haunt of many London boys, eager to earn a tip as guides or by carrying the baggage of a foreigner; but Thomas had an innate liking for order and good manners, which Pevensey had reinforced; low company had no charm for him.

There was another important quarter of London, besides the rich shops and the harbor. But good Londoners seldom went there, and did their best to forget about it. Where the eastern wall swept down to the river stood the Tower, astride the fortifications so that its garrison could enter or leave at will; and in the Tower lived the Sheriff of Middlesex, with his band of unruly and bullying sergeants. Three times a year he met the burgesses assembled in their shire court, and collected his dues. That was wrong, for any scholar would tell you that cities should collect their own taxes, as did the cities of antiquity. Nevertheless, the burgesses elected an alderman for each ward; and they all met in the folkmoot which had swallowed up the old shire court of Middlesex. There was enough local politics to be interesting, and Goodman Gilbert, who had served one year as a rather weak alderman for Cheap, was interested in it.

Intertwined with this mercantile city lay the London of the clerks, affected by business prosperity but holding aloof from commerce. Here was the greatest concentration of learned men in England, thirteen religious communities and the clergy of one hundred and twenty-six parish churches, all under the Bishop and the Chapter of St. Paul's. Unemployed clerks naturally collected round this great pool of benefices, which was also next door to the King's offices at Westminster. There were no less than three grammar schools, and by common consent the best of these was St. Paul's.

At St. Paul's Thomas worked very hard, but he found the study of rhetoric most unlike the silent application of Merton. He was set to learn by heart famous speeches of antiquity, or the unintelligible Greek names for various figures and modes of argument. He did this as well as his fellows, for he had a good memory; but then everyone in the school had a good and well-trained memory, or he would not have survived the rigors of elementary education. The chief object of a liberal education was to teach skill in argument; that was done by frequent disputations, extempore debates on set themes. In these debates a quick wit and a knack of making memorable assonances and jingles in rhyme counted for more than deep thought. Thomas proved an effective debater, and soon made his mark in the school.

At Merton he had never been positively unhappy; but he was quick to take the color of his surroundings, and in the quiet earnestness of the monastery he had been dimly sober and obedient. In addition there were physical reasons for his disciplined and unspectacular willingness to please. He had grown too fast; he was always cold and nearly always tired. Now, at St. Paul's, his strength had caught up with his height, and he felt an ever-renewed energy bubbling inside him every morning. Besides, the tone of St. Paul's was gay and flippant, and he became gay and flippant to match his company. He was still rather too self-centered and withdrawn to make intimate friends, but he became a popular and respected leader of schoolboy opinion.

As his character expanded so did his stature. By his fifteenth birthday, in December 1133, he had grown up to his large hands and feet. He was more than six feet tall, and growing fast. He remained very thin, and he felt cold so keenly that his extremities were usually purple. His mother, anxious, had him examined by a physician, but the doctor declared there was nothing to be done about it: Thomas had been born with a frigid temperament, and he must wear thick clothes and eat as much pepper as he could afford; even then he would seldom feel warm, but he would live as long as the next man.

During the Easter holiday of 1134 his father had a talk with him. It was time for him to choose either the tonsure or the life of a burgess; which meant in practice that his father would choose for him.

"I have been thinking," he said, "about the diocese you

should choose for your ordination. That is, if you are still eager to be a clerk?"

"Why, yes, Father. But a clerk does not need orders, at least while he is still at his books. The tonsure is enough to bind me to the Church, yet it does not commit me to anything. That's not the popular opinion, but it's sound canon law. Suppose that later on some great lord who has employed me should offer me a fief. Then, if I am only a tonsured clerk, I might let my hair grow and do knight-service for my land. I might even marry. All without breaking the canons."

"Well, I never knew that. I thought every clerk was a clerk for life. You will be telling me next that priests may marry and hold land in lay fee."

"They do, in some parts of England; though of course it's wrong. The King won't enforce the laws of the Church, and these English were always shockingly slack. You mustn't judge this country by the decent customs of Rouen."

"Then it's time we compelled them to follow the decent customs of Normandy, the customs of all civilized men. But you know more about the law than your father. I would believe anything of this country."

"We shall set it to rights when we have time. It's odd to think that after all these years the English still follow their own barbarous law."

"Yes, a long time since the Conquest. I suppose the last man who remembered it was the poor lord who died a month ago."

"Our Duke Robert? May he rest in peace. Though such a hero of Outremer hardly needs our prayers."

"More than eighty when he died," said Gilbert, comforting his own middle age. "When he was in his cradle there were no Normans outside the Duchy. Now a man can ride from Scotland to Apulia and sleep every night in the hall of a Norman lord. It's a great thing to be a Norman. Don't you ever do anything to disgrace us."

"I am as Norman as you, Father, for all that I can speak a little English. I shall live like a Norman, and I hope to die like one. I have been trained to arms, not to dressing hides."

It was rank bad manners to crow over his father so crudely. But the recollection of all the glory won by Norman swords in the last seventy years sometimes made Thomas lose his head.

"As a clerk you may not bear arms."

"Let me explain, Father. A clerk is not a priest. I want to study the law, all the law there is in the world. There is more of it every day, but one man working hard can still master the whole. At Merton they taught us some canon law, and at Pevensey I picked up a little of the customs of Normandy. In Paris and Lombardy learned doctors are lecturing on the old Roman civil law. If you will support me for a few more years I could attend those lectures. Last of all, at the folkmoot and the Exchequer, I could pick up the odd Saxon customs of England. Then I would know all the law in the world, and great lords would be eager to employ me."

"So that's what you want. And your mother thinks you are burning to be ordained! Well, it's not a very noble ambition, but it seems to have taken your fancy. You may stay at St. Paul's for two years more, and then perhaps I could afford to send you to Paris. I suppose in the end you will begin to earn money."

"Lawyers earn a great deal, as a reward for their long training. Seriously, Father, it's what I want to do. Of course I once had the usual boyish dreams of winning fortune with my sword, but no one can do that nowadays. England is a land of peace."

As he spoke of his vanished childhood fifteen-year-old Thomas looked very wise and mature; but Gilbert reflected that his training at Pevensey would make him hanker after knighthood all his life. Perhaps that chivalrous education had been a mistake, though his courteous manners would be useful to him whatever his position in the world.

"Don't count on too much peace in England," Gilbert went on. "For more than thirty years our King has kept good peace, but he won't live forever. Who will come after? The magnates have sworn to serve his daughter the Empress; but her second husband is an Angevin. Can you imagine Normans taking orders from an Angevin? It seems against nature."

"The Empress has a son," answered Thomas reflectively, "though I suppose you might call him an Angevin like his father. He could be reared in Normandy, to rule us as a true Norman."

"He could, if the King lives another twenty years. That baby is just about a year old. If the King dies while his grandson is a child there will be war. When I was alderman of Cheap I swore fealty to the Empress, so I am bound to her service. I hope she gets her rights without fighting, but I shan't be surprised if trouble comes."

"When I know all the law that can be known I shall serve her and her son with my pen. England is full of gallant knights, but there are very few good lawyers."

Henceforth Thomas had an end in view, the satisfaction of a cherished ambition. He studied with an ardor that amazed his teachers, until they congratulated Gilbert on being the father of a genius. That was a stroke of luck, for it saved Thomas's career even when the family suffered a heavy financial misfortune.

At harvest he paid a short visit to Pevensey, thus missing the great fire which devastated London at that time. During a September gale a house caught alight, and the wind carried burning thatch far and wide. It happened in broad daylight, when everyone was awake, and there was little loss of life; but St. Paul's Cathedral was utterly consumed, and with it most of the rented houses which provided Gilbert's income.

He must go back to his trade of drysalting. He was tempted to put his clever young son to work, but for all his mildness he had his share of Norman honor; he had given his word that the boy might complete his education, and his word must be kept. The visit to Paris was postponed for one year only; by the autumn of 1135 some of the little wooden houses were rebuilt and rented, and there was just enough money for the support of his son.

When at last Thomas sailed from Pevensey the top of his head gleamed white from the tonsure; for every student of Paris was a clerk, and he had received from the Bishop of London the lesser orders of exorcist and doorkeeper.

The journey through Normandy and France seemed a homecoming. It was strange to hear the poorest peasants speaking good French; but this was the land of his ancestors, and it was thrilling to see for the first time great castles and walled towns which had been the background of family conversation since he could understand it. Paris itself was smaller than London, cramped on its fortified island and just beginning to expand on the south bank of the river; there was obviously less trade than in the city of his birth. But this town was more alive. The King of France lived in it nearly all the time, since his magnates would not permit him to do justice within their fiefs, as the King of England did justice in the fiefs of his vassals. The great schools brought a multitude of clerks from every nation in Christendom. The town was always full of prominent visitors.

The foreign clerks were organized in clubs, whose chief purpose was to bargain with the lecturers over tuition fees. Thomas was advised to join the English "nation," and did so with reluctance; it seemed to reflect on his status as a Norman, but there was no "nation" for Normans only, and the north-French "nation" would take only vassals of the French King. Each "nation" haunted a particular tavern, and saw to it that there was always a senior scholar waiting there to give advice to newcomers. Thomas was told of the best lecturers in canon and civil law, and how much he ought to pay to be enrolled among their students.

In his private life he was completely free, for his tonsure placed him beyond the jurisdiction of the King's Provost. His teachers made him pay his fees, and enforced order in the lecture hall; but so long as he paid for his course no one compelled him to attend and listen. There was no authority to check the drunkenness and evil living of the young scholars.

Thomas had often wondered where the numerous pupils of the London grammar schools would find a livelihood. Now he understood that he had reached the stage at which most clerks abandoned the career of learning; boys who had commenced their education in the strictness of a monastery, and continued under the salutary discipline of home life, were turned loose in a foreign city where no one would inform their parents of their behavior. Some died of drink, many drifted into the furtive underworld of hired letter-writers or forgers of fake charters, a few even enlisted in bands of professional mercenaries.

Thomas himself was one of the selected band of hard workers and sober livers. He enjoyed the study of the law, and in private life he had developed a strong liking for neatness and order; debauchery repelled him by its sordid dirt. The courtesy of his manners marked him out as a youth bred in a castle; his few intimates were also young men of courtesy, cadets of great houses qualifying for careers in the law courts or the Church.

Though he was on the whole popular, as at Merton and St. Paul's, he made no close friends. His companions thought he carried into private life too much of the piety which to them was a professional qualification. These gently born scholars heard Mass when they should, frowned on affairs with prostitutes, and went to Confession once a month; but their chief interest was the study of the new code of chivalry, with its facinating conception that a man might love a woman's character, not merely her body. (In fact the more inaccessible the lady the more a true knight should love her.) They spent their evenings discussing which of the famous beauties whom they had never met they would choose as an ideal to be worshiped. But when Thomas was challenged to name the lady of his choice he replied that he served Our Lady only, which took all the fun out of the discussion, by reminding them that they were dedicated to a celibate career. Peter of Norwich observed crossly that if you believed what Thomas said he was too good for this world and already ripe for Heaven; but that in very fact he was so busy serving Thomas of London that he had no time to serve any lady.

There was enough truth in this to sting. Yet Thomas, examining his conscience that evening in accordance with the training of Merton, could not honestly see he was at fault. By accident he had the manners of a gentleman; in truth he was the son of a poor burgess, with his way to make in the world; a spotless reputation was a valuable asset. His companions never guessed how sternly he had to rule himself. Chastity was not too difficult; he had always known it would demand an effort, and that effort he was prepared to make. He was still a virgin, and a virgin he would die—provided he was careful with drink. There he had to watch himself, for he appreciated good wine; luckily the cheap drink of the students' taverns was too nasty to be pleasant and he could seldom afford anything better. Anyone who drank cold water in Paris quickly died of disease, and he formed the habit of drinking water in which lime blossoms had been boiled, which made it safer. He found that with a little resolution he could keep himself chaste and sober.

*   *   *

Old King Henry of England was dead at last, struck down at the dinner table during an enormous Friday meal of lampreys. For thirty-five years he had kept firm peace, but "the King's peace dies with the King," and England seemed once again a prize for the strongest sword. That was to be expected, since it was not the custom for the English crown to pass by inheritance. Duke William had won it in battle, Rufus had taken it by force from his brother Robert, and Henry had repeated the usurpation. The old King had planned for the succession of his daughter, binding his magnates by solemn oath. But before his body could be carried from Normandy for burial in his Abbey of Reading the magnates had agreed to crown Count Stephen of Blois, son of Duke William's daughter.

Thomas was not very interested. As a Norman, he thought first of the interests of the Normans of England. The male line of Duke William had ended with the death of young William Clito, son of Duke Robert. Count Stephen was not a Norman, but he had been reared in Normandy and England, and he was a gallant knight. The late King's daughter, the Empress, was herself Norman; but she had been reared in Germany, and after the death of the Emperor had married the Count of Anjou, the neighbor and therefore the hereditary foe of Normandy. Since a woman could not lead armies Count Geoffrey must rule in her name, a thing proud Normans found hard to stomach. There was much to be said against either claimant; though Thomas recalled that his father had sworn fealty to Matilda the Empress, and as far as he had any feeling he favored her cause.

In 1138 came news that Count Robert of Gloucester had renounced his allegiance and declared for the Empress, his half sister; for he was a bastard of the old King. What had earlier been only the threat of disturbance was now a regular civil war. Gilbert wrote that Count Geoffrey of Essex, Sheriff of Middlesex and Castellan of the Tower, ruled London with a heavy hand.

In June 1139 Thomas was surprised to receive a special messenger, a lad from his father's warehouse. The letter he carried said only that King Stephen had arrested the Bishops of Salisbury and Ely, and that the affairs of England were in a terrible state. His verbal message, too complicated to be put on paper by one used only to composing short business communications, was that Thomas's fortune was made. The metropolitan see of Canterbury had just been filled, and the new Archbishop was Theobald of Bec, a native of Thierceville in Normandy, a contemporary and playmate of Gilbert who still remembered his old comrade. Thomas should concentrate on those branches of canon law which would be most useful to a clerk in the household of a metropolitan archbishop.

The following spring Thomas had word that his mother was sick, and unlikely to recover. Quickly and efficiently he wound up his affairs, being careful to obtain explicit letters of recommendation from all his teachers. In midsummer calm he crossed the Channel, and reached home in time to stand by the deathbed of Rose Becket.

She made a good end, and died happy. Kneeling beside her were the prosperous matron and the dignified lady of Barking, her daughters; her decent, sorrowing elderly husband twisted his hood in embarrassed shyness behind them. But her eyes were fixed on her tall son, Master Thomas the lawyer. He stood under the highest ridge of the roof, six feet eight inches tall in his black legal gown; his fierce nose jutted from his hood and his hard black eyes blazed with a sorrow very like anger. As his lips moved in prayer the lines of his mouth deepened; in those lines a mother could read iron self-control and a savage temper continually curbed. But there was also honesty, courage that nothing could daunt, unswerving love of justice, and a courtesy that long training had made second nature. She died knowing that her twenty-one-year-old son was a good man, though virtue would never be easy for him.

Thomas arranged the funeral in St. Paul's Cathedral. His status as a clerk from the fashionable schools of Paris won him automatic respect from all English priests, and he knew better than his father how these things should be done. He looked cold and businesslike, and very much on his dignity; but inside the calm exterior his grief was genuine and deep. He saw the fussiness and futility of his father; home to him had been his mother. She had been utterly good; not remarkably devout in a generation of regular church goers, but honest and kindly and loyal. She served no saint except Our Lady the Mother of God; from her he had learned the same devotion, which had kept firm his virtue through all the temptations of Paris; when he thought of Our Lady he saw Her with his mother's face. He would never disgrace her, and he would never forget that from her place in Heaven she could see his every action.

Meanwhile there were earthly things to be seen to. His father pointed out nervously that a great scholar was a source of pride to the family, but that it was necessary now for his only son to earn money. The hope of patronage from the new Archbishop of Canterbury had been disappointed; while King Stephen was at odds with the Church, Archbishop Theobald preferred to keep his distance. He had not pronounced in favor of the Empress and her supporters, who now held all the west of England; but from London it was difficult to reach him. If Thomas could not as yet serve the Archbishop, what could he do to bring in an income?

Thomas's answer was vague. As a clerk he despised merchants, and as a lawyer he knew that very few of them were honest. He could not make anything with his hands, and he lacked the technical knowledge needed by a buyer of green hides. Unless he served some lord who needed legal advice there was nothing he could do except write letters for a merchant.

It was lowly employment for a scholar of Paris, but nothing better offered. Gilbert was no longer prominent in London politics, and the term as alderman which figured so often in his conversation was nearly forgotten; though he still had important friends in the city. One evening, as father and son were sitting by the fire, talking over the prospects of the leather trade and the rumor of a vacancy on the staff of St. Paul's school, Thomas's married sister called with a promising suggestion.

Margaret Tanner bustled in, telling the porter who came with her to dump his load of presents and hurry back to the tannery; as usual, she conveyed the impression that she was too busy to waste a moment, and then settled down to chat until cockcrow. But after exclaiming at the untidiness of the house, and vowing that Thomas must come back with her for a nourishing meal, she at last came to the point.

"A distinguished visitor called this afternoon. He came, as it seemed, on business, to order a score of leather bucklers for his serving men. But he asked politely after the health of all my family, and bade me convey his regards to my father and brother. Then he asked what Thomas was doing now, and said something about needing a well-educated clerk in his counting house, to write letters to foreign merchants. He had just got rid of his accountant, one of those Englishmen who know all the works of King Alfred and write a neat hand; but the fellow could only write English, and nobody oversea could read his letters. He told us all this just as he was leaving, and both Robert and I took it as a hint that he would like to employ Thomas but was afraid to make an open offer, in case you snubbed him. He is ridiculously vain, and a snub hurts him. But he reckons his money in sackfuls, and they say he pays well for faithful service."

Margaret rattled off this long speech and at last paused for breath. It was not often that a woman could hold the attention of two men, and she was determined to keep them on tenterhooks until they asked her for the name of this rich employer. Gilbert at last gratified her by grunting the question.

"Norman or English? Do I know him?"

"He speaks French, though it's the French of London. You ought to know him, Father. I believe he helped you to get elected when you were made alderman (what a ridiculous word!). He is Goodman Osbert, or perhaps I should say Sir Osbert, citizen and tanner, and knight in the retinue of Count Robert."

"Good heavens," said Gilbert, "old Huitdeniers flies high, pretending he needs a scholar of Paris to keep the sordid records of his business! But it's true enough that his money would make a full load for a mule, and if his accountant knows his master's secrets he must certainly pay the fellow well, or else cut his throat. You should take the post, Thomas. Let Osbert know, Margaret, that if he makes a civil offer he need not fear a snub."

Thomas had been one of the leading men of his year in Paris, and Margaret helped her husband to manage a prosperous tannery; Gilbert Becket's muddleheaded stupidity was made more noticeable by the intelligence of his children. But he was the head of the family; to Thomas it seemed natural that his father should choose a master for him.

"Huitdeniers—eightpence—what a curious nickname!" he said mildly. "I don't remember him. Of course I shall be honored to serve a master who is my father's friend. But you talk of his business as sordid, and Margaret seems to despise him. Please tell me the full story, in particular what he did with his eightpence to make him so famous."

"Oh, Osbert hasn't done anything with his eightpence," said Margaret, chuckling. "I don't think he ever got it. It was his trying to earn it that makes the funny story. Count Robert of Gloucester granted him a manor to be held by knight-service, and when the war broke out Osbert is said to have offered to fight for his lord, if he were paid the eightpence a day that is the standard wage of a knight. The offer was declined with thanks. Count Robert thought he could manage without the reinforcement of a London tanner who can't ride like a gentleman."

Thomas looked inquiringly at his father. Margaret thought only of mocking this burgess whom evidently she disliked, but there were gaps in the anecdote as she told it.

"It's all quite true, but not the whole truth," Gilbert said earnestly; since Rose's death he had forgotten how to talk nonsense. "This Osbert is a French Londoner, and I believe of sound Norman blood; though he was born here, and the French he speaks sounds odd. He was a tanner in a very big way until he went in for buying green hides wholesale all over the country. I used to deal with him, and he supported me at the hustings when I stood for election. He always has ready money by him, and he lent some to Count Robert. The Count could only repay by offering land, and Osbert certainly holds a manor in the West Country by knight-service, though the story about his volunteering to serve in person may be only a joke. His confidential clerk will have plenty of work, for Osbert is up to his neck in high politics."

"Dangerous business for a mere burgess," said Thomas. "Which side is he on? I suppose, since he is a friend of ours, he holds by the old oath of fealty to the Empress?"

"You couldn't call him a friend of ours any longer," said Margaret, sniffing. "He is a very great man, and he condescended to my Robert until I longed to set the dogs on him. As to which side he is on, what would you say, Father? Both at once is my guess, and I doubt if his guardian angel knows more."

"He has not been a very consistent partisan," Gilbert replied judicially. "But politics here in England are tangled, and you can't blame a merchant with a fortune in cash for keeping in with the lord who rules London. By the way, I should make it clear that he was never more than a business acquaintance, and as it happens we have not met for some years. If you serve him, as I think you should, it will be because we lack money, not to requite an old friendship."

"And his politics?" Thomas pressed.

"He used to favor the Empress, as I do. Because after all an oath is an oath, and her father was a good king who kept the peace. But he lives in London, and his coffers are worth robbing. So at present he is on very good terms with Count Geoffrey de Mandeville, who holds the Tower for King Stephen. Count Geoffrey will take money from him anyway, and I suppose Osbert would rather think of it as a friendly loan, which may be repaid later, than as a sheriff's tax."

"He doesn't sound a very honorable master to follow," said Thomas with a sigh. "But since we lack money, and he offers it, I may as well earn it as the next man."

Within a few days a delicate message had been conveyed to Huitdeniers, and the formal offer of a place in his counting house was formally accepted. The salary was quickly agreed, and for the first time Thomas began to earn his own living.

He could write quickly, in a hand that strangers could read; though he was not a trained scribe who could make beautiful books. In Huitdenier's office, however, speed was what counted. Often a discreet shabby man would come on foot with a letter and wait in the kitchen for the answer. The correspondence appeared to be concerned with the price of leather; but there was too much urgency and discretion for such a mundane subject. One day as Thomas was passing the Tower he recognized a sergeant as the discreet and shabby messenger. Then he understood that Osbert was acting as go-between for Count Geoffrey. But since Count Geoffrey openly supported King Stephen these secret messages must deal with a projected change to the party of the Empress. Since Thomas himself favored the Empress he was glad to lend his skill to what might otherwise have seemed a dirty business.

All that winter armies rode through England, sacking towns and plundering open manors. The Londoners strengthened their wall and reorganized their militia. One of the eight "viscounts" who commanded it was Osbert, but he would not allow Thomas to bear arms in his command. He said that even in the field he would need a confidential secretary, and Thomas was ordered to follow him with portable desk and inkhorn, not lance and sword.

On the afternoon of the 4th of February 1141 Thomas was at his desk when a strange clamor suddenly filled the air. For a moment the whole household, porters, workmen, and serving maids, paused in astonishment, for it was a sound that had rarely been heard in England during the reign of the late King. Then Osbert shouted above the hurrying rhythm which invaded every glassless casement: "That's the common bell, and it beats the tocsin. Let every man collect his shield and sword from my armory, and muster behind me where I stand at the folkmoot. Come on, Thomas. Bring a pen and your tablets. I shall need an accurate record of the decisions taken at the meeting."

The burgesses mustered self-consciously in arms, each behind his appointed "viscount." Thomas noted with interest that Huitdeniers led by far the largest and best-armed contingent, with a disciplined core of his own employees, armed at his expense. Among the excited, puzzled crowd in the churchyard of St. Paul's he alone seemed self-possessed; it was likely that London as a whole would follow his advice.

The gates of the Tower were closed, and there was no sign

of Count Geoffrey the Sheriff. After an indecisive pause the Senior Canon of St. Paul's called the meeting to order. There were murmurs of discontent, for the burgesses, who resented the domination of the King's Sheriff, were alert to the danger that the Bishop might seek to displace him in the rule of the town. But the Canon did not make a speech; he merely introduced a tired and travel-stained courier, who read aloud from a despatch.

The message was brief, and its tone carefully neutral. The Chapter of Lincoln Cathedral wrote to inform their brethren of St. Paul's that in a great battle fought outside their city King Stephen had been taken prisoner, and that it seemed probable that the Empress would shortly bring her power to the gates of London. In this crisis, with the civil government in dissolution, the clergy were charged with the duty of maintaining order.

The eight viscounts consulted together in private, but no resolution was put to the meeting. The gates were closed, and watchmen placed on every tower of the walls. Then the burgesses were dismissed to their homes, though every man was advised to sleep with his arms by his bedside.

During that gloomy Lent every burgess who had cash to be plundered or daughters to be raped continued to anticipate a sack of the city. But the Bishop of Winchester, papal legate, brother of King Stephen and cousin of the Empress, managed to arrange a peace conference in his cathedral city.

Goodman Osbert now came forward as the avowed leader of the Angevin party in London. When the folkmoot decided that London must be represented at the conference he was chosen to lead the burgess delegation; and of course he took with him his treasure of a confidential clerk.

On the Sunday after Easter all the magnates of England assembled in the great hall of the Bishop of Winchester's castle.

Thomas had ridden there with Osbert and a small escort, but they found to their annoyance that burgesses were not important enough to be admitted to the hall; they must wait in the courtyard with the common herd.

This was Thomas's introduction to high politics, and he was keenly interested to see all these great men. Osbert identified them as they dismounted in the courtyard. They all looked worried or dissatisfied except the Bishop of Winchester, who was disposing of the crown of England, and the Empress, who was about to receive it. The Lady of England, for that was now her title, was as splendidly dressed as a princess in a fairy tale. On her mantle of cloth of gold were embroidered in black silk the imperial two-headed eagles; her shoes were of purple silk, and her long tunic, also woven from the Imperial silk of Constantinople, was a vivid green; her fair hair hung low in two plaits before her shoulders (but Osbert whispered that these plaits also were of silk), and her head was covered with a white veil of very fine lawn, kept in place by the silver-gilt coronet of the County of Anjou.

Osbert muttered what a great many people were thinking. "The Lady of England goes in state, in the robes of the Empire and the coronet of Anjou. Is she ashamed of her grandfather, Duke William the Conqueror, that she wears no emblem of Normandy or of England?"

Bishop Henry received his cousin at the door of the hall. He was beaming all over his face, as happy, Thomas muttered with a certain lack of charity, as a magnate should be when his elder brother is in fetters. This sally at the expense of old King Henry and his treatment of Duke Robert brought a smile from Osbert, but it was not a topic to be discussed in public.

Except for Count Robert of Gloucester, the other magnates wore sour faces. For all of them this should have been a joyful occasion; they had sold their loyalty to King Stephen at a heavy price and now, less than six years later, they must be bought all over again. If they looked unwilling they must hate the Angevin party very bitterly indeed.

But there was nothing they could do. King Stephen was fettered in a dungeon and his armies dispersed. The holy crown of King Edward the Confessor was kept in the Treasury at Winchester, and the Empress had already taken it out to gloat over it. But only Coronation could make her a queen. Though that meant no more than that she must ride to London, for the party of Blois had no armed force to bring against her.

When the details of the coronation in Westminster Abbey had been settled, the delegation of London was called in to give their formal consent. Osbert demurred, pleading that he must seek instructions from the folkmoot; for though he himself supported the Empress he knew that London as a whole favored King Stephen. But Count Geoffrey of Essex reminded him that the Tower was now held in the name of the Lady of England, and he gave way gracefully. He agreed to fix the common seal of London to the treaty.

It was the duty of Thomas to heat the wax and impress the lead seal of the Viscounty of London, a little seal which he carried in a bag in his bosom. This was a piece of ceremonial most gratifying to Osbert's pride. He, who was too ignoble to be granted the spurs of a knight, had a chancellor to keep his seal, or at least the seal of his city. For the moment that put him on a level with great magnates like the Counts of Gloucester and Chester. Thomas also was pleased to have a task which excused his presence in the hall and allowed him to hear what was going on.

The magnates were still discussing the important question of the custody of royal castles, and what struck him immediately was how badly they discussed it. Bishop Henry had an accurate mind, trained by the discipline of the Church; he kept to one point at a time, seeking agreement before going on to the next. But the lay lords all talked at once, each about the district which most concerned him; even when two of them reached a compromise over some fortress the whole question was reopened when they began to discuss the next shire. These gallant warriors were incapable of ruling the country, though they were too independent to permit anyone else to rule it. What was needed at the top was a single man with a clear brain, to make up their minds for them. They were entitled to offer their opinions, for England could not be governed without their assent; but nothing would ever be done unless they allowed a strong chairman to rule their discussions.

On that same evening Osbert and his delegation began their ride back to London. Osbert was worried, and said so frankly. On behalf of his city he had recognized the Empress; but most Londoners were on the other side, and only the accident of King Stephen's capture had induced them to submit. If the Empress came straight to Westminster for her crowning, and made a gracious impression in London, the party of Blois would subside. But the Empress would not see that time was running against her, and she planned a long visit to Reading to offer prayers at her father's tomb. At her coronation she would not be gracious to the burgesses; she had been uncommonly haughty with Osbert, her leading supporter; how she would bear herself to the supporters of Blois did not bear thinking of.

At last came news that the Empress would reach Westminster on the 20th of June, and that the Coronation would take place on St. John's Day, the 24th. The frightened burgesses did what they could to appease her wrath. Every man who could bear arms or ride a horse came out to meet her at Knightsbridge, on the outskirts of Westminster; and of course the cavalcade was completed by the chest of silver which habitually made smooth any meeting between burgesses and sovereign.

Thomas remained in Cheapside, for he had been given the important task of supervising the making of the Empress's new Great Seal; the inscription, by her express command, was

MATILDIS IMPERATRIX ROMANORUM ET REGINA ANGLIAE, and even the silversmith grumbled at her for putting the Empire first and England as an afterthought. There was no doubt that she was becoming increasingly unpopular.

When Osbert returned from Knightsbridge, hot and chafed by the mail which never sat well on his paunchy figure, he was depressed by this fresh evidence of her lack of tact; but even more dejected by what he had seen.

"The silly old woman has come without her army," he grumbled. "She brings a glorious train, her uncle the King of Scots and her brother the Count of Gloucester, Brian fitzCount, and many more great magnates. But they ride unarmed, in splendid robes. Just to rub it in, the whole force of London met her in arms, so that the meanest halfwit in the city sees that London has the power to chase her away. Can't she understand that the burgesses don't like her? She made things worse by exacting full Imperial ceremony. When I knelt before her horse she graciously protruded her toe that I might kiss her stirrup. Why not make me kiss the horse? And I am supposed to be her friend! How do you suppose she will greet her enemies? I hear on good authority that she paraded King Stephen in fetters through the streets of Winchester. It was agreed in the treaty that his detention should be honorable. This is simply asking for trouble."

For three days, as angry men sought a way of escape from submission to a hated ruler, the city hummed with rumors. On the evening of the 23rd there was a great feast at Westminster, held with sublime but foolish self-confidence in an unguarded tent; as dusk fell, points of light could be seen in the southeast, and the word went round that the other Matilda, King Stephen's queen, was wasting the Kentish lands of the adherents of Anjou. Osbert took refuge in the Tower, and Thomas went home to his father. It seemed that St. John's Eve would be dangerous to Londoners who held by the Empress.

Sure enough, as the Beckets sat together in the privacy of their chamber, they heard the common bell beating out the broken hurrying rhythm of the tocsin. Gilbert, ever conscious of civic duty after thirty years as a burgess, made to rise; but his son restrained him. "Why bear arms against the Lady to whom you swore fealty? Don't say that because the bell summons you it is your duty to obey. It is never the duty of a Christian to obey without question. If your superiors are wrong it may be your duty to disobey them. That is my advice as a lawyer. Let us keep the house dark and hope the mob will forget us. Tomorrow we can learn the news."

All night they heard the mob cheering for King Stephen, vowing destruction to the Angevins and their henchman Count Geoffrey of Essex. For that was the root of their hostility; they would always be foes to the friends of Mandeville. Luckily no one remembered that the dark house in Cheapside sheltered Goodman Gilbert, the retired alderman who was faithful to the Empress. In the morning it stood unharmed.

The news, when they ventured out to learn it, was definite and final. The Empress and her companions had been forced to flee westward, leaving in Westminster their gay tent and all their baggage. Queen Matilda, wife to King Stephen, was within the walls, with the knight-service of her own County of Boulogne and the militia of Kent. The captain of her mercenaries, William of Ypres, was barricading the streets near the Tower against Count Geoffrey, and building siege engines on Tower Hill. London was lost to the Angevins.

At this crisis, when everyone else thought only of war and revolution, Thomas remembered the new Great Seal. He sought out the silversmith, and broke the news that the work could not be paid for; then he personally witnessed the melting of the seal, and drew up a certificate to that effect. The craftsman had tried out his handiwork, as silversmiths would in spite of all prohibitions. Thomas took this single impression, and wrapped the lump of wax in his certificate of destruction. The unlucky Empress might like to affix it to some grant to remind her of how nearly she had been crowned Queen of England, and he would send it to her as soon as he could do so in safety. But the destruction was imperative; a Great Seal of England abandoned by its rightful owner could undermine the title of every man to his own land.

The Londoners missed their chance to destroy the Count of Essex. That rascal offered to change sides, and his power made him worth buying. The party of Blois bought him, making him Sheriff and Justiciar of London, Middlesex, Essex, and Hertfordshire. Whoever might be on top in this eventful civil war, peaceful burgesses would always find themselves at the bottom.

Goodman Osbert Huitdeniers flourished like a green bay tree. He led the London contingent which marched against the Empress, but even during the blockades and counter-blockades of that campaign, which ended in an appalling sack of Winchester and the further flight of the Empress, he continued to insure against accidents. Thomas had been left behind to deal with letters in the London office; but when he was asked to copy a deed of the Angevin chancery, confirming Count Geoffrey in his rule over London and rewarding his faithful follower Osbert with land in Angevin Gloucestershire worth twenty pounds a year, he decided that he could no longer soil his hands with work of this kind. He filed his papers with care, wrote a civil letter of resignation, and returned to his father's house.

In November King Stephen was released, in exchange for Count Robert of Gloucester, who had been taken while covering his sister's retreat from Winchester. In December the King again wore his crown at Westminster, and for London the crowded year 1141 ended with both parties holding what they had held at its beginning. But this was the time of which the monk of Ely wrote: "It seemed that God and His Saints slept." In every shire of the south, from Dover to Bristol, armed bands pillaged and ravished in the name of one or the other claimant to the crown. Trade vanished and burgesses grew poor.

By the autumn of 1143 Thomas was twenty-four. He was a Norman of the race who ruled from Sicily to Scotland, his intelligence was exceptional, and he had profited by the best and most highly regarded education in the world; he was honest, sober, and industrious. But no one would employ him.

He lived with his widowed father, keeping the accounts of the moribund drysalting business and sometimes earning a small fee by drawing up legal documents for his neighbors. But these were rare, for the London wardmoots administered the old customary law of England, unlike anything he had learned in Paris. He could advise only in commercial cases, which were judged in the Church courts by international Roman law, or in matrimonial suits before the archdeacon. But with trade so slack there were few matrimonial suits; for they were fantastically expensive, and in hard times men made do with the wives their parents had chosen for them. To make matters worse, the Beckets were unpopular. Everyone knew they had favored the Empress, whose brief occupation had done such harm to London; and who was losing the civil war anyway.

One gloomy November day, as he sat in his father's hall reading a borrowed lawbook, Thomas heard the rare sound of mules entering the yard. He hastened to pull aside the linen window, hoping this was a pack train at last arrived from the west. It was something even more surprising, two prosperous clerks with servants and baggage. They must be strangers, ignorant that the hospitality of Goodman Gilbert was a poor introduction to the ruling circle in London. He ran out to do the honors in the absence of his father.

The visitors introduced themselves as Baldwin, archdeacon

of Boulogne, and Master Eustace his brother, come to consult the Archbishop of Canterbury in the matter of a will that disposed of land both in England and France. "I am told the Archbishop is at Harrow, not far from London," said Baldwin. "We wish to stay in the city, and when I heard that in Cheapside lived a burgess who had known the Archbishop in childhood, and that his son was the Master Thomas whose learning is still remembered in Paris, I thought this house would be our best lodging. Do you know the Archbishop intimately, and is he busy at Harrow?"

"My father and the Archbishop played together when they were children," Thomas answered, "and when my father waited on him three years ago the lord Theobald remembered him. Since then we have not seen him. In the troubles two years ago my father supported the faction that was beaten, and while the fighting raged the Archbishop kept away. I fear we shall not help you to forward your cause, though you are very welcome."

Master Eustace looked keenly at the tall, shabby youth, noting his fierce nose and disciplined mouth. "You are Master Thomas of Paris, I suppose? You upheld the losing faction in one of these futile civil wars for which England is notorious? And so you sit in your father's house with no real work for your mind? Young man, you take these squabbles too tragically. The Archbishop of Canterbury is above faction. If I find you work in his household will you accept it?"

"Sir, I will accept anything. Last week I drew up a deed to endow a sanctuary lamp with twopence a year, and that was my only legal work this month. But the Archbishop must have many clerks as learned as I, and my Angevin record will count against me."

"Don't be too sure of that," said the archdeacon. "London may think King Stephen safe on his throne, but in France we see more clearly. The Angevins grow stronger every day. In any case, no Archbishop has enough competent clerks. Your Paris training must not be wasted."

Then Gilbert came in from his vain search for customers, and the conversation turned to old days in Normandy.

Gilbert had been so discouraged by the decay of his business and his own unpopularity that he had forgotten his link with the Archbishop. Once reminded of it he could think of nothing else; Thomas would soon be a great man, and in that worthy cause they must make a show of prosperity. He sold a good horse, bought wine, engaged a good cook, and prepared to keep open house for any of the Archbishop's family who might have business in London. Naturally the first to come were the lesser servants, not the clerks who had their own friends in the city; but they pressed Gilbert to call on their lord. Theobald, who had been a holy monk and was not ashamed of his humble birth, rejoiced to see again the comrade of his infancy. It was taken for granted that the Archbishop would find a place for the son of his old friend. Thomas was to take up his duties at Epiphany 1144, immediately after the Christmas holiday.

At Christmas, of course, the Archbishop kept open house, and his dependents naturally stayed at home for the feasting. Only one of them put up with Gilbert over the holidays. He was Gyrth, woodchopper to the kitchen, whose aunt kept a beerhall by the river. He was a rough Englishman, who preferred boisterous jollity in the waterfront taverns to the good wine and long prayers of his master's hall; besides, at home there would be firewood to be chopped, even on a holiday. On the morrow of Epiphany, the 7th of January, he was sober and had outstayed the welcome of his aunt. He offered to show Master Thomas the road to Harrow, and the two of them walked there together.

Thomas knew he could do the work of an Archbishop's clerk, and do it well. But he was frightened at meeting a crowd of strangers. For more than three years he had lived among the burgesses of London, and he had forgotten the flippant superficial chatter which was the talk of clerks off duty. They would see him as dull, infected with the merchant's love of money, a clod from the counting house. Probably they would be right. The schools every year discharged a host of clever men with a promising future, who remained men with a promising future until they died of old age. The worst of it would be living in a crowd. He had not lived in intimacy with a group of equals since he left Pevensey, for at Paris he had passed his evenings in solitary study. He knew that his tall figure and angry eyes gave the impression that he thought himself too good for his company, and he was eager to avoid the appearance of pride. So when Gyrth, who was feeling poorly after ten days in the taverns, asked him to carry the heavy hatchet he had bought in London, he took it at once, in a glow of humility. He was carrying it when they reached Harrow; and that was a dreadful mistake.

Loitering under the eaves was a group of young clerks, chatting as they sniffed fresh air and sheltered from the January drizzle. On Gyrth's approach they all belched loudly, putting their hands to their foreheads; then they welcomed him with cries of sympathy, asking whether the maidens of London were as easily vanquished as ever, and whether Aunt Gytha still gave body to her beer by drowning her neighbors' puppies in it. It seemed that Gyrth was a character in the household; but not the most suitable character to introduce a serious and ambitious clerk.

Now they turned on Thomas. "Who are you, Gyrth's brother or his son?" called a short chubby youth with blue eyes and sandy hair, instinctively repelled by the tall, gaunt figure before him. "I see you have brought your hatchet. I suppose you are the woodchopper's mate?"

With an effort Thomas bottled up his rage. "I am Master

Thomas of London, not long from the schools of Paris. His Lordship the Archbishop has offered me employment in his service."

"I am Master Roger de Pont l'Evêque, clerk to the Archbishop. But, my dear fellow, are you sure you want to work in the office? We never use hatchets there, even to cut the pens. Now if you turn left you will find the kitchen, and a splendid pile of firewood waiting for you. I never knew the doctors of Paris lectured on the art of chopping wood, but I suppose it was the field of study best suited to your talents."

"Master Roger, will you be so good as to lead me before the Archbishop?" said Thomas, with icy calm.

"If you insist, Master Thomas Bailhache. Do you cling to your hatchet, or may Gyrth take it from you now you have it safely here?"

Thomas dropped the wretched tool as though it were red-hot; he was glad to be rid of it before he yielded to temptation and cut that silly sneering face in half.

But as he smoothed his gown and prepared to follow the other into the presence of his lord he knew, after long years passed with schoolboys and young students, that the nickname so lightly given, "Bailhache," the hatchet-bearer, would be very hard to lose.

CHAPTER III

The Young Knight

IN 1149 the garrison of Bristol was wary and experienced; for this was the twelfth year of the everlasting civil war, and since 1138 Bristol had been the headquarters of the Angevin party. When the gate commander saw knights riding over the down toward the city he gave the alarm, and saw the portcullis lowered and the gate closed. But he did not bother Count William in the castle; the whole southwest, from Wallingford to Land's End, was a solid block of Angevin territory. That had been the achievement of Count Robert of Gloucester, brother to the Empress; and since his death his son Count William

ruled this Angevin half of the realm. Strange knights, though
they should be received with caution, were not likely to be
raiding adherents of Blois.

As the knights drew nearer the gate commander raised his
portcullis. He ordered the guard to turn out, and sent word to
the castle that distinguished visitors were on the way. The
leader bore on his red shield the golden leopards of Anjou, and
that could only mean he was an envoy from Count Geoffrey of
Anjou. He need not be Count Geoffrey himself, for the design
on a shield was not yet strictly personal. Leopards stood for
Anjou, and the leaders of the party mostly bore them in some
form.

Then the guard saluted, while trumpets blew. For the youth
at the head of the cavalcade proved to be Count Henry, son and
heir of Count Geoffrey. The guard commander congratulated
himself that his men were clean and well armed, and evidently
alert; a good report from the young Count might get him another command, nearer than Bristol to the fighting and the
plunder.

The men gazed curiously at the youth riding under the gate;
they were faithful followers of Count William, and if he decided for King Stephen they would change sides without
demur. But the Count of Gloucester was the mainstay of the
Angevins, as his father had been; in all probability this young
man would be their lord all his life.

They saw a short pink-and-white boy of sixteen, with gray
eyes and sandy hair, and freckles on his nose. Though short he
did not look small, for his shoulders were very broad and his
frame muscular. He sat well down in the saddle of his gray
charger, with the firm seat of one trained to the joust; but his
horsemanship was not perfect, since his horse looked more
jaded than its companions. Here was one of those strong riders
with heavy hands, who tired a horse by too much checking. He
carried shield and sword, but was otherwise unarmed; his gray

tunic and hose were thick and serviceable, but too shabby for such a great lord.

As the young man rode under the gate he looked keenly at the guard. When he spoke to the commander it was in the forced friendly tone of a great man who is actually in a bad temper but thinks it profitable to be gracious to his inferiors. "Your sergeants are smart and well armed, as I shall tell Count William. But I recognize some faces from my last visit, five years ago. Do the same men remain in this garrison, without taking their turn in the exposed castles beyond Cotswold?"

The guard dismissed, feeling that this new lord would be a good leader to follow. All had noted, watching with the concentration with which all soldiers observe a new commander, how carefully he had avoided direct criticism of Count William, at the same time offering them the chance of plunder in the future.

Inside the castle, alone with Count William, young Henry spoke in a different tone. Since he was old enough to stand he had been the figurehead of his mother's cause, and whenever he saw soldiers he tried to make a good impression. But now he was taking charge of affairs. A little straight speaking would show Count William who was master; and by voicing his dissatisfaction he would relieve the appalling strain of controlling his temper.

"I have ridden from Wareham on the coast," he began. "When you have gathered a force for my escort I shall continue through the Marches of Wales right up to the border of Scotland. By the end of my ride I should have recruited an army, and then I march south to seek out Count Stephen of Blois. I shall bring him to battle, and finish this war on one decisive field."

Count William made a gesture of interest and assent. He could not see this stripling winning a pitched battle against Count Stephen, one of the best knights in Christendom, and he had no intention of risking the following of Gloucester in such a desperate enterprise. A decisive battle would be difficult to bring about; in the eleven years of the war there had been only two battles, at Northallerton with the Scots invaders, and at Lincoln where King Stephen was captured. Stephen would not run such a risk again. But there was no point in disagreeing with the boy; he would be cheated of his battle without unpleasant truth-telling here in Bristol.

"If we fight a battle we shall win it, I am sure," the boy continued. "But even if we are beaten that will make an end. We hold Normandy and Anjou, and we can manage without England. But we must end the war, one way or the other. I saw my father conquer Normandy, and since I was old enough to ride I have ridden over battlefields; but between Wareham and Bristol I have seen worse horrors than even in the ever-harried Vexin. We must bring peace, before the peasants eat one another."

"They don't often do that, my lord," Count William answered soothingly. "You think you have harried a village quite bare, but some of them hide on the waste; then they dig up their hidden seed corn, and scratch the ground again. If you ride there next year the place needs harrying again."

"In the last three days I have ridden through villages whose life will never return. When the dead are left unburied it means there are no survivors. That is what we have done, and we must do it no longer."

"Some places have been unlucky, but it isn't like that all over the country. At Tewkesbury, not far from here, they are building one of the finest abbeys in the world; and in other parts they build fine churches. The lords north of Trent obey neither Blois nor Anjou, and get on all the better with no taxes to pay."

It was a mistake to argue with Count Henry, though William of Gloucester was not to know it. He was only standing up for his native land, but the boy saw himself contradicted.

His whole aspect changed. His fists clenched on the arms of his chair, and inside his shabby brown leather shoes his toes curled; his freckled brow drew together in a frown, and red lights glowed in his gray eyes. As his answer tumbled out of him his voice jumped from a child's squeaky treble to an adult growl.

"You want the war to continue, don't you, Count of Gloucester? Things suit you very well as they are. You need not manage your lands, or foster good husbandry, while you can ride east and take anything you want from the miserable vassals of Stephen. It's less trouble to loot the seed corn of your enemies than to make your own tenants plow. You won't conquer Stephen, and he can't conquer you. That's why I see the same faces in Bristol gate that I saw five years ago. At Wallingford they are fighting. If you would fight with them Stephen must be driven back to Blois."

"My dear lord and cousin," began Count William, taken aback at such a sudden storm of fury.

"I am your cousin," the other cut in, still shouting, "but your father was base-born. My grandfather made him a count, and what has been granted may be taken away. Do not say 'Cousin' as though to an equal. My grandfathers were the King of England and the King of Jerusalem, and my mother is Empress of the Romans. One day I shall rule England and Normandy and Maine and Anjou. Compared to that, what is Gloucester?"

"You have omitted one of your ancestral titles, my lord," said Count William, also losing his temper. "Perhaps one day you will inherit Hell from your forefather."

"Yes, I am descended from the Devil himself, and you do well to remember it. I have come here to destroy Stephen the usurper. I shall summon all my vassals, and my mother's. If you neglect the summons even the demons of Hell will punish you. Oh, you tail-wearing English, never constant in any quarrel! I come to finish the war, and you thwart me to my face!

Here in your castle I can do nothing, but one day you will be disciplined as you deserve."

"The Empress is my lord, and I am her man," answered the other. "If she summons me I shall follow. But never did I swear to follow a boy who is not yet a knight, a child unfit to bear arms. Come back, my lord, when you are a man and a knight. Then you may give orders and I shall obey them."

That was the last straw. Henry threw himself on the floor, where he lay drumming his heels and screaming incoherently. His face was purple, and foam gathered on his mouth; but there was nothing childish in his rage. Count William took fright.

He knelt on the floor beside the writhing figure. "My lord, I shall follow your banner, as soon as you are knighted. Truly, I am a loyal servant of Anjou and the Empress. Now let me conduct you to your chamber. When you ride out my attendants will go with you."

Henry continued to scream. But deep inside him a great expanding cloud of wrath had burst like a bubble, and he was beginning to feel better. Whenever he was crossed it was always the same. First rage would fill his breast until he could scarcely breathe; then someone would remind him that the first Fulke of Anjou, Black Fulke, had married a daughter of Satan; and the memory of his diabolic ancestry would inflate his wrath beyond all bearing. He would abandon control, shrieking, kicking, writhing on the floor. Then . . . then his adversary would give in and apologize.

That was the method of self-expression he had perfected in early childhood, in the hate-filled castles where his father and mother bickered and screamed. If ordinary children shrieked themselves into hysterics they were slapped; but ordinary children were not descended from the Devil. His rage was noble, worthy of his ancestry. And the most important point of all, more important even than the deep relief of yielding to his passion, was that rage always got him his own way. It had worked in the nursery, and now it was working in Bristol castle.

Presently he came to himself, and walked quietly after his host to the chamber allotted to him. But he did not apologize. It was all to the good that Count William was frightened of his temper. Though now that he felt better he would have enjoyed a festive supper in hall, that would have spoiled the effect of his outburst.

For a few days, while the escort assembled for his hazardous ride to the far north, he wandered through the remembered streets of Bristol. He had known the town since he was old enough to tell one place from another, and his memories of it were chiefly pleasant.

In Bristol, when he was nine years old, he had first realized that learning could bring pleasure. Master Adelard of Bath, who had traveled the known world from the hot enclosed court-yards of Spain, tinkling with fountains under the fierce sun, to the mighty cities of Asia, where carved monuments marked the graves of rulers so ancient that their memory was forgotten —this Master Adelard had felt honored to teach all his lore to the son of the Empress, the great-grandson of the Conqueror. Before ever he came to England, in friendly Le Mans where merchants from Flanders bargained with merchants from Andalusia before the open gates, the poet Pierre de Saintes had sung to him of chivalry, honor, self-sacrifice, the service of God against the infidels of Outremer, and the service of fair ladies in the castles of the West. But in Bristol Master Adelard had taught him to read Latin, the key to all the great deeds of the past. To this descendant of mighty rulers he had spoken of statecraft, immutable law, the duty of protection and justice which the lord owed to his helpless peasantry. He had told of empires and kingdoms destroyed by weak rulers, and of re-publics overthrown by internal faction. Whatever example he chose, the lesson was always the same: Man is distinguished from the brutes because he lives in a State, and the State is only as strong as its ruler.

In Bristol, in that happy year 1142, when he was nine years old, he had been allowed to seal a charter as "rightful heir to England and Normandy." The charter was issued by his mother, and his seal was only a confirmation; but he had never forgotten the thrill of that first act of kingship.

When he was fourteen he saw Bristol again; but that was an unpleasant memory, over which he did not linger. The first campaign in which he had been nominal commander (though no one listened to him) had ended in shameful defeat. That was not his fault. He had led every man who would follow straight against the army of the usurper, the knightly way of fighting a civil war; and if at Cricklade his sergeants refused to charge against odds of ten to one the shame was theirs, not his. He had done his duty, to the admiration even of his foes. Why else should Count Stephen send him money for his return to Normandy? Base cynics said he had done it to get a tiresome rival out of the country; but the usurper had exacted no promise of peace in return for his silver, and Stephen, though he seized a realm which was his cousin's birthright, was acknowledged to be one of the most chivalrous knights in Christendom.

Two years ago he had been unworthy of victory, a child striving against dubbed knights. But for his next campaign everything would be different; next time he led his men against the usurper he would be a true knight himself, and then victory must favor the righteous cause.

Meanwhile here he was in Bristol, the scene of happy memories (though it could not compare with Le Mans). For these few days he might enjoy himself.

By Easter he was riding north, through the close-set castles of the Marches of Wales. This was the land of war, more often ravaged even than the Vexin. But here war had a pleasant face; every man was a warrior, and the castles could shelter the women and children. When you rode past burned huts the peasants were not corpses rotting in the rain; they had taken their spears to drive the cattle of their neighbors. In such country, where all life was based on cattle-raiding, even a good king need not impose perpetual peace.

By Pentecost he had reached the Scottish border, riding all the way through the lands of magnates who followed the Angevin leopards. While such a great belt of country defied him it was absurd to call Stephen King of England. The Empress might have given up the struggle, retiring in despair to the comforts of Maine; but she had despaired too soon. Even while his opponent was a boy, unknighted, Count Stephen could not control the realm whose holy crown had been placed unlawfully on his brow.

The despair of the Empress had wrought great harm to the Angevin cause; but then he had never had loyal help from his parents, whose quarrels had formed the constant background of his childhood. When he was four he had heard his father, a little drunk after supper, remind the great Empress that after their wedding he had sent her home to her father, as too proud and overbearing to make a fitting wife for a Count of Anjou. His mother, as she sat disapproving in the stiff hieratic posture of the Imperial court, had answered coldly that she remembered very well; she also remembered that when her father, the mighty King of England and Duke of Normandy, recalled Count Geoffrey to his duty he had come to heel like the half-trained puppy he was. His father had then wondered audibly whether there could be any truth in the rumor that the Emperor was still alive; men whispered that Henry V had staged a mock funeral, to go off and live as a holy hermit in the forest. If that were true, and there were men in Germany who believed it, then the Empress had been incapable of contracting a second marriage, "And that squalling brat is a bastard, heir to nothing." But he had never heard the end of that particular quarrel, for the Devil's rage had come on him for the first time, and he had been carried, kicking and struggling, from the hall.

Young Henry must battle alone for his rights, without help from his parents; and in England, whose men had been cursed with tails as an emblem of faithlessness, he could never count on true loyalty. He must do everything himself. But he felt in his bones that one day he would be a great king; and he had one asset, his devilish rage, the rage that scared waverers and convinced the doubtful. When things looked black he need only give way to the red mist that flooded his brain; he would make a remarkable exhibition of himself, but when he was calm again affairs would have altered for the better. It was a distinction to be descended from the Devil, a distinction to be cherished.

At Carlisle he found the motley army of the King of Scots: mailed Norman knights, English spearmen from Lothian, Viking mercenaries from the Isles, and the naked targeteers of Galloway. The chief part of the host were light skirmishing foot, who could never dispute the field with the knight-service of England; they would be useless for war against Count Stephen. But if the Count of Chester and the Marchers of Wales rallied to the projected invasion the Scots army would be a useful reinforcement.

King David, his great-uncle, was a queer ancient figure, long past active campaigning; he spoke bad French with his mother's English accent, and introduced odd Celtic terms in discussing war and politics. Sixty years ago the Celtic court of Scotland had set itself to learn English manners from the holy English Queen; now the courtiers were trying to be as Norman as possible, and the effort was visible in a disturbing uncertainty of etiquette. These were not seemly allies for a prince of Anjou.

But King David was a crowned king, for all that his realm was so barbarous. There was disagreement among learned clerks about the nature of the grace conferred by Coronation, but whatever it was, Uncle David possessed it. With a genuine king as an ally Henry felt himself nearer the throne which was his birthright.

On the 22nd of May 1149 the Mass of Pentecost was celebrated with fitting splendor in Carlisle Cathedral, in the presence of the Bishop, a crowned king, and the magnates of Scotland and Northumbria. After Mass, still fasting, all walked in procession to the great hall of the castle, and there Henry Count of Anjou knelt before King David. The old King spoke briefly of the duties of knighthood: a true knight must defend the defenseless, widows and orphans, strangers, and the clerks of God's Church who might not bear arms; a knight was one with the brotherhood of the Maccabees and Charlemagne, of King Arthur and St. George. Then he gave Henry the last blow he might accept without instant retaliation, whatever the odds. Sir Henry fitzEmpress, Count of Anjou, was led to the place of honor at the board, where at last he might break the fast of his night-long vigil.

As he sat in his place, while hairy Island chieftains and red-cheeked Lowland ladies drank his health and wished him luck, Henry felt within himself a glow of kindliness and courtesy. As a knight he had no superior anywhere in the world, but in compensation he must be gentle with equals and inferiors. For him in particular, that meant that he must control his devilish temper.

Presently, to change the subject from the analysis of his own virtues which seemed to dominate the table (for these Scots were determined to be as courteous as any Provençal) he inquired for news of the Count of Chester.

"Too much business spoils a feast," answered the King. "I have news of Count Ranulf, but we shall discuss it apart."

Henry knew at once that it could not be good news; good news would have been proclaimed aloud, to encourage the feasters. But he was now a knight, worthy to lead his mother's armies; he must bear bad news with calm. Until the end of the meal he talked light-heartedly with his neighbors, amusing the table by trying out the few English phrases he had learned by rote (in a ridiculous south-country pronunciation) on a merry young lady from Haddington who was so old-fashioned as to speak no other language. It seemed that he had been misled concerning the meaning of some of these phrases, but making a lady blush was one of the amusements proper to a feast.

At last the dinner ended, and the two leaders could withdraw to talk privately. Both were sober, King David because at his age he must be careful with the wine jug, Henry because he had talked too much to have time for drinking; he was flushed and excited, but by knighthood, not by wine.

As soon as they reached the only small room which was found in any castle where the lord might be private, King David groaned, and spoke in a ponderous fatherly tone. "My dear nephew, you must prepare for a disappointment. Count Ranulf writes that the men of Chester will not join with a Scottish army. He reminds me that in England the Scots are hated, since we treated them so roughly in that unfortunate invasion which ended at Northallerton. If that was the truth there would still be hope. The men of Chester are as fond of plunder as other men, and they might join us if we offered them the plundering of York. But I have agents in Ranulf's council, and they have told me why he wrote. He has changed sides again. I know he's a Blundeville, but he must have grown the same tail as the volatile native English. All Englishmen change sides for a trifle. What he did in fact was to write to King Stephen, saying that he had a chance to link up with a Scottish army for the ravaging of Northumbria. King Stephen understood. He offered Ranulf more, in money and land, than he could win from the most successful season of raiding. There it is. Ranulf has been bought, and we can't buy him back again. My poor realm cannot bid against the Treasury at Winchester."

Henry received the news with complete calm. As casually as if discussing the weather he answered: "Then what will you do, Uncle? Your men are gathered, and some lords of the Marches will join my banner, even if Chester hangs back. At least we can draw Count Stephen northward, by ravaging Lancashire. That will give relief to Brian fitzCount and his gallant garrison in Wallingford."

"No, I shall go back to Dunfermline. My light spearmen cannot face mailed horse, and I dare not provoke King Stephen to lead the knight-service of England against me. I have given you knighthood; more I cannot offer."

Henry had been struggling to preserve his calm. He must not disgrace his new knighthood by a display of Angevin rage, and when he learned that Count Ranulf had been bought, contempt for such a recreant preserved him from any stronger emotion. But King David's second speech was more than he could bear. His policy was based on two firm beliefs, that the King of Scots was a powerful ally, and that Stephen, Count of Blois, could never call out the knight-service of England. Now he heard his uncle proclaim, as a matter of fact universally admitted, that the Scots dared not meet England in the field; at the same time he gave Stephen the kingly title, and assumed that all England would follow his banner. Were all kings faithless, even his uncle? Must he ride tamely back to Bristol without drawing his knightly sword? Was there nothing he could do to win the throne that was his by right? Even more important, was there nothing he could do to save himself from looking ridiculous?

That question brought its own answer, the familiar answer which had solaced his unhappy childhood. The bubble of rage swelled in his breast until he was barely able to restrain it. If he yielded to it he would find comfort in the warm flood. Perhaps this was shameful for a knight, but he must lose his temper or burst.

King David was amazed. This stony-faced lad had heard the bad news with stoic calm until the end. Now he had fallen off his stool to claw the rushes on the floor while he screamed imprecations on the house of Blundeville, the house of Blois, and even his kin the royal house of Scotland. He kicked off his shoes, and shrieked through purple cheeks. The knights of the bodyguard crowded into the study, sword in hand.

While dignified Celtic chieftains hurried their King from the presence of this unseemly maniac the knights of the Angevin escort knelt in ecstasy beside their young lord. "Hear how he shouts, the offspring of Melusine daughter of Satan! Listen to those curses! No one in Carlisle can curse so strongly, not even the Bishop! Ah, there's a true son of Black Fulke. No matter if his mother is still wed to the Emperor, there's the lord who will lead his knights to rich plunder! Did you ever hear such roaring? The very sound gives me fresh courage!"

In May 1152 the nineteen-year-old Count of Anjou and Duke of Normandy paced the flat roof of the keep of Rouen castle, where he could be alone with his thoughts. He was dressed, as usual, in dingy hodden-gray tunic and hose, but now a baldric embroidered with gold thread crossed his right shoulder. The ducal sword of Normandy was a heavy ceremonial object, which he wore only for occasions of state; but the baldric demonstrated his right to wear it, the right that had come to him six months ago on the death of his father.

In fact he had exercised a good deal of power even during his father's lifetime. He was the sort of man a Duke of Normandy ought to be. In battle he was swift and determined, sitting well in the saddle; not outstanding as a lance, but up to the average.

For all that he passed many hours in hunting, he was willing to work at his task of governing the Duchy; men took their disputes gladly to his judgment, for they knew they would get a final decision as soon as the case was heard. (But the most eager litigants were those with a righteous cause, for Henry had a remarkable knack of getting at the truth through a tangle of conflicting testimony.) While he galloped the muddy roads of his Duchy there was peace in the land, firmer peace than the oldest peasant could remember.

There was war on the borders, for that was a normal condition. In that perpetual warfare the young Duke had played a worthy part. Of course there was never a hope of final victory; the best the Normans could hope for was that this time they would drive back their more powerful antagonist. Henry had led his knights gallantly against the French, even when King Louis was reinforced by Count Eustace of Blois, son of the usurper in England. By refusing to attack the person of his lord, when he surprised King Louis in the castle of Arques, he had given a much-needed example of the rights and duties of a vassal in rebellion. His cause was righteous, for he was defending the inheritance of his mother from invasion; but even a righteous cause could not excuse a direct assault on the person of his lord. The magnates of Normandy, his own vassals, would be wise to remember the lesson, for if they neglected it they might expect no mercy.

In the end the strong hostile coalition had agreed to a truce, at the small price of the Vexin, now in French hands—until the war began again. Externally he had given Normandy peace as the reward of honorable defeat; at home his firm rule brought wealth and prosperity.

But he was still no nearer the crown of England. Count Stephen the usurper had reigned for sixteen years, and it would seem that he must die with the crown on his brow.

If Henry rested content with what he had he would pass his

life as Duke of Normandy and Count of Anjou, one of the six lay peers of France, almost an independent prince. He was too powerful to be conquered by his suzerain, and he would transmit the Duchy undiminished to his heirs. But if he disturbed the balance of power he might unleash forces which could destroy him.

Because he now had a chance to alter the whole political geography of Christendom he had climbed to this lofty platform to think undisturbed. Word had come to him, secretly and unofficially but from a source he could trust, that the greatest fief in France, a fief much richer even than Normandy, would be his for the asking—if he could hold it. To take this chance would mean a renewal of the war with King Louis, and the jealous hostility of his half-dozen equals; but he might win the war, he might even make Rouen the capital of a principality more important than the Kingdom of France.

Of course the King in Paris would still be his suzerain. He had sworn homage, and that was an oath he would never break. He had the hard common sense to see for himself, what Master Adelard had taught him in childhood, that the power of every great magnate in Christendom rested on the sanctity of the vassal's oath; if he set the example of breaking it his own knights would no longer be bound to follow him.

But if he could add to the Duchy of Normandy and the County of Anjou the Duchy of Aquitaine, he would be the strongest prince west of the Rhine. And if after this accession of power he conquered his rightful inheritance of England he would be the greatest king in the civilized world, greater even than the Emperor. The stupendous chance had come suddenly, and he must accept or refuse without hesitation, knowing that if he refused Aquitaine would be offered to a rival; and with Aquitaine he must take a willful proud lady, who had already proved too independent for the pious King of France.

For nearly fourteen years the Duchess Eleanor, ruler of

Aquitaine in her own right, had been the quarrelsome and unmanageable queen of King Louis VII. In all that time she had never borne him a son, and even the supposedly lucky child conceived in Rome, after the reconciliation effected by a personal intervention of the Pope, had proved to be yet another daughter. The lady Eleanor was a famous beauty, now of mature age; she was fruitful, of most noble birth, an excellent ruler of her paternal inheritance, well known for her intelligence and force of character. She was also notoriously flighty, and said to be wanton; her temper matched his own, without the excuse of diabolic ancestry. After years of bickering and the most startling mutual accusations she and King Louis had agreed to part. As with every member of the high nobility who took care to preserve full details of ancient pedigrees, it had been easy to find a common ancestor a few generations back; that brought them within the prohibited degree of consanguinity, and without a papal dispensation their marriage was invalid. Instead of the dispensation they had asked for an annulment, which had been willingly granted. Now the lady Eleanor offered her hand to the Duke of Normandy, nine years her junior and almost unknown to her.

Of course it was not his prowess as a knight or the charm of his demeanor that had won her heart, though she was polite enough to say so in her secret message of proposal. Her Duchy needed an efficient protector, and of all the magnates of France he was the only one unmarried and about her age. She wished to marry Normandy, not Henry. Well, if he accepted it would be to marry Aquitaine, not Eleanor.

If he refused he might live peacefully, with plenty of leisure for the hunting which was his favorite amusement, and enough of the business of governing his lands, a business he was beginning to find absorbing, to allow him to feel that he was doing something with his life. But to the end of his days he would know he had missed a great opportunity. If he married this headstrong beauty he would find himself at war with the world; he would probably die in mail; he would struggle unceasingly; but he might become the greatest potentate in the West.

When he had posed the problem to himself in those terms he came down from the roof to dictate his letter of acceptance. He was an Angevin, a son of the Devil, descended also from Rollo the pirate; with such an ancestry he must inevitably choose power rather than ease.

Within a fortnight he waited on the lady of his choice to deliver the formal offer of marriage which good manners demanded, even though his lawyers and hers were already negotiating the terms of her dower as Duchess of Normandy. Once or twice at formal ceremonies he had seen Eleanor, Queen of France; but he had never spoken freely to her, or even looked at her closely; he met his promised bride for the first time while the marriage contract was being drafted.

There was nothing odd in that; it was the normal way in which an alliance of great magnates was arranged. If his father had lived to arrange a marriage for him he would have been sent off to a stranger without even the option of refusing to propose to her. What was unusual was the experience and knowledge of the world his lady possessed, her reputation as a beauty, and her age. When he was introduced into the bower where she sat with her damsels, modestly embroidering an altar cloth, he looked at her boldly, in a way which often made young ladies blush and bridle; but it was curiosity, not loving ardor, which made him stare so earnestly.

He saw a bold voluptuous beauty, with hot brown eyes in a white face. Her green silk gown was laced close to the figure, emphasizing her rounded thighs and swelling bosom; the fashion was for willowy slenderness, but Eleanor had the sense to see that she could not follow it; by stressing her unfashionable figure she achieved a striking singularity. Over her gown she wore a sleeveless blouse of blue silk, powdered with golden pomegranates. Her headdress was a white muslin wimple, within the ducal coronet of Aquitaine. Her hands were very white and slim, and she glanced first at his hairy freckled paws, scarred by the beaks of hawks and calloused by his charger's reins. He was conscious of his ungainliness, standing there sturdily, his square shoulders thrusting out the red cloak bearing three golden leopards which was the most splendid garment he possessed. She looked infinitely desirable, and not at all trustworthy. A splendid mistress, but not the woman a wise man would take to wife.

"Welcome, my lord," she said in a husky, throbbing voice. "It is noble of you to come at the call of a lady in distress. The King has treated me shamefully. Because of his double-dealing I am neither maid, wife, nor widow, and my inheritance lies at the mercy of every ravening wolf in France. Count Theobald of Champagne and Count Geoffrey your own brother pursue me. King Louis took me, and had his pleasure of me. Now, because he is not man enough to get a son, he has cast me off. I appeal to your chivalry to guard defenseless Aquitaine."

Henry would have preferred a more businesslike conversation. It was absurd to pretend that two people meeting for the first time were already deeply in love, and in his private opinion anything the lady had suffered she had richly earned. She had accompanied King Louis on his futile Crusade, which was one reason why Edessa was still in infidel hands; if half the stories of her adventures in Outremer were true she was lucky to have a head on her shoulders. It is the duty of any king to take vengeance on a faithless queen, lest the succession to his kingdom, that sacred trust, should go astray. Louis had merely got rid of her by a friendly annulment, and she had nothing to complain of. But since she had begun the interview on a note of high chivalry he replied in the same vein.

"My lady, your wrongs would rouse the blood of any true knight. When I knew you sought my aid I came as swiftly as horse could bear me. But if I am to protect you from your enemies it would be more seemly if you gave me the right to be with you day and night. This is a brief wooing, but you already know that every man who is admitted to your presence seeks to possess you. I am your peer in blood, and free to marry. I beg you to accept my sword as your defense, and my company to relieve your loneliness."

Eleanor rose from her cushioned chair, in a graceful rippling motion that brought out all the curves of her body. She made to clasp the young man in her arms, but he evaded the embrace by sinking to his knees.

"My true knight," she murmured. "With your sword to defend me I need fear no foe. As a helpless heiress I live in daily dread that some ruffian will carry me off and force me. Let us be wed as soon as the clerks can arrange it. Then I shall sleep in safety, and with a stout young hero. We shall be merry in Aquitaine, and you can help me to judge the suits my vassals bring before me."

"I am the happiest of men," mumbled Henry, who had bumped his nose on her jeweled girdle as he knelt.

The snow had turned to rain, which was if anything more unpleasant. There had been frost a few days ago, and half the war horses were coughing; a soaking would kill them as they stood at the picket-ropes. The sun had not been seen for a week, and it was difficult to measure time; but the gloom of the January day was thickening, and lucky men far away, under the shelter of roofs and walls, would be beginning to think of supper.

A numbed sergeant sat hunched on the river bank, his head drawn into his shoulders; over his rusty mail he wore a truss of straw, fixed like thatch to keep off the rain; but he had been wet through five minutes after he had taken post. His head was bent so low that an army might have paraded unnoticed in the next field, but what he watched was the thick brown flood of Avon at his feet. Reluctantly he rose, noting with disgust that rain water at once made a puddle of the dry patch where he had been sitting; but the twig he had placed by the water's edge had just been swept away by the current, and it was his duty to report.

Splashing through the slippery grass with the clumsy tread of a horseman, he reached the rag of sacking stuck on spear points which marked the bivouac of his captain. Several drenched straw-covered figures sat under it, too miserable to raise their heads at his approach; he addressed the group at large.

"Send to tell the Duke that the river is still rising: half a hand, by the marker I put in when I took post. We shall have to shift the horse-lines. By morning the stream will be ready to burst its banks."

"You need not send far to tell the Duke. Here I am. Now show me this flood. Do you know about rivers? What part of the world do you come from?"

The sodden warrior who had risen to answer him looked no better dressed or better fed than the mercenary sergeants round him. But the man immediately recognized his lord. There was no mistaking that broad-shouldered figure when it moved into its characteristic jerky action. The pink-and-white face, jaw and cheeks veiled by a thin scrub of sandy hair, looked younger than Henry's nineteen years; but the square freckled hands, with their thick distorted fingernails, might have belonged to a middle-aged craftsman. Obviously, when there was no one to fight and nowhere to ride, one might expect to find the Duke of Normandy plodding on foot round his outposts. The sergeant felt glad that under his lord's eye he had shown himself alert.

"I serve among the Brabançons, my lord," he answered. "But

I myself am a Fleming, Robert of Courtrai. The river Dyle drove me from my holding and made me a mercenary. I have seen mighty floods many times in my life."

"Then walk with me by the river bank. I must be sure Stephen's men cannot cross tonight. If there is any doubt we must stand to arms, but perhaps this rain will give us a night's rest. Tell me the truth." His hand on the sergeant's shoulder could be felt through the links of his mail. "You want a night in blankets, like every other mercenary. If you tell me the river is impassable and I find tomorrow that even one man has got across, I shall gut you like a salmon, with my own knife."

The Fleming squinted wisely up and down the flooded Avon.

"There's a ford just here, my lord, as you can see from the tracks. It's seldom used, probably a local short cut. Look, horses cross, but never a wagon; so it must be deep at the best of times. No one would chance it with the river raging like this. There's another crossing half a mile upstream. I can't be certain of that until I see it close."

They called for horses, and rode by the water. Presently Robert pointed out a shelving margin, where deep ruts were roughly filled with stones. "That's a wagon-ford, my lord, where the wheels have scored the bank. There's no road to it. Probably one man holds land on both banks, and sometimes he will take his team across. Oxen too, I see, and they flinch from what a horse will face. At a pinch I might cross here even in this weather, on a good horse and without my mail. But no man could cross armed. We may sleep sound tonight."

"It can be crossed, you say? Then we shall cross it. Do you want to make your fortune, Robert of Courtrai? Then you will strip off your mail, and choose any horse in the army except my own mount. You can keep him afterward. You and I will ride together unarmed through the flood. We shall take a rope, and fix it to a tree on the far side. Our foot will throw in brushwood to make a sound bottom. With the rope and the brushwood men can cross, even armed. That's it. By dawn tomorrow we shall be before Malmesbury, and you will hold richer land in England than the Dyle took from you in Flanders. Or of course we may be drowned. But it's by risking death every day that we soldiers earn our suppers."

The sergeant grinned with delight. This was what made soldiering the best of trades, in spite of the low pay. A few hours of risky work and he would be set up for life. He was glad that his band had come ashore in Devon, and so enlisted in the Angevin cause; but for an easterly wind they would have made the Solent to join the army of King Stephen. He liked this gallant young lord, and looked forward to a life as his landholding vassal.

Unfortunately he was drowned instead, and Duke Henry had a very narrow escape. It proved impossible to ford the flooded Avon, and the army remained in the same waterlogged camp for several days, peering through the mist at the castle of Malmesbury where King Stephen and his forces lay awaiting battle.

But the effort to force a crossing kept the Angevins interested and keen, while Stephen's men sat about in the rain with nothing to do. When at last the rain ceased and the river subsided Henry forded an unguarded stream, to find Malmesbury lightly garrisoned and willing to surrender at the first summons.

King Stephen's army had gone home to get out of the wet. It was made up of English knights reluctantly performing their feudal duty, who knew that if they all deserted in a body the King could not punish them; and there was a general feeling that soon King Stephen would be unable to enforce his will even on individuals. Latterly he had captured some Angevin castles, but the war still dragged on without an end in sight; and the whole Church now backed Duke Henry, from the Pope in Rome, who had openly forbidden the crowning of Stephen's heir, to the Archbishop of Canterbury, who must officially obey the crowned King but who could find ways of letting his sentiments be known. In any civil war public opinion is the deciding factor, and public opinion had declared against Stephen, the enemy of the Church.

In high spirits Duke Henry's army rode eastward until they reached the faithful castle of Wallingford, for many years the farthest Angevin outpost. They drove back the besiegers to their counter-fortress at Crowmarsh on the opposite bank of the Thames. The faithful castle had been at the extremity of endurance, and there was great rejoicing when the leaders of the relieving army were feasted in its hall. The Angevins were not only encouraged to find themselves winning at long last; their fervor for the cause was also increased by the lucky accident that the Castellan of Wallingford, Brian fitzCount, was perhaps the only disinterested and chivalrous leader who had fought on either side through the treasons and maneuvers of the long, sordid struggle. Ever since, fifteen years before, he had sworn homage to the Empress, he had upheld her cause, seeing his lands ravaged to the last haystack without heeding the tempting offers of King Stephen.

The cause for which the lord Brian had given everything seemed the more noble in consequence. The old game in which powerful magnates put themselves up for auction, or supported the weaker claimant to keep the war alive—that old game was now outmoded. When they heard that King Stephen was marching on Wallingford the Angevins faced the impending battle with high hearts.

There was no battle. Stephen's army would not fight, and the magnates of both parties arranged a truce. Obviously the war was ended at last, and King Stephen was the loser.

During that summer Henry rode through the midlands, receiving the homage of doubtful magnates and seeing the leopards of Anjou hoisted on the keeps of strong castles before his besieging army had time to unsaddle. It seemed that God Himself intervened to end the war, by removing irreconcilable contestants. Matilda of Boulogne, Stephen's queen and the best man in her party, died in her bed; the aged David, King of Scots, was dead at last; the double-dealing Count of Chester was sick to death and would never ride again. That gave the parties something to bargain with, for King David and Count Ranulf had accumulated claims to half the fiefs in England. Then Count Eustace, Stephen's heir, was struck down by disease as he ravaged the monasteries of the fens. King Stephen was old and sick and lonely. When the Archbishop of Canterbury suggested another peace conference at Winchester, he agreed to attend.

The Winchester conference of November 1153 had been arranged by the Church. It was to be held in the castle of the Bishop, who was brother to King Stephen and cousin to Duke Henry, but it had been summoned by the Archbishop of Canterbury, and Archbishop Theobald was naturally anxious that it should open smoothly. On the feast of St. Martin, soldier and bishop, he said Mass with special fervor and at breakfast afterward ran over the arrangements with his most trusted assistant, the new Archdeacon of Canterbury.

"These men have been fighting one another for fifteen years, and it will be a great thing if we can start them talking peaceably together in one hall. What I fear is that in the first half-hour someone will insult someone else, and then one side will sweep out in a huff. After that we may never get them talking again. You have arranged that they shall enter separately?"

"Yes, my lord. King Stephen will be seated on his throne, among his supporters, when Duke Henry and the Angevins come in by the main door; it will be opened by the Deputy Constable as a herald cries: 'Make way for the Duke of Normandy and Aquitaine.' The King will then rise from his throne and advance to meet the Duke. Then both parties seat them-

selves on benches, with a long table between; and the throne
on the dais will remain empty."

"You yourself arranged these details, Master Thomas? You
have an instinct for ceremonial."

"I was greatly assisted, my lord, by Master John of Salisbury,
who is familiar with the protocol of the papal Curia."

"Of course, of course. But my dear John would never have
won agreement from all these hot-tempered magnates. You
deserve our thanks. That is, if you are certain both sides will
abide by their agreements. Are you sure Duke Henry won't
change his mind at the last minute?"

"No one can be sure of that. They say the young man has the
temper of a devil. But he has given his word that he will do
what has been laid down for him, and by public repute he
is a knight who keeps his word of honor. I was careful to negotiate only with his clerks, never meeting him myself; in that
way I could press a point without rousing his famous wrath.
And by this procedure we avoid the most dangerous crux. The
high and puissant prince Stephen of Blois sits on a throne, and
I expect he will wear a crown. But no herald proclaims him
publicly as King of England. That is the one condition on which
Duke Henry insisted."

"Stephen is King, all the same. I myself placed the crown on
his brow, and Coronation alone confers royal power. Duke
Henry may call the realm an hereditary fief, but it has never
yet passed by hereditary right. By Henry's argument his grandfather, from whom he claims, had usurped the right of poor
Duke Robert."

"I hinted as much to the Angevin clerk, without putting it
as bluntly as Your Grace puts it to me. He took the point at
once, but I imagine he did not pass it on to his lord. *We* know,
all clerks know, that Coronation makes the King. But Duke
Henry thinks differently. His theory is that the throne is

never vacant, because at the moment a king dies his heir becomes king. Nonsense, of course, and contrary to received legal opinion. But that is what he and his mother fought for, and we can't expect them to abandon the point before the conference opens."

"No, the great thing is to stop the war, on almost any terms. But I hope we can get Duke Henry to admit that Stephen *has* been King. Otherwise every legal decision of the last seventeen years will be invalid, and no man will enjoy a clear title to land."

"I hope that admission will be the fruit of this conference. The best compromise we can hope for is recognition of King Stephen, with Duke Henry named his heir, and some arrangement to give the young man a share in the administration in the meantime. But we can do no more than bring the two sides together. We have no armed force, and Canterbury will look undignified if we sit helpless while matters are arranged against our wishes. For that reason, among others, I wish to avoid taking part in the conference. There are also arrears of business waiting for me."

"As you wish, Master Thomas. I must remain, to put the seal of the Church on the best peace they can arrange. But you will be more useful in Canterbury, doing the work that awaits you. If the Church needs an army the Bishop of Winchester is the man to levy it. You may go when you are ready, but I must repeat my thanks for your skillful negotiation of the preliminaries."

As Master Thomas of London, Archdeacon of Canterbury, withdrew from the presence of his lord, Archbishop Theobald reflected once again on his luck in finding such an efficient lawyer and diplomatist. Canon law was a mass of undigested and conflicting precedents, badly in need of codification (though they were making a start on that in Italy); Thomas remembered every decided case, and his own decisions were seldom upset on appeal. He had a good head for figures, so that the revenue of the See came in very regularly, considering the disturbed state of the country. Most important of all, he was a really superb negotiator. Pleading before a tribunal (and he had twice journeyed to Rome to plead before the Curia) his arguments were clear and comprehensive; his language was not eloquent, but lawyers distrust eloquence, and his trick of presenting a weak case almost apologetically made the judges feel that he was treating them fairly and that even his weak arguments should be given their full weight. But it was in compromising cases before they came into court that he really shone: as he had shone in arranging the preliminaries for the conference of Winchester. He always saw his opponent's point of view, he could give way gracefully without arguing to the bitter end, and he sounded so reasonable that he never gave personal offense.

It was a pity that he lacked the gift of getting on with his fellow clerks. In the household he seemed definitely unpopular, though Theobald found him pleasant enough. What was it Master Roger called him—Bailhache, the hatchet-carrier? What a curious nickname! There must be a story behind it. It was unfortunate that at Lambeth or Harrow one could not ignore his vulgar birth, since his father's old friends were always dropping in for a chat. If he had traveled farther from his birthplace he could have passed as a gentleman, for his manners were courteous, though stiff. He was a good man, who prayed regularly and kept the Commandments. But Theobald, an experienced director of souls, saw that Thomas was obeying the rules, not serving God for the love of God.

He made a very good archdeacon; but archdeacon was about his mark. An official whose chief duty was collecting money due to the See, and judging those sordid matrimonial cases, must be tainted with worldliness. What a pity Roger had picked up the story of that mock disputation in Paris, when the leading lecturers debated together in a tavern after supper! The real object had been to advertise the speakers, who seized the opportunity to be merely facetious; but the question in dispute had been: "Can the soul of an archdeacon be saved?" and the verdict of a hilarious audience had been overwhelmingly in the negative. Roger was always coming back to the topic, though one could see that Thomas found it hard to control an exceptionally fiery temper.

The young man deserved promotion, and the next step must be a bishopric. Theobald hesitated; he had promoted the last archdeacon, who was his own brother, to the unimportant See of Rochester; Walter was not really competent to run a diocese, but even the most upright prelate owes something to his kin, and at Rochester, under the eye of Canterbury, he could not get into serious trouble. But with Rochester filled there was nothing of that kind left for Thomas. If he was made bishop he must be in independent charge of his see. He would quarrel with his chapter, excommunicate laymen whom tact and kindness might have brought to repentance, and end up with half his parishes in sullen discontent. No, he did not deserve to be made bishop.

Theobald's thoughts ran on. He himself could give the young man nothing greater than a miter, and when you came to think of it the office of bishop, successor of the Apostles and shepherd of his flock, was the highest in the world. But Thomas would appreciate a post where he could give orders and get things done, without spending too much time on spiritual affairs. In fact what he deserved, and what he would like, would be an important post in some secular government. Kings were always stealing Theobald's most valuable clerks, as King William of Sicily had stolen that excellent Master Thomas

Brown; here at last was a competent servant whom he would be glad to recommend to a secular prince.

With the future of Thomas neatly docketed in his mind Theobald turned with a sigh to the more intractable problems of the government of England.

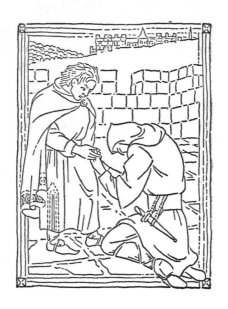

CHAPTER IV

The Fair Promise of a New Reign

O N the 19th of December 1154 Henry, Duke of Normandy and Aquitaine, Count of Maine and Anjou, was crowned King of England in Westminster Abbey. Henry had peacefully attained the crown for which he had fought since he was old enough to sit a horse, and he owed it chiefly to Theobald's diplomacy. At the Coronation banquet in Westminster Hall the Archbishop sat at his right hand, as was his due; and the two greatest men in England discussed affairs of state.

"You have kept the peace for me, my lord Archbishop," the King said graciously. "For the last two months, since Stephen died, you have in fact been King yourself, and you hand me over a realm in remarkably fine order. No rebels, and only the usual brigands. I shall deal with them by pulling down the castles in which they store their plunder. I owe you much, and this joyful occasion seems a good time to repay it. Is there anything I can do for Holy Church? Any wrong that needs redressing?"

"We want nothing, my lord, except peace and good order," Theobald answered. "Since Duke William conquered this realm there have been times when the Church was oppressed. In particular the law of the Conqueror, forbidding bishops to go oversea without the King's permission, was a constant source of friction. You may recall that even I was forced to quarrel with King Stephen on the subject. But King Stephen gave way, and now the Church enjoys complete liberty. Maintain the good customs you find in this realm, and especially the good customs introduced by King Stephen, and all will be well."

King Henry frowned at this plain speaking. It was against all right that Count Stephen of Blois, the usurper against whom he and his mother had battled for eighteen years, should be recognized as having been lawful King of England. His acts should be annulled, and King Henry II should be written in the lawbooks as immediate successor of his grandfather Henry I. But at Winchester he had compromised, yielding this point in return for a peaceful succession; in the rolls he would appear as heir to King Stephen, bound by the customs of that feckless ruler—until he could persuade the magnates to alter them. It was the price he had paid for the support of the Church; once again the Archbishop was making this clear.

The Coronation banquet went on and on. All the magnates of England were seated at long tables under the lofty roof of the Hall, the largest and most famous secular building of modern times; they must be served without unseemly haste, and they should be given plenty of time to gossip among themselves, for this meeting was a parliament as well as a feast. King Henry had sat down fasting, since Communion was part of the ritual of Coronation; and in consequence he was hungry as well as bored. It was ironical that he should go hungry at the most splendid banquet of his reign; but this was an occasion for show, when the sergeant-cook might let himself go in creating elaborate fantasies of almond paste and sugar. Humble spectators in the doorway cheered to see a pasty from which, when it was opened, living doves fluttered out; but Henry reflected gloomily that a cook who was encouraged to put back all the plumage on a roast peacock, and add sugar eyes to the boar's head, always forgot to provide a plain everyday joint that would make a square meal for a hungry man. If he pushed down any more ginger or pistachio nuts his stomach would revolt, and he had not found a decent haunch of venison within reach of his knife.

He felt his anger rising, anger at these smug pudding-faced English magnates who had changed sides in the civil war until it made you dizzy to watch them, who had lain dry in warm castles while he camped by the flooded Avon, who had written friendly noncommittal letters while his mother rode for her life in a man's saddle or slid down a rope to escape on foot through the snow. They needed a master to subdue their pride, and by God he would be that master if he had to live and die in his mail.

The angry self-pity in his soul colored even his conversation with the Archbishop. "My lord," he said with a formal smile, to show he was opening a new topic, "you must be my fellow governor in this realm, for I am singularly without colleagues in my own family. My mother has willingly resigned her claims into my hands, and it would be unwise to allow her to meddle in public affairs. She has a remarkable facility in getting herself disliked, especially by the English. As for my wife, she is quite untrustworthy. She sees everything from the point of view of Aquitaine, and would reduce the rest of Christendom to a desert if she thought that would benefit the burgesses of Bordeaux. And for various other reasons I am never sure she is honestly on my side."

That is his own fault, thought Theobald to himself. He knew consanguinity was only an excuse for the annulment. He married a trollop for her lands. Of course he fears that the whole world, except himself, knows him a cuckold. Serve him right for marrying for money. . . . He smiled, to encourage the King to continue.

"My brothers are no help to me," the complaining voice went on. "My first task when I am secure in England must be to expel my brother Geoffrey from Maine, which he unjustly detains. My brother William may help Geoffrey or he may help me, but more likely he will try to betray us both. My house is descended from the Devil, and I would be foolish to look to my kin for help. In England the most famous statesman is the Bishop of Winchester; but he is the brother of the late usurper, and my followers would be angry if I sought his counsel. Of course I can't trust any lay magnate. Some of them fought for my cause, but more because they wanted to rebel against the King in London than because they recognized the lawfulness of my claim. I need an intelligent colleague, someone I can trust. He will be well rewarded, but he will have a great deal of work. Can you suggest a clerk, a good man of business, honest enough to serve me before himself?"

"I hope my Province will never lack intelligent and honest clerks," answered Theobald, a little huffily. "I can call to mind several at this very moment; the Bishops of Hereford and Chichester, for example, or Master John of Salisbury. But they are already busy on important work, the care of immortal souls; which matters more than whether Henry or Louis rules the Vexin. I am sorry to be so blunt with you, but the work of the Church must come first."

"I don't want a Bishop. In fact, I don't want a holy clerk. Bishops and holy clerks never serve a temporal ruler with their whole hearts. I want an ordinary intelligent man of business, who happens to be a clerk. Is there one you can suggest?"

The Archbishop was struck with a happy thought. This was the very opening for young Master Thomas of London. The young man deserved promotion after his excellent work as Archdeacon of Canterbury. A great post at the King's court would be a splendid promotion for the son of a burgess of Cheapside, but he had the manners of a gentleman and would not jar on the high-born nobles round him. It was just the field for his talents, a secular career where his blameless life would reflect luster on the Archbishop who had brought him forward, and his lack of spiritual fervor would be no stumbling block to the laity who looked to him for example.

"I have in mind a suitable clerk," he said slowly. "I shall present him to you in a day or two, for he is now in Canterbury. He is a competent official, but no great loss to the Church. His birth is humble, I am afraid, but his manners will pass in any company. They tell me, for example, that he knows a lot about hawking. Master Thomas, called of London, or of Cheapside, or Becket."

When Thomas heard that he was to see the King to consider the offer of an important appointment his first thought was of the clothes he should wear. He hoped this preoccupation with his appearance was not caused by vanity, a branch of the mortal sin of pride. He knew in his heart that he was not really proud. But he was abnormally self-conscious, always aware of how he would look to a casual bystander; and if he was well dressed he found it easier to talk well and make a good impression.

In the old days, in Paris or working for the merchants of London, he had kept himself neat and clean, but he had never minded an undistinguished shabbiness. The need of splendid dress to bolster up his self-esteem was the result of perpetual teasing from Roger de Pont l'Evêque. He was never allowed to forget the unlucky impulse that had brought him to the Archbishop's manor with a hatchet in his hand; he was "Bailhache," an eccentric of low birth, who might at any moment break out into further examples of unconventional behavior; in fact, as far as Roger could sway opinion, he was a joke.

He found the best way to deal with these gibes without losing his temper was to put on an extra layer of dignity. When his tall, thin, aloof figure was dressed in fine black cloth relieved by the scarlet hood of a Master of Paris he knew he looked imposing. Then he could smile indulgently even at Roger's gibes.

Roger was the only member of the household who disliked him, but he had no close friends. On the whole he was pleased to see the other clerks, but he would not have felt very sad if he knew he would never meet them again. Their talk was so full of unprofitable speculation, on how the human race would have been continued if Eve had refused the apple, or whether savages who lived solitary without a lord could be said to possess private property, that a busy archdeacon sometimes became impatient.

He had found the niche that fitted him. Canon law was at last being codified, and soon a Church tribunal would be able to judge every case concerning marriage, or testaments, or the legitimacy of infants, untroubled by local custom, whether the parties came from Scotland or Sicily, or anywhere else in the Patriarchate of the West. In the archdeacon's court he applied canon law, strictly and without favor; that was his duty as a judge of first instance; and since from his court appeals could be taken to the Archbishop, and from him to Rome, he need never temper his justice with mercy. Proceedings in his court were expensive, since the fees of the litigants must keep all the unsalaried officials; but he was so obviously honest that he had never been offered a bribe. As regards his work he was completely happy. It had to be done, it was worth doing, and he did it well. He did not seek promotion.

But he could not remain Archdeacon all his life; the post

was normally the first step to a bishopric. He knew that Archbishop Theobald considered him unworthy of a miter, but if he stayed where he was while other clerks became bishops the passing over would in time look like disgrace. A place in the secular royal service offered a convenient way out; it was the fashion in intellectual circles to despise clerks who deserted the logic of canon law for the haphazard mixture of precedent and magic which ruled the secular courts; but even secular courts would be the better for a trained legal intelligence to preside over them. If the King offered him a post which an archdeacon might accept with honor, he would enter his service.

In the end he set out for the fateful interview wearing his best deacon's gown and his red hood; his costume was completed by a red girdle and red shoes, in breach of the canon forbidding clerks to wear bright colors. That added to his self-confidence, as showing that the Archdeacon of Canterbury was a little above the law, though not very much. He rode to the Tower on a showy war horse, with an armed sergeant of the Canterbury cortège to hold it when he dismounted; a soft-paced Spanish mule was the smartest mount for a rich clerk, but he had been taught to ride like a gentleman, and he might as well display the accomplishment.

He was told that the King awaited him on the roof, a pleasant retreat on a fine day. As he climbed the spiral stair he wondered whether this might be a test of his wind and energy, for the King could mark how long he took over the ascent. But he dismissed the idea as too subtle; he must not fall into the habit of seeing everywhere the deviousness of Master Roger.

Then he was out on the high windy platform, with London and the river and the flats of Essex far below him. This had once been the eyrie of that foe of burgesses, Count Geoffrey de Mandeville; now Thomas of Cheapside was there by invitation while Count Geoffrey's unburied and excommunicate bones rotted in some ditch of the fenland. But where was the King?

Could he be that squat shabby figure, energetically clearing a blocked gutter with his bare hands?

The young man turned and scrambled to his feet. He was nearly as broad as he was long, with arms as big as thighs bulging the sleeves of his tunic. His red hair and gray eyes gave him an English look, and his hands, now black with stinking leaf mold, were as calloused and rough as those of any peasant. But he looked Thomas up and down with such certainty of his own superiority that he was evidently a great lord. As Thomas bent his knee he spoke quickly, the French words tumbling out in a high excitable voice.

"Are you the clerk the Archbishop spoke of? Master Thomas, isn't it? Do you know other things beside canon law? What happens when a gutter is blocked by rotting leaves, so that rain lies on the roof?"

"Why, water collects in hollows, and presently seeps through a worn part of the lead. Then I suppose the roof beams rot, and in the end the whole roof falls in."

"And the King has lost a castle. So the King himself must clean gutters. If he wants to be sure they run free."

He waved his filthy hands expressively.

"I see, my lord. And you wish me to resign the archdeaconry of Canterbury to help you to clear drains?" Thomas was always quick to catch the tone of a conversation. This high-spirited boy of twenty-one was in the mood for chaff.

"I want someone to help me clear drains, and pull down nests of brigands, and hold off the French, and keep the peace, and count my money, and give each man his due and no more. Would you care to do that?"

"Certainly. They are all things that must be done. Let us begin with this gutter. You poke with that bit of stick while I shovel the leaves."

The gutter ended in a most amusing gargoyle, a face under a mail coif bellowing boundless rapacity through its open mouth; presumably the mason who carved it had remembered Count Geoffrey de Mandeville. Getting it clear was an absorbing task, and only when daylight showed through the throat did Thomas notice that his fine black gown was stained, and his red girdle foul and stinking. The enthusiasm of this boy was catching; he had not felt so carefree since his student days in Paris.

The King chuckled as a lump of mud landed by the sentry in the courtyard far below. "That's done," he said. "What's next for us? If you are to be Chancellor you ought to come and look at the seal."

"What, my lord?" gasped Thomas, "your Chancellor? Do you know I am the son of a burgess, a drysalter in Cheapside? I hold no land, and I have served only in the family of the Archbishop."

"I know a lot about you, Master Thomas. All the gossip in the world comes to a King's court. For example, I know that your father took oath to my mother many years ago, and preserved his loyalty when London turned against her. I know that you took thought to destroy her seal lest it fall into the hands of her enemies. I know you were faithful to Anjou when those beastly burgesses followed Count Stephen, and left the service of that scoundrel Osbert in disgust at his treachery."

"Forgive me, my lord, but he was *King* Stephen. Your seal proves as much, on the Treaty of Winchester. For nearly twenty years judgments were given in his name, and there will be anarchy in England if his acts are void."

"So you also say that. But then you are a lawyer. I know his judgments must stand, but I can never think of him as King. However, that doesn't matter. I thought from your record you would make a good chancellor, and now we are met I like the look of you. Come down and see the condition of my archives. I need a chancellor even more than I need a clean shirt."

"Willingly, my lord. But there is something comes first. I am a lawyer, remember. My lord, will you please stand still."

As King Henry paused in his darting to and fro Thomas dropped to both knees, stretching out his joined hands. The boy stood still and grave, holding the clasped hands between his own.

"I swear to be the man of Henry, King of England, in field and court, as long as my life shall last; saving only the rights of God and His Church." The words rang out with the solemnity a trained orator puts into any formal statement.

"Good. You are my man and I am your lord. I don't like that last clause, but I know you clerks always put it in. Well, will you at last come and look at *our* seal?"

CHAPTER V

Thomas the Chancellor

BY the first summer of the new reign the King and his court were back in Westminster, after that famous winter circuit which brought the Angevin peace to every corner of the realm. Traveling had been unpleasant, and both warriors and clerks found it hard to keep up with their new master, who rode from dawn far into the night, galloping over unknown tracks from castle to abbey to walled town, halting wherever he saw a closed gate to demand by what right the lord had shut it. A guarded gate implied the right to wage war, and young Henry was determined that in England no one should wage war save himself, if he had to ride day and night until he had covered the whole land. No other king had ridden as he rode, not even the Conqueror. England had a new master.

Everyone was glad of the change, even the great magnates of the north who had coined their own money without reference to Stephen or the Empress. After nineteen years of self-help it was a pleasant experience to see the hedge keep the cow and the latch keep the door. The whole realm was eager to obey.

On the morrow of Pentecost 1155 Thomas the Chancellor was dressed by sunrise, ready for a long day in his office. Yesterday had been a holiday for the solemn crown-wearing, and the court was still crowded with visiting magnates; but feasting had continued late, and the early Mass was poorly attended. Only the clerks of the court, and a few clerkly visitors, stood in the tent while the chaplain muttered through his Collects; just before the Canon, at the latest moment which allowed him to say he was hearing Mass, the King pushed his way in. He was dressed for hunting, and as usual fiddled with a bit of leather between his fingers, this time a broken spur-strap. With any luck he would ride back to Westminster after the chase, though no one could be certain. At noon, or even at vespers, the whole court might learn that they were to meet the King at some hall forty miles away. Henry of Anjou seldom slept twice in the same bed.

As the Mass ended the King strode out, without a word even for his close friend the Chancellor. The officials gathered by the door of the tent for the customary meeting, known to the irreverent as morning prayers.

Within a stone's throw loomed the great bulk of Westminster Abbey. It seemed rather silly to erect the chapel-tent so near a great church. But in all busy organizations it is easier to follow routine than to change it; and in fact there were few permanent buildings anywhere in his dominions which could

house all the various branches of Henry's court. Because there
was plenty of room for tents the village of Westminster was a
more convenient London headquarters than the cramped fortress of the Tower.

After Mass the heads of departments exchanged views and
gossip, and planned the division of their labors. There were
the Barons of the Exchequer, about to sit in the Tower; but no
one had much to say to them; they were hidebound bureau-
crats, and everyone conspired to keep as much as possible of the
King's revenue out of the clutches of their slow machinery.
There were the Judges, about to sit in Westminster Hall, to
decide an important suit concerning land; they must check
with their colleagues to be sure that neither party owed
money to the King; if one did the land would be kept in the
King's hand until the debt was satisfied. The Keeper of the
Wardrobe must arrange with clerks from the Treasury at Winchester about safe custody for the robes and jewels the King
had worn yesterday. A junior but confidential clerk of the
Wardrobe whispered quietly to a clerk of the Chancery about
a small fief which must be granted to a certain country knight,
the father of a handsome daughter; but the Chancery must
not make the mistake they made when they drew up the grant
for Madam Alice; charters are public documents, and tongues
would wag. There must be no mention of the service rendered
in return.

Messengers hovered behind the meeting, waiting to be told
the office which would receive their reports. The King's court
was always being remodeled, as new secretariats and bureaus
broke off from the household; no messenger who had been
on a long journey could be certain of finding the organization
unchanged on his return.

In another group were the servants of the great officers of
state. The Justiciar and the Chamberlain and the Constable
could not be expected to appear at these dawn Masses, but

their clerks must keep in touch with the Wardrobe and the Marshalsea (which managed the royal stables). This was the only time when responsible officials from every department could meet and talk together.

The center and focus of these groups was the Chancellor. He stood, chatting easily, with a polite smile on his lips and a courteous inclination of his immensely tall figure, as one worried clerk after another came up for a private word in his ear. He alone in the clerkly gathering looked like a layman. Thomas was already known for the splendor of his dress. To-day he wore a long red tunic embroidered with the golden leopards of Anjou; its sleeves fell to his knees. His hood also was red, and his boots of soft red Spanish leather; but the silk shirt which appeared only on his forearms was yellow to match the leopards on his tunic. Under his red mantle peeped a sword whose hilt was inlaid with silver and bound with gold wire. From top to toe he was scarlet and gold.

When Treasury, Judges, and Chancellor had agreed that a lord who held of the Count of Toulouse, even though he was a most rebellious vassal, could not claim the dower lands of his English-born mother, the meeting dispersed. Thomas walked across Palace Yard to the house by the river which had been hired as a temporary Chancery.

It crossed his mind that it would have looked more fitting if he had ridden even this short distance. But if the second greatest man in England walked to his office, perhaps that showed a secure greatness which took no heed of public opinion. Besides, he could not ride in this long tunic and mantle, and changing his clothes would be a nuisance. All the same, that was a promising idea; suppose a page waited with his riding clothes outside the chapel, and he changed during the usual morning discussion? That would show the world that Thomas the Chancellor was accustomed to being waited on.

It would impress the vulgar, but perhaps the great who

were now his equals would laugh at this fresh evidence of the airs he gave himself. The King, and Richard de Lucy the Justiciar, both walked short distances if there was need. He saw that a great man who had been great all his life might frequently be irked by the conventions of state. One of the attractions of warfare was that on campaign even kings might lead the simple life. Even now, in peacetime, it was hard to persuade young Henry to dress in a manner befitting his rank. It was difficult to strike exactly the right note. Especially while he was so near London, where hundreds of burgesses could remember a hungry and unemployed clerk of Cheapside, he must keep the state required by his position. But those born to grandeur were always eager to cast it aside; when he was in Normandy, where his origins were unknown, he would try the effect of careless simplicity.

He was never for a moment free of this anxiety about his public behavior, for never for a moment could he forget that he was now the second magnate of the realm, and most emphatically not born to the position. When in doubt he chose grandeur. No magnate would ever forget his humble origin, but display would impress the populace. All through the day he was consciously the Chancellor, the busy statesman who was also a deacon, splendid without debauchery. In his youth he had seen a great household at close quarters, and his own household was luxurious and dignified; he chose the wine for his table himself, after careful tasting, and it gave him enormous pleasure to see knights of high birth drinking the best Bordeaux at his expense, while he, the master who was above such indulgence, sipped boiled water flavored with lime-blossom. He was served by noble pages, who presented the cup on bended knee; and if they did it awkwardly they were sent home, for many great families were eager to place a son in the household of the Chancellor, the seat of power that was also a center of courtesy and good manners.

He could say with truth that his household gave any noble youth a sound training. It was magnificent, but it was also decent and clean-living. Ladies of sufficient dignity were welcome at his table, and he could converse with them courteously, mingling a touch of the ardor of Provence with his stately North French speech. But his courtesy never went further than conventional praise of the lady's beauty, and that in public; unlike most powerful clerks in comparable positions, he had not taken a mistress. When he received the order of subdeacon, which bound a clerk to celibacy, he had added a private vow of chastity from devotion to Our Lady and in memory of his mother. His body obeyed his will, and at the age of thirty-six he was still a virgin. Chastity and sobriety reigned in his hall.

Now, as he walked through Palace Yard, he was satisfied with the impression he made on the numerous onlookers. Here was the great Chancellor, whom the King delighted to honor. He filled his high position worthily, but he could not be accused of profusion or unseemly pride.

At the Chancery a pile of work awaited him. While he sat at the head of a trestle table, clerks on either hand read aloud despatches from France or the north, applications to buy a royal writ as the opening of a lawsuit, begging-letters from scholars seeking benefices, stiff notes from bishops or archdeacons who accused the King's Judges of encroaching on their jurisdiction. Meanwhile other clerks engrossed the minutes of decisions taken in the royal council: grants of land, marriages of royal wards, every decision of the King which must be put on record in a manner binding on posterity. At the far end of the table stood the Great Seal, its silver faces held in the olive-wood screw-press. Beside it the chafe-wax tended his brazier and his copper box of sweet-scented green beeswax. Thomas enjoyed the ceremony of affixing the heavy green seal, gazing with affectionate and protective pride at the pompous little effigies on either side: Henry, King of England, Duke of Normandy and Aquitaine, Count of Anjou and Maine, riding fiercely in mail and brandishing a drawn sword, or sitting, full-face and a little popeyed, on his royal throne. The seal reminded him of the occasion when he had supervised the destruction of the seal of the uncrowned Lady of England, the deed that had brought him the favor of the Angevins. It also reminded him of the dear, lovable, rather absurd boy it depicted.

Just as he himself acted the part of a first-class chancellor, so he was glad to recognize the energy with which young Henry threw himself into the part of a busy king and statesman. The boy was willing to work, that was the great thing. Even hunting took second place to his chosen task of bringing peace to England. He was never idle, and made up his mind without delay (if the decision were unwise, a trusted chancellor might pursue the matter further before the binding document was sealed). He was not afraid of war, but, thank God, he was not eager for glory. Since he was big enough to ride he had ridden through sacked villages, the wrecks of his rightful inheritance; and the horrors he had seen had given him a passion for order. He was greedy and harsh, as was to be expected in a son of Rollo the pirate. But he did not take pleasure in inflicting pain, and the prosperity of his subjects was his greatest care. With enough patience and tact, which might be supplied by his trusted advisers, he would be a king worthy to rule the realm of Arthur.

If only his private life were a little more decorous! For his silly behavior with women Thomas almost despised his young ruler and friend. Henry was married to the most beautiful lady of her day (or at least the most beautiful reigning duchess); if the stories of her conduct at Antioch were true she must be very attractive to normal sinful men. She was years older than her husband, and there had never been any pretense that they had married for love. It was also true that her temper, when it was roused, matched his. But he had the freedom of her bed, which made him the envy of many knights and of all the best troubadours; she had given him a male heir, and the more children he begot on her the better. If anyone had a safe outlet for his passions, young Henry was that lucky man.

Yet he was always chasing young damsels. He would often take his pleasure among the trollops of Thames-side, asking Thomas, as a native Londoner, to show him the most amusing taverns; that did no great harm, for he left the trollops no worse than he had found them, and it was a sin most kings committed. What might be dangerous was his habit of seducing young ladies of good family. It gave him, poor fool, the illusion that he was being loved for himself alone, since in theory the damsels might have repulsed him. As if any simple knight's daughter would repulse the King of England! So far the parents had felt flattered, rather than insulted, at his attentions. Sir Roger de Akeny had accepted with gratitude the fat fief that came to him after his unmarried daughter made him the grandfather of two lusty boys. But one day some father would decide that honor demanded death for the girl and bloodfeud with her seducer, in accordance with the custom of his high-minded ancestors.

Thomas had drifted into a reverie; for he had cleared up current business, and work must pause while his clerks stitched fair copies to the Great Roll of the Pipe; that was the only way of keeping a file in a mobile office without shelves or cabinets. He was brought back to the present by a clatter of hoofs.

The horse sounded as though it were inside the room. Thomas's acute hearing seldom deceived him: the horse was inside the room.

Thomas saw first the neat alert head of a brisk little palfrey, his rider crouched flat over the withers to avoid the lintel of the door; then the pony collected his hind legs, and, from a stand, popped neatly over the table. There was just room for him by the inner wall; he stood like a statue while the King straightened in his stirrups and waved to a clerk who crawled out from under the board.

"Don't panic, Master Eustace. Quicksilver could have cleared you seated upright at your desk. He never puts a foot wrong. He is interested in my Chancery and he wants to know why you all spend a fine day sitting here among the parchments. So I brought him in to have a look. What *are* you doing, by the way? It can't be more important than flying my new gyrfalcon. She is a present from a Baltic shipmaster. I promised to excuse him toll for the rest of his life, but if his gift flies off home at the first cast I may change my mind. Come on, Thomas. You are better at luring a falcon than anyone else at court. We should find kites down by Barking. We can ride through the town, and call in at the Tower on our way back to visit the Queen. Anyway, come out and give me your opinion of Snow Maiden."

"A new gyrfalcon is a distinguished visitor, my lord, and I shall be honored to meet her. That letter you bade me write to Count Geoffrey is also important, but it will not be engrossed until this evening. Give me half an hour to send for a horse and change into riding clothes."

"Half an hour? You would loiter for half an hour before trying a gyrfalcon straight from Iceland? Quicksilver will never allow that; he is already impatient. There is a good hackney outside, and you must ride as you are. That mantle and tunic are not too good for the first meeting with such a great lady."

"My dear Henry," answered Thomas with a smile, "if I am correctly dressed then certainly you are not. What will the minstrels say of a great king who goes hawking in gray fustian and a tattered mantle? Is that the way to make friends with a lady from Iceland, where even shepherds wear ermine?"

It was a nuisance to be interrupted in the drafting of that
tricky letter to Count Geoffrey, the King's younger brother
who was claiming the whole County of Anjou as his price for
not raising a sedition in England. They were trying to persuade
him to withdraw without open war, though he spoke truth
when he claimed that his father had intended the County to be
his property. But all his life Thomas had been trained to fall in
with the moods of his superiors. The clerks could finish drafting
the letter, and if it was wrongly engrossed nothing was lost but
a fair sheet of parchment. It would be pleasant to ride hawking in magnificent scarlet; it would show the burgesses of London, who still told stories about the obscure childhood of
Thomas of Cheapside, that the great Chancellor recked nothing
of splendid robes. He smiled as he walked behind the well-
trained palfrey to join the group of horsemen in the street: the
sergeants of the bodyguard, the chief falconer with the new
treasure on his wrist, and a groom leading a smooth-paced
hackney for the King's friend to ride.

When she towered in pride of place and stooped to the kill,
the gyrfalcon was as wonderful as all her kind. But like all her
kind she was self-willed and slow to the lure. Her recovery
was a long business, the cause of hard gallops and hard swearing. Thomas reflected that his own peregrines really gave better sport; they were under the control of their master, and you
felt that you shared in their hunting; to ride after a gyrfalcon
was merely to be present when a wild bird hunted her prey.
But gyrfalcons were an emblem of kingship. Kingship was
still a novel experience to young Henry, and anything that reminded him of it gave him immense pleasure.

Of course they did not stop for dinner. Henry's courtiers
were used to that. Their eager young master grudged time for
meals, especially when he was hunting or hawking. Presently
he would feel hungry, and eat enormously of any coarse food

they set before him; but first he must burn up the energy the Devil his ancestor had given to all the house of Anjou.

After a long chase over the Essex marshes the King turned for home. He himself was not tired, but his horse had done enough; and except in the stress of war he was careful of good horses. Since they were east of London they called at the Tower before passing through the city; and Thomas had his first private meeting with Henry's Queen.

She had remained in the Tower during all the hard riding of her husband's winter circuit; for her first-born son had died in infancy and every care must be taken to ensure the continuance of the line of Anjou. Now little Henry, heir to England, Normandy, and Aquitaine, was in his third month, a sturdy infant who roared with something of his father's rage. But the Queen had picked up a touch of some fever from the crowded city; she lay in the state marriage-bed in her chamber on the topmost story of the Tower.

That was symbolical of her married life, as Thomas reflected. He knew, as the whole court knew, that there was little affection between husband and wife. While Henry lay at Westminster his Queen would prefer the Tower. Yet if she was not with him she must be within an hour's ride of him; for the Duchess of Aquitaine was immensely valuable, a prize to be kept constantly under the royal eye. She had none of the comfort of marriage, and no freedom to console her for its absence. Well, she was still Duchess of Aquitaine, and this was part of the price she must pay for it.

She was thirty-three years old, which many would consider late middle age. But as she lay among the fine-textured furs and silks of her bed she looked a damsel of sixteen. Though she had borne four children her breasts under the ermine bed-gown were high and firm, and her waist slim; the light in her eye summoned all true knights to joust for her glory, and the curve of her wrist was an incitement to high adventure. Any man who looked on Queen Eleanor felt himself grow to the stature of Lancelot (with her husband in the part of King Arthur). Even if the stories about her conduct in Outremer were true, the kindness of such a lady would be rich payment for the wrecking of a great Crusade.

Hitherto Thomas had seen her only at state functions, glowing from afar, a fair face in a setting of smooth silk and massy jewels; the unattainable princess, as worshipful and as remote as the image of Our Lady behind the altar. Now, looking into her face, he saw resolution, courage, and high ambition looking back from those sultry brown eyes. She was all woman, and yet she would have fared better as a man; every man of spirit must desire to possess her, but it was impossible to see her as a dutiful wife.

But that was none of his business. He was vowed to celibacy, and even in the eyes of this sinful world, which condoned many broken vows, she was the wife of his dearest friend. Temptations of this sort had been beaten down many times; if they stirred again he must tire his body further, by harder work, more strenuous hunting, longer prayers.

The lady spoke to him graciously. Her nature compelled her to draw any strange man into an intimacy directed against her husband. "I am pleased to know the King's comrade and coadjutor, of whom all England is talking. But only Henry would have arranged such an introduction. Here I lie in my old bedgown in this gloomy keep, and you are hot and muddy, and, I expect, hungry. Have you dined? I thought not. I can offer you only bread and wine and honey, but that is more than some courtiers get who ride with my impatient husband. Look at his mantle! When he put it on clean this morning it was unworthy of a beggar, and now he wears it wet and torn and filthy in the bedchamber of a lady. If you dress so meanly you will lose the respect of your subjects."

"My subjects respect the Chancellor, who dresses very splendidly. So long as they respect him they will obey me," answered Henry laughing. "But I can dress splendidly if the occasion demands it. You should have seen me yesterday, when I wore my crown for Pentecost. My vassals were most impressed."

"I suppose you sat smiling while the magnates of Aquitaine renewed their fealty. No man ever allows a woman the power that is rightly hers."

Thomas spoke up, to avert a family quarrel. "The King did indeed look most kingly at the crown-wearing, my lady. And he guards Aquitaine for you. Someone must wield the sword from which your sex debars you. Since your father is dead, that is the task of your husband."

"Oh, but I can wield a sword, Master Thomas. At Antioch I led a troop of ladies, all mailed and mounted on war horses. If we had encountered the infidel we should have charged, but since Prince Raymond guards his border we could only joust with one another."

"All Christendom talks of your exploits in Outremer, madam," Henry said hastily. "Such tales grow in the telling, and it would be wise to allow them to be forgotten."

The Queen shrugged her shoulders, with a conspiratorial glance at Thomas. Those tales were indeed well known, including the story that her uncle Prince Raymond of Antioch had been her lover, under the eyes of King Louis her husband. She was rash to remind her present husband of that episode.

A waiting-lady brought in bread and wine, and conversation ceased while Henry gulped down great mouthfuls, standing. Thomas, like every clerk, was trained to long fasting; and though he was very hungry he ate daintily and slowly, talking easily to the Queen in the flippant gallant tone he remembered hearing at the high table in Pevensey. Then Henry announced that it was time to get back to Westminster, where the magnates assembled for Pentecost would expect to see him at supper. Thomas perceived that an hour ago Henry had been eager to visit the Queen, whom he still pictured as the beautiful and valuable princess who had fallen into his lap while he fought for his inheritance; but that as soon as he was actually in her presence he was as restless and ill-at-ease as a schoolboy in the presence of the novice-master. It was a great pity, and a danger to Henry's soul. But the husband of such a masterful wife would be naturally tempted to seek consolation from ladies who were more easy to please.

They rode back through Cheapside, but nowadays that meant nothing to Thomas. After his father's death the old house had been sold, and he did not know where at the moment his married sister was living. For more than ten years his only home had been the household of Archbishop Theobald; now it was the household of King Henry; in any case it was no longer Cheapside.

But as they rode up the familiar street, two happy and prosperous cavaliers, their attendants some distance behind, Thomas noticed an old man waiting to accost them. For a moment he feared embarrassment from some acquaintance who would remind him of old days together in Osbert's counting house; then he saw the man was only a beggar, a miserable waif leaning on a crutch; he was nearly naked, and as he scuttled up to the horsemen he complained, in good French, of the cold.

"Hallo," said Henry, reining up, "here is one of my vassals in want, and a Frenchman by his speech. Where were you born, fellow?"

Of course the man came from Le Mans, and had been reduced to beggary by the plundering knights of Blois. Thomas proudly appreciated the quick wits of this Londoner, who had composed exactly the right story to appeal to the King. The man finished by asking for clothes, not money, which always sounds better from a beggar. A great lord would not know that the alehouses by the river would sell drink as readily for a mantle as for silver.

King Henry was less experienced in the wiles of beggars. But since he had been old enough to sit a horse he had led forays which must have ruined countless peasants; his Christian charity was under firm control. Thomas looked for him to ride on, perhaps with a curse.

Instead the King turned to his Chancellor. "Do you hear, Thomas? My vassal calls on his lord for aid, besides which a true knight cannot refuse the widow or the orphan. You are of course an orphan, my good man? And what you want is a mantle? Unfortunately you are begging from the wrong lord. Today both my Chancellor and my wife have told me that my mantle is not fit to give to a beggar. I am a little tired of the advice, but I must accept the opinion of my trusted counselors. My mantle would be no use to you. However," he continued, as gravely as though giving judgment from his throne, "I know of a very good mantle, quite near at hand. In fact I have been admiring it all day. This is Master Thomas of London, a deacon of holy life. I wish to share in the merits of his alms-deeds, so I shall help him to give you his mantle."

Leaning from the saddle, he strove to pull the great scarlet cloak from Thomas's shoulders.

Thomas was at first taken unawares. His long training in obedience to lawful superiors and in the suppression of his own desires inclined him to do as his lord wished; but the voices of all his Norman ancestors clamored in his brain that here was a lord encroaching on the rights of a vassal. If Henry had been in earnest this would have been tyranny; even as a joke it must not be allowed to pass without protest. He seized the thick hairy wrists at his neck, and struggled to pull Henry from the saddle.

While the beggar skipped to the shelter of the wall the two

greatest men in England wrestled like unruly urchins; until the sergeants of the bodyguard arrived at full gallop, and Cheapside was blocked by excited horses.

Henry fitzEmpress, that thick-muscled warrior, easily overcame the tall and slender clerk. As the scarlet mantle flashed through the air, making the eager horses plunge and rear, the King called in the trumpet-shout of a knight victorious in the joust: "Here, beggar, take my alms, the spoil Thomas could not withhold from me. And don't interfere, men. This is felonious assault—but committed by the King—on the person of the Chancellor."

There was laughter all round, and they rode in good fellowship to Westminster. That night Thomas instructed his steward to order an even more splendid mantle from the best tailor in London, and to send the tally to the Wardrobe as a private debt of the King. If the Wardrobe would not honor the tally that did not matter very much. In addition to his salary as Chancellor (five shillings a day, sixty times the wage of a foot-sergeant) Thomas might use for his legitimate expenses as much as he liked of the royal income which passed through his hands. He lived in great state, as a chancellor should; and he was not particularly accurate in keeping his accounts.

What was more interesting was this fresh demonstration of Henry's affectionate intimacy. When they began to work together they had hit it off very well; but this was the first time the King had joked with him as if with an equal. He was accepted, not merely as a useful official but as a close friend. He need no longer guard his behavior, as had been his custom for every moment of the day.

He resolved to increase his already splendid household. He could not be accused of gluttony or personal luxury; he still drank lime-water from choice, said most punctiliously the daily office of a deacon, and heard Mass every morning. But his mind held a clear picture of the perfect household for a dignified magnate, and his instinct as an artist, an artist at least in ceremonial, could now have free play.

On a sunny afternoon of June 1158 the burgesses of Paris crowded the Rouen Gate to see the great procession. The envoy of England came in state, to beg the hand of the lady Margaret for the lord Henry, son of the King of England; and rumor ran that this was the most splendid embassy that had ever come out of Normandy.

It was said that the expedition contained more than a score of splendid carriages, loaded with rich presents for deserving Frenchmen. That attracted the idlers. But wise men came also to see a remarkable sight, an expedition riding in peace from Normandy to Paris. For a hundred years there had been war, or at best truce, between the Ile de France and those pirates downriver. Now the turbulent Duchy had a new ruler, a civilized Frenchman from Anjou; perhaps he would honestly keep his oath of fealty, and there would be enduring peace between Rouen and Paris. It was a good augury that his envoy was a clerk, instead of a hot-tempered warrior; he had studied in the schools of Paris, the best schools in the world; he would appreciate the civilized festivities arranged to entertain him.

Sergeants made a lane through the crowd, and there arose a sound of singing. The onlookers were a little disappointed to see the van of the procession marching on foot. But these singing men were so well dressed, and walked in such good order, that there must be better to follow. There were five hundred of them, walking two by two, clad in scarlet with the golden leopards of Anjou embroidered on their breasts; they were all yellow-haired young Englishmen, a very handsome sight; and as they walked they sang a wedding song, their scarlet legs flashing in unison to the lilt of the music. It looked almost as enchanting as if they were dancing.

At last the line of foot ended, and there was a ripple in the

crowd as sergeants cried that holy relics were approaching, before which all good Christians must kneel and uncover. A tall
spearman swaggered slowly at the bridle of a huge pack horse;
everyone recognized the familiar shape of a portable altar under the silk covering of its load, and the gilded bronze chest by
the saddlehorn must contain treasures from the rich halidom
of the Kings of England.

This horse, chosen for his size, bore the most honorable load
in the procession. His shoes were of pure silver, and gold thread
was plaited in his mane and tail.

Behind the furniture of the royal chapel came eleven other
pack horses, whose burdens were less sacred but more immediately interesting. Sicilian silk covered their saddles and
reached to the ground; but the small heavy barrels whose shape
showed through could only contain money. That must be
given away, or at least spent in the shops of Paris; for no one
carries money to bear it home again. This should be a most
rewarding embassy. On the peak of each saddle sat a captivat-
ing little monkey; these were dressed in the same livery as the
footmen, down to tiny Angevin leopards on their tunics; and
though they were kept in place by chains of gilded bronze they
seemed very happy, chattering at the crowd and throwing
sweetmeats from little bags open before them.

After the monkeys came the famous four-wheeled carriages
of which rumor had spoken. There were only eight of them
after all, but even that was a large number in days when goods
were normally carried by pack horse. Each was drawn by a
team of five horses, and their sides were decorated with figures
of the saints. The loads were hidden under rich carpets, but
it was known that they bore the baggage and supplies of the
mission.

Now the procession declined into the commonplace. Two
hundred knights were more than most burgesses saw at one
time, and these were very well armed and mounted; but there

was no lack of knights in the Ile de France. Only the more intelligent observers realized that this was a remarkable sight; all these knights served Master Thomas of London, a clerk who held no land but depended for everything on the favor of his lord.

After the knights came the clerks of the Chancery, most of them riding on well-paced Spanish mules. They made up a large group, but a life spent stooping over parchment in a bad light makes a man look dim and unimportant. The crowd began to think the glory of the procession might be over.

But at the end came Master Thomas of London, Chancellor to the King of England. The crowd cheered again, and wise men looked keenly at the real ruler of the greatest state in Christendom, a dominion extending from Scotland to the Pyrenees. He rode a very tall black war horse, so fiery that he needed two scarlet-clad grooms at his head to keep him at a walk. He himself was so tall that the great horse seemed a pony. He alone did not wear the King's scarlet livery; he was clothed from head to foot in bright green (a color most unfitting for a deacon); even his hood was green, for here no one need be reminded that he was a scholar of Paris. On his feet were spurs of solid gold, and his horse's bit, as well as its shoes, were of silver. A heavy sword hung from a baldric of golden thread, and from the jeweled chain at his waist dangled a purple silk purse containing the Great Seal of King Henry. But even the jeweled collar and the ruby ouche which fastened his mantle could not distract the gaze of the onlookers from his face. His thick black hair, too long for a deacon, was confined by a jeweled net; black eyes flashed from his thin white cheeks, and the curve of his nose jutted forth like an eagle's. The cheers died away; before such a worshipful lord cheering seemed too familiar a greeting.

Nineteen years ago, when Thomas of Cheapside left Paris hurriedly to attend the deathbed of his mother, he had worried over how to pay for the journey. Now he was back again. He had never felt so happy in his life.

He knew he was wasting the treasure of King Henry, and he knew he was wasting his own time. The embassy was completely pointless, for the details of the French marriage, the treaty, and the dowry of the bride, had been settled already by correspondence. A good knight with a small escort could have guarded the baby on her journey to her father-in-law.

But Henry had ordered him to make a display. It was important to impress the French, and the King himself refused to pay a state visit. For one thing, it was awkward to be the guest of his Queen's first husband; Henry had snatched Eleanor after King Louis had considered her unworthy to share his bed, which made social chatter difficult. He would not improve matters if he boasted that he kept her under constant surveillance, so that she would never be free to cuckold him as she had cuckolded Louis at Antioch. However the subject was phrased, both kings must be aware that Henry had injured his honor by marrying a light woman for her dower.

In the second place, Henry genuinely disliked the state necessary to a king on a visit of ceremony, and he knew Thomas would enjoy it. To Henry, nominal ruler of Normandy since the age of four, pomp was a tiresome reminder of fatherly tutelage.

But Thomas, born well-to-do and then very poor in his youth, reveled in luxury and state. He was indifferent to comfort, or he would not be riding a hot war horse and carrying a heavy sword; but fine clothes, a swarm of overfed servants, an army of disciplined knights, all reinforced the self-assurance he needed before his mind would work clearly.

He had himself designed this pageant, and there were critics who held that his arrangements betrayed the burgess spirit of a drysalter aping nobility. The monkeys on the pack horses might be a legitimate touch of fantasy, but silver bits and silver horseshoes mocked the dignity of a well-bred charger; no knight who was the son of a knight would have ridden thus.

Thomas was glad to see his procession directed right across Paris to the splendid fortress of the Templars, the most noble lodging that could be offered to a distinguished visitor. The King of France was entering into the spirit of this comedy of grandeur. The embassy had no business except to entertain and be entertained, and the lord who gave the most splendid banquet might consider himself victorious. King Louis had struck the right note at the start.

That evening, when Thomas sent out his stewards to buy provisions for a great feast, they returned almost at once with a disturbing report. Butchers and vintners had shown them the best, but when it came to discussing prices they had refused to name a figure: in his good town of Paris King Louis was host to the envoy of his vassal the Duke of Normandy; let the guests take what they would, and the King of France would pay.

"Now that's a very pretty gesture," said Thomas. "I wish I had foreseen it. But King Louis forgets that I know Paris. Go out and wander by the south bank of the river among the scholars from Normandy. You ought to find them in a tavern just to the left of the bridge; it used to be the Green Man, but the sign may have altered. When you find a Norman tall enough for me to wear his gown fetch him here at once."

Late that night, after the shops were closed, a tall middle-aged scholar in a shabby gown disturbed the rest of the greatest vintner in Paris.

"Goodman Peter, if you saw the Norman embassy arrive you will have noticed certain wagons loaded with silver. I am not connected with that embassy, I am a humble scholar planning a party to celebrate a successful disputation in the schools. However, I have access to the silver-chests of Master Thomas the Chancellor. If you send me as many tuns as I choose of your very best wine (and I can tell the best at one sip) you

will be paid in silver before sunset. On the other hand, if you
take the tallies to the Treasurer of King Louis, how soon do
you think you will be paid? These are the pennies struck by the
English King; pure silver and even weight. You need not weigh
them one by one, as with the deniers of France, minted by a
score of different magnates, all greedy. Is that settled? Then
you may lead me to your cellars."

Thomas also produced a novelty to make his party a success.
He had brought with him two wagon-loads of English ale. The
casks were broached at the main gate of the Templars' fortress,
where all comers might sample the new drink while the King
of France was feasted within.

The great party was an unqualified success. With the friendly
advice of Norman scholars Thomas had chosen the most fashionable cooks and provision shops; the crowd at the gate pronounced the new drink to be if anything better than wine,
"equally strong and of a more pleasing flavor." Of course
they said that because they had got it for nothing, but even so
the brewers of London might reap some advantage. As for the
food, it pleased even the discriminating palates of the French
court. Thomas had chosen a Friday for his feast, since anyone
with a forest can offer his guests sound venison but only a con-
noisseur can plan a good dinner on a day of abstinence. Among
other things, he had bought up all the eels in the Ile de France,
at a total cost of a hundred pounds.

Such profusion smacked of vulgarity. But the money was
there, and Thomas had been ordered to spend it for the greater
glory of his master. He could not spend it on his own dress or
the livery of his household, for both were already suitable for
an exceptionally prosperous emperor; a dinner such as no
reigning prince could match was the easiest way of proving
that Henry of England was the greatest king in the world.

During the next week the French court did what they could

to match the splendor of this magnificent servant of a magnificent king; they could not hope to surpass him. In the intervals of ceremony Thomas visited his old lecture rooms. At thirty-nine he still felt a young man, and thanks to clean living and temperance he looked younger than his age; but of course to the scholars he was a revenant from a past so ancient they could hardly conceive it, an epoch when the gray beard of the janitor outside the school of civil law had been brown. They talked to him freely, but found it hard to believe that twenty years ago the schools of Paris had been much as they were today.

Thomas had considered paying the debts of those scholars who were King Henry's vassals. That would enhance the glory of his master more than banquets; a scholar free from debt was a rarer marvel even than a dish of eels worth a hundred pounds. But his steward told him that even his wagon-loads of money would not be enough to pay the debts of all the Norman scholars, from Normandy or England, who thronged the schools of Paris. They could manage, for their creditors were patient. Then a clerk said in jest that the real benefactors of learning must be these patient creditors, and Thomas was pleased with the idea. He gave a great feast to all the booksellers, tavern keepers, and owners of lodging houses who had allowed Norman scholars to run up bills. It was a remarkable party, much talked of in Paris; so it could be considered part of the campaign to enhance the prestige of King Henry. It helped the scholars also, for after such a public compliment to their forbearance their creditors were unlikely to press them in future.

Presently it was time to return to Normandy with the lady Margaret of France, two years old and betrothed to Henry fitzHenry aged three. It had been an enjoyable visit, and a great deal of money had been spent. The King of England, and his mighty Chancellor, would be famous throughout Christendom; and if nothing useful had come of the embassy no harm had been done.

Thomas had behaved correctly. His habitual state might be rather too grand, in fact a little vulgar; but the mob must be dazzled, and if King Henry preferred the simple life the dazzling became his Chancellor's duty. In Paris he had mixed easily with the highest in the land, talking falconry with the King and jousting with the great magnates, as though his father had been a count instead of a drysalter. He owed these easy manners to the lord Richer de l'Aigle; he was grateful, and remembered him daily in his prayers.

In October 1159 Henry King of England lay encamped with his power in the thrice-ravaged Vexin, the ever-disputed borderland between Normandy and the Ile de France. The army of France lay within a day's march, and a battle might decide the war tomorrow. But Henry knew there would be no battle. Battles hardly ever happened; in all his mother's long wars there had been only one battle, at Lincoln, and it made no difference to the final outcome. If Louis marched against him it would be because the French were stronger, and he would retire to his nearest castle; if the French stayed where they were they might presently be driven by lack of food to retire, and then he could advance to ravage deeper into their land. But probably the clerks would soon fix up a truce, so that everyone could go home before winter. It was hard to remember what this war was about, and no one was very interested in it.

This evening, as King Henry strolled from the horse-lines to his own pavilion, he was not really thinking about the next step in the campaign, the excuse on which he had dismissed his attendants; he was thinking about his Chancellor.

Who would have guessed that the busy archdeacon, the clever negotiator, the learned lawyer who could advise on every code, civil law, canon law, or the queer unwritten customs of England, would also find himself at home in the unfamiliar business of campaigning? Of course he was a Norman, and every Norman was a warrior born; he had passed part of his youth in a great castle, but he had been learning so many other things as well that he could hardly have enjoyed much knightly training.

Yet now he led the largest force in the army, seven hundred knights, fourteen hundred sergeants, and four thousand foot. He paid the men himself, though presumably with the King's money which he used as his own. Since his force was the best disciplined and best equipped, as well as the strongest, the money was well spent.

His men were well led too, and followed him eagerly. At the capture of Cahors he had ridden in front like a gentleman, and then taken trouble to see the booty fairly distributed. It seemed there was nothing Thomas could not do, and do well.

He was never out of temper, or sulky, or wanting to sit quiet and nurse a headache. It was hard to remember he was more than forty years old, which was middle age by any reckoning and senescence unimaginable to the twenty-six-year-old Henry. He was as thin as a lad of fifteen, and fit enough to ride with the King, who had grown used to seeing strong warriors pull up during his amazing forced marches. He was the best companion any young king could desire.

Perhaps even on that morning at Northampton he had not designed to make Henry feel uncomfortable. The affair was not of the King's contriving; it had been a practical joke among the junior clerks in the Chamberlain's department. Everyone knew about the young woman in Northampton; of course it was sinful, but kings must not be judged by the standards of ordinary men. It was not as though he lived regularly with a mistress, like some wicked rulers; there were just these girls dotted about his domains, available when needed but not forced on the attention of society; the Queen had no cause for complaint. After all that gossip about the Chancellor being still a virgin at the age of forty it had seemed a good joke to push him into Mahault's lodging when they rode into Northampton after dark, in pouring rain; there had been bets on the result. Henry had known of it but the idea was not his in the first place. In fact he had pointed out that it was a poor subject for betting, since no one could trust the account Mahault would give in the morning. All the same, it was a harmless practical joke, the kind of thing any clerk must bear with good grace if he chose to live among lusty warriors.

It had not seemed so funny in the morning, when a group of gay young men called to inquire how the Chancellor had slept, sharing a single bed with one of the less important of the King's whores. They had found the bed undisturbed; Thomas was on his knees by the screens and Mahault kneeling in prayer at the far end of the little house. She would tell them nothing of what had passed; all she wanted, she said, were the wages due to her; with that money for dowry she would be accepted in a good nunnery.

Thomas had never since referred to that night; unless when he said a few days later that a King must think of his subjects as persons, not as things put into the world for his convenience; as though anyone except a preacher could think of that little strumpet as a person, with a soul. But then a clerkly training often broke through in the conversation of the most worldly official. With Thomas you never knew where you were. Perhaps that was part of his attraction.

At present he was throwing himself into the task of helping his friend Henry to make head against Louis of France. It was really wonderful how he produced money when it was needed, and kept the army fed and contented. His only fault was that he seemed too eager for glory; such a useful life should not be imperiled in petty skirmishes at the outposts. But Henry, like every other warrior, knew that most of his friends would die in battle, and it might be tomorrow.

After four years of friendship Henry felt he understood Thomas's character. The Chancellor was always standing outside himself, looking to see how a man in his position was expected to behave. His chastity and sobriety showed that he was not really devoted to a life of luxury; he thought the chancellor of a great King should live splendidly, and he kept such state as he considered fitting. For the last year, campaigning first against Toulouse and now against France, he had seen himself as a valiant knight. At any moment he might think it his duty, in his capacity as a noble warrior, to undertake some desperate enterprise. And yet, his friend felt, Thomas was not either a royal official or a gallant knight; those were only the capacities in which he chose at present to appear. What he was underneath Henry did not yet know, and probably Thomas did not know either.

Meanwhile it might be a good idea to ride out for a last look at the French; he should be able to tell from the size of their cooking fires whether they were thinking of breaking camp. But as Henry turned back to the horse-lines he was halted by a remarkable sight. Riding through the camp, surrounded by cheering sergeants, was an immensely tall warrior in full mail. In the glare of torches that figure was unmistakable, though the newfangled close helm hid his face completely; three birds blazoned black on his shield confirmed his identity, for Thomas had remembered that in some parts of England red-legged crows were known as beckets, and he had chosen his arms in proud emphasis of his obscure origin. His horse was blown and sweating; he carried no lance, but with his right hand led a riderless charger beside him.

"Thomas, have you been jousting while I pottered round the horse-lines?" shouted Henry. "Are you the King, and I the clerk?"

"It was nothing of importance, my lord," Thomas answered, catching very well the quiet matter-of-fact tone in which the best knights recounted their exploits (no boasting, of course; but give every detail so that the troubadours can boast for you later on). "I knew you were busy, and I did not wish to disturb you. When a champion rode out from the French camp to challenge us I thought I would try my luck. His challenge had to be accepted, or our army would have been discouraged; and I was the man of highest rank present. I was lucky. At the first encounter he went over the tail of his horse. He was unhurt, but when he scrambled to his feet and drew his sword I thought the affair had gone far enough. So I didn't try to bring him in. I just took his horse as a trophy of victory. The horse-trappings are those of the lord Engelram de Trie. Is he a well-known jouster?"

"Engelram de Trie? Not a famous champion, but a useful man with a lance all the same," said Henry, who knew by repute every prominent jouster in Christendom. "You were lucky to overthrow him so quickly. I would have backed him to unhorse any clerk in the world. So don't you accept any more challenges. Now is the time for you to retire, with an unbeaten record."

"Oh, I shan't do it again. It doesn't really agree with me. But I am glad to know I can joust if I am put to it."

Thomas was thankful for the close helm hiding his face. His cheeks streamed with sweat and his lips were bleeding where he had bitten them in his struggle for self-control. He had won a harder battle than any joust. Something about the swagger of the French champion had made him lose his temper, and he had ridden out in a reckless fever of rage. The red mist, which had not risen for twenty years, had come back in full force. When that beastly Frenchman was stretched on the ground he had longed to trample him under the hoofs of his war horse; the warrior's fury in his breast had been terrifying. He had ridden back at once because he had no idea what he would do next if he continued to fight.

But he could not explain this to Henry, who gloried in losing his temper.

He noted also that the King was a little put out to see his Chancellor win fame as a jouster. There must be some field in which the younger man could outdistance his vassal. The difference in their ages was the awkward one of fourteen years. Had he been definitely of an older generation he might have received the deference even kings owe to age; now he spoke and thought of himself as a contemporary, but half the events he mentioned in casual conversation had happened when Henry was too young to be aware of them.

The immediate past, the years before Henry reached the throne, was an awkward topic. Henry frowned if he heard mention of *King* Stephen, though he had recognized Stephen as King when he sealed the Treaty of Winchester. Yet if you spoke of the Empress as the rightful ruler of England Henry must feel uncomfortable about her present situation; supplanted, without any formal act of abdication, and living powerless in a quiet Norman castle.

Fighting his inclination to unreasonable rage, fighting the wiles of luxury which appealed to his dramatic instinct, fighting the temptations of the flesh to which most clerks in his situation would have succumbed, Thomas found life as the King's closest counselor and friend a considerable strain. But it was worth it, to restore order in England, to use his mind at its utmost stretch. Now it seemed the more worth while; he was a knight, who had at last found a lord worthy of his loyalty. He had given Henry his fealty; together they would spend their lives on the difficult and rewarding task of welding England, Normandy, Maine, Aquitaine, and Anjou into the most prosperous and best-governed dominion in Christendom.

*   *   *

In November there was a truce with France, which in 1160 became full peace. For the first time in more than twenty years no English lord might lawfully gather his vassals for war. But after such an interval of anarchy only the eye of the King could enforce the King's Peace, and Henry rode incessantly from province to province of his wide-flung dominions. He must do justice from York to Bordeaux every year.

Where the King rode, his Chancellor must ride also, carrying his papers with him. When they stopped, seldom for more than one night, there was never room enough for everybody; half the court must lodge in peasants' huts, or bivouac in the open air. For offices the Chancery used tents, great pavilions of strong canvas stretched on many poles, the peaked roof line resembling a row of gabled cottages; the effect was of a spacious hall, though stifling hot in summer and bitter cold in winter.

Henry had no capital city. You could not leave the archives in Westminster, or Rouen, or Le Mans, until the government finished its tour; for the government was always on tour. Every current record must travel with the court, though the King rode sixty miles a day.

There was a great deal of work, for the dominions of Anjou bordered nearly every important power in Christendom. It was wise to keep on good terms with the Emperor, to safeguard English trade with the Low Countries; the Kings of Aragon and Navarre expected help in their perpetual warfare with the Moors; raids over the northern border called for frequent correspondence with the King of Scots; and the King of France, with the Counts of Brittany and Toulouse, were always raising intricate questions of boundaries or allegiance.

But the Norman world extended far beyond the borders of Anjou. Every Norman magnate had cousins in the crusading states of Outremer, and Sicily was ruled by an independent, parallel Norman aristocracy (for its original conquerors had

been middle-class adventurers). Relations with that rich kingdom were delicate, for Henry, as Duke of Normandy, felt that
he should rule the whole Norman race, a point of view the
King of Sicily did not share.

Besides foreign affairs the Chancery managed the King's
dealings with the Church. That meant in practice financial
dealings only, for a secular ruler could not meddle in spiritual matters. When bishoprics and abbacies lay vacant their
revenues were paid to the King, and when the vacancies came
to be filled, by the free election of the canons or monks concerned, the King's wishes carried great weight; how much
weight was better left undefined, so long as the electors did not
flout him deliberately. Thomas knew that by the letter of
canon law the secular lord had no standing in an election; but
if his desires were discreetly made known they were usually
discreetly fulfilled.

Negotiations with the Pope might be considered both foreign policy and Church affairs. But in prosperous times there
should be no such negotiations. Archbishop Theobald was Legate for all England, including the Province of York; if the
Pope wrote to the King direct it must be either to rebuke the
sins of his private life or to reiterate the everlasting appeal for
a Crusade.

Documents dealing with all these subjects passed under the
Great Seal, and while the court was constantly on the move
the best place to file them was in the memory of the Chancellor.

Thomas passed his mornings at work in the Chancery; in the
afternoon he usually rode with the King, either hunting or to
keep up with the journeys of the wandering court. Only in
the evening was he his own master.

Even that was an innovation. The old establishment which
fixed the Chancellor's wage at five shillings a day (ten times
the pay of a knight, and the highest wage in the government),

added elaborate regulations for his diet on the assumption that he would dine in the King's hall. When this wage was fixed the Chancellor had been the King's private secretary, not his chief minister. Now Thomas was the second ruler of the realm. Wherever the court might halt, the Chancellor dined with his own household.

This might be in one of his pavilions, but if it were possible he preferred a permanent building. In most places a magnate or religious community would be glad to offer hospitality to such a great man. Of course his baggage contained appropriate furniture. Even when he stopped only for one night he was surrounded by familiar possessions, trestle tables, long benches, a few high chairs with carved backs for distinguished visitors, windows of linen against the draft, an oratory with folding pictures of saints, a press for his breviary and lawbooks.

Very often the halidom was housed in the next room. The halidom was the collection of holy relics that accompanied the King of England to bring him luck; the collection had been founded by St. Edward the Confessor, but every King after, even the wicked Rufus, had added to it. There was nothing in it quite so divine as the hood of St. Martin of Tours which brought the King of France victory over his enemies, but it was a very great treasure; and the Chancellor was its official custodian.

Thomas's hall was noted for comfort as well as splendor. Every day the old rushes were thrown out, and fresh brought in; they were scented with meadow flowers in summer, and with sweet hay in winter; at the end of the room they were heaped up in bundles, to serve as seats for unimportant or uninvited guests who could not find room on the benches.

For the Chancellor's kitchen was as famous as his hall. Troubadours admitted that even in Provence one did not dine so well. The wine was chosen personally by the host, and his cooks were the most skillful in the realm; any stranger was admitted without question, and the doorkeepers would allot him the place appropriate to his rank.

King Henry dined with his Chancellor whenever he could, which was not very often; usually he had his own distinguished guests to entertain. But foreign envoys were never eager to dine with the King, since his food was notoriously poor and he himself so impatient that there was never time to eat it. Henry complained, in jest, that ambassadors to his court were nearly always to be found sharing the luxurious meals of the Chancellor.

The pomp of the Chancellor's household was as magnificent as the food. Thomas knew how things should be done, and he was determined that no carping foreigners would find anything amiss in the hall of England's greatest magnate. Even in time of peace two hundred knights lent splendor to the scene, and the servants, in scarlet liveries, were clean and expert at their trade. King Henry admired a pomp he himself was too impatient to endure; in the winter of 1160 he sent his heir, five-year-old Henry fitzHenry, to be "nourished" and trained in courteous living by the Chancellor. Other magnates followed his example, and soon there was a crowd of noble youths and children sitting gravely at a lower table, learning to listen patiently to troubadours, to refrain from throwing food to the dogs, to offer their neighbors the wine cup while it was still full.

It was hard work presiding with dignity over all this state, after a busy morning in the office and a long afternoon in the saddle. But Thomas enjoyed it. He was the Chancellor, and for every moment of the day he behaved as such. He hardly thought of himself as a person. The Chancellor must ride a fierce charger, the Chancellor must give generous alms to the poor, the Chancellor should dress in splendid clothes which indicated that he was at the same time clerk, warrior, and lawyer; since he was the Chancellor he must do these things.

Except for his dear friend Henry fitzEmpress he was quite alone in the world. He never saw his sisters, and he had no other kin save remote cousins he had never met. Occasionally a merchant would turn up at his door with a story of having befriended an obscure clerk in the London of King Stephen; these ancient kindnesses were amply repaid, for Thomas made no secret of his early struggles; but he had finished with mercantile life, and he was glad of it. He was too busy to talk over old times.

He had little in common with the other courtiers. Dashing warriors were frightened of so learned a clerk, though if he had nothing better to do he could chat with them easily about jousting or falcons. The clerks at court were a frivolous set, devoting what leisure they could spare from their mistresses to composing silly riddles and catch questions in theology; they avoided the company of this enormously wealthy deacon who had preserved his chastity, because he made them feel uncomfortable. On the other hand, holy abbots and bishops who visited the King to discuss ecclesiastical appointments took it for granted that such a splendid figure must be a worldly debauchee.

Being Chancellor to King Henry, and his most trusted friend, occupied all his time.

Occasionally there came a reminder of his old life. Archbishop Theobald was ailing, in his palace at Canterbury; but he heard tales of the Chancellor's magnificence. To a holy monk of Bec such a life seemed unworthy of his old Archdeacon; but there had been good in the lad, and if he were recalled to his duty his soul might yet be saved. The Archbishop sent messengers summoning Thomas to Canterbury for a long visit. Thomas replied that he could not spare the time.

It was hard for an old man sitting quiet in Canterbury to find out the truth about Master Thomas the Chancellor. There was nothing to go on except his public record, and that might be interpreted in many ways. Certainly he had opposed the great wickedness of the marriage between the lady Mary, daughter of old King Stephen, and Count Matthew, younger brother of the Count of Flanders. That had been a revolting business; not consanguinity for once, though that was the usual bar to a marriage within the ruling class. This was much worse, for the lady Mary was a professed nun, actually Abbess of Barking. The marriage had gone through, because this is a wicked world. The magnates favored it, glad to get a daughter of the late King out of the country before someone raised a rebellion in her name. Perhaps the Pope had dispensed her from her vows, though the story was told in more than one version. At least the Chancellor had spoken against it in full council, so strongly that the Count of Flanders had sworn to be revenged on him.

Thus his good advice had been overborne, though when he gave wrong advice it was immediately carried into effect. At the outset of the War of Toulouse Thomas had spoken in favor of a proposal to levy scutage from those abbeys which held land by knight-service. The abbots had been screwing up their courage to refuse, and his intervention tipped the scale against them. Perhaps his advice was sound in law, for there was no precedent. But Master Thomas had advocated taking money from abbeys to give it to a lay ruler. Whatever the exact letter of the law that showed a reprehensible levity, a willingness to desert the clerkly order. Every clerk should stand by every other clerk, without bothering over the rights of the matter in dispute. Master Thomas was not wholehearted in his calling.

The old man roused himself to write a really stiff letter, bidding Master Thomas drop whatever he was doing and come at once to Canterbury; if he disregarded the command of his Archbishop, who had conferred on him the order of deacon and received his oath of obedience, let him beware of excommunication. That should fetch the lad as fast as a ship could carry him. Here Theobald paused, to recall that the lad was now forty-two years of age, and engaged on important business. But at Canterbury he was needed for important business: there must soon be a vacancy in the Metropolitan See, and the Archbishop considered it his duty to look over a possible successor.

In March 1161 the court lay at Rouen, for once fairly stationary. Thomas disregarded the stream of letters from the Archbishop. He was not anxious to return to a household where he had been mocked: "Bailhache," indeed! Roger, who had mocked him, was now Archbishop of York, still as spiteful toward the King's Chancellor as he had been toward the Archdeacon; but at Canterbury there would be other clerks who remembered the old unpleasantness.

Finally came a letter threatening excommunication unless he obeyed the command of his Ordinary. Thomas was in half a mind to comply, until Henry persuaded him to stay where he was needed. The King pointed out that archbishops were inclined to give orders to every clerk anywhere, without considering the bounds of their canonical authority; Theobald of Canterbury had no standing in the Province of Rouen. If Thomas had been asked to come, for the sake of old friendship, then he might have gone; but in face of an order he must stand on his rights.

In April Theobald died. Thomas mourned the old friend of his father, the kindly master who had started him on his great career. He was sorry he had been unable to visit his deathbed. But now there were other things to think about. After twenty-two years the Metropolitan See of Canterbury was vacant. For the present its revenues would flow into the King's Treasury, but unless it was filled within a reasonable time the Pope would complain.

CHAPTER VI

The Archbishop

CANON law lays down only one method of filling a vacant bishopric. The canons of the cathedral chapter must meet to elect a new bishop. In theory their choice is unfettered; any male Christian of full age, whether clerk or lay, is eligible. If the chapter neglect their duty, and the see remains vacant for a scandalously long period, the Pope may provide a bishop of his own choice. No one else has a voice in the matter.

But facts do not always square with the letter of canon law. In fact, the monks of Christ Church who formed the Chapter of Canterbury Cathedral were unimportant clerks in a backwater of England; and the Archbishop whom they must choose would be the first magnate of the realm, the traditional representative of the people in face of an absolute ruler. Since St. Anselm had openly rebuked Rufus for sodomy the Archbishop of Canterbury had been more than merely head of the clergy in the south of England.

The Chapter might not hold an election until they had received specific permission from the King; and the King would not grant permission until he had come to some unofficial understanding with the Pope. Meanwhile the King enjoyed a great increase of revenue, and for at least a year there was no need to take a definite step.

Of course Thomas talked over the question with his dear friend Henry. "Luckily," he said, "we have an obvious candidate, born in England, of good Norman family, and already a bishop. He is also a devout monk, trained at Cluny, a clerk of exemplary life and a competent man of business. In case you are too intent on repairing that broken dagger to guess the man I mean I shall tell you his name. Bishop Gilbert of Hereford is clearly destined to be the next Archbishop of Canterbury."

Henry grunted, for he held an end of waxed thread between his teeth. The two friends sat alone in the greenwood, munching bread and cheese; at the end of the glade huntsmen were busy round the carcass of a stag, and grooms walked horses lest they take cold after the gallop.

The King looked round to make sure they could not be overheard.

"I respect Gilbert," he answered. "He's intelligent. He kept Hereford straight during the years of anarchy. He has done homage to a king of England, though the king was Stephen. Still, that binds him to me. I must have an Archbishop who is already my man. Look at the fuss they make in the Empire over bishops doing homage to temporal rulers. We avoid that in England by electing only those clerks who have already done homage. And yet I don't know. Gilbert is a dry old stick. Have you ever heard him make a joke? And he was very unhelpful over that London affair. He directly refused my request."

"He was quite right, as you know very well. London needs its own bishop. The money comes in very handy, but we can't expect the See of Hereford to pay a bishop to look after London. We shall have to find someone for London sooner or later. If we can't think of anyone better I might take the job myself."

"What would happen to my Chancery? I wouldn't know whether I had any money or not. I can't understand your accounts, my dear merchant of Cheapside, and privately I suspect you don't understand them yourself. But with you in charge there always seems to be silver in the Treasury. Probably some of it comes from your benefices, if the truth were known. You see why I can't do without you?"

"Accounts were never my strong point, even when I worked for that scoundrel Osbert Huitdeniers. I never remember how much money I have, or whether it came from your Exchequer or my benefices. If it goes farther than it used to that is because I keep an eye on my subordinates. But of course I can't plan ahead when I don't know which magnates will die during the year and what relief their heirs will pay. If you had Euclid for your Chancellor he would be beaten by that same trouble. You ought to arrange a scheme by which the magnates pay you a regular sum every year, instead of a relief whenever a fief changes hands."

"And get them to pay reliefs in addition, eh? That sounds a good idea, if the magnates would stand for it. But no Norman gentleman who carries a sword would pay taxes every year; the greatest tyrant on earth couldn't make them do it. So you can't have London, my bold and covetous deacon. And Gilbert can't have Canterbury because I couldn't stand his saintly monkish face at every meeting of the council. Why don't you take Canterbury? You could hold it with the Chancery."

"My dear Henry, you're crazy," said Thomas, without bothering to look up from the blade of grass he was chewing. "For one thing, I am known far and wide as the most worldly clerk in your realm; the whole Church would be shocked. For another, I couldn't do the extra work. Keeping your conduct within the broad limits allowed to a Christian king takes all my time. If I had to fit being an archbishop into the odd hours of the day I should never again sit at my ease in the greenwood."

"While things go well, Canterbury has less business than most diocesan bishops, though he must look after his own diocese. Nowadays all the appeals go over his head to Rome. The Curia would appreciate a metropolitan who was busy with secular affairs. The cardinals could deal direct with the bishops, and everyone would be satisfied."

"You make it sound attractive. Thomas Becket of Cheapside, Primate of All England! Well, Caligula made his horse a consul, but I can't think of another parallel. Poor old Theobald! He was a holy monk, and a great scholar. How angry he would be to hear us agreeing that the Archbishop of Canterbury has very little business! He worked all the hours of daylight, and never caught up with his arrears; but then before I took over the archdeaconry his papers were in a frightful muddle."

The subject dropped while they sat silent, watching the flight of a jay. In the distance a forester blew a single note, the signal that his hound had found the trace of a hart. The King sprang to his feet, brushing crumbs from his tunic. As he rose also, Thomas spoke casually: "You must make up your mind about Canterbury. The monks of Christ Church will soon be pressing for leave to elect. In the end who will you choose? Gilbert of Herford, I suppose. There isn't anyone else."

*   *   *

Hunting in the woods of Normandy during that peaceful summer, the King several times returned to the question of the vacancy at Canterbury. Henry disliked to feel that his mind was being made up for him; the fact that everyone took it for granted that Gilbert Foliot of Hereford would be the next Archbishop was one reason why he turned against it.

Gilbert possessed every qualification; not only was he a monk of unblemished life, and a gentleman of Norman blood, connected with all the great houses of the Welsh Marches; he was second only to Thomas as a lawyer and man of affairs. He would make a saintly ceremonial head, and at the same time look after the legal and financial affairs of the Church in England. During the civil war he had followed the Bishop of Winchester; that meant frequent changes of side; but on the whole, like the Bishop of Winchester, he had supported the Angevins more often than the party of Blois. There seemed to be nothing against him.

Unfortunately he was ambitious, and surrounded by flatterers who saw him as the next Archbishop. Indiscreetly, he began to talk of what he would do when he was installed at Canterbury, and boasted that his opposition to the King's plan for London had been justified by events. This boasting, and the reminder of his past opposition, decided the King.

One morning, when Thomas was working as usual in the Chancery, Henry strolled in to stand over him, cocking one leg on the table. "Well," he said cheerfully, "what is it this time? Another letter to the Emperor about the wrongs of those goldsmiths in Cologne? Let it wait. The Emperor usually takes a month to answer my letters. Why should we answer his complaints on the day we receive them? And while we are on the subject of the Emperor, can you tell me who is his chancellor?"

"Why, my lord, I thought you knew. The Emperor has two chancellors, since his realm is spread so wide. His chancellor for Germany is the Archbishop of Mainz, and for Italy the Archbishop of Cologne."

"I knew. I thought you might have forgotten. You see that it is the very latest fashion to have an archbishop for chancellor. Does the Church in Germany complain that these archbishops neglect their spiritual duties? On the contrary, everyone is pleased to see great clerks so highly placed in the councils of the Empire. Why shouldn't I have the Archbishop of Canterbury for my chancellor?"

"Those clerks were already archbishops, who took office because they knew they had time to perform those duties. The Emperor does not administer his realm as you administer England. I have never heard of a king's chancellor who took an archbishopric as his second, less important, work. In any case, Gilbert is your man."

"Gilbert Foliot is out of the running. I have let him know as much, unofficially."

"Well, you must find someone. Otherwise the Pope will appoint. Let me see. Gilbert himself got Hereford from the Pope because the See had been too long vacant, and that ass Hilary got Chichester in the same way, on the excuse that his predecessor died in Rome. That's two papal appointments, out of less than twenty Bishops in all England. The Pope will be appointing to London unless you hurry up. If you let Canterbury lapse also, your power will be greatly diminished."

"As you say, someone must have Canterbury, and soon. But if the Pope knows a nomination is under consideration he won't do anything in a hurry. Once again I suggest that you take it. At least see how the proposal is received by the clergy of England. I have already taken steps to find out that. I told Walter Map, in strict confidence. Walter is incapable of keeping a secret. In a month or so, when the news has leaked to the most remote rectory in the realm, we shall know what they think of it."

"I can tell you that now. They will think that an avaricious king has found a way of rewarding his chancellor at no cost to the Treasury. It will be regarded as yet another plundering of the endowments of the Church. Perhaps that is how you see it yourself?"

"Well, you know, it *would* be an economy. But the Archbishopric would also be in good hands. You could easily do the work in your spare time, and with the same man at the head of both spiritual and temporal affairs there would be no danger of a conflict of jurisdiction."

"But I don't want to be an archbishop, and your loving subjects among the clergy don't want me over them. Do our wishes count for nothing?"

"My dear Thomas, I wouldn't offend you for the world. I shall even take note of the sentiments of my subjects. That is why I launched the rumor. If it causes a great uproar I shall deny it gracefully, and start looking for another head for the English Church."

"Then I'm safe. If you wait for public approval before promoting me I shall die a simple deacon."

Then it was time to ride thirty miles in the general direction of Aquitaine, hawking by the way while the baggage caught up. For the rest of the day Henry did not refer to the Archbishopric, and Thomas hoped that the outburst of indignation which must greet the rumor would convince him. But he was not sure. Sometimes opposition only confirmed Henry in his obstinacy.

By autumn they were back in Rouen, Henry's favorite residence. It was the most comfortable station for the court; the castle could shelter the King and all his knights, in the town there was a market hall big enough for the Chancery, and the Archbishop always lent Thomas a spacious lodging. This even possessed a private room behind the dais, where the Chancellor might amuse himself in private. Thomas never relaxed where the public could see him; before a crowd his acute sense of the behavior fitting in a chancellor always kept him self-conscious.

On this particular evening Henry was away; the hunt had led him farther than he had intended, and he would pass the night in a forester's hut. The unfortunate courtiers might find what shelter they could, or sleep in the open. That was one of the penalties of court life, worth enduring for the sake of catching the King's ear when he was in an affable mood. The Chancellor, who had been too busy to go hunting, might for once pass the evening in privacy.

In the little room he gathered a few intimates for a game of chess. They were mostly knights of his court, not clerks. For he passed all his working hours in the company of clerks, and for amusement in the evening laymen struck a lighter note. Besides, at chess most clerks could beat him; he had only taken up that frivolous game after he had become an archdeacon, able to afford heavy wagers; the average clerk of the court had played it since he was big enough to sit at the table. So had the average knight, but the average knight was not intelligent; Thomas found that his wit enabled him to hold his own with laymen.

Chess was the most fashionable gambling game. Young debauchees could dissipate a fortune quicker at dice; but that was definitely wicked. Chess was a game of skill, though frivolous. It was a little daring for a sober official like the Chancellor to indulge in it, but no one could say it was positively wrong. Of course it should not be played too earnestly, or the fun of the gamble would be lost. In this room a troubadour sang a lay of the Crusade, and the player must make his move before the end of each stanza. Thomas's opponent was the captain who led his cortege, a player of his own level of skill. Since the lesser knights standing round held definite views about the capability of their leader, the board was plastered with gold and silver, the stakes and the side bets of the onlookers.

Then a fool of a new chamberlain made a serious mistake. The door was thrown open, and this ass announced that Master John of Salisbury craved immediate audience of the Chancellor; John followed on his heels, pausing in the doorway to take in the tableau.

It could hardly have looked worse. The Chancellor sat behind a winking heap of money; on the table were flagons and wine cups, and some knights showed by their manner that they had been drinking steadily all evening; everyone was dressed in the extravagant garb of the court, and the Chancellor outshone them all. Over a tunic and hose of his favorite scarlet cloth he wore a long gown of sky-blue silk trimmed with sable; on his red leather shoes gleamed knightly spurs; the sleeves of his tunic followed the new fashion from Provence: cut with increasing width from elbow to wrist, their open ends swept the floor as he sat; inside they were lined with gold tissue, and the wrists of his shirt, thus exposed, were caught up with little gold chains. Round his neck, and on the front of his tunic, were other chains and brooches; as he moved he flashed like a man in polished mail.

There was nothing for Thomas to do but to carry off the interview as best he might. Springing to his feet, he pushed his stake across the table.

"Sir William, I concede you the victory. You would have beaten me anyway, but I must not let this game delay my greeting of Master John, the learned lawyer of Rome and Canterbury. Come here, John, and sit beside me. What can your old friend Bailhache do for you?"

That gave Master John all the advantage he needed. After a successful career in the Roman Curia he had entered the household of Archbishop Theobald. He had been present when Master Roger, now Archbishop of York, had bestowed that opprobrious nickname. He knew Thomas hated it; he would only use it, in that deprecatory manner, because he was already ashamed of himself. So he ought to be ashamed of himself, and John was the man to drive it home.

He waited, standing in silence, until the household had withdrawn. Then he sat down carefully on the little stool facing the Chancellor across the gaming board. "Thomas," he began portentously, "I shall tell you my errand, and then you can judge the effect of your conduct. I have been sent, on behalf of the abbots and bishops of England, to see for myself how our prospective Archbishop amuses his leisure. We heard of your extravagant embassy to Paris; that might be excused, since you were carrying out the instructions of your ruler. But there were stories of your magnificent private life, stories which do infinite harm to your reputation, which I wish to be in a position to deny. What do I find? You are a deacon, of a rank next in honor to the priesthood itself. Yet as Chancellor you divert to the secular Treasury the endowments of three wealthy sees, London, Worcester, and now even Canterbury."

"Worcester isn't wealthy," Thomas interjected. "It's one of the poorest sees in Christendom, vacant because no one will accept it."

John was a trained orator, not to be halted in his eloquence by a mere mistake of fact. The speech rolled on.

"You are a Prebendary of Beverley, Dean of Hastings, the holder of many rich benefices. The Church supports you generously, and you should support the Church. Instead I find you gambling with a group of bloodthirsty drunkards, gambling away, for all I know, money which is the property of some cathedral. You yourself are not drunk, I am pleased to see; but your companions were intoxicated, and you provide strong wine to make their condition yet more disgraceful. As to your dress, I beg you to recall that you are in major orders. You look like an exceptionally profligate knight, with gilt spurs and a silk gown and sleeves trailing on the floor. There is no more to be said. I did not come to seek favors from you; I did not even come to speak to you. I came to see you, and to tell the clergy of England what I had seen. If you will call for my horse I will leave immediately."

Thomas was too angry to feel ashamed. He knew that in the face of great temptation he lived chastely and soberly. He was doing difficult work remarkably well. He had shed luster on the arms of Normandy by unhorsing Engelram de Trie. Now this fat windbag, who had never faced anything more dangerous than the splutterings of a rival advocate, was telling a grown and learned man of forty-three, the most successful clerk in France or England, how he ought to behave. The red mist of anger rose in his brain, though by long custom he controlled it. When he answered his face wore a pleasant smile.

"Master John, since you are come on a grave errand I have heard you patiently to the end. Now I will tell you a secret. I did not seek the burden of the primacy; I considered it too heavy for me, and I was determined to refuse. Your wise advice has changed my convictions. Now, if Canterbury is offered to me, I shall accept. And I shall show you, and every other gossiping idler in my province, what it means to be ruled by an archbishop who knows his rights and intends to enforce them. Go back and advise those who sent you to begin making friends with their new master. Oh, and by the way, if you happen to see that pompous Archbishop Roger, will you remind him of the rule about metropolitan crosses? He may display his cross in his own province, but not in mine. If you want your horse I will send for it. But why don't you stay here for the night? You might enjoy a good game of chess."

There was a twinkle in the Chancellor's eye, and John smiled in return. He saw that Thomas had been angry, but it was really amazing how that man could control his temper. He was once more the gay scholar of Paris, the witty spark who had kept them laughing in the Archbishop's office at Harrow. After all, he did know the rights and duties of Canterbury, after his training as archdeacon; and he had the business experience to become a capable administrator, if not a specially saintly shepherd of his flock.

When Thomas thought over what he had said he realized that there was still one great obstacle to his accepting the proffered promotion. St. Augustine, the first Archbishop of Canterbury, had been a Benedictine; it just so happened that nearly every succeeding Archbishop had been a monk also. A monastery of black monks formed the Cathedral chapter, with the Archbishop as Abbot *ex officio*. Thomas knew he could not endure the monastic life, after six years of delicate food and luxurious beds. He would never stand the rising at midnight, the fasting, or the straw pallets. No, after all, he was not fitted for Canterbury.

During the next Lent he had his last chance of refusing the great office. At Falaise Henry held court to entertain the Cardinal of Pisa, a special envoy from the Pope. That fitted in very nicely, for the Cardinal could convey the papal endorsement necessary for the chosen candidate for Canterbury, whoever he might be.

The Cardinal knew of the proposal, for the Roman court took immense trouble to be well informed about the leading figures in every realm of Christendom. Thomas was surprised to find that he favored it, for usually papalists disliked the custom of rewarding a king's ministers from the endowments of the Church. The reason for this approval was a simple matter of power politics. Though everyone spoke of the "Roman" court and of appealing to "Rome," the Pope, as had often happened before, was in exile. On the death of the Englishman Adrian IV, the patron of John of Salisbury, the cardinals had elected Alexander III to succeed him. But the Emperor had organized a rival election, and proclaimed his creature "Victor IV." The chief supporters of Alexander III were the Kings of France and

England, and a cardinal of this party would go to great lengths to please King Henry.

At the end of a long banquet Henry summoned Thomas to his royal seat. Thomas had expected this, and had deliberately attended the banquet in his most splendid and most secular dress. If they insisted on making an archbishop out of him they must see him for what he was.

When the King began to speak loudly, in the hearing of all, of his desire that Thomas should accept the See of Canterbury, the Cardinal graciously added his entreaties. Thomas listened quietly until these speeches were finished, and then glanced down at his gown. "My lord," he said with a grin, "do I look the kind of man who should be put into such a famous bishopric? Do I look the kind of holy monk who should be made Abbot of Christ Church?"

"Certainly not," Henry muttered under his breath, "but you haven't always dressed like that. Thomas, I know you can do this. Do it, to please me."

"Shall I please you? Are kings usually pleased with their archbishops?" whispered Thomas in reply. Then he went on, in a loud voice that all the company might hear: "If I accept, the love you now feel for me will turn to bitter hate. For I know you will require of me many things which I shall not bear quietly."

Then he muttered again: "That's my last warning. If you press me again I must accept. At least you know what you are in for."

"I know that my best friend will be the most powerful clerk in my dominions. That will bring peace to the Church. Of course you must accept, and we shall hurry on the election. Bear witness, all of you, that I nominate to the electors of Canterbury the learned deacon Master Thomas of London, my Chancellor."

"In the name of the Pope I endorse that excellent choice," added the Cardinal.

"Very well, my lord. I shall leave for London immediately. Will you come also? The election cannot be complete until the King has given his assent."

"Or the King's representative. You forget that now I have a viceroy in England, capable of these purely ceremonial functions. Little Henry fitzHenry will assent in my name and receive your homage."

"But an archbishop may not do homage to a king," put in the Cardinal anxiously.

"That is arranged, Eminence," Thomas said smoothly. He was once more the Chancellor, finding the quickest way out of one of the muddles caused by Henry's impetuosity. "In England we have found a way round the difficulty. I shall do homage as a simple deacon, after election but before consecration. In my native land no bishop does homage. Perish the thought! But every bishop is a man who has done homage, and homage endures for life."

"Ah, the famous English levity," said the Cardinal. "We grave Italians could never invent these frivolous evasions. But now all ends happily, and such amity among his children will be specially pleasing to His Holiness."

For the rest of the banquet Thomas sat silent. That night he paced the floor of his chamber for many hours, thinking of the future.

There had been plenty of time to get used to the idea, and yet it came as a shock. He was forty-three years of age, and for more than twenty of them he had earned his bread as a scholar and lawyer; he was not a priest; and in a few weeks he would be Archbishop. He had lived in the household of a holy archbishop, and he knew how seriously and devoutly Theobald had performed his duties. Come, that was something; he knew what an archbishop should do. Richer de l'Aigle had shown him

what a knight should do, and when he had to do it he had un-
horsed Engelram de Trie. At Merton he had been taught how
a holy man should comport himself; incidentally his old comrade, novice Robert, was now Prior of Merton; he would appoint him confessor to the Archbishop, and such an example
would keep him up to the mark. In Paris he had obeyed his
teachers. In Theobald's household he had behaved in a manner fitting to his position. When he was made Chancellor there
had been no precedents to guide him, for never before had the
Chancellor wielded such power; but at least no one had been
surprised at his conduct. It was quite simple, at least for a
scholar who had been taught to use his mind. In a novel situation you must find out how you were expected to behave; you
then behaved in that manner, and everybody praised you. It
needed self-control, but self-control was his strong point.

With his memory of Theobald, and with Robert of Merton
to tell him the latest theological theories, he could be a model
archbishop. At present the obvious thing to do was to pass the
night in prayer, especially to Our Lady his patron. When his
valet came to call him in the morning, he found the Chancellor
kneeling beside an untouched bed. The valet was not surprised;
if his master wished to pray he would of course pray all night,
for his master never did anything by halves.

At last the monks of Christ Church, Canterbury, had the
royal permission to proceed to election, without which they
could do nothing. But there was no pretense that this was a free
election, and in consequence no need for them to consult in
private over their choice. For a purely ceremonial function
they jumped at a chance of a visit to London. All the seventy
choir-monks rode up, and the election was held in the chapter
house of St. Paul's.

Though only the monks were electors, this was a matter that
closely concerned all the bishops of southern England; they

were entitled to be present and speak, though not to vote. In the chapter house Gilbert Foliot, Bishop of Hereford, counted all the other bishops of the Province of Canterbury, besides three visiting Welsh prelates. He was glad to see such a distinguished audience for his protest.

For he must protest, as publicly as possible, against this cynical misapplication of a great office in the Church to provide an endowment for a royal official, a deacon who had never exercised a cure of souls, a warrior and administrator, unfitted to bear rule in spiritual things even if his exacting work as Chancellor left him the time to perform the duties of his charge. Conscience compelled Gilbert, though he knew jealous enemies would misrepresent his stand for righteousness.

A bishop faithful to his charge, who rebuked sinners and held the lazy to their duty, must have plenty of jealous enemies. A monk would not accept a bishopric if he thought the throne would be only a pleasant seat. Gilbert had abandoned the monastery of Cluny, that outpost of Heaven on earth whose spiritual life fitted all the needs of his soul, only because the Church on the war-torn Marches of Wales needed a zealous supervisor. A profitable servant might not spend his days and nights chanting in the blessed choir of Cluny if his talents would be useful in a wider sphere. Making his sacrifice of inclination and desire, he had accepted a miter.

Even the world admitted that he made an excellent bishop. Otherwise the King would not have offered him that hole-and-corner semipromotion, to administer the See of London at Hereford's expense. Of course as far as he personally was concerned the money made no difference, though it grieved him to see the endowments of the Church vanishing into a secular Treasury. He had been compelled to refuse, antagonizing the King, who could make or mar his career, because any trained canon lawyer could see that London was not really vacant. Canon law permitted a bishop to resign, though it seldom happened; or a bishop overcome by age might consent to the appointment of a coadjutor with right of succession. But poor old Richard of London had lost his wits through sheer senility; by the time the King noticed that he was incapable of performing his duties he was also incapable of giving consent to his own replacement. Until the dotard died London must remain without a bishop.

That refusal of an uncanonical responsibility had cost Gilbert dear. It had been taken for granted that he would be the next Archbishop of Canterbury; but for the King's dislike the bishops would have recommended him, the Pope would have given his formal assent, and the electors would have considered no other name. What made the disappointment more bitter was that his friends had congratulated him in advance.

That was not the reason for his protest. No clerk had a right to Canterbury, even though he was best fitted for it. The protest must be made because the King was giving the rule of the Church to his boon companion, a secular clerk notorious for luxury, who would place those who had vowed their lives to God under the control of the sinful royal court. The Prior of Christ Church had just finished reading the letter patent under the Great Seal (a seal affixed by that sinful Thomas, no doubt with unholy glee). Now he formally sought the advice of the assembled bishops. Gilbert rose to address the meeting.

It was not an easy speech, even for a trained preacher. Of course no one there present would accuse him of ambition, for he was well known to them all. But a Goliard, one of those dissolute wanderers who disgraced sound learning, could make a very funny song about the envious monk who attacked his successful rival. Gilbert persevered, for he was willing to put himself in an unfavorable, even ridiculous, light if duty demanded.

An obstacle he had not foreseen was the dignified bearing of the worldling. Thomas managed to look worthy of his promotion, though no well-informed man could ignore his hunting and hawking and jousting, and the scandalous luxury of that embassy to Paris. He was as magnificent as usual, in wide-sleeved scarlet tunic, scarlet gown trimmed with ermine, pointed shoes and gilded spurs; but he wore also the hood of the Paris schools, and under it his pale face, the jutting nose and flashing eyes, seemed that of an ascetic Doctor of the Church. He was very thin, and he stooped courteously from his great height with a composed smile of assent as Gilbert pointed out his manifest imperfections.

The monks of Christ Church took refuge in the letter of the Rule, sitting with bent heads enveloped in cowls and hands hidden in wide black sleeves; the other bishops and attendant clerks stared stonily ahead. Only the Chancellor seemed to listen as Gilbert, overcome by a mounting sensation of embarrassment, stumbled to a faltering conclusion.

There was a minute of dead silence.

Then Thomas himself came forward and spoke: "My lord Prior, you have read the letter of our lord the King, and you have sought the advice of those bishops who owe obedience to Canterbury. The Bishop of Hereford alone has thought right to advise you; and I agree with all he has said. I hope you follow his advice. But since no other bishop wishes to speak it is your duty to proceed to election."

The Prior looked round nervously; but he was accustomed to taking a chief part on occasions of ceremony, and he spoke out with a firm voice: "My lords, brethren, we have heard the wish of our lord the King, and we have been informed of the concurrence of our lord the Pope. Taking note of the advice offered us by the Bishop of Hereford and the King's Chancellor, we note also that they are advisers only, with no vote in this election. We unanimously elect Thomas of London, deacon, to be Archbishop of our Cathedral and Primate of All England."

"I accept," Thomas answered at once, "provided I receive

the assent of the King's deputy in England, King Henry fitz-Henry. Will you come with me, my lords, to seek it?"

Seven-year-old King Henry was usually known as the Young King, for it seemed absurd to call him Henry III while Henry II was yet reigning. Now he sat in Westminster Hall, carefully rehearsed in what he must perform.

All the same, when the group of bishops and monks approached the throne on which the self-conscious child sat stiffly, an unrehearsed incident intruded. As Thomas knelt before the boy, his long bony hands between the chubby fists, Bishop Henry of Winchester stepped forward to speak.

In the absence of an archbishop, Bishop Henry was the unquestioned leader of the clergy. His see ranked second in the southern province, but Henry of Blois was great in his own right; brother to the last King, he had been for some years papal Legate, which made him superior to Canterbury. This honor he no longer held, for such an arrangement had proved unworkable; but he had resigned gracefully when asked, and in temporal politics all knew that it was largely through his efforts that Henry of Anjou had succeeded peacefully to the throne. There were few assemblies in England where he would not have first place.

Now he spoke formally, facing the boy-king but addressing the magnates round his throne. "My lord, our Archbishop-elect is also the salaried servant of your father. Let him come to the service of God untrammeled by wordly cares. It may be many years before the Exchequer finally passes his accounts; grant him now a release from the claims of his secular employment. Only thus can he devote all his energies to his great task of ruling the Church of God in England."

The child looked round his councilors. He must never grant a favor, or refuse one, without their assent; and usually he was told beforehand exactly what to do. But there had been nothing about this in the morning's rehearsal. However, he saw the

Justiciar nod and smile. That was enough; he took a deep breath, and his childish treble could be heard through the hall.

"My lord Thomas, we release you from the burdens of your Chancellorship. I am sure your accounts will look very nice when you present them. The King is your debtor for loyal service, and I also am indebted to you for a pleasant winter passed in your hall. I hope to visit you later in Canterbury."

He looked round again, proudly. On the spur of the moment he had made a gracious speech, all composed in his head without rehearsal.

The Bishop of Hereford muttered sourly to his neighbor: "Does this mean that our new Metropolitan can spend the King's money as he likes?"

The Justiciar overheard, and answered soothingly, anxious that harsh words should not mar this occasion of state. "Our little King's answer means nothing. Thomas is still Chancellor, and of course the Chancellor must account for his expenditure. The word of a seven-year-old king will not weigh with the Barons of the Exchequer. But it doesn't matter. Thomas keeps accounts, and we all acknowledge that he is an honest man."

Bishop Gilbert was not so certain, but this was not the time to pursue the matter. Servants were bringing in long tables, for such a numerous gathering of magnates merited a feast of exceptional splendor.

The procession to Canterbury attracted every idle sightseer for miles round. Since the King never ceased his journeying, men were accustomed to galloping parties of horse, knights, sergeants, and crossbowmen. But fourteen bishops in one cavalcade, even though three of them were Welsh foreigners who didn't count—that was something the oldest Kentishman had never seen, and the youngest would never see again. The new Archbishop-elect they were bound to see often, as he rode from Canterbury to London and back again; but it would be pleasant to tell the neighbors you had seen him when he was only a deacon.

First came a small advance guard, made up of knights and sergeants of the Chancellor's military household; wearing the scarlet livery of their lord instead of armor, they were obviously there to add dignity, not for protection. Servants followed, mounted or leading pack horses, loaded with the great leather trunks, ironbound and studded with brass nails, in which magnates packed their robes and clerks their vestments. Heavy chariots creaked along, burdened with the carcasses of harts and boars, or with ponderous tuns of Gascon wine (which would taste very nasty after the ruts of Watling Street had stirred its dregs); for Canterbury would be scantily furnished after a vacancy of more than a year, in which dishonest stewards could plunder without a master. The consecration of an archbishop called for a greater feast even than that which had celebrated his election.

Then came a horde of clerks, on mules if they were wealthy, hackneys if they were moderately prosperous, donkeys if they were genuinely poor. Last of all came the bishops, in ecclesiastical order of precedence with the place of honor at the rear. Thus the visiting Welsh came first, followed by Walter of Rochester, whose diocese was almost a part of Canterbury; there followed him the suffragans of Canterbury, ten in all, for London and Worcester were still vacant. These great men rode tall Spanish mules, whose gentle paces could bear an elderly clerk over the roughest road without discomfort.

Last of the bishops, riding alone, came Henry of Winchester. In his gorgeous appearance the emblems of noble birth seemed to war with his natural humility. His traveling cloak, of fine silk, was a monkish gray in color, and the Benedictine habit below contrasted with the jeweled splendor of his miter; on his hands were gloves of soft leather, set with rubies; on his unspurred feet Benedictine sandals; he held it unclerkly to ride a horse, but his mule was worth a King's ransom. The bene-volence of his countenance held no hint of the woolly kindliness of poor old Theobald: at sixty years of age he was an intelligent and experienced politician, still in full command of his facul-ties.

At the very end, just before the military rear guard, came the Archbishop-elect. Thomas was still a deacon, and he had made no change in his secular appearance. His scarlet tunic and riding cloak befitted a gallant knight as much as the gilded spurs on his heels and the hooded falcon on his wrist. His war horse, a black stallion, played gently with his silver bit; had there been other stallions in the procession he would have screamed and fought to get at them, but mules and gelded hackneys were beneath his notice. Prior Robert of Merton, on a cheap little jennet, might ride in safety beside him.

Thomas had tasted the first delights of his new authority when he sent for the Prior of Merton. No prior who took thought for the welfare of his community would neglect an opportunity to be constantly in the presence of the Archbishop of Canterbury, and Robert had immediately agreed to stay with him as long as he was wanted.

Thomas chatted easily, telling of hurried journeys over this same road on the King's service, or recalling their shared schooldays. As he talked he slipped into the old intimacy, and presently opened his most inward thoughts.

"I am too excited to think straight," he said casually. "If I begin to make a fool of myself in public you must stop me. This great promotion haunts even my dreams. Last night I dreamed that a venerable figure, clothed in white and wearing a halo, bowed low before me, offering ten talents wrapped in a napkin. I don't know what a talent looks like, though I have often read of them; but in my dream I knew these were talents. Now I might easily start talking of that as a vision from Heaven; when it only means that I can't stop thinking of my own greatness, even in sleep."

"Thomas, that was a vision," the Prior answered earnestly. "But you were not receiving the congratulations of the saints, which you have done nothing to deserve. Can't you see? It was a warning. The steward who received ten talents was required to return them thirtyfold. God has given you health and brains and courage, good luck and the respect of your fellows. In return you must serve Him as the best Archbishop ever seen in Canterbury. If you fail in that task you imperil your salvation."

"The best Archbishop ever seen in Canterbury? The first Archbishop, Augustine, is a canonized saint; and later there were St. Alphege and St. Anselm. Is it my duty to surpass these?"

"It is your duty, for you can do it. St. Augustine came to a pagan land, St. Alphege was martyred by pagan invaders, St. Anselm strove with a wicked king. You control the spiritual life of a Christian land, whose king is your friend and an adequate Christian. You can do anything you set your mind to. Give to God's service the determination and astuteness which impressed your teachers at Merton. As your confessor I point out your bare duty. I ask nothing extra, for the love of God."

"I have chosen a stern confessor, though I had all England to choose from. This needs thinking over."

Thomas rode the rest of the journey in silence. But that night in Canterbury he spoke to his valet apart.

"Guido, I have a commission for you. You can find your way about a strange city. I want you to buy me a hair shirt with drawers to match. In this holy place such things must be made from time to time. Stay, you had better buy two of each, so that they can be washed. I must do my duty, but it is no part of the duty of an archbishop to stink in hot weather. Take what money you need from that coffer in the corner, and get these things without telling anyone. I shall wear them for the first time tomorrow, at my ordination."

Guido was an excellent valet. Next morning he brought in with his master's other clothes the hair shirt and drawers. As he returned a few coins to the coffer he remarked: "They were cheap, my lord, for they were woven by a widow vowed to poverty. She showed me how they should be washed, and I suggest, if you wish to keep them secret, that I wash them myself."

That was the morning of the Saturday within the Octave of Pentecost. As soon as he was dressed, in his richest deacon's vestments over the secret hair shirt, Thomas rode fasting to the Cathedral. There the Bishop of Rochester ordained him priest. The other bishops were present to lend luster to the function; but it was a warm May morning, and yesterday these elderly gentlemen had ridden a long journey; the service was cut to the minimum, and Thomas went to breakfast without saying Mass.

He passed the remainder of the day in prayer and meditation. He prayed decorously, on his knees before a crucifix, or flat on his face with arms extended. That was not very difficult. He merely ordered himself to pray, and obeyed his own orders. But when he tried to meditate he could not fix his mind on heavenly things; his thoughts turned to the neglected Chancery, and he could not help wondering how Henry was getting on in Normandy without his most competent adviser.

In the evening the bishops called him from his chamber to decide as Chancellor a trivial dispute. Gilbert of Hereford, making things as difficult as only a pedantic and uncooperative canon lawyer could make them, had pointed out that on the rare previous occasions when a priest had been consecrated Archbishop of Canterbury the consecration had been performed by the Bishop of London; he inferred that the consecration of the Primate was a privilege of the See of London. At present that See was in the hands of an imbecile. Should they wait until it was filled by a competent bishop before proceeding further?

Thomas was inclined to think Gilbert wrong in his facts. In any case the implied slur, that it was unusual for a priest to become Archbishop, was patently absurd. St. Anselm and Lanfranc had come straight from the cloister to the primacy.

But who should have the honor of consecrating him? Luckily there was an obvious solution. Henry of Winchester stood first among the bishops of England. But a professional courtier like Thomas must avoid the suspicion that he deferred to a bishop because he was brother to a king. Instead of naming Winchester, he suggested that the senior bishop, in point of consecration, should have the honor of consecrating his own Metropolitan. Henry of Winchester had been a bishop for thirty-four years, and was by a long way the senior.

On the Sunday after Pentecost, which at Canterbury was kept as the special feast of the Holy Trinity, Pontifical High Mass was sung with great splendor before the high altar of the Cathedral. Then Bishop Henry consecrated Thomas of London, priest and Chancellor and a knight besides.

Now that he was among the successors of the Apostles, Thomas could no longer delay saying his first Mass. It was queer to find himself performing the actions he had seen done every day of his life. He had thought of priests as a class apart, saved from many of the temptations of secular life by the grace of their orders. An archbishop was nothing extraordinary; in the Chancery he often had dealings with the archbishops of Rouen and Bordeaux, and as archdeacon he had pleaded before a whole bench of Cardinals. Archbishops were magnates, independent and willful and always seeking to defy their temporal lords; you might not make war on them, and you had to be especially careful of their dignity, but otherwise they behaved very much like counts. But a priest—a priest could bring down God's Body to the altar.

As he genuflected and moved his arms in the ritual gestures

his mind could dwell on the significance of what he did: he, Thomas, was an intermediary between God in Heaven and man on fallen earth. At each pace he took to right or left the pricking of the hair shirt reminded him that he was entering on a new manner of life.

The altar at which he celebrated was the easternmost in the lengthy Cathedral, in the apse behind the High Altar; he had chosen it because it was dedicated to the Blessed Trinity, Whose feast was kept today in Canterbury. An odd feast, typical of the queer English customs that sensible Normans had been unable to root out from this insular Church; every Christian prayer was addressed to the Trinity, and to celebrate this special feast seemed to argue that on other days you might worship some other god. But perhaps it was not a bad idea that a clerk should once a year fix his thoughts on God alone, without seeking the intercession of the Saints. Thomas was now set apart to serve God alone, without seeking the favor of any earthly power. Henry had been his lord, now he was God's knight only. This was really a very helpful and timely feast; he would order it to be celebrated throughout the Province of Canterbury.

The Mass was quickly over. He had arranged with Prior Robert, who knew his way through all the complicated maze of the Missal, that he should always say the shortest Mass liturgically permissible. At his age he could not keep his thoughts fixed on heavenly things for more than half an hour, and he was determined that while he said Mass he would think of nothing else. On this first occasion his thoughts did not wander, and yet when he made his reverence and left the altar he found that a great decision was fixed in his mind. Henceforth he would be a priest first and all the time. If he had the leisure he would also be a businesslike archbishop; it would leave him no time to serve his friend Henry fitzEmpress.

For the rest of that day nothing was demanded of him beyond the ceremonious manners which cost him no effort. He sat through a long banquet, remembering not to squirm as the hair drawers pricked his flesh; he replied politely to the polite speeches of bishops, and accepted their homage with grace. The only unpleasant note was struck by Gilbert of Hereford. When it was his turn to render homage he pointed out that he had sworn an oath of obedience to Archbishop Theobald; since that oath must endure for life there was no need to renew it. The instinct of the trained politician made Thomas agree at once, without argument. Gilbert escaped a ceremony he disliked—and all the other bishops went home remembering him as a cantankerous bad-tempered man, who could not stop struggling when he was beaten. That would be valuable the next time he tried to oppose his Archbishop.

In the morning Thomas said Mass again, as would be the unvarying ritual of every morning for the rest of his life. After he had broken his fast he sent for the Prior of Christ Church, for Prior Robert of Merton, and for Herbert of Bosham, who seemed the most intelligent and sympathetic of the clerks he had inherited from Theobald. He conferred with them at one end of the long hall which housed his business administration; at the other end lesser clerks were already bent over their desks, drawing up the first of the mass of documents that must be read and approved every day by the Archbishop of Canterbury.

"I know something of the work in an archbishop's household," he began. "After a vacancy of more than a year there must be thousands of cases, matrimonial or probate, awaiting my decision. There is also the ordinary work of the diocese, Confirmation and visiting. I am newly a priest, and I need some time daily for meditation and spiritual reading. Then as Abbot of Christ Church I ought to attend part of the daily office. Let us draw up a time table."

Prior Walter of Christ Church looked up in wonder. He had heard the usual stories of this new Archbishop, that he was more knight than clerk, a jouster and a chess player, who kept higher state than the King. Now he proposed to live even more seriously than the holy Theobald. But his Abbot had ordered him to relate the daily time table of his monastery, and he plunged into it, thinking only of holy obedience.

After hearing Walter, Robert and Herbert on the claims of their respective departments Thomas announced his first decision.

"Draft a civil letter to King Henry, explaining that I haven't time to be his Chancellor. When he pressed the monks of Christ Church to elect me he knew that the rule of the Church in England was a full day's work. He cannot complain that I refuse to hold another great office in addition."

They all knew King Henry would complain; but they did as their lord had ordered.

For the rest of that summer and autumn Archbishop Thomas followed a regular routine. He rose at dawn, though there was nothing odd in that; so did King Henry and every other busy man. His day opened with an hour of spiritual reading and discussion with Herbert of Bosham. Then came his Mass. After breakfast the rest of the morning was filled with work in the office, deciding every disputed testament and doubtful marriage in the south of England.

He dined shortly after midday. This was the time when the Archbishop of Canterbury chose to remind the world in general that he was the greatest magnate in England, second only to the King. He no longer paid wages to seven hundred knights, but the military tenants of Canterbury made up a powerful force, and every day a number of them dined in their lord's hall. There were more than two hundred servants and chamberlains, clothed in scarlet. The numerous clerks of the household, with visiting clerks who came on business or happened to be passing through, dined at the clerks' table, with the Archbishop at their head. Here conversation was discreet, and a monk read from a holy book; though the food was as lavish and as exquisite as at the knights' table, where a troubadour recited some epic of love or war, and men of the world might laugh over wordly stories without interrupting the serious discourse of the clerks. Every day the floor was covered with fresh rushes, and the wine was the best in England.

Thomas loved neatness as much as splendor, though he was indifferent to comfort; nowadays he was never comfortable, under his hair shirt. He loved to sit in his high chair, watching poor clerks take their fill of Gascon wine, while himself he sipped the abstinent brew which a puzzled cook described as "water in which hay has been boiled." He ate very little, but that little must be of the best. He had tried the Benedictine diet of Christ Church, and almost at once suffered from fainting fits and violent internal pain. He could not get through his work in those conditions, and soon he went back to roast pheasant and the best cuts of venison.

After dinner every clerk rested; as did most laymen of the upper class, since even the rich rose at dawn. Thomas went properly to bed, since his health was beginning to worry him. He never felt warm, and his hands and feet were usually covered with chilblains; his stomach was easily upset, and if he missed a meal he felt worse than if he had eaten too much.

In the afternoon, for exercise, Thomas would ride out on a tall war horse. That was the outcome of a compromise with Robert of Merton, reached after considerable argument. His confessor maintained that it was sinful for a bishop to spend the afternoon hawking; Thomas replied that nearly every bishop of his acquaintance hawked regularly; Robert turned up the relevant canon, which laid down that the clergy might not hunt for pleasure, though in an emergency they might hunt to get food. Thomas then admitted himself beaten, and dispersed his splendid mews of falcons in presents to all his lay friends. But when Robert went further, claiming that it was unseemly in a bishop to ride any mount more warlike than a mule, Thomas challenged him to find the canon forbidding horses. Since one could not be found Thomas, deprived of his favorite sport, consoled himself by riding the hottest and fiercest chargers he could find.

Even on these rides, his sole recreation, spiritual business intruded. When his habit became known the priests of the countryside marshaled their parishioners to meet him for Confirmation. It was only if they happened to live near a bishop that poor Englishmen could hope to be confirmed; which did not necessarily mean if they lived near a cathedral, for some bishops rarely visited their sees; the Bishop of Ely, for example, had been for many years Treasurer to old King Henry, and after that in prison under King Stephen. It was a happy chance to find an archbishop who resided in his own city, and was accessible every afternoon.

The little groups would wait at some crossroad, the parish priest in front to assure his lord they had been adequately instructed. There was no time for individual questioning, but Thomas always dismounted and put on his stole. He was the more punctilious over this when he heard that Gilbert of Hereford, who could never conceal his impatience with any function that took him away from his prayers, was accustomed to ride his mule through the crowd, tapping any head within reach.

(All the same, something should be done for poor Gilbert. It was absurd to leave the best bishop in England stuck in that unimportant western see; the ignorant might attribute his lack of promotion to personal spite. He had persuaded Henry to promise that Gilbert should have London, with its full endowment, as soon as senile Richard ceased to cumber the earth.)

When the Archbishop came back from his ride he would sup and converse with his household clerks, the most intelligent talkers in England. But he went to bed early, for his nights were broken. Nocturn and Matins, beginning at midnight, was the only office he had time to attend, in his capacity as Abbot of Christ Church. It was a wrench for one who felt the cold as he did to leave a warm bed in the middle of the night; but once in the choir of the great, empty, echoing Cathedral he appreciated the beauty of the service. Seventy monks, huddled in black cowls, carried each a candle; they made a little island of light and peace in the darkness of the long building, as in the wickedness of the surrounding world. When they chanted the psalms the Archbishop could join in, remembering the lessons of Merton. This was the good life, as every wise man knew; he was not worthy to live it, but for an hour or so every night he might join those who did. The cares of the day fell away, and he felt a foretaste of the timelessness of Heaven.

When he left the Cathedral there was one more ceremony before he went back to bed. He washed the feet of twelve poor men, and fed them with his own hands. This was the Mandatum, performed by every great lord on Maundy Thursday, and it caused no surprise that a conscientious archbishop should perform it every day. Thomas would have liked to do the thing in earnest, really cleansing the filthy scarred feet of the poor, really carrying stew from the pot until his guests were satisfied. His stewards would not permit it. By the time he reached them, towel in hand, the twelve pairs of feet were clean and scented; and the portions of food were already prepared in wooden bowls, each with its horn spoon, so that he could do no more than carry them from the serving table. Even that was better than nothing, for it served to remind him of an important duty.

By tradition the Archbishop of Canterbury was the spokesman of the humble and oppressed. St. Anselm had faced even William Rufus to plead the cause of the poor against the royal tax gatherers; Theobald had defied King Stephen to defend the peasantry from the ravages of civil war. It was fitting that Thomas should come of a humble family. Among the great he was the champion of the humble.

After he had followed this model regime for a few weeks he was suprised to find his clerk, Herbert of Bosham, himself a monk of Christ Church, wait on him with a tentative and cautiously worded complaint from the Prior. The brethren, instead of being edified by the sight of their Abbot sharing the most inconvenient of their daily offices, were distracted at his appearance. It had not occurred to Thomas to alter his dress; when he rose in the middle of the night to hurry down to the cold Cathedral he put on his thickest mantle over a warm tunic; the tunic was scarlet and the mantle of bearskin turned up with ermine. These, with his ring, his soft shoes, and the long gold chain over his shoulders, made him a greater figure of pride and luxury even than the picture of Dives on the wall of the refectory. The more frivolous members of the community were laying bets on what he would wear next.

He dressed splendidly because he considered splendid dress to be part of the expected state of an archbishop. He was quite willing to make a change if his brethren preferred it. The trouble was that he lacked a suitable garb, because he was the first Archbishop of Canterbury for many generations who was not himself a monk. It would be absurd if he took Benedictine vows when he was in no position to live the Benedictine life; and it would be equally absurd to wear his Abbot's cowl as a kind of fancy dress. Then Robert of Merton reminded him that once he had been a child of the cloister; by the letter of ecclesiastical law he had never ceased to be a student of Merton. For office in the Cathedral he took to wearing the dress he had worn at school, the black gown and white surplice of an Augustinian canon.

That solved another problem, that of keeping warm in the

midnight chill of the unheated church. He put on gown and surplice over his everyday tunic. Since he was so very thin even two complete sets of clothing did not make him look bulky.

He remained at Canterbury throughout that summer and autumn, giving all his attention to his see. It was many years since an archbishop had devoted all his time to episcopal work, and the laymen who brought suit before his ecclesiastical court found it an amazing improvement. But he could only do this because it happened that England was being governed from Normandy, and the Archbishop of Rouen represented the Church at the court of King Henry. When the King crossed the Channel to keep Christmas in England Thomas was reminded that it was the privilege of his office to act as chief adviser to the crown.

At Southampton he awaited the landing of his old friend, in some doubt of his reception. Henry had advanced him to be head of the English Church because he was a faithful royal servant, and he had expected him to retain the chancellorship. It would be no use telling a busy ruler that he had dreamed of ten talents, or that Prior Robert of Merton had given him excellent spiritual advice. His resignation of office, and his long absence from court, must look like desertion. If Henry chose to indulge his Angevin rage there would be an unpleasant scene.

But all passed off happily. The King was delighted to see his friend again, and they chatted about old times. At twenty-nine Henry was on the whole pleased to be finished with his mentor; he felt himself capable of ruling without advice, and it was a great weight on the right side of the balance that he could count on the friendship of the head of the Church in his realm. For the moment he was not at war with anyone, and he had come to England principally to hunt and to amuse himself. He had left the Queen in her favorite castle of Poictiers, and a great part of his amusement would be in toying with the more broad-minded ladies of his court, so he could get on without an archbishop who seemed to be setting a record for a holy ecclesiastical way of life. After two days the friends found they had nothing to talk about except the past, but they parted in all friendship.

Thomas returned to Canterbury, to keep Christmas in greater state than had ever been seen by the oldest inhabitant. It was a decorous, clerkly state, of costly incense in the Cathedral and delicate wine served in moderation to sober guests. In many monasteries the annalists, filling the short space devoted to the events of each year, wrote that on the Octave of Pentecost Thomas of London was consecrated Archbishop of Canterbury, and then turned to the calendar for 1163; nothing had happened after.

Every morning at Mass Thomas tried to recapture the spirit of devotion that had filled his mind at the first Mass he had celebrated. As a memorial, he planned a special feast for the following Trinity Sunday; but when the anniversary came round he was in France. It was one of the most embarrassing days of his life, one of the very few occasions when he felt unequal to his responsibilities.

With the anti-Pope reigning in Rome under the protection of an army of Germans and Ghibellines, Pope Alexander, a refugee in France, summoned a Council to demonstrate to the world that the Kings of France and England still acknowledged his supremacy. In compliment to King Henry the Council met in his city of Tours, and of course the bishops of England attended in full strength. When they were assembled they found nothing in particular to discuss; the object of the Council had been to prove that they would come when summoned. But since they were still in session on the first Sunday after Pentecost the Pope, as a graceful gesture, invited the learned Archbishop of Canterbury to preach before the assembled Doctors of Christendom on the first anniversary of his consecration.

Thomas had never preached a sermon in his life, and he was not going to begin before the most critical audience in the world. He could prove a point of law, or argue in favor of a policy; but the graceful, empty flow of rhetoric expected on an occasion like this was beyond him. He refused, politely but stubbornly. His refusal gave keen pleasure to certain lawyers whom he had defeated before the Curia. He wondered whether the invitation had been prompted by these rivals; or whether King Henry had suggested it, to remind his old friend that there were things he could not do.

If Henry had in fact planned to make him look foolish it was a proof of continued friendship, the sort of prank young men play only on their intimates. The King's visit to Canterbury last Palm Sunday had evidently been intended to demonstrate that the old intimacy still continued. It was unfortunate that a storm blew down all the decorations in the streets; wiseacres called it an evil omen, though the climate of England was explanation enough. They had walked together through pouring rain, and in one way the foul weather had been an advantage; Henry could wear the comfortable clothes he liked, instead of the splendid robes prepared for him by the Archbishop's embroiderers.

Henry had not mentioned the one awkward subject that lay between them. It was most unfortunate that the great heiress Isabel de Warenne, widow of King Stephen's son, was unwilling to marry King Henry's brother William, as her lord the King required of her. It was the King's right to give heiresses in marriage, and a son of Anjou was her peer in blood. All the same, in spite of the rules of feudal inheritance, Christian marriage demands the consent of the bride. Thomas had to intervene. Luckily he could find that affinity forbade her to marry that particular suitor, and no one had to bear witness in public that she hated the sight of the lord William of Anjou. William took his disappointment very hard, and some young knights of his retinue swore revenge on the Archbishop. But the King allowed the matter to drop and their friendship remained unimpaired.

Thomas was discovering that though the administration of his province gave him plenty to do, his duties as first counselor of the crown made it inadvisable for him to pass all his time at Canterbury. When next he met Henry, at the Parliament held at Woodstock, there was an unfortunate collision; just because the two rulers of England were becoming strangers to one another.

The matter in dispute was unimportant, and the trouble would never have arisen if Henry, who spent most of his time on the Continent, had not lost touch with the public opinion of England.

All over the country there were estates burdened with petty little dues, once the main livelihood of ancient Saxon kings and now paid to the king of united England. These little taxes, a basket of eggs or a litter of piglets, were not worth sending to the Treasury at Winchester, so they were collected by the sheriff of the county. That gave the sheriff almost unlimited power to make himself a nuisance. He might collect his dues at inconvenient seasons, or he might harass landholders by endless suits in his shire court. During the last century sensible Norman landholders had worked out a friendly compromise with their Norman sheriffs; each sheriff received an annual subsidy from the landholders in his shire, on the understanding that he would not bother them unreasonably.

Henry got it into his stubborn head that his sheriffs were intercepting a tax which should rightly go to the crown. He proposed to his magnates that the Sheriff's Aid should be paid directly to the Exchequer.

Thomas, sitting on the King's left (for the Justiciar sat on his right), tried earnestly to break into the announcement; for he knew that when Henry had spoken in public it was very hard to make him admit he was mistaken. But he had not been given advance notice of the royal decision; the intimacy of the Chancellorship, when Henry talked over with him every public decision before he announced it, was gone forever. All he could do was to catch the royal sleeve as the King sat down, and whisper in his ear while the Council watched in hostile silence.

"Don't you see?" he whispered urgently. "These men *must* keep on the right side of the sheriff, or spend their lives as defendants in the courts. Of course every landholder subscribes to an annual present for the sheriff; if you take this Aid they will have to raise another subscription in addition. How do you think your sheriffs live? They get no wages, and yet they pay you large sums for the appointment. If you persist I must oppose you in open Council. Please, my dear Henry, withdraw your pronouncement at once."

The King shook his head angrily. By his own wit he had discovered this fraud; because Thomas, when Chancellor, had never spotted it, he now pretended it wasn't a fraud after all. But Henry knew himself a grown man, free from tutelage; he would show the ungrateful Archbishop that he could get on very well without his advice.

With a shrug of despair Thomas rose to his feet, to address the Council formally. None of the magnates approved of the King's pronouncement, partly because it touched their pockets but even more because it seemed to be an innovation; and they were against all innovation, on principle. When they heard the Archbishop of Canterbury, whom they knew to be a learned lawyer, reminding them that by the ancient custom of the realm new taxes might not be imposed save with the unanimous consent of the magnates, they decided that to pay the Sheriff's Aid to the Exchequer made it a new tax, and that certainly it lacked their consent. As Henry looked round the circle of stubborn faces he recalled that these men had a background of twenty years of civil war; if he flouted them they might take up their arms again. He announced that he had been persuaded by the learned Archbishop of Canterbury, and that the Sheriff's Aid might continue to go where it would do most good.

But that evening, at the feast which ended the Parliament, he allowed Thomas to see he had lost the King's favor. There was no Angevin rage, no screams or writhing on the floor; cold and formal politeness, instead of warm intimacy, was the due of a clerk who had been raised from the gutter by a gracious lord, and, after he had been promoted beyond his deserts, openly opposed him in council.

In the autumn of 1163 the King toured the English Midlands, before going oversea to keep Christmas in Rouen. Every day he rode forty or sixty miles, and wherever he passed he did strict and bloody justice. That was what the country expected from a king, and he enjoyed the esteem which it brought him; but his courtiers did not share his passion for order and in his loneliness he thought with regret of his late Chancellor. Thomas had basely deserted him, and at Woodstock he had dared to speak openly in opposition. But he was the only colleague who had ever seen the importance of Henry's work, who made the dull business of day-to-day administration an exciting and romantic sport. In addition he had been a good companion out hawking, and as Henry hawked in the water meadows outside Northampton, where he would sleep that night, he missed him continually.

But a chance incident reminded him that he had a serious quarrel with the Archbishop. He noticed a new peregrine among the royal birds, and asked the cadger about it. At the answer that she was one of the forfeited chattels of Canon Philip de Brois, his mind was flooded with his grievance.

The Sheriff of Bedford was convinced that Canon Philip de Brois had committed murder. He had done his duty in bringing the culprit to trial, and judgment and hanging should have followed immediately; for as a rule no prisoner was acquitted if the sheriff considered him guilty. But the Archbishop of Canterbury had intervened, on the irrelevant ground that the prisoner, a clerk, was within the jurisdiction of the Church courts. The end of the matter was that Philip got away oversea, and though the King had seized his chattels there was still a murder unavenged, a blemish on the King's Peace.

Thomas was using his own judgment; that was the root of the trouble. It was a new experience for Henry, who had never been thwarted save by open foes against whom he could ride in arms. In the old days Thomas had never disagreed with him; they had talked things over, and perhaps in the end the Chancellor had persuaded the King; but it had always been done delicately, and the policy announced had been what the King of England had decided of his own free will. Now the Archbishop of Canterbury seemed to be claiming that he alone ruled certain aspects of English life; and his knowledge of the law sometimes made it possible for him to assert this claim successfully. All the same, Thomas had been a most stimulating companion; it was unfortunate that his exaggerated sense of duty made him stay most of the year in his own city. They would soon be good friends again if only he would travel with the court, as the King's adviser should.

At that moment there was a stir among the sportsmen, and the sergeants of the escort shortened their reins. A strange band of horse was approaching.

"Talk of the Devil," muttered Henry. "Here I was wishing Thomas would come to court, and there's the metropolitan cross leading a troop of horse. The effect is very like a cortège riding behind the banner of their lord, but I suppose Thomas can't forget that not long ago he was a gallant knight."

The King cantered forward to meet the Archbishop alone. Thomas ordered his men to halt, and also rode forward alone. But each rode a charger, trained for war; and a trained war horse knew his duty when his master cantered out between the armies to encounter a rival champion. Both beasts reared on their hind legs, striking with steel-shod forefeet and darting open-mouthed heads to seize the hostile rider by the thigh. Then curb-chains tightened, and long gilded spurs sank into their sides. As they drew apart Thomas was relieved to see Henry laughing.

"What, my lord Archbishop," he called gaily, "do you take me for Engelram de Trie? You shall not have my horse as a trophy. I will defend myself, unarmed as I am, even if you take that tall cross from your squire and joust against me."

Thomas dismounted in haste, and a groom led away his excited horse. The King also jumped down, and approached smiling.

"What will they say at Citeau when they hear that the Archbishop of Canterbury rides a war horse, so fierce that it must fight all other stallions? A mule is the mount that befits your rank."

"The monks of Citeau think poorly of archbishops as a class. We need not worry about their opinion. But I have a valid excuse. To catch the most hard-riding king in Christendom I must mount the fleetest charger in my stable."

"You always have an answer. But what is the reason for your haste? Have you decided to let me hang that murderous canon? You should, you know. It is wrong for the Church to protect murderers, even though clerks must stick together against the laity."

"My dear Henry, Philip de Brois has been punished for insulting your judge, which was the only crime proved against him. We can't hang him because there was murder done and the local sheriff doesn't like his face. I came to discuss the case, certainly. I want to have it out with you in private, before you strike an attitude in Council and find it difficult to withdraw gracefully. Your sheriffs are trying to alter the law of England when they claim that clerks must plead in their courts. That is wrong. You can't alter the law. You didn't make it; it was there from the beginning, and the English are entitled to be judged by it. That law lays down that clerks may be judged only by clerks. There's no more to be said."

"There is a great deal more to be said," Henry answered hotly. "The law as you describe it was defined by Stephen of Blois, and what that usurper made I can unmake."

"It is the law of King Edward," Thomas interjected.

"Nonsense. Besides, the King must keep the peace. Murder is a crime against the peace, *my* peace. Why do you think I ride the land until my bottom grows corns and my horses founder? To keep my peace. Remember the England of twenty years ago! Your father suffered oppression from Geoffrey de Mandeville, in walled London under the eye of the King. How did that Geoffrey treat the fens? Under my peace the hedge keeps the cow and the latch keeps the door, from Cornwall to York. You rode here from Canterbury, with ten sergeants for escort and a great silver cross borne before you. There were no brigands, and in every castle the gate stood open and the portcullis raised. While I work for every minute of my waking hours, work harder than any plowman, I can just keep the peace in England; but only if the whole realm, clerk as well as lay, acknowledges my power and submits to my judgments."

"You keep good peace, and work hard to keep it. My dear Henry, I admire you, as you know I love you. But your grandfather kept good peace, as I remember. When I rode as a boy to Merton the road was safer than it had been in the memory of man, as safe as it is now. Yet your grandfather allowed full liberty to the Church of God."

Henry felt a glow in his heart. Thomas had gone out of his way to pay him a compliment, and he was always delighted to hear praise of his grandfather's rule. They would be friends again. He answered, smiling: "Then if I keep the law as it was in my grandfather's time you and your clerks will be satisfied? I cannot remember that England, my dear Thomas, but you remember it. Together we shall work to bring back the old days, and we shall be friends as before. That's settled. Now I must ride back to my cortège and you to yours. I shall be King of England and you Archbishop of Canterbury, and we shall enter Northampton in state, my lord the Archbishop beside my lord the King. But let us never forget this meadow, where we talked together as Thomas and Henry."

As they rode side by side through the crowded town Thomas recalled that in fact the question of clerks charged with felony had not been settled; that was typical of Henry, who hated to yield ground openly. But their friendship had been reaffirmed, and while that endured awkward cases could be settled as they arose.

It was unfortunate that mere day-to-day administration kept Thomas too busy in Canterbury to draw up the detailed statement of the rights and immunities of the clergy which he ought to provide for Henry's guidance. Their broad agreement in principle, to return to the condition of affairs under the first Henry, was all right as far as it went; but the Lion of Justice had been dead for twenty-eight years, and it was hard to find an official who could recall the correct precedent in every doubtful case. Besides, the settlement was vague in one important aspect. Would Henry claim only the powers exercised by his grandfather, or would he say he might do what any of his grandfather's predecessors had done?

At Canterbury there were copious records, and when Thomas looked into them he was appalled at some of the things done by earlier kings of England, without protest from the Church. This was easily explained. William the Conqueror had favored the new Gregorian reforms; the Pope had therefore permitted him to enforce the discipline of the Roman Curia. As for Rufus, in his time the bishops had yielded everything, hoping only to avoid bloody persecution; but no honest ruler would appeal to precedents established during that unhappy reign.

All the same, his predecessors at Canterbury had overlooked some shocking usurpations. He found, to his amazement, that if he rebuked his flock for purely spiritual offenses the offenders could seek protection from the King's Council. The lord William de Eynsford had put himself hopelessly in the wrong, as any lawyer must admit. He claimed an advowson, the right to present the clerk of his choice to a certain benefice. Thomas disputed the claim, and investigated it in his own court. Eynsford, after he had lost, intruded his nominee by force. Whereupon Thomas excommunicated the lord William, as a despoiler of the property of the Church. At once he received an angry message from the King, demanding William's absolution; since it had been agreed in the days of William the Conqueror that no tenant-in-chief might be excommunicated without the previous consent of the King.

That was absurd. Eynsford had been guilty of a spiritual offense, and spiritual punishment was the appropriate penalty. Of course no true shepherd of souls would keep a Christian under the ban if he showed contrition or tried to make amends; it is the business of bishops to get sinners into Heaven, not to keep them out. As soon as Eynsford admitted his fault he would be absolved. The King demanded that the ban be lifted at once, for an excommunicate might not perform knight-service, and the sinner was lost to his army. That was unfortunate for the King, but his obvious remedy was to keep his tenants-in-chief under better control. The Archbishop was doing his duty as laid down by canon law; a local agreement with a long-dead King could not supersede that universal code.

After a few weeks Eynsford withdrew the intrusive clerk; his excommunication was lifted immediately, and peace was restored between King and Archbishop. As Thomas said to Herbert of Bosham, this proved that canon law and the law of the land need never conflict; after all, every Christian was bound to obey both codes.

At Michaelmas the military tenants of Canterbury rendered homage to their lord. To Thomas this was a new experience; the seven hundred knights he had led as Chancellor had been hired soldiers, owing obedience only while they were paid. Now he undertook the lifelong responsibility of a lord, and these noble Normans swore lifelong duty to the son of a drysalter in Cheapside. But he also was a Norman, of free birth; they owed him obedience, as he owed them protection. As they came up one by one to place their hands within his clasped hands he vowed to himself that he would be their true lord and protector. At Pevensey he had been trained in chivalry; he had fought for his King and earned the spurs of knighthood; he was capable of protecting them.

All the same, it was unfortunate that some knights should hold from so many different lords. For example, here was the attorney of the Justiciar, doing homage on behalf of his lord for some small fief of the Honor of Canterbury; Richard de Lucy held far greater fiefs from the King, and everyone knew that he thought of himself as the King's man only. So he was making a promise that perhaps he would not fulfill, which any lawyer knows is the greatest source of contention in the world. It was a pity. England would be a tidier country, easier to govern, if each knight held only one fief from one lord.

But you could not deprive Lucy of his fiefs to make things tidy; while he performed his due service he must keep his land. Yet a prudent Archbishop should bear in mind that some promises did not mean all they said.

At the end of September 1163 Thomas rode from Canterbury to Westminster. As always, he was sad to leave his own city, where work filled his daylight hours and the monastic office in the Cathedral comforted his soul. He knew that all England considered him the most efficient archbishop who had ever occupied the chair of St. Augustine, but he could only keep abreast of his work if he remained constantly at home.

Cantering down Watling Street on his charger he discussed this with Herbert of Bosham, pattering beside him on a monkish little mule. "This realm lacks competent magnates, Herbert, that's the real trouble. The best Normans rode south to Italy, where they could be free of all government; only the second-rate followed Duke William. As a result they lay too many duties on the Archbishop. I must rule the Church in the greater part of England, which is a full occupation for a busy man; at the same time I am expected to be in constant attendance on the King. Whenever he holds a Council I must be there, lest my successors lose their rightful place as the first magnates of the realm. We have nothing of importance to discuss at this Council, and yet I must go, neglecting the plans I had made for the due celebration of Advent; just because all great decisions must be ratified by my seal. Well, Henry is even busier than I am, but it only proves once again that one man can't govern both Church and realm. You might remind me to make that point if the King tries again to encroach on my rights. But I don't think there will be an opening for speech ranging over general affairs. What exactly are we called on to decide?"

"Only quite ordinary questions, things that come up time after time. The Abbey of St. Albans seeks to be placed immedi-

ately under the control of the Pope; the Curia has agreed, but
the Abbot very sensibly desires a formal grant from the King's
Council. I presume you will support him, my lord?"

"If the Curia agrees, I have no option. It is a good principle,
though only too often control from Rome means no control at
all. But that is not exactly a question that comes up time after
time. I suppose you were thinking of some other matter?"

"The Archbishop of York seeks a clear-cut definition of his
rights and privileges, from the King in person. Thus in the future unedifying disputes will be averted." Herbert looked
primly down his nose.

"Aha, so Roger's at it again! Nothing will make him admit
that he is inferior to me in dignity. But he's a trained clerk.
He will argue and dispute and perhaps offer bribes; but when
a definite decision arrives from Rome he will obey it."

Thomas fell silent, thinking of all the trouble Archbishop
Roger had caused him, and would cause him in future. The
government of the Church in England had been frozen into a
very queer pattern, for historical reasons that were now out of
date. Once each petty Saxon kingdom had enjoyed its own
bishop; as the kingdoms coalesced, the number of bishoprics
had diminished, until now they were too few. The last two kingdoms of any importance had been Wessex and Northumbria.
With the supremacy of Wessex had come a vague supremacy
of Canterbury over York, though both remained Metropolitan; one was Primate of England, the other Primate of All
England. In short, their relationship did not make sense. But
it was not for Thomas, temporary holder of a great office which
would continue after his death, to diminish the power entrusted
to him. The Archbishop of York was Metropolitan, but he was
not the equal of Canterbury. So it must remain, and the less
Roger's power was analyzed the better.

Besides, there was something flighty about Roger. He had
a good mind, and he lived a godly life, causing no scandal. But

he despised everyone less intelligent or less highly born than himself, which meant that he despised the greater part of the human race; he lived in great luxury; and he thought too much of the King's favor. These last faults might be imputed to Thomas, but that made him all the more aware of them in Roger.

CHAPTER VII

Clarendon

AT WESTMINSTER on the 1st of October 1163 all the
bishops of England were present; but though the business before the meeting was chiefly ecclesiastical it was a meeting of the *King's* Council, and the clerks were outnumbered
by lay magnates. The King presided in person, seated on the
throne at the end of the great hall built by Rufus.

The meeting opened soon after sunrise, to allow for a long
session before the light faded. Thomas had warned the bishops
to say their Masses early, and when they took their places they
had all breakfasted. It was a well-known trick, in these mixed
gatherings of clerks and laity, for the lay magnates to bring

snacks in their wallets, keeping the proceedings going until fasting clerks gave in through sheer hunger. But the early Masses were noticed, as a warning that the Council might be contentious. Thomas regretted his precaution when he saw that Henry was already in a bad temper.

The first business was the exemption of St. Albans. There was little opposition, but a too-ingenious monk of the community insisted on going into precedents, and Henry took a keen interest in the authorities cited: this had been done on the authority of our lord the Pope, but that on the authority of our lord the King of England. To a legal mind it was a glorious confusion; Pope and King seemed to have held equal and concurrent jurisdiction in every ecclesiastical question of the last hundred years.

After the Abbot of St. Albans had been granted his franchise there was a pause before Archbishop Roger opened his plea. The Archbishop of York was behaving correctly, Thomas was pleased to note. He had come to the meeting in cope and miter, the full vestments of his rank, for this was a state occasion that demanded full dress. But no cross was borne before him, as was the privilege of most archbishops; the Archbishop of York, in virtue of his undefined inferiority to Canterbury, was not permitted to display his cross outside his own northern province. He made a seemly reverence to the crucifix which topped the cross of Canterbury, and embraced his rival. Thomas felt safe whenever an occasion called for a display of good manners, since he knew his manners were as good as Pevensey could make them; it was only when great men began to lose their tempers that he felt at a disadvantage. His rage was so strong that he dared not allow it to wake, and he found it a trial to remain calm and smiling while others shouted and banged on the table.

While everyone waited for Roger to introduce the advocate who would advance his plea the King suddenly took a hand in the proceedings. He rose to his feet (a nuisance, for etiquette compelled all others to stand also) and spoke in a loud voice to the whole company.

"In judging the plea of the venerable Abbot of St. Albans we have heard much of the ancient custom of the realm of England. In accordance with this ancient custom we decided in his favor. Yet there were voices raised against us, though they were overborne by argument. It is a very shocking thing to disregard the ancient custom of the land. We did not make it, and, unless we obtain the consent of every free man in England, we cannot alter it."

He looked at Thomas, standing to the full extent of his enormous height, splendid in cope and miter, with the pallium of metropolitan authority dangling on his breast. The King's malicious smile reminded his old comrade of the armory from which he had drawn that argument concerning the unalterable nature of the law of England.

The King continued, his cheeks red and fingers twitching, signs that he was making ready to overcome any disagreement of his councilors.

"The ancient custom must stand; and the ancient custom was best enforced during the reign of my grandfather, whose peace was the strongest England has ever known. Therefore I propose that, before we go any further, all my councilors here present swear to uphold that ancient custom. First I shall ask the opinion of my knights and lay magnates."

There was a roar of agreement from the laymen, who held their land by ancient custom, and disliked any change. Besides, they could guess what was coming next, and they looked forward to the humiliation of these haughty bishops.

"Now I ask the same of my spiritual councilors. My lord of Canterbury, you are learned in the law. Will you be the first of my bishops to give adherence to the ancient custom of England, as it was in the reign of my grandfather?"

Many thoughts raced through Thomas's head. First came resentment at an old friend who should spring this proposal on him without warning, as though deliberately to make him look foolish. Then his legal training warned him not to commit himself without careful study; King Henry I had reigned for thirty-five years, and it would be dangerous to approve everything he had done. Then, as he was about to open his mouth, he saw the next point standing clear, as he had seen the end of an involved argument while he thought on his feet in the schools of Paris long ago. Even if the custom of England were the best code of laws conceivable in a fallen world, that did not matter; it rested on the authority of the King, and for the Church to acknowledge it would mean the submission of the Church to lay control.

"My lord," he said firmly, speaking distinctly that all might hear, "your grandfather was a great king, who kept good peace as I remember. But the clergy, who are ruled by God and His Vicar the Pope, may not swear to abide by the customs of any king."

From time to time that needed saying; though it was an obvious truism, with which, after reflection, every Christian must agree.

Without reflection Henry would not agree to it. Thomas saw he was working up one of his famous rages.

Thomas continued to think on his feet. Henry in a rage might do literally anything. Obviously he had summoned this Council with malice in his heart, or he would have discussed his surprising proposal in private beforehand. It was unfair to call on the bishops of England to commit themselves, unprepared, to such a far-reaching agreement. The unfairness was so evident that no one would blame him for using guile to turn aside the King's wrath. Well, there was a formula, known to all lawyers, which met the case; it might mean anything or nothing, but then so might the King's claim to enforce a custom which his oldest councilor could not remember.

After a pause Thomas continued: "My lord, this land has been Christian for more than five hundred years. Its customs should be Christian customs, though I, a Norman, cannot be expected to know all of them. Nevertheless, for the sake of peace, and to prevent a conflict which might overturn the secular authority (as the authority of King Stephen was overturned after he had persecuted the Bishop of Salisbury), I will swear to follow your custom, saving of course the rights of my order."

King Henry turned purple, while the Bishops of Winchester and London, trained clerks who could appreciate every nuance of the speech, smiled in delighted recognition of Thomas's thrusts. It was necessary to bring the exchange to a close, before the King bellowed some absurd threat from which he could not withdraw. Bishop Henry of Winchester stepped quickly into the breech. Ceremoniously he swept up to the foot of the throne. "I also will abide by the old custom of the first King Henry, the ancient custom of England," said he, "and I also make this reservation: saving the rights of my order."

Every bishop made the same promise, with the same reservation; except Hilary of Chichester, who hung back as though trying to make an independent decision. At last he swore also; but instead of the usual reservation he said he swore "in good faith," a phrase strange to lawyers. The King did not know whether to take this as an amendment in his favor, or as a stronger expression of dissent.

By this time everyone had forgotten the next business, the claim of York to independence. The King was in a fury. He strode from his place, glaring at the bishops; when he had left the magnates looked at one another, uncertain whether the Council was in fact ended.

The Bishop of Winchester was less flustered than his colleagues. A gallant knight, a holy monk, a king's brother, he could not be disgraced and he did not fear death. He spoke mildly:

"I take it, my lords, that the Council is terminated. The King may be unwell, or he may have been called away by urgent business. Let us disperse to our lodgings, until we are summoned to the next Council. Since the lay magnates are in full accord with the King they obviously have no more to discuss. But I noticed some difference of opinion among my episcopal brethren. I invite you, my lords, to meet again in my lodging over the river."

Then he sat quietly, his lips moving as he got through his daily office, until a servant announced that his horse was waiting.

That evening, in his great town house across the river from London, he faced an excited gathering of men who screeched and chattered to shake him from his calm. Thomas alone said nothing, because he could not trust himself to speak; he did not know whether that morning he had surrendered the liberty of the Church by his improvised submission, or whether he had insulted the King so gravely that there could be no forgiveness. That was one of his handicaps; if a telling phrase came into his mind he could not keep it to himself. He was always more anxious to win the debate than to convince his adversary.

Bishop Henry, however, was all praise for his behavior. Thomas was Metropolitan, and Bishop Henry a stickler for form; but it was absurd for a middle-class man of forty-five to exact continual deference from an elderly royal prince; after a short contest of politeness the Archbishop and his most important suffragan sat side by side in a window, where they could talk privately.

"You did well in a tight corner, my lord," began the elder man. "It was discourtesy in the King to open such a grave matter without warning. Your assent 'saving the rights of our order' means nothing at all, but it was wiser than a blunt refusal. My only regret is that you included what sounded like a threat, which by the way was not wholly accurate. My unfortunate brother died King of England, for all that he oppressed the Church until I thought it my duty to oppose him. Though perhaps if the whole Church were united we could overthrow a king." He glanced across the hall at Gilbert of London.

"Gilbert made the same reservation," answered Thomas. "He feels ill-used, and that is in a way reasonable. He would be a better archbishop than I am. But the monastery of Cluny trained him in obedience. He will never disobey the command of his lawful superior, however unworthy."

"Gilbert will never fall into the sin of canonical disobedience, though if he advises your adversaries his plans will be hard to circumvent. However, our real danger, if you will pardon a warlike metaphor, is not that our knights will desert to the other side, but that through fear they may flee before the onset."

To Thomas this was a new idea, for he had never been afraid in his life; neither had Bishop Henry, but during the civil war he had seen fear in others. Now he looked hard at Bishop Hilary of Chichester. "That's a frightened man," he murmured. "He will do anything to escape death, and certainly he will not risk his life in your cause."

"Young Henry lost his temper this morning," Thomas replied easily, "but he won't do anything rash. I know him. He'll kick and scream and bite the blankets on his bed. But the crown of England is very dear to him; he will never imperil it."

"Don't take my word alone," the older man persisted. "Collect the opinions of our colleagues."

Thomas was surprised to find many bishops truly frightened. After all, as William of Norwich pointed out, the King's father had castrated the Bishop of Seez and all his chapter. That showed what an Angevin might do when his blood was up. The Bishop of Norwich was a holy and elderly monk, who constantly regretted the unsought promotion which had torn him from the cloister; he considered laymen capable of any wickedness; if they had not been wicked they would have become monks. He protested that he was indifferent to personal risk; but in the interest of the realm as a whole they must not tempt the King into the grievous sin of sacrilege.

Bishop Hilary of Chichester raised another point, and a sound one as far as it went. He had been trained in the Roman Curia, and he always thought first of the temporal interests of the Holy See. He reminded Thomas that only two kings of the first rank supported the rightful pontiff. Alexander III, living in exile under the protection of King Louis of France, was financially dependent on revenues remitted by the King of England. While Italy and the Empire acknowledged the usurped sway of the anti-Pope it would be disastrous if the Church picked a quarrel with King Henry.

Since his consecration Thomas had neglected foreign policy. Now he remembered with a start that even a good cause may need the help of unworthy allies. At Tours he had met Pope Alexander, and he guessed that the Holy Father would be less concerned with his revenue than with upholding a great principle. Even so, a good Papalist should not maneuver the Pope into a position where he must make unwelcome decisions.

Next morning the bishops learned that the King had left London, riding no man knew whither; he might even now be raising an army to harry their lands, or sending envoys to transfer the allegiance of England to the anti-Pope. Even Henry of Winchester begged Thomas to make peace at once, on the best terms he could, before great harm came to all the souls in his care.

*　　*　　*

In the cold dawn of a rainy January day the hunting lodge of Clarendon looked as though besieged by an army, so many were the pavilions crowded round it. If the King wished to summon his Council he could have lodged all his bishops and lay magnates at Windsor or Winchester or Westminster; but it pleased him to make them camp here in the January rain. There was even a reasonable excuse, if someone complained of such an uncomfortable meeting place. A magnate with a guilty conscience might fear to enter a royal castle, lest the gate be barred when he wished to leave; no one might avoid unwalled Clarendon on that excuse.

As King Henry strolled out, wrapped in a sheepskin cloak against the rain, he heard a chorus of coughs from the pavilions, and smiled to himself.

He was determined not to use force; but he could only get his way by playing on the fears of the bishops, and if they suffered from colds in the head they would yield the quicker. They were going to yield anyway, though as yet they did not know it. That was the best stroke of all. These holy men had ridden at great inconvenience to support the Archbishop in his defiance of the King; and the Archbishop would not defy the King. He shivered with joy in his secret knowledge.

He hated Thomas, who had been his friend. He was going to humiliate him, utterly, before all England. Thomas deserved the worst that could happen to him, for he had committed the unforgivable sin; he had told Henry to his face that there was a power to which even the King of England must bow.

Henry knew he ought to bow to God. He was a Christian who heard Mass every morning. But he had been crowned King of England, and that made him responsible for the welfare of his whole realm. He had sworn to govern justly, but how could he govern justly if a large part of the population refused to be governed by him? Once he had thought that the problem might be avoided if the Archbishop of Canterbury

was a friend who knew his ways; they could talk over diffi-
culties together, and he would magnanimously permit Thomas
to act from his own authority, provided Thomas did what the
King required of him. Henry knew the history of his adopted
country; he knew that a hundred years ago the Pope had permitted William the Conqueror to govern the Church because
William did exactly what the Pope would have done in his
place; he had planned to permit Thomas to do what Henry
would have done.

It had worked badly, because Thomas would not spare the
time to talk things over with him. That was absurd. No previous Archbishop of Canterbury had found it necessary to sit
in his cathedral city all the year round, merely to administer
the affairs of his province. It was not necessary, but Thomas
pretended it was; because Thomas was an actor, always standing back to look at himself, watching himself perform the
functions of the great office his talents had obtained for him.
There was a queer word in the New Testament, a Greek word
for which St. Jerome had found no Latin equivalent:
hypocrite, meaning an actor. So he had been told by Master
Adelard of Bath, when Bristol was his mother's capital and
he had learned his grammar there. Thomas was an actor, a
hypocrite.

He was a good actor, and a very thorough one; he played his
part so carefully that he became the character he was imitating.
Could hypocrisy make a bad man good? Henry considered the
idea for a few minutes, without reaching a definite conclusion.

The humiliation of Thomas had been carefully planned, and
now it was certain to take effect. The Pope himself opposed the
Archbishop who was standing up for the rights of the Papacy.
As soon as news of the quarrel at Westminster reached the
Papal court at Sens, Alexander had sent over Master Robert of
Melun to bring the Archbishop to reason. Henry giggled to
himself, thinking of Robert's promotion to the vacant See of

Hereford; it had been amusing to hear Thomas plead the cause of his old tutor, in ignorance that the retired lecturer from Paris had come to England to oppose him. Then, in the privacy of the King's study, Thomas had bowed to the advice of the Pope's envoy. He had promised that next time he was asked in public he would publicly agree to the old custom of King Henry. It showed that in high politics the son of a London burgess could not compete with the great-grandson of the Devil.

The beauty of it was that Thomas had no inkling that the old custom was now written down. He must suppose that after he had given his formal assent he could still haggle over particular cases. But there it would be, in black and white; and for each claim there could be adduced a precedent of sorts. After all, his grandfather had claimed all the rights of his predecessors, and if you could show that Rufus, in an access of drunken rage, had imprisoned a bishop or hanged a clerk, that would bind Thomas—once he had sworn.

The camp was stirring. Soon the bishops would be hurrying through their Masses, to eat breakfast before the meeting opened. Henry, who had already begun working, had finished his bread dipped in wine, all he ever ate before dinner, the first real meal of the day. It would undermine the resistance of these clerks if he opened the Council early, interrupting their breakfast. He went back to his cozy bedchamber to don his robes of state.

Three days later King Henry once more went out to sniff the dawn. He was not feeling well, and he hoped the cold air would revive him. His eyes were bloodshot, looking out on a world filled with floating specks; his neck felt twice its normal thickness; he ached all over, and a disordered liver had given him a raging thirst; yet he dared not drink for fear of apoplexy. For three days he had surrendered to the luxury of a royal

Angevin rage, which was as exhausting as fighting a battle.

All the same, though the physicians warned him that his lack of self-control endangered his health, this outburst had been profitable as well as enjoyable. Thomas, after breaking his pledged word to assent to the old custom, was now weakening under pressure from his colleagues. It was a waste of time trying to frighten Thomas himself, though Henry could not forgo the pleasure of attempting it; but the Bishop of Norwich was genuinely afraid of any form of violence, and the Bishop of Salisbury had a guilty conscience, which reproached him for his old treasons in the days of King Stephen. The bishops must bring their leader to heel. If not, he might proceed to extremes; he had not finally made up his mind. It would probably cost him his throne, but it might be worth losing a throne to see William of Norwich scream with terror on the scaffold. If he himself did not know whether he might not in the end mutilate or hang these silly old men, then they could not know either. They would feel afraid, and they would be right to feel afraid.

Yielding to overpowering rage was as exciting as galloping over rough country on a bolting horse. Anger impelled him to kill, while common sense strove to hold him back; in the end he did as common sense advised, but meanwhile the struggle had the exhilaration of danger overcome. It was more enjoyable than the stimulus of heavy drinking, but with the same kind of dangerous joy.

It was difficult to keep his rage at the appropriate heat, for events were falling out as he would have ordered them had he been omnipotent; no one blessed with such amazing luck could continue to feel angry. Thomas had lost his head, to put himself completely in the wrong. Soon, when the fears of his colleagues compelled him to yield, he would be exposed to the derision of all Christendom as a cantankerous fool who could neither give way gracefully nor maintain his quarrel with firmness. An archbishop who floundered so clumsily could never hurt him.

The happy result was entirely due to his skillful shift of position at the last moment. Before the Council opened, the Pope, and every responsible statesman who wished to avoid a breach in the Papalist ranks, had put pressure on Thomas to agree to the old custom. But everyone, except the King himself, was thinking of relations between England and Rome, the question which had caused friction since the days of the Conqueror. The right of appeal to the Roman Curia, the right to attend a papal Council without first seeking leave from the King, these were the rights which had led to disputes between Lanfranc and the Conqueror, between every king of England and his archbishops, until even the timid Theobald had been sent into exile. No one had given a thought to the problem of clerks accused of grave crimes; that had remained an open question, too unimportant for a serious quarrel.

But the version of the old custom he had reduced to writing dealt almost entirely with the problem of "criminous clerks." Of course he dared not claim that they should be tried and sentenced in the ordinary courts; he might as well introduce the worship of Mahound as claim that there was no legal difference between clerks and laity. His vassals would rebel if he tried anything like that. He had only proposed that clerks who had been found guilty in the Church courts should be sent to the King's court for punishment. That seemed fair, on the face of it, as the lay magnates had at once agreed.

Only that foolish Thomas had refused to swear to these new customs, such an improvement on the old custom which had in fact been enforced by his grandfather. He had made the technical point, only apparent to a pettifogging ecclesiastical lawyer, that the new system would punish clerks twice for one offense; they would first be deprived of their orders, and then mutilated by the King's hangman. In a sense that was true, if loss of orders could be regarded as a punishment. Most laymen did not so regard it, but that was not an argument you could use to an archbishop.

Nevertheless, the new proposal had broken the united front of the Church party, and Henry knew that very soon the extremists must give way. To the lay magnates the important thing was that in future criminous clerks would forfeit their chattels to the King. All sensible laymen favored a scheme which would increase the revenue the King drew from the Church; less would be demanded from the laity. The bishops as a body probably thought it wrong in principle that anyone who had been a clerk should suffer on the secular gallows. But bishops as a class are not thieves or assassins; the new customs would not affect them personally. They would not embark on a dangerous struggle with the lay power just to make life easier for a few debauched scholars or runaway novices who had taken to a life of crime because they were unfitted for the clerical state.

At this moment the more dignified bishops were probably begging Thomas to give way, though they would stand by him until he did so; and Salisbury and Norwich would be squealing with unworthy fear. It was the third day of the deadlock, and more than once Henry had wondered whether to offer some small concession to get the negotiations on the move once more. But he was bound to win. His only difficulty would be to work up a convincing rage before the Council met; that was hard when he was on the brink of success.

A few hours later he sat crowned on his throne, in the timber hall of that meager little hunting lodge. By meditating on the double dealing of his old comrade Thomas he had worked himself into a rage never surpassed by any Angevin son of the Devil. There was a man who owed all to the royal favor, an unemployed and unemployable scholar, son of a poor burgess of Cheapside; the King had snatched him from his undignified trade to make him one of the greatest magnates of the realm. (At this point the Devil his ancestor reminded Henry that Thomas had attained the archdeaconry of Canterbury by his own merit, without royal influence; the reminder that his picture was false made the King angrier than ever.) It was Henry alone who had made him Archbishop, and he had done it only because he thought he was rewarding a faithful supporter. Thomas had cheated him as soon as he was safely consecrated. All that flaunting in public as a holy man, the ostentatious riding out to confirm great throngs, the attendance at monastic office in the Cathedral, had been a scheme to build up his own influence in opposition to his lord's. Thomas was making himself a rival to the King. There was no room for two Kings in England, as all would agree who remembered the civil war. When ordinary decent Norman gentlemen understood what Thomas was up to they would desert him, and when he was deserted he would give way. If he remained obstinate there would be nothing for it but to risk excommunication by killing him; his power was greater than King Stephen's had ever been, and he might be able to keep his throne until he came to an arrangement with the Pope. Or, better still, the Archbishop might be murdered by loyal vassals, without orders. It would be necessary to condemn the murder, and punish the murderers. But they could be rewarded later, when the world began to forget.

He was daydreaming. Worse, the thought of what might one day happen to Thomas had brought a smile to his lips. He must build up his rage, or the submission might be postponed indefinitely. He turned to the lay magnates who stirred uneasily in the semicircle of seats round his throne; they would have sat all day in the saddle without complaint, but they were becoming dreadfully bored with this long Council.

"My lords," he said in a low, grumbling voice, "do you remember my poor brother William? Doesn't the anniversary of his death fall about this time? Let us say a prayer for his soul."

"Remembering also the Archbishop in our prayers?" put in Hamelin de Warenne, another of the King's bastard brothers.

All caught the allusion. Thomas had forbidden William's rich marriage. William, who was said to have died of disappointment, had their sympathy.

The King was satisfied. He had reminded the magnates that Thomas was not only a bad servant to the crown: he was capable of interfering in the private lives of great vassals. As they recounted his misdeeds they worked up a rage equal to the King's.

This was the third day they had spent sitting in Council, awaiting the Archbishop. Even for the winning side this was a most tiresome Parliament. There was nothing they could do to hasten a conclusion, save send envoys to the other hall at the far end of the ramshackle hunting lodge where the bishops were gathered round their obstinate leader.

At last, about midday, there came an interruption of their nagging boredom. The Prior of the Temple bustled in.

The chief of the Templars in England was an obvious intermediary between lay magnates and bishops; himself a knight, he was also a clerk, and the wide estates he ruled for his order gave him a place among the magnates. For three days he had been scuttling up and down the long passages of Clarendon, carrying messages.

He ran to the dais, to whisper excitedly; instead of standing at the door to shout at the top of his voice, as he would have done if he had been entrusted with a formal message. This was odd, and the Council craned to hear.

"The Archbishop is on his way," he gasped out. "Suddenly he got up, without a word to anyone, and asked if the King were still in his hall. I ran on to warn you. Look, here he is."

Thomas towered in the doorway, haggard and hollow-eyed.

Over his Augustinian gown and surplice he wore cope and pallium, but they were in the somber purple of Advent, a month past. He was bareheaded, his tall skull climbing through a fringe of hair now gray; but his black bushy eyebrows and beak of a nose were as fierce and commanding as ever. He gazed round the assembly in dead silence, his gaunt bloodshot eyes searching the face of every man present; the King received the same sweeping glance, neither more nor less than his neighbors. Then he walked proudly forward, but with such a rigid stiffness of leg that Henry looked for him to faint. Behind him Herbert of Bosham wrestled with an enormous book, but otherwise he was unattended.

At the foot of the dais he made a stiff little bow, as though greeting an equal; and signaled to Herbert to hold the book open before him. Those magnates who knew their letters could distinguish the gold and red capitals, *Initium Evangelii Secundum Sanctum Matthaeum,* sprawled round a great purple angel. With his hand on the open page Thomas spoke into the waiting silence.

"I, Thomas, Archbishop and Legate, swear by the holy Word of God that I will observe the ancient custom of the realm, as that custom was observed during the reign of King Henry the grandfather of King Henry now reigning."

In the hush which followed Thomas made another little bob to the throne; then he stalked out. All eyes followed him, and it seemed an anticlimax when the other bishops, who had entered unobserved while their leader held all attention, came forward one by one to take oath on the same book.

Except for the oath, not a word was spoken; only King Henry made a rude sound with his lips as the last bishop, Walter of Rochester, turned away at the close of the ceremony.

In the palace at Canterbury there was a cramped little study at the back of the hall, the only place where the Archbishop could talk in complete privacy. On a wet and cold March evening Thomas sat there, hunched over a brazier of charcoal. Nowadays he was never warm, though he wore more clothes than ordinary men. Across the fire Prior Robert of Merton sat decorously upright on a stool, his hands folded in his lap; but in that private place they might talk as equals.

"You had better hear my confession before Matins," the Archbishop began. "I have received a direct order from the Holy See, commanding me once more to say Mass daily."

"I am glad. It is for your confessor to say when you have sinned. I told you you were too scrupulous."

"The Pope agrees with you," Thomas answered bitterly. "My suspension is not lifted, because the Curia will not admit that I was ever suspended. The Pope writes a friendly, unofficial letter, begging me to make up my quarrel with the King because it interferes with certain developments of papal policy; in a postscript he tells me not to be silly. I know that what I did was not right, and the Pope says I have done no wrong. I suppose my actions are as blameless as those of any other idiot. I have perjured myself, I have sworn away the liberty of the Church in England. But it's only poor Tom, what he does can never be serious."

"That's nonsense, Thomas. More than thirty years ago we sat at the same desk, and I know you well enough to contradict you to your face. The Pope holds you blameless, because in swearing to the custom you were following his instructions. That's true, isn't it? He does not mean that the custom is harmless. As a matter of fact he doesn't know what it is."

"That's true, but Henry has put it into writing. One day the Pope, or perhaps his successor, will read the full enormity of what Henry considers should be the custom of a Christian land. If I did not sin in swearing to it, the Pope sinned gravely in ordering me to swear."

"Then the Pope sinned gravely. He is not the first Pope to

sin, since the day when St. Peter thrice denied his Lord. You
have nothing to worry about. You only obeyed orders."

"I concede it," Thomas said gloomily, in the language of the
schools. "Since I was carrying out the order of my lawful superior the sin cannot be put to my account. But my incompe-
tence is more shameful than the gravest sin. Think of it! The
great Thomas of London, the famous Chancellor, the skilled
negotiator, the eminent lawyer, the archdeacon who judged
the suits of all England! I was given a simple task, to smooth
over any difference between the Pope and his faithful son King
Henry, who is committed to support him against the anti-Pope.
Just to make it perfectly easy I am instructed to grant Henry
everything he asks, though even those Italians on the Curia
know that he asks more than the Church should concede. Well,
I give in, I swear away the liberties of the Church, for which
St. Anselm suffered persecution, for which even poor old Theobald endured exile. And at the end, when I have lost every
stake with which I began to play, the King remains a bitter
enemy to Pope and Church. I was ordered to buy peace, at
much too high a price. I paid the price, and there is no peace.
In the most important negotiation of my career I failed ludicrously."

Robert of Merton knew that the Archbishop was in great
need of consolation, but truth was always to him more important than sympathy. "You failed, and you failed ludicrously,"
he assented sternly. "Do you know why? Because you yourself
wanted war, not peace. You followed your instructions, you
granted the King all he desired. Yet you did it so grudgingly
that now he hates you, though not so long ago he was
your friend. Do you remember Palm Sunday only last year,
here in Canterbury? How the King came here specially, and
how he walked beside you through the rain, though the gale
had destroyed the garlands hung in the streets? Now, as I said,
he hates you. All the same, you have carried out your instruc-

tions. He has the friendliest feelings for Pope Alexander. At the present moment he is probably writing to ask him to remove you from your archbishopric. No harm has been done."

Thomas smiled bitterly. "The Pope and the King are united in a common enmity to Canterbury. Perhaps I shall be remembered as a peacemaker. A queer kind of peacemaker, whose enemies make peace with one another. But at the end you went wrong, my dear Robert. At Clarendon a great deal of harm was done, not to me personally or to the strength of the Pope in his struggle with the Emperor; just harm to the ordinary obscure Christians of my province. I must write to the Pope, pointing out what will come from these customs if they are accepted without protest from the Curia."

"You can't write to the Pope without permission from the King. That is one of the customs you swore to accept."

"Which proves that these customs are absurd. But I will not commit further perjury just after I have been absolved for swearing to them. I myself will visit the Pope at Sens, which is handier than his usual residence; and explain my attitude to the whole Curia."

"You can't do that either, without the King's leave. No intercourse whatever with the Pope, either personally or by letter. It is all down in black and white in the Customs of Clarendon."

"This is schism!" shouted Thomas. "Whatever I swore, the Pope remains my superior. I have not sworn myself right outside the Christian Church! I don't know these customs as thoroughly as you, for it is a subject that repels me. But if they are as bad as you say, I must warn the Pope against them."

"If you go, you should go secretly; otherwise the King will stop you. It is my duty as your confessor to remind you that recently you swore to obey the King."

"It can never be a sin to warn my lord of pressing danger; as any knight would do, though he were a prisoner released on parole."

"I cannot consider hypothetical cases," answered Robert with a smile. "You have sworn to obey the King. If you cross the Channel you break that oath. Whether you are justified depends on the urgency of the danger. You are the best judge of that."

"In other words," said Thomas, more cheerfully, "you think I ought to go secretly to the Pope. Even poor Theobald did as much, when Stephen tried to keep him from a Council. They say he actually crossed the Channel in a dinghy rowed by two fishermen. If he could cross in a rowing boat, I can swim! We shall see how my faithful pirates in Romney obey the King's orders."

Soon after, when they separated at bedtime, Prior Robert reflected on the one curious failing of his admired master and penitent. Thomas had every accomplishment. He was a good archbishop, a good priest, a good diplomatist, even, so they said, a good knight. But he was blind to the effect of his actions on public opinion. He had shocked and dismayed the bishops by his abject surrender at Clarendon, when a little explanation beforehand would have prepared them for his sudden change of front. Now he was about to break a promise, in such a good cause that his act would not be sinful; but his breach of faith would shock every chivalrous knight in England. The exploit was in fact silly. He would never dare to return unless the King forgave him; and if he considered exile better than submission he might have fled to France earlier, without ever swearing to those sinful customs.

When rumor reached the King's court that the Archbishop of Canterbury had fled oversea Henry was delighted. It was dangerous to arrest an archbishop, in spite of the threats a king might utter in his wrath; while he remained in England it was even more difficult to silence him. Now he was oversea, and would presently be forgotten.

The lands of Canterbury must send their profits to the Treasury, as though the See were vacant; but there might also be valuable chattels in the palace, for the Archbishop had fled in haste. Three knights of the King's household rode at once to Canterbury, to seize in the King's name all he had left behind.

These were knights who remembered the luxury of the Chancellor, and they were eager to see how Thomas had lived when he was something even greater. Rumor spoke of servants by the hundred, and the most openhanded hospitality in Christendom. The man who demanded fresh floor-rushes daily when he was on campaign would keep an interesting palace as first vassal of the crown.

They found the city gate of Canterbury standing open and unguarded. Before they could show the King's seal on their letter they had to search out a watchman. But they feared to be accused of private plunder unless their commission was known, and they insisted on reporting to the city authorities. Inside the walls it was not far to the Archbishop's hall. Here also they rode unquestioned into the yard and dismounted unattended, without so much as a groom to run to the horses' heads. The whole establishment was deserted. But there were no signs of plunder. King Henry kept good peace.

The knights were wet through; for the last week the weather had been foul, with driving rain and gales. They left their sodden cloaks on their tethered horses, and entered the palace in search of a fire.

Even the great door was untended, the door where daily the poor of Canterbury were marshaled to receive the leavings of the Archbishop's lavish dinner. The screens between hall and kitchen were deserted. Only at the far end of the empty hall a smoky fire of damp wood smoldered feebly in the great chimney. As the envoys reached it they were aware of a solitary figure seated on a pile of rushes, a figure huddled in a black

Augustinian gown, so still and shapeless that at first glance they had taken it for a heap of cast-off clothing.

Then the figure moved its head; and the knights recognized the unmistakable Norman beak. Their leader remembered his manners; on bended knee he fumbled for the right hand of this miserable creature and raised the sacred ring to his lips.

Dully Thomas offered it, then raised his hand in a shaky gesture of blessing. His voice was a weak croak. "You come from the King? I see you wear his badge. I am sick; I cannot answer the King's message. Seek my steward, in the little house across the court. In the meantime, leave me alone."

The last sentence came out venomously, with such an under-tone of hatred that the knights were glad to withdraw without warming themselves at the little heap of damp sticks which seemed to be the only fire in the place. The little house across the court was likewise deserted, but presently they found the steward of the temporalities of Canterbury, Sir William fitz-Nigel, drinking in a city tavern. From him they learned what had passed, and carried their message swiftly to the King.

Henry was disappointed to learn that the archbishopric was not abandoned after all, and that the law would not yet permit him to seize the Archbishop's chattels. But something must turn up soon, for Thomas seemed determined to defy him.

By the beginning of September something had turned up. Thomas had refused to attend his lord's court when summoned.

CHAPTER VIII

Northampton

IT WAS a glorious autumn day, with bright sun and a strong
wind to dry the water meadows. Showers had washed away
the mist, and the red-gold woods seemed solid blocks of color
against the paler gold of the stubble. In fact it was a very good
day for hawking.

Green-clad astringers beat on foot through the thorns by the
river, and shaggy spaniels splashed among the reeds; a bowshot
from the bank, where the grass was firm for riding, noble fal-
coners sat chatting in the sunshine; they lounged in their padded hunting saddles, bird on wrist, more at their ease than in

any other seat. As the beaters dislodged a duck one of the lesser short-winged hawks would be loosed to pursue it, following its jinks and turns in a stern chase until the quarry escaped to cover or was caught and killed. This was not a sport you could bet on, and in fact it was not very exciting; but every courtier trained his own hawks, and took pleasure in seeing them fly better than his neighbor's.

High overhead a gyrfalcon waited on, towering in her pride of place. King Henry, sitting easily in his saddle, half-turned in conversation with that amusing young man of letters, Walter Map, occasionally glanced in her direction. Superbly trained, she hovered awaiting his signal.

Presently the spaniels put up a great cob swan. Instantly the river was alive with splashing men, frightening him away from the water. This was the real thing, the cream of the day; and it was made all the better when the gyrfalcon missed her first stoop. Each courtier gathered his reins and rammed his toes home in the stirrups; soon they were galloping over a wooded ridge, all eyes turned to the sky. The swan flew strongly searching for the gleam of open water; while the falcon mounted for her next stoop. Then she struck, falling out of the sky at breathtaking speed, an embodiment of ruthless power; she bound to her quarry, and both came crashing to earth. Before she had opened the entrails of her prey the King arrived at a thundering gallop, and she came obediently to the lure as soon as he waved the gay little toy.

"A model flight, young Walter," the King said with satisfaction. "All went off perfectly because my bird did as she was bid. You know, you could make a conceit out of that. The rage I inherit from my ancestors is the falcon towering in the sky, frightening but harmless until she is signaled on her quarry. She kills, but at my command. Then she comes back to me, harmless once more until I need her the next time. So it is with my rage. I am never overcome, unless I will it. Certainly I cannot control all my feelings, any more than the best falconer alive can control all the motions of his falcon. But I can order her to stop, and roughly speaking she does as I tell her."

"And that falcon, your rage, is always in the sky," answered Walter, with a glance at the towering gyrfalcon. "You never carry her, hooded, on your wrist, as do lesser men with their lesser hawks. When you have bound to the swan who awaits you at Northampton you will still hunt unsatisfied."

"You should not make Thomas a swan, unless you invoke the imaginary black swans of the poet. He was once a jay, decked in bright colors and chattering incessantly to mislead the other fowl of the forest; then he changed to a gloomy black crow . . ."

"And soon he will hang upside down from the husbandman's snare, a scarecrow for his brethren." Breathlessly Walter completed the figure, glad of a chance to show off his rhetoric.

"No, he won't hang," the King answered seriously. "I have no right to hang an archbishop, no matter how richly he deserves it. He shall have strict justice, the very letter of the law. But that will be enough. After this Council he will never again trouble the peace of England."

"Has he put himself in the wrong, my lord?" Walter asked vaguely. It was his pose to despise great affairs, and affect ignorance of politics. If you kept to that line you would never make dangerous enemies. "It's odd if he has, for they say he is a clever lawyer."

"He hasn't a leg to stand on, my boy," the King chuckled jovially. "He has refused to plead in his lord's court, and there can be no defiance worse than that, unless he were to unfurl his banner and summon the tenants of Canterbury to ride against the King. The beauty of it is that this case has nothing to do with religion. It's a straight denial of justice, proved on oath. No clerk can claim that such a case should be tried by canon law. Yet Thomas neglected to attend."

Walter saw, even as the King spoke, that there could be a great difference between refusing to plead and neglecting to attend. The Archbishop might have a valid excuse up his sleeve, waiting to spring it on the court. But he was too wise to say anything of this to King Henry.

The King seemed disposed to hawk the length of this new stream, where the swan had been seeking refuge when the falcon caught him. Count Hamelin of Warenne, his half-brother, urged by a group of serious clerks, presumed on his relationship to ask the King to ride on. But Henry would not be hurried, even when Hamelin reminded him that the Council had been summoned to meet at Northampton on Tuesday the 6th of October, and that today was the 7th. He replied that it was already too late to start business today, and that it would do no harm to keep Thomas waiting two days instead of one. Even if they hawked every stream they would reach Northampton by evening.

"Then you must do your share, my dear brother," he continued. "I shall not judge the Archbishop; if all goes well I shall not even meet him. This is a secular case, concerned with a lay fief. The suitors of my court must give judgment and pass sentence. You all dread my rage," he added in a burst of frankness, "I know that. It's why I am so careful to keep in the background. But you must do your duty, and judge him as you would any other landholder who has broken my law. Just forget that he is an archbishop."

"Brother Henry, you are my lord, and I owe suit to your court," the young man answered doubtfully. "I must do my duty, and when it comes to the point I suppose I shall. But I wish he were not an archbishop. You ask too much in asking us to forget that."

"Never mind. I intend to keep my temper. In this crisis I need an unclouded judgment. I depend on you to keep your peers straight; and if a point of Church law comes up (though

it can't) you can rely on the Bishop of London, who is as good
a canonist as Thomas. There will be nothing to frighten you."

Next morning, Thursday the 8th of October 1164, the magnates of England both clerk and lay stood ranged in the great
hall of Northampton castle, with the King on his throne in the
midst. The first business was the hearing of the appeal of John
the Marshal against his lord the Archbishop of Canterbury; a
mere formality, hurried over before Thomas arrived. On the
15th of September last John the Marshal had taken oath that
his lord denied him justice in the matter of the manor of Pagenham, held of the Honor of Canterbury; and the Archbishop
had not answered, either in person or by a sufficient attorney.
John the Marshal once more gabbled quickly through his oath,
and the court waited for Thomas to arrive and make what excuse he could for his defiance. It seemed quite straightforward.
Thomas must be put in the King's mercy.

But Gilbert of London left his place to whisper in the King's
ear. "My lord," he said, bending over the throne, "this John
is a great rogue, and his claim to the manor would fail if it
were tried by the Grand Assize."

"What of it?" Henry whispered back. "He does not charge
that his lord gave judgment against him, but that his claim was
not heard. That is 'denial of justice.' He has taken oath on the
Gospels that justice was denied to him. Every formality has
been fulfilled."

Bishop Gilbert, that skilled lawyer, felt a little nettled to
hear the King explain to him the elements of feudal law. He
answered in a damp and agitated whisper. "The forms have
not been fulfilled. That rascal John never swore on the Gospels.
I have been talking to him. The book he held in his hand was a
collection of tropes, pointed for singing. He explains that, since
he can't read, all books like alike to him; and he was told that
this troper was the Gospel. I don't believe it. He knew he was
swearing falsely, and he thought to avoid the sin by avoiding

swearing on the Gospel. If the Archbishop hears of this he can claim that the case was not properly heard, and that therefore his presence was not necessary."

Henry enjoyed a neat legal quibble, but only if it went in his favor. Now he brushed aside the objection. "Don't mention it again, Gilbert, though you were right to warn me. The Archbishop doesn't know, nor the other suitors of the court. John Marshal is a rogue, and I don't care whether he gets justice or not; but the Archbishop thought he was lawfully summoned, and he defiantly disregarded the summons. This case has nothing to do with the rightful ownership of the manor of Pagenham."

When at last the defendant arrived, in the full state of an archbishop with his metropolitan cross borne before him, Henry looked with interest to see if his old friend seemed ready to give in. Thomas was certainly very lined and harried-looking but he appeared actually to have put on weight. Then Henry remembered how he used to complain of the cold, especially when he was nervous. Thomas was wearing an extra tunic under his cope; that was a good sign, proving that he was weakening.

However, the great thing was to observe the forms of law. As soon as the case was opened Thomas threw himself on the mercy of the court, the only thing he could do since he had no answer to the charge. The King withdrew to allow the suitors to reach their verdict without royal pressure. The Archbishop also asked permission to withdraw, and this was granted provided he did not leave the castle.

The castle of Northampton possessed the rare luxury of two halls and two private studies. The court was assembled in the great hall on the lower floor, and the Archbishop withdrew to the adjoining study; the King climbed the winding turret stair to the study above. The suitors used the upper hall for informal discussion, which made it easy for Henry to know how their private discussion was going.

At the outset the clerks among the magnates sought to dodge their responsibilities; but Henry had expected nothing better of them, and his temper remained unruffled. The bishops and abbots pleaded that they had in the past sworn obedience to Canterbury, and every true knight agreed that it would be wrong for vassals to sit in judgment on their lord. The clergy then left the private discussion, and most of them returned to gossip in the lower hall; but Henry was disturbed to hear that a few had joined the Archbishop in his study, as though to demonstrate that they supported him.

Among the lay magnates opinion was quick to declare itself. In the shifting groups who discussed their verdict informally, to make sure that the sentence of the Justiciar would embody the sentiments of the whole court, Thomas had few friends. The lord Richer de l'Aigle was surprised to find the magnates of England so hostile to their archbishop. The lord Richer had recently returned from pilgrimage to Outremer, and he found that politics had moved swiftly in his absence. Since he was more than sixty years old, and too deaf to follow casual conversation, he maneuvered his old friend and neighbor, Reginald de Braoze, into a window seat. He tried to persuade him that Thomas must have a case; but Braoze was not to be persuaded.

"You are out of touch, my dear Richer," he said soothingly, speaking clearly into the old man's ear. "This Thomas was a good knight while he was Chancellor, and when he became Archbishop we all looked for peace between King and Church. But since that Parliament at Clarendon last winter, when you were oversea, he has changed greatly for the worse. For one thing, we all thought he was as fearless as Roland, yet when the King threatened him he agreed to everything that was demanded. I suppose he was afraid of the mutilation the King's father inflicted on the unlucky Bishop of Seez. You remember the old story?"

"I remember it, and we who serve Anjou would do well to

be ashamed of it. Count Geoffrey gelded the whole chapter, and their candidate, because they had elected a bishop without first asking permission from their temporal lord. It's not a precedent to be proud of, but it seems to be in everyone's mind. You are the third to remind me of it today. But we in England are more faithful to the Church than those Angevin robber barons. If the King behaves like his father there will be broken relations. I say that in public, and you may repeat it if you wish."

"I fear the King no more than you. If I wish to sever peaceful relations in a worthy cause I shall do it, and hold Bramber by my own power. But I won't risk my fiefs to help a coward, who swore to what he thought wrong because he feared the King's vengeance."

"That's nonsense," cried old Richer in great indignation. "You met Thomas at Pevensey, and you ought to remember him. He has never been afraid of anything or anyone, in all his life."

"Then why did he swear to the Customs of Clarendon?"

"There must be a secret reason. Perhaps he had orders from the Pope. Come to think of it, that's very likely. Thomas would defy the whole world for what he thought was right, but in France they say Pope Alexander will swallow anything to keep the support of the King of England."

"That's a plausible explanation of a puzzling business. As you say, Thomas is not the man to yield from fear, and I was surprised when he collapsed."

Richer fetched a deep sigh, contemplating the downfall of the young page whose rise had been so gratifying to his pride. Then another thought struck him.

"We know Thomas has declined to answer in his lord's court, and for that he must be condemned," he said slowly. "Why did the King summon all his tenants to pass a sentence that should be merely a form?"

Reginald shrugged his shoulders, and made to leave the window. Then he saw a knight standing in the crowd, and beckoned him over to explain. "I don't understand high policy," he said. "Once things go beyond the King of England I keep quiet and remember only my sworn homage. It's something to do with an appeal to the Holy See. The Prior of the Temple here is the best man to explain it."

The Prior was glad to greet a returned Crusader, and pleased to show off his knowledge of foreign affairs.

"We Templars are genuinely neutral," he said earnestly. "Since we owe no obedience to the Archbishop I can remain a member of the court; yet the obedience we owe the King is highly qualified. This is how things stand. In England the Archbishop has no support worth speaking of, but in Christendom at large a great many people blame King Henry; and the King has made all Christendom a party to the dispute, when he might have kept it a domestic matter. He forbade appeals to Rome without his consent, and got all the Bishops to agree to this invasion of their rights. Then, presumably because without Thomas he has no competent lawyer to advise him, he went and laid his customs before the Curia, seeking papal approval. In other words, he himself made the very appeal he had forbidden to all the clerks of his realm."

"So that's it," said Reginald. "I wondered where the Pope came into it."

"The King brought him in, and he must be cursing his impulsive action. Of course Henry is vain, and rightly proud of his good rule in England (he does rule well, you know). He wanted the Pope to tell him what a fine fellow he is, since the King of France is putting it about that he is a savage persecutor of the Church. Now he will have to submit to the Pope's commands, or declare himself a schismatic. The Emperor can rule in opposition to the Holy See, but if King Henry tries it he will go the way of King Stephen."

The Templar swaggered off, pleased to display his independence before these Sussex landholders. As local representative of an international order, and at the same time leader of a powerful court, he could not easily be harmed by any power in the world.

"What a muddle!" said Richer unhappily. "If the King quarrels with the Pope I suppose I must support the Church. To put it on the lowest level, I have been a Christian since I lay in my cradle, but I was a grown man and a knight before I swore homage to Henry. Yet I wish I could avoid taking a side."

However, in this clear case of defiance the lay magnates could reach only one verdict. The Archbishop was in the King's mercy, and the only question to be discussed was the appropriate penalty. It might have been perpetual imprisonment, or death; but after a short discussion they fixed on a merciful sentence, forfeiture of all personal chattels. The King could not disapprove, though to him it seemed a light punishment. Nothing remained but for the spokesman of the court to apprise the culprit of its findings.

Here came a check. The Justiciar refused to deliver the message, explaining frankly that he feared excommunication; that set off all the other magnates, who began to invent frivolous excuses. Henry grew angry, until he recalled that the bishops, who had avoided their duty as his councilors, could not be blamed for the sentence. Bishop Henry of Winchester undertook the unpleasant task, and accomplished it without trouble.

"So now he has no chattels," Henry murmured with glee. "Not a hawk, not a horse, not even a plate for his dinner; if I enforce my full rights, as believe me I shall. We'll see Thomas lose his dignity at last. By the way," he added to the Bishop of Winchester, "we mustn't let him return to Canterbury. He might bury his jewels before my sheriff can take over. Let him stay here under guard until he has been stripped of everything."

Bishop Henry had listened politely. Now he drew himself up to his full height (it was most unfair that the usurper's brother should look like Charlemagne in a romance, while the true heir of England was short and stout, covered with red blotches and red hairs). "You need not hold the Archbishop under guard. I offer the whole property of the See of Winchester, the richest see in England, and the plate I inherited from my father the Count of Blois, as surety that my lord the Archbishop will pay his amercement. If you, my lord, should not think the wealth of Winchester sufficient, every bishop of the Province of Canterbury will join me as surety."

"Do all the suffragans of Canterbury stand by the faithless Archbishop against their true lord the King?" asked Henry, more to gain time than for any more important reason. Looked at in cold blood, this offer ought to help his Treasury; for he was certain to find an excuse to make Winchester pay heavily after he had taken all the movables of Canterbury. But this nobly born bishop made the King of England look, and feel, like a boor; that was a genuine grievance, which would excuse a little properly controlled bout of rage.

"Not quite all," Bishop Henry answered gravely, his voice completely neutral. "The Bishop of London declines to join with his brethren. He takes the view, which is tenable, that as tenant for life only of the property of the Church in the Diocese of London he is not justified in staking it all on the honesty of one man, even though that man is his lord and Metropolitan."

The Bishop of Winchester was determined to conceal the disgust he felt at Foliot's petty malignity; because the See of London was the equal of Winchester, and it was not for him to condemn his peer as though he were a subordinate. But the excuse he had invented gave Henry an idea, and the news that he had at least one supporter among the bishops encouraged him to allow free rein to his anger.

"You speak of the honesty of one man," he spluttered, while flecks of foam gathered at the corners of his mouth. "What can you know of the honesty of Thomas of Canterbury, Tom of Cheapside, Tom Becket the burgess? I know him, for he was my chancellor, and I do not trust his honesty. Thousands of my pounds, millions of my silver pennies, have passed through his hands, and he has never shown me a quittance. Now I am poor and he is rich. He shall not leave this castle until he has rendered account for every penny he scattered as my chancellor."

The Bishop of Winchester looked even more dignified than before.

"My lord the Archbishop was summoned here to answer in the cause of John the Marshal," he replied stiffly. "It is unlikely that he has brought his accounts for the last nine years, if indeed they are still in his possession and not in your Chancery. Your Council will think it unreasonable that he should answer today, unprepared."

Henry snatched at his self-control. He longed to luxuriate in a noisy fit of rage, to roll on the floor and scream until someone told him he might have his way in everything. But when the greatest magnate in England said to his face that his Council would think a certain course of action unreasonable he could not ignore the danger signal. He must go carefully, keeping Thomas on the wrong side of the law; and leaving the question of his accounts as an unsettled threat for the future.

Therefore the King ruled that the Archbishop might withdraw, on condition he came to court tomorrow with a summary of his accounts. Just to make everything more unpleasant he added that by the ancient custom of the realm a defendant who left the King's court with a charge unanswered should give substantial bail for his reappearance; the lands of Canterbury might not be alienated for such a purpose, and Thomas had been deprived of his chattels. So he might have been in an awkward position. But the Bishop of Winchester once more intervened to make the King look both foolish and greedy; he offered bail in his own bond for two thousand marks.

On Friday the 9th of October the court reassembled, and remained in session all day. But by nightfall the magnates complained that they were kept hanging about this castle merely to provide an audience for the King's rage. For the question of the Archbishop's finances had got no further. This time Reginald de Braoze sought out Richer de l'Aigle to listen to his grumbles.

"Here we are," he said, as they leaned together against the wall of the crowded upper hall, "here we are, just after harvest, when the stubble at Bramber is full of partridges. We have been edified by hearing the King accuse the Archbishop of Canterbury of embezzlement, a rare occurrence that may be worth telling to our grandchildren. Otherwise nothing has been done. It's a charge that can never be proved, and never refuted. Why should the Chancellor keep accounts? If the King doesn't trust him he should get another chancellor. Could you render account of the money you spent on your journey to Outremer, though your neighbors contributed to the cost of the pilgrimage?"

"I remember your generous contribution, my dear Reginald. You can be sure it was spent on my journey, for I was penniless when I got back to Pevensey. All the same, I wish Thomas had attempted to answer the charge. It seemed to me mere English levity to reply that the King himself didn't know where his money went."

"I thought it rather amusing. It's funny to think that Thomas was drawing the revenue of two great Honors at the King's pleasure while the King sought to ruin him. Eye and Berkhamstead, they are rich baronies, yet the King never missed them. Next time he asks us for another tax we can tell him to look again at his records and see if he isn't really quite well off after all."

"No," said Richer firmly, assuming the pompous expression of an elder statesman instructing a younger colleague, "Thomas came out of it badly. It was the wrong kind of point to make before the King's Council. We are none of us lawyers, thank God; just simple warriors advising our King as every landholder must advise his lord. When Thomas explained that the King had forgotten to withdraw grants made during pleasure I saw the Archbishop for the first time as a lawyer, a wily debater from the schools of Paris. A clerk trained in Paris might very well cheat a simple bluff warrior like King Henry."

"Simple bluff warrior my foot!" Reginald answered crudely. "If you ever dispute with the King about money I advise you to hire the best lawyer you can find. Even then he may prove that your horse is rightly his, and send you home on foot."

"All the same, I am sorry," said Richer with a melancholy sigh. "I used to think of Thomas as a brave knight, now I see him only as a clever attorney. And I'm not alone. There are other lords who will recognize that perhaps he's too clever by half, too clever to be a worthy archbishop. I wish it was all over. This has been a beastly embarrassing day."

It had been an embarrassing day for everyone except the two principals in the dispute, each of whom was so convinced of his own righteousness that he had no time to consider his dignity. The King showed himself petty and vindictive, but the Archbishop was disingenuous in claiming that he could fetch from Canterbury accounts he had never bothered to keep.

The Archbishop was not frightened, but he was a little troubled in his conscience. In a dispute over the rights of the

Church a clerk had only to stand firm, to the death if need be; in the next world, if not in this, he would be proved right. But here was a dispute about his financial policy as chancellor, at a time when he had been only a deacon; he might perhaps be at fault. Whatever happened, the King would seize the chattels of Canterbury. Perhaps, to bring peace to the Church, he ought to acknowledge his fault. It was unfortunate that he had answered the King so hotly, but when he heard Henry's sneering reproaches he remembered only that he had been trained in debate in the sternest school in the world, Paris; and he gave as good as he got. That oblique reminder that Henry had stolen the crown of England from his own mother was especially unforgivable, because unanswerable. For if he claimed by descent from the Empress, while she lived her claim must be better than his. On Saturday morning the Archbishop held a meeting of his trusted advisers in the guest chamber of the Priory of St. Andrew, where he lodged. Today he would not attend the court in person; he would negotiate only through envoys, who would not be tempted to insult the King to his face.

All the Bishops crowded into the guest chamber, and all approved his plan to keep out of the King's way. But if this Council were ever to end there must be some definite act of reconciliation or apology; otherwise Henry would rake up another breach of the law as soon as the last had been purged. Though no one really knew the whole law of England in all its archaic and superstitious ramifications, he knew enough of it to put in the wrong any magnate who had offended him.

What was the best way to win the King's forgiveness? Bishop Henry of Winchester had his answer: they must buy it. In his view the King did not really care about the punishment of criminous clerks, the ostensible ground of the quarrel. But the King received the chattels of convicted felons, and what he disliked in the claims of the Church was that a clerical felon convicted in a Church court did not part with his chattels to anyone. Accordingly Bishop Henry began to reckon up how much money all the bishops of the province could raise as a peace offering; even Gilbert of London, who attended the conference as an almost open representative of the other side, offered to contribute. But Thomas forbade it. He pointed out that the King had already seized the chattels of Canterbury, and would probably find an excuse to confiscate the two thousand marks Bishop Henry had put up as bail. He must not be incited to rob the whole Church in England; as he would be if they tried to buy his good will.

Bishop Henry suddenly remembered the solemn release from all secular obligations that the Young King had pronounced on the occasion of Thomas's election. Thomas objected that at the time he had still been Chancellor, intending to continue in office; the release had been a graceful gesture, but in the last analysis meaningless. Still, if the King were willing to end this undignified quarrel, here was an excellent opportunity for him to save his face. It might be worth trying. The Bishops, without Thomas, rode the few hundred yards from St. Andrews to the castle.

Thomas knew he had committed a grave breach of the law by refusing to appear in the case of John the Marshal. He could not give a convincing reason for such pointless contumacy, which had of course entailed his conviction. He had been ill, so ill that he did not feel equal to arguing before a hostile tribunal; but he had not asked for an adjournment on grounds of ill health, though such an adjournment was usually granted. In truth, as he now realized, he had grown tired of struggling to keep the peace. At Woodstock and Clarendon he had bowed to injustice for the sake of peace. But since then the course of events had shown that the King would never live in peace with him. It was better to bring the quarrel to a head.

But if he was glad that the lists were drawn for a pitiless encounter between King and Archbishop, he realized that in
the whole of England only King and Archbishop were eager to
carry on the quarrel. The Bishop of Winchester was anxious
to buy peace with all he possessed. The Bishop of London had
broken the united ranks of the hierarchy because he did not
wish the Church as a whole to be committed to this quarrel.
As for the lay magnates, the whole world knew they would
eagerly endorse any compromise put before them. If Henry
would he content with peace, victory, and the chattels of Canterbury, it was his duty to yield as gracefully as he could.

He was relieved when the bishops rode back, to announce
that the King refused to recognize the release granted by his
son. He was within his rights, for the formula had been meaningless. Now it was open war, and Gilbert of London had at
last openly joined the enemies of his Metropolitan. For Gilbert, proud of his wit, had been unable to suppress a wound-
ing impromptu; though he knew very well that the matter of
the old release had been brought up only to save the King's
face, and that Thomas himself did not take it seriously, he had
flashed out in open Council, before all the lay magnates of
England: "The Archbishop of Canterbury thinks episcopal
consecration absolves from debt, as baptism absolves from
sin. As a theologian, I deny it."

Here was all the excuse Henry needed to refuse the proposal; the bishops could get no better terms than an adjournment until next Monday. On that day Thomas must produce
his accounts, or admit that he was again at the King's mercy.

Still the Bishop of Winchester had not abandoned hope of
a settlement. His new proposal recognized that there could be
no peace between Thomas and Henry, and sought only to
leave the Church in general outside the dispute. He wanted
Thomas to resign his see, going into exile as a titular arch-

bishop. Then his successor might settle the question of clerical felons without the handicap of the King's animosity.

There was much to be said for this scheme. In his imagination Thomas saw a distinguished confessor, an archbishop exiled from his see, traveling as a poor scholar from Paris, by way of Chartres and Salerno, to Bologna; the clergy greeted him in every city, and he was invited to lecture in every school; he would enjoy leisure, dignity, and the sympathy of educated Christendom. But he saw farther; he saw a procession of ex-metropolitans, compelled by precedent to resign as soon as they disagreed with their secular lords, crossing the Channel by every tide. If the archbishopric of Canterbury were to be held at the King's pleasure, like the Honor of Berkhamstead, the Church would be wholly subject to the lay power.

He refused to resign, even at the entreaty of the Bishop of Winchester. Bishop Henry dwelt on the terrible condition of Christendom, and the danger that the exiled Pope might lose his wealthiest supporter; he reminded his lord that the first duty of a bishop is to save souls, and that to continue on a course which must bring interdict and excommunication to all England might be regarded as a betrayal of trust. But Thomas stood firm. He would suffer persecution without resistance; but Henry must know, without a shadow of excuse, that the man he persecuted was the Archbishop of Canterbury.

By Sunday morning every magnate in the realm, clerical or lay, was searching for a formula to avert the breach. Unless a formula was found the Council must give judgment on Monday, and then every suitor would have to support one party or the other. That was what they all dreaded. For the division between clerk and lay was anything but clear-cut; the Justiciar's brother was Abbot of Battle, the Bishop of Winchester was born a great lord; everywhere the contest would sunder families and friends. For that matter, the lay magnates were decent practicing Christians, who would be reluctant to follow their lord to the point of excommunication. If only a formula could be found!

As he said Mass that Sunday Thomas was assailed by a conviction of sin. Here in Northampton were assembled the great men of the realm; all were ardent for peace, save the two greatest of them. Henry and Thomas alone sought conflict; which seemed to put the Archbishop in the same class as the angry and sinful King.

Thomas knew he had a quick temper. So far he had kept it reasonably well, by the cowardly expedient of staying away from his enemy; a more saintly archbishop might have apologized so humbly that the King's wrath was appeased. As instigator of the quarrel he must be at fault. But when he considered the matter more calmly he could see no way of conceding with honor all the points at issue. As for the simple question of his accounts as Chancellor, he would not seek to defend himself. But his real offense was that he was Archbishop and would not resign, and there he knew he was in the right. All the same, at St. Andrew's he was in a minority of one, and the fear that his obstinacy might be obstructing a peaceful settlement set his heart pounding against his ribs.

On Monday evening, alone with Prior Robert, Thomas spoke straight to the point: "Have I sinned against King Henry? If I have, how shall I make restitution?"

Prior Robert was a tough, middle-aged monk, who never compromised with the world into which duty had called him; he made time to say his whole office every day, and lived, by himself, the regular life of an Augustinian canon. All day he had sat in a corner over his breviary, hearing what was said but taking no part in the discussion. His answer was as direct as the question.

"You have not sinned against King Henry, and you are not

called on to make restitution. The Council may find you guilty of a breach of the law; but what you have broken is a penal regulation. Anyone may break a penal law without sin, provided he is willing to pay the penalty."

"Then what is your advice?"

"You have heard advice all day, probably more than is good for you. Why do you seek more from me, who can tell you nothing of politics?"

"I don't want your views on politics. I want the moral counsel of my confessor. What shall I do in court tomorrow?"

"You have a choice. You may yield to the King. If you crawl abjectly enough, and pay enough money, he will forgive you. And you will not be doing anything that I, your confessor, can pronounce sinful. But," and he waved a horny thumb to emphasize his point, "if you wish to serve God as a good knight serves his lord, joyfully doing more than your bare duty, you will defend the liberties of Canterbury, defying the King even in his strong castle."

"And that's what I'll do, old comrade. It can't be more frightening than jousting against Engelram de Trie. I shall ride to the castle and defy them all. By the way, whose feast falls tomorrow? I hope he is a saint who will lend me courage."

"St. Edward of England, King and Confessor," Robert answered with a sardonic smile. He was Norman enough to feel some dislike of the newly canonized Saxon. "A very meek man, though holy. Not perhaps the most inspiring patron of a perilous enterprise."

"Then I shall say a votive Mass. What patron do you suggest?"

"Let me see. What about St. Stephen, the first martyr? He spoke fearlessly in the council of the Jews, as you intend to speak fearlessly in the Council of England."

"That's it, my dear Robert. Tell the sacristan to put out crimson vestments. St. Stephen will fortify my courage. My mind is made up! No more compromise, no more politics! They can't do more than kill me; and I must one day die and face the Judgment, though King Henry were my loving friend."

"True enough," answered Robert calmly. "But if you provoke them you tempt them to the sin of sacrilege. Your duty is to make the magnates of England behave as Christians, instead of going about the place threatening archbishops. You should ride to the castle in all your state, to remind them what manner of man they are judging."

"Leave that to me," Thomas said eagerly. "I shall plan my appearance in court as I planned the famous embassy to Paris. The world will remember the visit of the Archbishop of Canterbury to King Henry in Northampton castle."

Early on Tuesday morning the bishops of England assembled at the Priory to escort their lord to the castle. But the Archbishop of York, with his single suffragan, might go straight to court, since he owed no obedience to Canterbury. The Bishops were poorly attended and simply dressed, for they hoped by a show of humility to turn away the King's wrath.

They were informed that the Archbishop had risen early from his sickbed, and was already saying his Mass. They at once set off for the chapel, to join in the prayers of their lord. But as they reached the side-altar where Thomas celebrated they halted in amazement. They themselves had said the Mass of St. Edward, in the white vestments appropriate to his feast; but their Archbishop was vested in the crimson of a Martyr. He had already said the opening psalm, by which these veteran clergy could recognize any Mass, and they did not understand what he was about until be read the special Gospel. *"Ut veniat super vos omnis sanguis justus qui effusus est super terram,"* he thundered, and his voice took on a tone of triumph a moment later: *"Ecce relinquetur vobis domus vestra deserta!"* (That upon you may come all the righteous blood shed upon the earth. . . . Behold your house is left unto you desolate.)

"God save us," whispered William of Norwich. "He expects martyrdom this very day!"

"He exaggerates," replied Henry of Winchester. "They say that when he entered Paris on that embassy he looked more like a jongleur than a statesman; today he thinks more of appearing as a splendid figure of defiance than of the welfare of the Church. But he has great need of our prayers. Let us kneel."

When Mass was finished and Thomas went to breakfast the bishops were relieved to discover that he was not at all angry. Neither was he frightened. Only Bishop Henry, recalling the struggles of the civil war, recognized his mood. That controlled exaltation, that glittering eye and slightly shaking hand, were the marks of a brave knight about to charge in a doubtful battle.

Before the bishops could disperse Thomas called them before him. He sat on a little stool, munching bread and honey; but he made it clear that this was a formal Council, and that he was giving orders to men subject to his obedience.

"I am Metropolitan of Canterbury, and I am within my province," he began, sweeping the little group with a steady eye. "It may be that before I leave Northampton some layman may sacrilegiously use force against the person of his Archbishop. As you know, such a crime brings instant excommunication. But perhaps not every layman knows as much. I therefore command that any of you who should witness the wicked deed shall at once pronounce public sentence of excommunication, as I shall myself if I am permitted to speak. You have heard my formal command; if you disobey it you commit the sin of schism."

He could see that his order was disliked. There was a little stir, and Gilbert of London opened his mouth to protest; after a sharp exclamation he closed it again, for there was nothing he could say unless he was prepared to rebel against his lawful superior.

After a pause Thomas continued: "Furthermore, even if these men shrink from laying hands on my person, I understand that they intend to pronounce some penalty against their spiritual pastor, which is sacrilege and a breach of canon law. Therefore I give public notice, before my brethren as witnesses, that I appeal to the Pope against any sentence unjustly passed on me by this tribunal of laymen."

"Remember that at Clarendon you swore never to appeal to the Pope without first seeking leave from the King," Gilbert retorted at once.

"Nevertheless, I appeal."

"Then I appeal also," the Bishop of London went on. He paused to frame his sentence in legal form, and continued: "I appeal to the Pope against my Metropolitan, who has commanded me to excommunicate loyal servants of the King if they execute the lawful orders of the ruler to whom they have sworn homage. Until my appeal has been determined I am free to disregard this command of my Metropolitan. My brethren, have I stated the law correctly?"

"That is the law," said Thomas before anyone else could speak. "You are free to disregard my command, until the Pope orders you to obey it. Do any more of my suffragans appeal against me?"

He could feel the red mist stirring in his brain, but with a mighty effort he calmed his anger. Today above all days he must remain unmoved, even when a subordinate defied him to his face.

The other bishops heard their orders in glum silence. Only Robert of Hereford muttered, more to himself than to his companions, "God save us all. We cannot hope for peace, now that our Archbishop has broken the King's customs. Yet when war starts I must follow my lord, like the rest of us." He straightened his shoulders as he glanced down at his Benedictine sandals. A promoted monk, still hankering for the cloister, he was the most peace-loving of the Bishops; but he also had been born of the warlike race of Rollo, and when the trumpet sounded he would not shirk his duty.

Now the Bishop of London announced, with a formal reverence to his Metropolitan, that it was time for him to ride to the castle, where the King wished to consult him before the court opened. This gave notice that henceforth he would be on the King's side; but so much was already public knowledge, and Thomas felt that Gilbert had been courteous in thus making his position clear before the trial resumed. He was now in full command of his temper, and he graciously acknowledged Gilbert's genuflexion.

Bishop Henry of Winchester stayed behind, with Bishop Jocelyn de Bohun of Salisbury. Both were great magnates by birth, and friendly with many lay magnates of the Council. They wished to advise the Archbishop on his demeanor before the King; even if there was no hope of a friendly outcome Thomas must be persuaded to change his present angry mood of defiance.

They could not change his mood; but they prevailed on him to refrain from provoking the King before the court opened. He had proposed to ride to the castle in Mass vestments of Martyr's red, with miter, cope, and pallium. Bishop Jocelyn pointed out that such a deliberate appeal for sympathy might alienate more laymen than it persuaded, and Thomas agreed that a Bohun must know more than a burgess about the sentiments of great magnates. Instead of a chasuble he wore under his cope his customary black Augustinian gown; though he insisted on a stole as well, and hung a little pyx inside it. This was to make certain that he would receive communion if the King should kill him on the spot. Bishop Henry agreed reluctantly that there was nothing actually wrong in this dress, especially as stole and pyx would be hidden by his cope; but it seemed a reflection on his clerical supporters. The whole hierarchy of England would be present, yet Thomas assumed that not one of them would have the courage to attend him if the worst came to the worst.

"He is very obstinate," muttered Jocelyn. "He goes out of his way to anger the King."

"We must remember that he is not a gentleman born," answered Bishop Henry. "He is in fact in danger of death, though I hope the King will be sensible. If he wishes to make a display of his peril let him do so. It may win him friends among the populace."

A flight of stone steps led from the court of Northampton castle to the double doors of the great hall. The court was crowded with grooms and sergeants, all hoping to be eyewitnesses of a famous historical event; but the steps were left clear for the magnates, and on them, as the appointed time approached, lounged the Bishops of London and Hereford. They had a clear view of the first remarkable event of that remarkable day.

Through the outer gate rode the clerks of the Archbishop's household, two by two on well-paced hackneys. On entering the courtyard they dismounted, and grooms took their horses. Behind the senior clerks came the processional cross that was the emblem of metropolitan authority; Dom Herbert of Bosham, in black Benedictine cowl, bore the tall silver-gilt pole, banded with gleaming enamel and surmounted by a silver-gilt crucifix; as high and conspicuous as a battle standard, it announced, to any who might have forgotten it, that behind it came the spiritual ruler of southern England, which included the town and castle of Northampton. In normal times any well-mannered layman would uncover and kneel at the passing of a metropolitan cross, and even today many of the grooms paid it due honor; while those who ignored it, looking steadily at the horizon, were plainly embarrassed.

Behind the cross rode Thomas, Archbishop of Canterbury, in cope and miter and jeweled gloves, his right hand raised to bless the muttering crowd; while his left managed the reins of a great roan charger, a more warlike mount than clerks were used to ride on occasions of ceremony. He sat low in his peaked war saddle, his toes forward and his back straight; Gilbert whispered flippantly to his brother bishop that this cavalier seemed listening for the trumpet to sound the onset.

When all were within the courtyard there was a creaking of stout oak timbers, and Gilbert gripped Robert of Hereford by the arm. "See," he hissed, "they have locked the gate. Thomas is trapped in the King's strong castle."

But Robert was not listening. With a little moan of distress he sprang forward, arms outstretched. "Our Archbishop himself carries his cross, as did Our Lord at Calvary," he called. "Most gracious master, permit me to be your cross-bearer."

"My dear fellow," said Gilbert with a shrug, "the man was always a fool, and he always will be. Pay no attention."

For Thomas had seized the weighty cross from his astonished cross-bearer. He had never carried it before, and he was too impatient to hold it in the correct ceremonial fashion, bolt upright a foot before his nose. There was something else of roughly the same weight and shape which once he had carried frequently; he tucked the butt inside his elbow, as a knight bears his lance when the foe spurs against him.

The Bishop of Hereford made an ineffectual grab at the cross, and as Thomas brushed him aside Bishop Gilbert intervened more brusquely. "Here, give me that," he called sharply. "If you wield your cross so, the King will wield his sword; and then who shall make peace between you?"

Thomas glared fiercely, but his steps did not falter.

"This cross is the emblem of peace, which I carry for the protection of the Church," he rapped out.

He swept up to the lower hall, then plodded through it to the little study beyond. Within the study he sat huddled on a bench, grasping the cross between his knees. Most of his clerks lingered in the hall, fearful of the King's vengeance; only Herbert of Bosham and Robert of Merton followed him into the inner room.

Meanwhile another great train of clerks mounted the steps to the hall; the onlookers barely had time to take their eyes off the Archbishop of Canterbury before the Archbishop of York marched by. The Bishop of London genuflected to this metropolitan cross, for his monastic training made such reverence second nature. But he bowed his knee with a sarcastic smile. Roger of York was behaving characteristically, which was to say with foolish pomposity. In the first place, he had purposely delayed his arrival until a great crowd had gathered to witness his glory; in the second, he had taken advantage of the crisis to invade the rights of Canterbury. His cross should never be borne before him except within the bounds of his own province; even Gilbert, glad to see his own Metropolitan slighted, felt a shock of distaste at this insult to the province which held his allegiance; every subject of Canterbury must bristle at the trespass.

A clerk who had overheard his passage with the Bishop of Hereford whispered in Gilbert's ear: "You said our Archbishop carried his cross like a lance. Here is the lance of the champion who will joust against him."

Every move of that day of climax had been carefully planned in advance, to ensure that Henry and Thomas should not meet face to face. The Council met in the upper hall, with the King in the adjoining study; the Archbishop remained in the lower study; and the lower hall made a useful lobby, where delegations could revise the wording of messages passed from one study to the other.

In the upper hall Richer de l'Aigle was glad to rest in a window, apart from the crowd of jostling magnates. He knew that today would bring long hours of standing in ordered ranks of precedence, with probably no proper interval for dinner. At present the King's study was filled with bishops, making a last appeal for peace and concord. That was expected from bishops, and it would be very shocking if they slackened in their search for peace; but it would also be very surprising if they found it. A wise man with gouty feet should sit resting until they were dismissed.

Suddenly a roar from the study startled even his deaf ears. He glanced inquiringly at the young lord beside him, who spoke up obligingly. "That's only the King indicating a mild annoyance. He isn't chewing the rushes, so it doesn't really count as anger. He has just learned that every bishop in England spent the morning appealing to Rome, in spite of the Constitutions of Clarendon. He will roar for a little, but the diversion won't last. He is too eager to get on with sentencing the Archbishop."

Richer was shocked to hear a vassal speak so lightly of his lord. That was not how young knights discussed affairs of state forty years ago. He could not decide which side he supported, and this further evidence of the degeneracy of the times increased his disquiet. For many years he had been a suitor of the King's court, and never before had he felt any doubt in a case of felony; for such cases did not reach the King's court unless the culprit's guilt was flagrant. The normal duty of the magnates was merely to pronounce sentence; after which they would be normally bound to enforce the penalty, with their own retinues if necessary. Today he could not help wondering whether the Archbishop might not have right on his side; though of course King Henry, that expert on the custom of England, was sure to find a way to put him in the wrong. If he, Richer, were asked on oath whether Thomas had denied justice to John the Marshal, and had then appealed to Rome without the King's permission, he could only answer Yes. But did that make his old pupil a traitor? Perhaps as the day wore on a solution would emerge.

Presently the Count of Warenne led a group of young knights to the lower study, where they stood in the doorway reminding one another of what had happened to bishops who had defied earlier kings of England. The gelding of the Bishop and Chapter of Seez was trotted out again as a precedent, as though the King were proud of his father's revolting vengeance; and of course there was the imprisonment of the Bishop of Bayeux, nearly a century ago in the days of the Conqueror.

Before they began Richer could have told them they were wasting their time. You could not frighten Thomas of London. By the middle of the morning they had all trooped upstairs, sheepish and crestfallen; Thomas had ignored them completely, continuing to recite his office with that scowling monk beside him. It was getting on for dinner time, and Richer searched his wallet for the lump of salt beef he had brought. A wise courtier always came to these bad-tempered sessions prepared as for a campaign.

Still from the King's study came angry raised voices, and from the Archbishop's the mutter of psalms. There was constant coming and going on the winding turret stair, as peacemakers hurried in search of a formula. Nearly everyone present longed for peace; unfortunately two exceptions were the King and the Archbishop.

Presently Richer scrambled to his feet to bow to the metropolitan cross of York. For a moment he hoped the council was ended, but he was quickly undeceived. As Archbishop Roger formed his clerks in procession he addressed them in a loud voice. "You will return with me to my lodging. I advise my brethren of the Province of Canterbury to withdraw also. The slaughter of a consecrated archbishop is a sight no clerk should witness. But if the King wills it we cannot prevent it; and the King has good reason for his anger."

The steep winding stair marred the pomp of his procession; but he walked through the narrow door with all the dignity he could muster.

King Henry could sense the changing moods of his vassals. He had demonstrated his wrath, but without losing his head. He knew that if he lost the allegiance of his magnates he would be as powerless as King Stephen; and he knew that if he murdered an archbishop half the castles in England would hoist banners of defiance. He had been trying to frighten Thomas into withdrawing his appeal to the Pope, encouraged by the fact that some bishops were already beside themselves with fear; Bartholomew of Exeter, an unworldly scholar, had fallen on his knees to beg his Metropolitan to save many lives by a timely surrender; even Henry of Winchester besought him to go into exile of his own free will. But Thomas would not yield; he was willing to face martyrdom, knowing that his martyrdom would cost Henry the throne. Both sides had gone too far to withdraw with dignity.

When Gilbert of London proposed a way out, Henry snatched at it. After all, this business of appeals to Rome was an unforeseen distraction. When it was out of the way he could proceed with more definite charges, charges on which the Court must find Thomas guilty.

Gilbert proposed that Thomas should be given leave to lodge his appeal with the Curia. At the same time all the suffragans of Canterbury should lodge an appeal of their own, begging the Pope to remove their Metropolitan.

Nothing in canon law forbade such an appeal; though there was no precedent, for an archbishop did not usually unite all his suffragans in opposition. It would be a most resounding insult; and if the Pope valued the support of England in his struggle with the Emperor it should end in the transfer of the factious clerk to some undistinguished titular see.

In the early afternoon it was announced that the King permitted appeals to the Curia from every bishop in England, including the Archbishop of Canterbury. The court might now convene to hear the charge that a great magnate had refused to answer in his lord's court when summoned.

Everyone was tired and cross and hungry. When Richer de l'Aigle heaved himself to his feet he felt all around him a fierce determination to make an end of this troublesome affair. The matter of criminous clerks was tangled, and it did not interest lay magnates who would never dare to compel clerks to answer in their own courts. But a lord must be able to compel attendance at his court, or the foundations of law would collapse. Most of these magnates had come unwillingly to Northampton, because their lord commanded it; unless they could compel their vassals to attend their own courts they would lose the power which made them great. The Archbishop was plainly guilty, and must suffer for it.

Suddenly everyone began to shout that Thomas was a traitor. The Justiciar, as eager as all the other magnates to finish this unsavoury business in time for supper, announced at the top of his voice that the tenants-in-chief of the King, the highest court in England, held Thomas, Archbishop of Canterbury, to be guilty of treason, and advised their lord to punish him with lifelong imprisonment. The cause was not rehearsed in open court according to law (though the suitors, who had discussed nothing else all that long morning, were thoroughly conversant with it); and some clerical magnates, who might not sit in judgment on their lord, had no time to get out of the hall and down the stairs. In fact, Richer noted, this discussion had been so informal that it might be argued that the case remained untried. Probably the Justiciar and the more responsible counts were aware of this, glad to leave an opening for an appeal later on. But in the meantime the Council of Northampton had got through its agenda.

Or very nearly through its agenda; there was still one formality. Though hysterical shouts of "Treason!" could be heard all over the castle, the culprit had not been officially informed of verdict and sentence. Until he had been so informed the proceedings remained incomplete. It was a task for the Justiciar, and boisterous young knights pushed Richard de Lucy to the head of the stairs.

Since he had dismounted in the courtyard that morning, when the Archbishop snatched the metropolitan cross from his hands, Dom Herbert of Bosham had realized that this was the greatest day of his life. It looked as though it would also be the last; but he strove to be a good monk, and much reading in the Lives of the Saints had shown him how a Martyr should face death. At the beginning he had been nervous and discomposed, which he knew was wrong; then the Archbishop had ordered him to join in reciting the office, and in reading his psalter he had recovered his composure. This is a fleeting world, and soon to be destroyed; he concentrated on reaching the end of each verse, looking no further into the future.

There had been minutes of great strain, when the Archbishop sat still as a statue, his great cross between his knees, while fierce knights threatened or saintly bishops begged him to be meek. It was hard for a simple monk to remain undismayed when the Bishop of Exeter wept tears of genuine terror.

Now his vigil was ended. The persecutors had worked up the requisite pitch of rage (for these men were baptized Christians, and many of them had fought to defend God's Sepulcher in Outremer; when they were sober again their remorse would be ghastly). He heard shouts of "Traitor!" and a rush of feet on the stairs; they were coming, swords drawn, to make an end of the chief servant of God in England, and presumably at the same time of his cross-bearer and companion. Well, they would find Dom Herbert recollected and ready.

But this unforeseen delay was very trying. As the crowd shuffled in the entry Dom Herbert raised his eyes, which had been fixed on the Host hanging from his lord's shoulders. The ruffians, undecided, were pushing one another, each reluctant to be the first to invade the study.

Now they had found a ringleader. The Count of Leicester stood forward in the narrow doorway. But, good heavens, the man had begun a rambling extempore speech, not even in the dignified Latin in which a formal sentence should be couched! He babbled in sloppy French of the Two Swords of Temporal and Spiritual Justice, and the divine origin of kingship, founded on the annointing of King Saul! Must a brave man, about to die, first hear these tendentious and misleading arguments, the stock-in-trade of miserable Ghibellines who divided the Seamless Robe of Christ by setting up their private imitation of the true Pope? Perhaps he was not about to die, after all? The Count of Leicester was stumbling to a close. It looked at though he had begun with a conclusion in mind, and collapsed from nervousness before he could reach it.

Now the Count of Cornwall took up the speech, still in that clumsy French of England which was unfitted for legal pronouncements. Herbert understood what these magnates were about. They were trying to promulgate the sentence of their lay court, which by God's law could have no jurisdiction over an archbishop. The sentence could hardly be death, or they would not have bothered with this formality; but so far they had not even rehearsed the crime they were proposing to punish. Naturally they would make a mess of it, for since the bishops and abbots had withdrawn they had no skilled clerks to hold them to the forms of even their secular and unwritten law.

Herbert felt more cheerful, and at the same time more worried. Martyrdom was a final act, soon over, which any good monk could face with fortitude; lifelong imprisonment, and probably a beating to begin with, would be harder to bear with dignity. Glancing at his lord, he saw stoic resignation beginning to give place to anger, the anger of a proud knight who must listen to a string of unjustified and insulting reproaches. He hoped Thomas would have the self-control to keep silence; if he answered his accusers this historic occasion would dwindle into an exchange of vulgar abuse.

The Count of Cornwall was as unable to reach a conclusion as the Count of Leicester; young knights at the back shouted blasphemous obscenities which should have no place in a court of law, but the responsible magnates clustered in the entry of the study could not bring themselves to pronounce the Primate of All England guilty of treason and felony.

At last the Bishop of Chichester pushed his way through the throng. "Make way, my lords," he shouted. "I am a lawyer trained in the Curia. I will deliver your sentence in proper form."

Herbert looked again into his lord's face. Bishop Hilary was a veteran foe, but it was the boast of legal training which caught the Archbishop's attention. A scholar of Paris, who had pleaded before the Curia when Hilary was a papal clerk, must gather his wits to meet that challenge. Herbert saw his lord no longer resigned to suffer with dignity whatever a tyrant might inflict; he was thinking of how to get the better of Bishop Hilary.

All the laymen fell silent, pleased that a bishop had undertaken their burdensome duty. Hilary cleared his throat, bowed to the seated Archbishop, and spoke formally, in clear Curial Latin. But before he had completed his first sentence, explaining that the magnates of England, his peers, held the Archbishop of Canterbury to be a traitor, Thomas intervened with a curt bark of *"Tace!"*

It was the word used by an angry judge to call an impudent advocate to order, and Hilary, the veteran lawyer, stopped in the middle of a phrase, his mouth hanging open. Thomas burst into a torrent of legal Latin. By the universal consent of Christendom no bishop might pass sentence on his metropolitan, he shouted; what answer had Hilary to that? The two lawyers forgot their uncomprehending lay audience in the crackling exchange of rebuke and excuse. Then Bishop Hilary, knowing himself in the wrong, stepped back, plowing a gap through the crowd in his anxiety to get away.

In the instant Thomas was on his feet, the metropolitan cross in both hands, as a knight bears his standard into battle. As he strode to the door Herbert followed.

Before them stretched the long hall, filled with knights and grooms and magnates; at the far end the outer door stood open, and beyond it lay the yard and the gate and the Priory of St. Andrew and a respite from persecution. Herbert was praying. If they could win their way to the open the King might be cheated of his prey.

He caught a low whisper from the Archbishop. "They have no order to arrest me, and they may fear to act without it. Let us make straight for St. Andrew's, stopping for no man."

Thomas drew himself to his full, immense height, raising the cross far above him. His cope billowed out behind, and his fierce eyes were fixed above the heads of the tallest spectators. In that crowd of enemies, the King's most loyal adherents, no one was anxious to be the first to lay hands on an Archbishop.

Herbert, pattering beside him, began to hope for the future.

If the Archbishop could awe the crowd for a few minutes they would be safe. His dignity was certainly awe-inspiring; knights and grooms shrank back as though before an angel with a fiery sword. But once he was past, when they could see only his back, their courage began to revive. A young page made a rude noise with his mouth, and threw a handful of muddy rushes plucked from the floor. They hit the Archbishop square between the shoulders, leaving a foul stain on the crimson cope. Thomas checked his stride as though to round on the offender; but Herbert, forgetting he was a humble choir-monk in attendance on his Abbot, dared to offer advice.

"Take no notice, my lord," he whispered. "If you stay to quarrel this will be the beginning of such bloodshed as England has never seen."

The Archbishop, with a gesture of assent, continued to stalk toward the door.

Others had noticed his hesitation, and quick wits among his enemies set to work to drive him to frenzy. Young Count Hamelin of Warenne was the boldest; as Thomas passed he shouted "Traitor!" into his face, and seemed about to spit. Walking on, the Archbishop answered his tormentor over his shoulder. "I could prove on your body that I am no traitor," he answered, "but my hands are consecrated. Furthermore, a man of my condition cannot joust against a nameless bastard."

The Count turned away. He was a feeble jouster, but what really quelled him was the reminder of his birth. At his brother's court he passed as a great man, but he was ever conscious that in the world he had no place of his own.

Nearing the door Thomas stumbled over a bundle of faggots, litter dumped by lazy servants. That was the most dangerous moment of the dangerous day, for a snigger came from the back of the crowd; they would beat him to death if they began to think him ridiculous. But his dignity overcame even this mischance. Still with his cross erect in both hands he descended the steps to the castle yard.

Herbert looked anxiously at the gate. But the Archbishop, without losing the immovable carriage of his head, had taken in the situation with an even swifter glance.

"We must ourselves unlock the outer gate. The porters have run away, to avoid the responsibility of stopping me. Don't waste time, but don't look frightened. Get mounted as quick as you can."

Beside the gate more than a score of horses stood picketed in a row, an overflow from the crowded stable. Herbert had a vague recollection of seeing his own horse tethered there that morning; but in his agitation he could not remember what it looked like. He had a clear picture of a rough mane and scarred withers, which he had seen when he rode, bearing the cross, to this horrible council; but he could not for the life of him recall its color. Before that line of restless rumps he hesitated, and some of the beasts, sensing a frightened man behind them, drew up their hind legs to kick.

The Archbishop dodged calmly among the restless stallions to unhitch his own war horse. Still hampered by his great cross he jumped at the saddle, and lay balanced over the animal's back. As his right foot felt for the off stirrup he called softly: "If you can't find your own horse leave him. In a minute the King will order them to stop us. We must be away before that. Here, jump up behind me, and hang on to my cope. If you fall off I must leave you lying."

The tall charger was trained for war; confusion all round him and the excitement of his own rider made him the more willingly obedient to leg and rein. Under his double burden he walked sedately to the closed gate. It seemed that the Archbishop intended to burst it open by a charge; but that desperate step was unnecessary. Beside it, where the porter had left them when he fled, hung a bunch of keys.

The hostile crowd was now more willing to take action; the sight of the Archbishop balked by a locked gate reminded some bold spirits that the King might give a handsome reward for his capture. Herbert, in desperation, suggested that they should dismount and try to clamber over the wall.

"Then we should look silly, and they would be on us at once," answered the Archbishop. "Just lean over and see if that key fits the lock. Pray to God we find the right key quickly. It must be there, but we cannot linger."

Leaning dangerously from his perch, wishing he had learned to ride properly before he entered the cloister, Herbert snatched at a key, thrusting it in the direction of the gate. At that moment the charger passaged sideways, and the key seemed to enter the lock unguided; as it turned, the gate swung open toward them.

Of course the right key must have been in that bunch, and it was pure chance which he seized first. But if it was not a miracle it was a piece of very good luck. As they thundered through the archway Herbert shouted *"Deo Gratias"* in pious gratitude; but the way he shouted it made it sound very like a war cry.

At the Priory of St. Andrew, Thomas ate his first meal since breakfast. He was completely unafraid, and not even tempted to lose his temper. In the morning, while his enemies insulted him, he had felt so angry that only concentration on his psalter had given him the strength to sit unmoved. But now the campaign had reached its crisis; he was all warrior.

While he ate the boiled fish with egg sauce which was the most luxurious supper St. Andrew's could produce, the porter announced that two separate deputations wished to see him. First came the Bishops of London and Chichester, his opponents. They showed no credentials, but spoke as though in the King's name, and Thomas did not doubt they were his envoys.

They suggested that if Thomas would resign the lands of his see to the King (who already had his chattels), he might live unmolested in a monastery until the Pope had settled the dispute. Gilbert of London, a monk who cared nothing for money and very little for legal rights, seemed to think this a reasonable compromise. But Hilary the lawyer delivered his terms with a hangdog air; he knew that a bishop had no right to impoverish his see by granting its land to a secular lord. For Thomas to accept these terms would be to buy his personal safety with the property of the Church; he indignantly refused the suggestion.

The two bishops went back to the castle. Thomas was delighted to see them go, but he could not accuse them of betraying their ecclesiastical superior. They were entitled to support the King in a purely temporal dispute over the bookkeeping of a retired chancellor; they were competent diocesan bishops, and though they made plain where their sympathy lay they had not broken any rule of canon law.

It was odd that the second delegation, his friends the Bishops of Rochester, Worcester, and Hereford, should bring him substantially the same proposal. They also suggested that he should abandon the lands of Canterbury to the King; but instead of staying in a monastery they wanted him to visit the Pope. So even his friends would be glad to see him leave England!

There was a great deal to be said for this plan, since at present he could not rule his province unmolested by the secular power. But when he sent to King Henry for a passport the King would neither grant nor refuse it. It was a grave matter, he said; he would sleep on it, and give his decision tomorrow.

When at last he was alone, the only bishop within the Priory of St. Andrew, Thomas consulted his confessor. Would it be desertion to leave his flock unshepherded, exposed to that ravening wolf, King Henry? Robert of Merton, as usual, gave him a straight answer.

"It is never wrong to flee from persecution, since no man can be certain that his courage is equal to martyrdom. This can be proved from the Scriptures. St. Peter followed his Lord, at peril of his life, to the house of the High Priest; and before the cock crew he had denied Him thrice. St. John fled from Gethsemane, and so avoided the sin of denial. You would be right to flee. But I believe you cannot, for a scullion tells me that the city walls are guarded to keep you in."

"They may be guarded, but they will not keep me in. The men of Cahors could not keep me out," Thomas answered stoutly. Now that it had come to open warfare he felt gay and clearheaded. "Let us question my cross-bearer. Herbert has been wandering through the streets to test the sentiments of the people."

Herbert was cheerful. It was all over the town that the King had given strict orders to respect the Archbishop's sanctuary. The burgess militia would enforce the order, or send warning at once if zealous knights tried to curry favor with their lord by disregarding it. A discreet innkeeper had hired him another horse to take the place of that abandoned in the castle, and the charger was fit for a journey. As for the guarding of the town gates, that was the King's command, which must be obeyed; but quite by chance the captain of the town watch had encountered this monk whom he recognized as the Archbishop's clerk. "He told me that there had been a regrettable muddle at the north gate. As a rule the Castellan finds sentries for it from his garrison; tonight, with the King to guard, he relied on the burgesses. But the captain forgot to muster enough men to guard it. It will remain unguarded until dawn. The captain was very worried about it. He hoped his negligence would not bring harm to your lordship."

"I see," said Thomas. "The burgesses of Northampton are loyal to the King. But, to a burgess, peace and good order are the most important blessings. Even my warlike fellow citizens in London might leave a gate unguarded if they were sure the disturber of the peace would use it to leave, not to enter. But we must not expose the Priory to the King's vengeance. Let us see if we can hit on a plan."

When the Archbishop requested that his bed might be set up in the chapel, so that he might hear the midnight office though he was too exhausted to join in it, his wish was of course granted. The bed was placed behind the High Altar, hidden from the monks in choir, and he could get to it most easily through the vestry door. But if he did not mind the discomfort no one else could complain. Not until the sacristan went to light the candles for the Morrow Mass soon after dawn was it discovered that the Archbishop had left his bed during the night. It was probable that he had left the town also, but on account of that unfortunate muddle about the north gate no one could be sure. Of course no one could be blamed.

CHAPTER IX

The Challenge

IN high spirits the Bishop of Chichester lounged by the fire. But as the other members of the delegation entered the luxurious anteroom he held himself straight and dignified, and greeted them with a slightly patronizing smile. Though he had never before visited the city of Sens he was a veteran of the Curia; already he felt at home in the busy, intriguing, crowded bishop's palace which at the moment sheltered the exiled Pope.

The lay magnates of the delegation seemed pleased to see him; they returned his smile politely, and allowed him to keep his place at the end of the room, with his back to the great hooded fireplace, where he automatically assumed the position of chairman. But a few minutes later the Bishops of London and Worcester, entering together, greeted him more coldly. He had raced through his Mass, to be first in the room where he might take this position of pre-eminence; the lay lords accorded it to him without a thought, for they must have a clerk for spokesman and they did not care which clerk. But Gilbert of London was a strict monk, and Roger of Worcester a royal official who carried out his duties with dignity and care. They had said their Masses slowly and carefully, to make a good beginning to such an important day. Now they regarded the Bishop of Chichester with a slight shadow of contempt, as a worldly and lukewarm shepherd. Hilary began to feel nervous.

This was his great chance to win the King's favor; he was determined to push himself into the position of spokesman for the whole delegation. He began to murmur, as though musing to himself, but loud enough for the whole group to hear: "Thomas of London is certainly our Archbishop, by canon law and the law of England. We do not plead that he is not Archbishop of Canterbury, or lay any complaint for which there is a legal remedy. We ask His Holiness to do us a favor, to do a favor to King Henry, the most powerful king in Christendom, to do a favor to his realm, the Dowry of Mary, a land pre-eminent in fidelity to Rome and completely unspotted by heresy. We seek a friendly arrangement by which Thomas is translated to some titular see, and given responsible work in the Curia if that is necessary to save his dignity. He might even be made a cardinal . . . Oh, was I talking aloud? I hope you agree with me?"

"Certainly we must ask a favor. There is no point of law we can call on," Bishop Gilbert said firmly. "Is there any reason why the Pope should grant us this favor?"

"Perhaps no real reason, but he will be influenced by political factors in the world at large," continued Bishop Hilary.

He recalled with delight the days of his youth, when as a clerk of the Curia he had talked wisely with his fellows about political influences, and discovered devious reasons for the most straightforward papal decisions. "The Emperor lurks in the background, with his anti-Pope. Of course we shall never waver in our support of the true successor of St. Peter, but if you allow me to make the first speech I can work in a hint that our lord, whose rage is famous throughout Christendom, might be driven by anger to approach Victor IV."

"If he does, he won't stay King of England," the Count of Leicester broke in bluntly. "He has my homage in all things temporal, but that does not give him the right to lead me into schism. The magnates of England will agree with me."

"Oh, I am not suggesting that we should encourage the King to lead a schism. For all I know he himself would be horrified at the suggestion. But one must use against the Curia the weapons they expect to see used. That is an obvious point, and if we omit it the cardinals will think we are not really in earnest. If you will pardon what may sound like a boast, I know the Curia very well indeed, and you secular magnates do not." Hilary felt happier than ever before in his life. To the scandal of all Christendom a worldly clerk had been thrust into the greatest see in England; now that cunning and ambitious lawyer was about to be thwarted by the simple eloquence of one of his suffragans.

That made all the more stunning the blow delivered by the Bishop of Worcester, who now cleared his throat and spoke formally to the whole group.

"Have I been summoned to a conference under the presidency of my brother of Chichester, to discuss our strategy before the Curia? If so, the summons must have gone astray. But since we are all gathered here for breakfast, and the talk is now of our plans, I must make plain one awkward but undeniable fact. His Holiness feels a strong personal dislike for my brother Hilary. If we wish our petition to succeed he should remain in the background, and silent."

Six months ago Bishop Roger had been a distinguished member of the royal administration, and he had not yet lost the habit of plain speaking in private without which no civil servant can get through his work. No one else would have put it quite so crudely, but when it had been said the other clerks present could only agree. Pope Alexander and Bishop Hilary had been clerks together in the Curia of Pope Adrian, and it was notorious that they had been on bad terms.

"There is the further point," Bishop Roger continued, disregarding the stir caused by his plain speaking, "that our lord Thomas, when he was Archdeacon, frequently argued before the Curia, and that he also is personally known to His Holiness. But the Pope likes and admires him, as a man and a lawyer. Luckily we are laying our complaint in his absence, but we don't want to remind the Pope of old friendships and dislikes. Our spokesman should be a learned lawyer, famous for sanctity, but personally a stranger to the Curia. I don't mean myself. I have never practiced in the Church courts. I mean my brother of London, who has the further advantage that he was reared in holy Cluny. His Holiness is notoriously well disposed toward Cluniacs."

Bishop Gilbert had been thinking along the same lines; though wondering, under the promptings of his alert and well-trained conscience, whether the thought was the offspring of unworthy ambition. But it was necessary that this quarrelsome and shifty Archbishop be removed. At Clarendon the man had agreed to everything. Now he jibbed at the inevitable consequence of his surrender, in a hysterical manner that might bring the whole English Church into contempt. To effect his removal was the duty of the speaker best fitted for the delicate task; to hang back now would not be modesty, it would be shirking a responsibility. When the Count of Leicester turned to him in inquiry he answered with a gesture of assent, and at once fell to composing in his mind the speech which would bring peace to England.

The disappointed Hilary was too well trained in self-control to sulk. He abandoned the commanding position before the fire which made him seem head of the delegation, and with a sigh and a shrug drifted over to a group of lay magnates who sat quietly talking French in a corner.

(For the bishops had spoken Latin, the unambiguous language which left no room for misunderstanding. The laymen, like all other eminent men accustomed to attending important conferences, could understand it, though themselves they used the shifting nuances of their mother tongue.)

Hilary was annoyed to hear his new companions discussing the exploits of that tiresome Archbishop, almost as though he were a hero whom chivalrous knights should admire. Or rather, the Justiciar, Richard de Lucy, was trying to relate the story of Thomas's journey from England to the Ile de France, while others chipped in to interrupt him with tendentious and untrustworthy anecdotes, mere rumor put about by the enemies of King Henry.

"They say the gates of Northampton opened of themselves when he approached." . . . "Rot, the portreeve left them open on purpose, fearing disturbance in the town if we arrested the Archbishop." . . . "Anyway, he rode openly from Northampton to Lincoln." . . . "He left Lincoln in the cowl of a canon of Sempringham. Probably some angel closed the eyes of the King's servants, for no one recognized him on his journey." . . . "Rot again. The King had given orders for his arrest, but we all knew they were not to be taken seriously. This is the best solution. He has left the country of his own accord, and we won't let him in again in a hurry." . . . "Of course no one recognized Thomas of Cheapside in a Gilbertine cowl. Do you remember how he used to dress? Scarlet slippers, and ermine wherever he could stick it on his mantle." . . . "Thomas of Cheapside is too grand a title for him. His father was a merchant named Becket." . . . "Thomas Becket then, if you want to be insulting. Anyway, he wore this Gilbertine cowl, and no one recognized him. That bit is perfectly true. Of course when he reached a monastery and said who he was, the monks passed him on. All clerks stick together against the King." . . . "Thomas is their lord. You can't blame them for being true to their oath. I hope my vassals would follow me against the King." . . . "Which reminds me, Richard. Haven't you done homage to the Archbishop? Aren't you by rights his man?"

"So I am," said the Justiciar, in confusion. "Lucky you reminded me. So far I have done nothing against him, and when next we meet I shall formally sever relations with him. Then I can hold my Canterbury fief in his despite, defying him to seize it from me."

"And a lot he can do against you, stuck in the Ile de France."

"All the same, that is my legal right," continued the Justiciar. "If I defy him, and hold my fief against him, no one may call me recreant. However, to go on with the story. He persuaded the pirates of his own town of Sandwich to ferry him over to Flanders."

"He got across in a little nutshell of a boat, rowed by two men." . . . "But if the two men came from Sandwich they were pirates. They are all pirates. If you doubt me, ask the men of Rye." . . . "Anyway, he landed on the dunes of Flanders, still dressed in his cowl. That was a risky step. The Count of Flanders is after his blood, because of that old grudge about the marriage of his brother." . . . "He had no choice. Where else could he land? From Normandy to Navarre the whole coast owes obedience to our King Henry."

"Never mind," continued the Justiciar, struggling against these interruptions. "Our King Henry rules from the Pyrenees to the Cheviots, and the Count of Flanders rules from the Rhine to the Somme. But Archbishop Thomas may travel unmolested through their lands, because vassals forsake their lords to serve him. He was recognized again and again, but no one reported him to the viscounts. We must bear that in mind as we lay our plans. The Pope can subdue him, or we may come to some friendly arrangement to keep him out of the realm; but kings and counts cannot suppress a bishop if the people support him."

"What are these stories about his being recognized?" asked Hilary, hoping they would prove mere unfounded gossip.

"There are two in particular, which I believe myself," answered the Justiciar. "They are not the kind of thing people invent to prove the holiness of a persecuted confessor, and in fact they don't show him in an especially good light. That's why I think they are true. Once he arrived at the hut of a poor fisherman, and begged a share of his supper. He was on foot, with a few companions, all disguised as monks. The worthy fisherman handed over his pot of fish stew before any of the family had tasted it, hoping the monks would leave enough when they had finished. But when the leading monk had eaten he told a companion to give the pot to a beggar who happened to be passing. Then the hungry fisherman knew he had entertained a great man in disguise, a great man who always sent the leavings of his meal to the poor at the gate. After that it was easy. He knew that the Archbishop of Canterbury is one of the tallest men in the world, and that he was hiding from his enemies. But he did not tell his count, though he might have received a rich reward. Yes, the poor always sympathize with a bishop in distress."

"Poor fishermen may be against us, but I can't see that really matters," said Bishop Hilary. "All the poor fishermen in Christendom could do us no harm."

"Maybe, though that is not a thing to say in the anteroom of the Curia," said John of Oxford, a clerk in the King's service. "His Holiness might remember that he is the successor of a poor fisherman. The Curia is already too much inclined to help the poor against the powerful, without inquiring into the merits of the case."

"Perhaps fishermen don't matter," continued the Justiciar. "But my next story concerns a knight, a man of honor who would normally keep faith with his lord. This Flemish knight rode out with his hawk, and met a party of monks on foot. It seems that in Flanders monks walk on a journey, instead of riding, as with us. He took no notice of them until he saw their leader looking hard at his hawk. She had damaged a pinion, which he had mended after a new German fashion. As he rode on he thought it odd that a choir-monk should be interested in hawks' pinions, since even in the laxest communities the brethren never go hawking. Then he recalled the enormous height of the strange monk, and something chivalrous in his bearing. He put two and two together. The story goes that he rode after the party, to inquire if the leader was the missing Archbishop. A clerk put him off with some joke about the splendid state and gorgeous raiment affected by the Archbishop of Canterbury, adding that he was not in the habit of plodding through sand dunes on foot. But since he carefully avoided saying who they were, the knight was all the more certain he had stumbled on the famous fugitive. Yet he kept quiet about his discovery until the party was safely out of the district. It's not only the poor who support Thomas. Decent knights of the countryside favor him, even though they must break faith with their lords."

"That is unfortunate," admitted the resilient Bishop of Chichester, who could not keep silent even after a devastating snub. "But if we handle them rightly we can turn these stories against our Thomas. The first shows him absurdly pompous, forgetful of his duty to his host and of the welfare of the poor;

the second will remind anyone who has forgotten it that he is more of a sportsman than an archbishop."

"None the less we have a difficult task," muttered a frivolous young knight. "We must persuade the Pope, and the whole College of Cardinals, that Thomas is a bad Archbishop; and in fact he is a damn' good one."

Hilary admitted to himself, though he said nothing publicly, that their task was difficult indeed. It seemed that even the members of the delegation sent to demand his dismissal secretly admired him.

When at length the learned and holy Bishop of London opened the plaint of all the responsible clerks and lay magnates of the realm of England against their troublesome Primate, Hilary saw from the start that he was making a hash of a strong case. They should have left this speech to the most experienced curial advocate, even if the Pope was most unfairly prejudiced against him; instead of allotting it to a rash and opinionated prelate who never bothered to conceal his feelings or to conciliate the prepossessions of the bench. Gilbert began by suggesting that Thomas's election to Canterbury must have been tainted with simony, since it had been procured by pressure from the King. He was probably the only man in that crowded hall who forgot that the appointment had been welcomed with delight by Pope Alexander himself, whom he now accused by implication of condoning simony. He went on to accuse Thomas of private immorality, playing on the two meanings of the Latin word *luxuria,* which can signify either luxury or lust. Thomas was known all over Christendom for two things: he was the tallest bishop in the world, and at forty-six he was still a virgin; the accusation was so absurd that it must weaken his stronger arguments.

Finally Gilbert reached the genuine complaint against Thomas, the point on which the lawyers among the delegation had pinned their hopes. The Archbishop of Canterbury had left his see by stealth, neglecting his flock and throwing the English Church into great confusion. There was no reason for his flight, since no one menaced him (though a monetary penalty had been adjudged against him for a flagrant breach of feudal law). That he had left secretly was evidence of malice. He had not waited to see whether the King would give him leave to go; he was parading himself as a persecuted confessor while no one sought to harm him. Gilbert wound up with a neat peroration: "The wicked flee when no man pursueth."

The cardinals listened attentively; they were connoisseurs of rhetoric, they had never before heard Gilbert of London, and he was speaking very well. But now the Pope himself interrupted.

"Deal gently, my brother of London," he said with deceptive mildness.

"Since Your Holiness commands it, I shall deal gently with Thomas of Canterbury," answered Gilbert, too busy thinking of what he should say next to notice the reaction of his audience.

"I do not ask you to deal gently with the Archbishop. I ask you to deal gently with your own case, which is damaged by your violence," said the Pope, with a sardonic smile that would have frightened a more self-possessed advocate than Gilbert.

The effect was devastating. The unfortunate Bishop of London stammered and made ineffectual gestures with both hands; then, torn by hiccups and remorse, he begged to be excused from further speech.

At once Bishop Hilary came forward to fill the gap. He had no speech prepared, because of the disgraceful way in which Bishop Gilbert had silenced him that morning; but that made all the sweeter his task of showing a silly old monk how a trained veteran addressed the Curia. He got off to a flying start before the cardinals had shifted on their bench to face him;

and he flattered himself on his good sense in sticking to points where Thomas had been genuinely at fault, without inventing unfounded and incredible accusations against his private life. He need not dwell on the unnecessary flight from England, for Gilbert had already dealt with it; but it was only right, in fact it was his duty, to point out that Thomas seldom consulted his suffragans, the constitutional advisers who should have formed his Council.

Hilary knew what he wanted to say; it was forming in his head while he spoke, without preparation. When he got it out Thomas would be crushed unanswerably. But it was unfortunate that he had spent the morning listening to lay magnates talking French, for now he found himself thinking in that tongue and translating in his head as he went along. It was years since he had addressed the Curia. Once or twice he hesitated, trying to remember the correct termination of some unusual word; but his hesitation only made the speech sound the more earnest.

Now he was thundering along splendidly. When Thomas arrived he would find the Curia with its mind made up, and made up against him. But really this switching from French to Latin was most exhausting, and he had not yet recovered from that horrible Channel crossing. How should it go? The Archbishop's Council should never have allowed him to behave as he did; they *ought* to have advised him better. *"Oportuebant,"* he shouted, to stop in dismay at the gale of laughter which swept the bench.

"Your ship seeks the wrong *port*," shouted a cardinal through the uproar, while all his colleagues slapped their thighs and dug their neighbors in the ribs. The Count of Leicester was extremely puzzled. He had been following the speech with careful attention, for he knew the meaning of most Latin words, though he had never bothered his head with the complicated rules of grammer. It seemed to him that Bishop Hilary had been putting the magnates' case very fairly, with none of the venom shown by Gilbert of London; but someone seemed to have made a joke which he had not heard.

"What are they laughing at?" he inquired of his neighbor, Master John of Oxford.

Master John answered readily, under cover of the noise which still filled the courtroom. "Hilary's grammer is too much for them, as it is too much for me. How can I explain in French? Let me see. '*Oportet*' means 'It ought to be,' and you must never conjugate it. Hilary said '*Oportuebant*,' a word that cannot exist; as though in French you said 'They used to ought.' It's not very funny in itself. But to think of it coming from Hilary of Chichester, the eminent canonist, the veteran advocate, the proud scholar specially appointed by the Pope to bring a little learning to rustic Sussex . . ."

"Does a mere slip of the tongue matter as much as that?" the Count of Leicester persisted.

"It depends on who makes it, and when. Look at the pompous old windbag. These cardinals live dull lives, and they haven't had such a good laugh for years. . . . To think that the spokesman of the King of England can't string together two sentences of correct Latin! . . . Hallo, our Hilary has had enough. He's off. What do we do next? Our first spokesman was silenced by the personal intervention of the Holy Father, and our second string has forgotten his Latin. Who now volunteers to make a fool of himself in public?"

"I do," said the Count of Leicester calmly, stepping forward as the blushing Hilary made for the door. The interests of his lord King Henry demanded that some other magnate should continue the complaint. In study Anglo-French, stuffed with obsolete words and archaic pronunciations, he began to explain the black treason of the Archbishop.

The court heard him patiently, though he spoke through a constant mutter of conversation, as French-speaking clerks translated to the Italian cardinals. When he had told the Pope, in brief soldierly words, that the magnates and tenants-in-chief of England unanimously pronounced Thomas to be a traitor, he stopped. His Holiness graciously thanked him for his assistance; but he explained that the court must hear the Archbishop's defense before sentence could be pronounced. That was the signal for adjournment, and the English delegation returned to the anteroom where they had breakfasted.

It was all up with their appeal, as the lawyers among them at once explained to the lay magnates. When the Pope spoke of hearing the Archbishop's defense he was treating the case as a trial at law, and legally they had not a leg to stand on. They had sought a favor, the removal of an obstreperous primate; His Holiness had not refused outright, but his reply was a polite way of indicating that Thomas had done nothing contrary to canon law. The clerks added that they would like to start for home at once, before the Archbishop reached Sens; it would be irksome if the lord to whom they had sworn obedience found them here, advocates for his enemy King Henry. That was an argument every vassal could understand, and the English delegation left Sens after dinner on that same day.

A few days later the Roman Curia sat once more in state. But in the supreme court of Christendom there was now a more friendly and informal atmosphere; the holy and persecuted Archbishop of Canterbury was received as a friend rather than a suitor; descending from his throne the Pope embraced him, and engaged him in private conversation. But there were legal-minded clerks who had noted the point made by the Bishop of London, that the last election to the See of Canterbury had been achieved irregularly, by royal pressure. You did not often get such an admission from the representative of the King who had brought it about, and a valuable precedent should not be wasted. It was a neat little score, which appealed to the legal mind of the Archbishop himself as soon as he was apprised of it. To drive it home, and to forge another weapon for the armory of St. Peter, Thomas formally resigned his see into the hands of the Pope, by the tender of his episcopal ring. The Pope solemnly replaced it on his finger, making Thomas of London Archbishop of Canterbury by the direct appointment of the Vicar of Christ. He held by the strongest title in the world, and henceforth no one could challenge his position.

On a fine April morning in the year 1166 the spring sun, shining on the Cistercian Abbey of Pontigny, lightened even the gloom of Lent; though Lent in a well-ordered monastery is rather sad than gloomy, since religious spirits rise at the approach of God's greatest victory on earth. In a fortnight the monks would be celebrating the most joyous feast of the year.

But in the principal guest chamber the round of liturgical mourning and rejoicing made no difference to a routine that had scarcely varied in eighteen months. At a desk under the narrow window the Archbishop of Canterbury sat writing in the morning sun, as he had written by the light of tall wax candles even before the dawn. Save when he dined at the Abbot's table, or joined the brethren in choir, Thomas was always to be found at his desk; he took no exercise, and since Christmas he had not left the enclosure.

He was dreadfully bored, after what had seemed the longest year of his life. He also felt ill, a new experience. In consequence his anger glowed within him, and he could scarcely behave with the outward charity demanded by his position. Now he sat nibbling the end of his pen, and brooding over the wickedness of King Henry, who had once been his friend.

Henry's nerves must be in a shocking state. It was the only excuse for his petty vindictiveness. Thomas recalled with a shudder that miserable episode last year, the arrival of his exiled supporters. Four hundred decent men and women, including the two sisters he had not met since he became Chancellor, all turned out of England penniless and landless, under oath to seek him out and show him the full extent of their misery. Only a man whose soul was sick would display such pitiful spite.

Henry must have felt even worse when the exiles received safe harborage, amid the sympathy of all Europe. Sicily was ruled by exiles driven forth by the wrath of past dukes of Normandy, and there all Norman exiles were sure of a welcome. Perhaps they were better off than they had been in England. Certainly their sufferings had not tempted the Archbishop to yield.

But it was time, for Henry's sake, that this horrid quarrel was ended. He had been a good king, and if only he would admit himself beaten he might become the best king in the world. It was time to press him, now that the Pope had restored full authority to the exiled Archbishop. In a fortnight, at Easter, he would be free to excommunicate his oppressors. He had a long list of them.

First must come the Broc family of Saltwood castle, the scoundrels who at present farmed the lands of Canterbury as escheators on behalf of the King. That in itself was evidence of malign rancor; Henry was entitled to the lands of a fugitive archbishop, but he could have appointed honest custodians who would have collected the income while holding the fiefs intact for the Church; the Brocs were notorious ruffians, who had already begun to intrude their disreputable friends into the monastic community at Christ Church.

Those who plundered his faithful followers must also incur the ban. He need mention no names, for the cap would fit one man in particular. Bishop Gilbert of London administered all benefices declared vacant because their holders had adhered to the Archbishop. Thomas felt a spasm of anger at thought of the harm done by that envious clerk. If the Brocs did not rob the Church of Canterbury they would rob someone else, and when they came to die their only hope would be the Mercy of God. But Gilbert Foliot was a learned bishop of exemplary private life, a worthy son of the zealous Abbey of Cluny; he should have been his Archbishop's right-hand man. He had been seduced into opposition by nothing but envy, the envy of a first-class mind for the genius which put his own talent in the shade; his was the sin of Lucifer, the sin of ambition.

As he sat hunched over his desk, composing political manifestos with the surface of his mind while its depths worried over the question of excommunicating his old friend, Thomas shivered with the unnatural cold which perpetually tormented him, and a sharp pain stabbed at the ulcer in his stomach. In his own chamber he wore the black gown of an Augustinian canon over the long tunic which was the informal dress of his rank, and over that a Cistercian cowl which the Pope had sent him with a special pontifical blessing; it was thrice the clothing of an ordinary man, and underneath were the stiff folds of the hair shirt. He looked so bulky that stray visitors from England thought him grown fat in the idleness of exile; and still he shivered.

He shivered more violently when his thoughts returned to the question he could no longer avoid: should he excommunicate King Henry? There was good in Henry, if only he would control his temper; excommunication would render him reckless of consequences. He would die cut off from salvation, and unless saved by the uncovenanted Mercy of God he would go straight to Hell. Thomas could not pass such a sentence on the comrade with whom he had ridden against Toulouse, the boon companion of Cheapside, the ardent reformer who had been his colleague in bringing peace to England after the long wars.

When Herbert of Bosham brought his dinner he found the exhausted Archbishop asleep on his knees. But he brought news as well as food, and he did not scruple to wake him. The news was that King Henry lay dangerously ill in Normandy; tidings of his death were expected from every messenger. Thomas was relieved to find one question settled for him.

"I won't excommunicate a Christian on his deathbed," he said at once. "That would be to deprive him of the opportunity for repentance, to sentence him to Hell. You know, Herbert, I may yet persuade the King to be a good friend to God's Church and to me. He is a gallant warrior as well as a greedy lawyer, and he does not bear malice when a war is ended."

"That may be," answered the chaplain doubtfully. "I have never borne arms, and I don't know the ways of warriors. However, though he is sick unto death, his servants persevere in his cause. His followers among the clergy have drawn up an appeal against the exercise of your legatine powers, and they plan to serve you with notice of this appeal before you have time to excommunicate anybody."

"Until my legatine power has been restored their petition will be invalid," pointed out Thomas the lawyer.

"They are aware of that. They are also aware that your powers will be restored, and soon; for the Pope makes no secret of it. This is what will happen. In Rome, on Easter Day, the Pope will seal your letter of appointment, and despatch it by messenger. The King's men will watch the roads, but they will not hinder the messenger. As soon as he arrives the King's messenger will follow, to serve on you notice that Henry appeals against any sentence you pass as Legate. Then he and his followers may disregard your excommunication until their appeal is heard before the Roman Curia."

"Aha, they quibble over legal forms with *me*, who have been Archdeacon of Canterbury and advocate before the Curia!"

Thomas stood erect, hand on hip, in his eye the eager look of a jouster accepting the challenge. Herbert was delighted at

the change in his lord, whom he had found on his knees in the
lassitude of boredom. The cause of the Church must be safe in
the hands of such a warrior.

"On the feast you will see me in Vezelay, where I shall pronounce sentence in due form. But in the meantime I shall go
on pilgrimage to a holy shrine where Henry's messengers will
not look for me."

In an aisle of the Cathedral of Soissons stood a small shrine,
poorly ornamented and seldom visited by the clergy. But there
were usually a few supplicants before it, and a curious collection of votive offerings hung on a neighboring pillar. All the
chivalry of France knew that if a knight must face his accuser
in mortal duel, to prove by victory his innocence of a charge of
felony, he would be well advised to pass the night before the
encounter at the shrine of St. Drausius.

On the 8th of June 1166, the Wednesday before Pentecost,
a very tall clerk slipped quietly into the cathedral and approached the shrine. Thomas did not pray for victory. There
was no need to pray for it, since he could not be defeated. The
Pope holds the keys of Heaven and Hell, and the Pope had
delegated certain powers to his Legate the Archbishop of
Canterbury. Henry could not turn aside the bolts launched at
him by due authority; whatever was bound at Vezelay would
be bound in Heaven.

He prayed that his dear friend Henry would recognize defeat, and accept it in the spirit in which a good knight accepted
his overthrow by a better: St. Drausius, save my dear friend
Henry; lead him to acknowledge his own weakness; show him
that he is vanquished before the joust begins; bring him once
more into the peace of God, and into true friendship with all
Christian men!

After a night of prayer the Archbishop of Canterbury
mounted his horse. In two days he rode ninety miles to Vezelay,

the crowded shrine where lay the relics of St. Mary Magdalene. There, on the Day of Pentecost, the 12th of June 1166, he excommunicated first Ranulf de Broc, the despoiler of the lands of Canterbury, then John of Oxford and Richard of Ilchester, the royal clerks who had waited on the Emperor at Wurzburg and there taken a schismatic oath of obedience to the anti-Pope, then the Bishop of Salisbury who had given preferment to John of Oxford, and finally "those who enjoy the benefices unjustly taken from my adherents," which the whole world knew to mean the Bishop of London. But of King Henry, lying sick and in danger of death, he said nothing either good or evil.

CHAPTER X

The Lists Are Set

IN December 1167 King Henry, restored to perfect health, lay at the castle of Gisors, on the Norman border of the ever-disputed Vexin. It was hoped that an interview might be arranged with King Louis of France, and that at this private meeting between the two kings an agreement could be drawn up to regulate the position of the border castles, the dowry of the lady Margaret of France, married to the heir of England. It was in those days the fashion to hope that a personal inter- view between lifelong enemies would settle questions which had baffled professional diplomatists trained in negotiation, and public opinion was eager for this meeting.

King Henry was indifferent. He did not fear King Louis, and he did not desire a settled peace; ever since he could re- member the French King had been the rival and foe of the

House of Anjou. But a few years' truce would be convenient, and there would be no harm in another treaty about the Vexin. It would be broken as soon as it was sealed, but then it might be possible to show the French as the aggressors; and the few square miles of harried borderland were not worth a full-scale war.

King Henry was far too busy governing his dominions to have time for the ceremonious state more frivolous kings employed every day. But he enjoyed a rare formal occasion, if he had plenty of warning to prepare for it and knew it would not continue too long. He was a magnificent horseman, not yet too fat to look well in the sumptuous robes which were among the treasures of his Wardrobe; he spent freely on jewels and golden ornaments, knowing that in an emergency they could quickly be turned back into money; and he flattered himself that the force of his character would wring a profitable agreement out of the gentle and well-mannered King Louis; though of course the counselors of the French King would break it or repudiate it as soon as was convenient. In this solemn interview he would cut a good figure, and he might pick up some useful private information. He looked forward to the grand occasion.

But he had just learned of another approaching interview, which would be much less enjoyable; and he was giving a private display of the famous Angevin rage as he discussed it with his counselors. Now that he was thirty-three years of age the anger which had seemed mere high spirits in a ruler of twenty-one was beginning to appear childish in the bad sense. His sandy hair had grown very thin on top and his ruddy cheeks were seamed with purple veins. He sat with his advisers at the high table in Gisors castle, withdrawn into privacy by the buzz of conversation from the body of the hall; as his big chapped hands twisted a broken spur he pricked a chilblain, and swore vividly.

He turned the oath into a complaint about the matter in hand, and continued his address to his most intimate advisers.

"Cardinals! What the devil have I to say to two cardinals! Let them stay at home and manage the Roman Church, until the Emperor marches and once more they take to flight. If they come only to inspect the Church in Normandy, to compel those loose-living parish priests to put away their concubines, let them get on with it. Why should they bother me? I will never crawl to Thomas Becket of Cheapside, and the Pope won't translate the confounded rebel to some titular see where he would have no subjects to misrule. So the dispute will endure until one of us dies. I suppose Thomas will die first, since he is many years my senior. I've a damned good mind to tell these cardinals to go away and convert the Saracens. Why must I waste time on them?"

The Justiciar and the Archbishop of Rouen sighed together. They must always endure this drip of whining complaint before they could persuade the King to deal with any matter that displeased him; and it did not really make things easier that, when Henry had at length been persuaded to deal with the facts as they were, his plans were usually practical and ingenious.

"Nevertheless, you must meet these cardinals, my lord," the Archbishop said firmly. "They have taken a whole year to reach you, dodging I don't know how many Ghibelline bands before they could get over the Alps. Their pains prove that the mission is important. And their proposals may even turn out to be useful. Cardinal William of Pavia is an opponent of that stubborn Archbishop; they say that before he left Rome he was already convinced that Thomas is in the wrong."

"But Cardinal Otho set out convinced that no archbishop can do wrong. That's typical of the way the Curia muddles everything it undertakes. Fancy sending on an embassy two men of opposite views, without a third envoy to be arbiter! The Pope deserves to be chased out of Rome again. I bet he is, too, within the year."

"Yes, yes, my lord, it is a poorly chosen delegation," said the Justiciar, who took less trouble than the Archbishop to soothe his King. Richard de Lucy was a great magnate in his own right, who did not care if he was dismissed from his laborious office; and he was very tired of this particular subject. "But Cardinal William is on our side, remember. The other point is that they have already met Thomas. They wouldn't bother to come here unless they had some feasible proposition to offer, and they must have gained his consent to it when they met him at Sens."

"I'm tired of the whole affair!" The King bent the spur in his hands until it snapped, and threw it pettishly on the table. He picked up a little silver salt cellar in the form of a dolphin, and began to straighten the tail; he could not sit still unless he had a piece of work to occupy his rough nail-bitten hands. "If I could have a talk with Pope Alexander himself we would settle the matter in a day. He's a sensible man who knows where his money comes from, now that the Empire is in schism and all Italy a battleground. But I know Thomas through and through. I know that if a settlement waits on his consent then the dispute will never be settled. He can't bring matters to a head, excommunicate me in form and incite my vassals to rebellion; because the Pope won't let him. But the Pope won't suppress him either. There it is. I see no end. And I don't care in the slightest." He glared defiantly at his advisers.

"All the same, my lord," replied the Archbishop of Rouen, "If the dispute continues the Church in England will get into an awkward tangle. Even the holiest bishops sometimes disagree with their brethren, for example about the boundaries of their sees or the exemption of religious houses; and the less holy ones quarrel constantly over money. As we sit here the Abbot of St. Augustine's in Canterbury is claiming exemption from the control of his metropolitan; the Bishop of London, most unwisely in my opinion, is preparing a plea in Rome to get himself declared the third Archbishop in England; there is a serious quarrel between the Bishop of Hereford and an abbey within his jurisdiction; and in Wales the whole organization of the Church is at the point of collapse. These are all matters that can be settled only by the Archbishop of Canterbury. If you keep him out of your realm for many more years you will have no Church, only a collection of quarreling clerks out of communion with one another and refusing obedience to any superior at all."

"What maddens me is that we never get on with the quarrel," put in Lucy. "Look at what happened eighteen months ago! When the Archbishop pronounced all those excommunications at Vezelay we seemed to be going somewhere, even if it was in the wrong direction. But within less than six months the Pope had withdrawn his legatine commission, forbidden him to excommunicate anyone else, and remitted the sentences of Vezelay. We are back where we were two years ago. It isn't as though the Pope would silence Thomas for good. Now and again the Archbishop gets back his powers; then he excommunicates his enemies; then the Pope takes away his powers once more and pardons everyone he has banned. Thomas can't win that way, but he never sees that he is losing; for he blames every setback on halfhearted support from the Pope, who should be his leader."

"He has taken a few knocks, all the same," said the King, putting down the salt and rubbing his hands in satisfaction. "I drove him from his snug quarters in Pontigny. That made the whole Order of Citeaux look very foolish. It probably caused Thomas himself as much grief as the sufferings of his English adherents. All Christendom sees that the arm of the King of England reaches far."

"In all those things, my lord, your actions weakened your cause," said the Justiciar firmly. Ignoring the red flush on the King's neck, and the spasmodic working of his fingers, he continued to point out past mistakes with a smug air of reason.

"When you exiled the Beckets you gave those confounded land-pirates in Sicily a chance to flaunt their independence of their natural lord, the Duke of Normandy, who should be head of the Norman race wherever it happens to rule; and the Beckets are probably better off now than they were in England. Your threats against the Cistercians made enemies of the most eloquent preachers in Christendom, who have said some very nasty things about you in every pulpit from Hamburg to Lisbon. And Thomas himself, who used to be a true Norman, is now the pensioner of France. It's true that the Pope remitted the sentences of Vezelay; but he went out of his way to proclaim that he considered them lawful and just, and that he remitted them only by his clemency. As a result the Bishop of London, the most useful of your English supporters, is suffering from a disturbed conscience. His mind tells him Thomas is wrong, but his heart tells him a persecuted confessor may very well be right. You should leave Thomas to make his own mistakes, disgusting public opinion by his unappeasable rancor. Every time you try to harm him you harm yourself instead."

That ended the conversation, which had been the aim of the bored Justiciar. King Henry rose, his hands clawing the air; then, foaming at the mouth, he subsided to the floor and scrabbled among the rushes. Servants came running to escort their lord to his chamber, but the diners in the body of the hall scarcely looked up from their flagons. It was only another of the King's tantrums, they decided; probably someone had been reminding him of the Archbishop of Canterbury.

That same evening the cardinals deputed by the Pope to make peace between King and Archbishop reached Gisors from Sens. Nobody told them that the Justiciar's impish teasing had put the King in a worse rage than had ever been seen. They asked for a private interview in the morning. That interview was so private that no one among the courtiers ever learned what had passed; but when the cardinals emerged the King, very red in the face, escorted them to the outer gate in stony silence. As he turned away he shouted, so loud that even the sentry on the drawbridge overheard: "I hope to God I never set eyes on another cardinal!"

It was presumed that the cardinals' mission had ended in failure.

The next year, 1168, passed in stalemate. Thomas continued to be the guest of King Louis in the royal Abbey of St. Colombe at Sens. King Henry remained in his continental dominions, riding like a hurricane from Bayeux to Bordeaux, bringing order to lawless Poitou, and showing the magnates of Aquitaine that their hereditary Duchess could not protect them from the wrath of her husband. Men were beginning to forget the beautiful and indiscreet Queen Eleanor; King Henry kept her in seclusion that was almost imprisonment, and nowadays she seldom took her rightful place at court. The spiteful said it was the only way to treat a light woman, if you had been so greedy as to marry one for her fiefs; a piece of gossip which reached Henry as it was meant to do, and did not mend his temper.

Pope Alexander was still eager for peace, and far more willing to compromise than was his supporter the Archbishop. To avoid an irreparable breach he forbade Thomas to inflict the penalty of excommunication on any of his subjects; though he promised that his powers would be restored next Easter. It was a warning that Henry must make peace while there was yet time.

King Louis of France was also earnestly seeking after peace. He had everything to gain by a continuance of trouble in England, but that had no influence on his chivalrous soul. He deplored the persecution of a holy archbishop; but he was himself a king, and he did not think too hardly of a king who took steps to punish a clerk who defied him. It seemed to him a great pity that two gallant knights who had once been companions in arms should be thus estranged. Surely if they met on their chargers in some fair meadow, as did the Paladins in the epics of chivalry, brotherly love would wake again in their stubborn hearts. With noble impracticability he set himself to bring about such a meeting, not bothering to negotiate preliminary terms of agreement.

Noble and impractical though the French King may have been, he was more desperately in earnest than any of the other peacemakers, and his energy was rewarded. The King of England agreed to meet his exiled Archbishop, at Montmirail in his County of Maine, on the Feast of the Epiphany.

The meeting would not be private, though since both would be mounted they might if they wished ride apart for private conversation. The King of France would be present, and the Pope had sent a commission of two learned lawyers as witnesses.

Thomas rode to the meeting with his little train of faithful clerks. Since there had been no preliminary negotiations he had no idea of what sort of terms would come from this interview; but he was beginning to see that the present situation could not continue indefinitely. His own clerks were eager for peace at any price.

They were the cream of the educated clergy of England; that was why they had been chosen for the household of the Archbishop. They were Normans, bred to the unswerving loyalty to an oath freely given which was the foundation of Norman honor; that was why they had followed him into exile, abandoning rich benefices into the greedy hands of the King. They would never desert their lord, but they expected their lord to heed the advice of his followers. If they, even they, thought it was time he tried to make friends with the King, it meant that in the opinion of all educated Christendom the quarrel had gone far enough.

Thomas himself had no plans for the meeting. He was desperately weary of the whole sordid argument, and troubled in his conscience lest pride had led him to refuse earlier offers of a reasonable settlement. He had seen for the last three years that the Pope, though he could not abandon his supporter, considered him too intransigent; there could be no other explanation of the long suspension of his power to excommunicate. King Louis, the most honorable knight in Christendom, also thought it was time to make peace. Hitherto he had discounted these opinions, because neither the Pope nor King Louis knew King Henry; they had never experienced his pettifogging insistence on the last ounce of his legal rights, or his atrocious wrath when he was thwarted. But these clerks, Herbert of Bosham, Henry of Houghton, and the rest, knew the King well; only he, Thomas, once his dearest friend, knew him better. It must be time to give in.

Yet how could he give in, and allow Henry to rule the Church in England? Henry was not a bad ruler. Certainly there was peace throughout his realm, for he allowed no rivals to oppress his people. But in financial matters he was quite unscrupulous; and his itch to interfere in the personal affairs of his vassals would lead him to invade the legitimate sphere of his bishops and parish priests. Besides, powers granted to Henry would be claimed by every succeeding King of England; young Henry fitzHenry was a brave child, with his mother's ambition added to his father's vigor; but no one could foretell what kind of men would succeed him.

A Church ruled by the temporal power would be a mere branch of the administration, its endowments misapplied to reward politicians, and its teaching edited to justify the personal failings of the ruler. Though the whole of Christendom were against him, and even the Pope lukewarm, Thomas knew that it must be his duty to stand firm.

The place appointed for the meeting was the usual grassy meadow, where great men might ride apart in private conversation while their secretaries and advisers conferred in a group. When Thomas arrived behind the tall metropolitan cross which was his ensign he saw already standing side by side the red flag bearing the golden leopards of Anjou which was the personal standard of King Henry, and the flag of Our Lady's blue sown with Her golden lilies which for ages past had been the standard of Christian France. The two Kings had taken this occasion for another discussion of the never-settled question of the Vexin border castles; a polite and exquisitely dressed chamberlain asked the Archbishop to wait until this first conference had been concluded.

Presently the two kings rode forward, clear of their advisers. Both were dressed in the full state of royalty, with thin golden circlets round their purple hoods and ermine mantles of sovereignty flowing over their saddles; they were mounted on warlike chargers, and Henry's in particular, fretted by the restless hands of his impatient rider, pranced and curvetted, his neck lathered by the reins. The stately war horses walked forward side by side, until all could see them; then their riders swung them apart and turned them face to face. They pricked their ears and pawed the ground, ready for the fight; but their riders restrained them, forcing them gently forward until they met and halted head to tail. It was a tricky business with a war horse, trained to fight with forelegs and teeth against hostile stallions. Thomas recognized with admiration the skill of the riders who kept them at peace.

The two kings dropped reins on the saddlebow, and simultaneously leaned from their saddles, each to his right; their arms came forward to rest on each other's shoulders, and for a moment the two purple hoods, each with its gleaming crown, touched and nestled side by side. Then they wheeled their horses apart, and returned self-consciously to the group they had left.

Ah, the Kiss of Peace, thought Thomas, recognizing a ceremony he had often heard described, though as it happened he had never seen it. It must mark the conclusion of an agreement, and therefore the time had come for his own interview. As he rode forward he recalled that to knights and warriors that ritual embrace was more binding than any sacrament. Enemies might seal a treaty and agree to live in peace; but only those who intended to be true friends would exchange the Kiss of Peace.

It was worth remembering, in these present negotiations. Henry would not commit open and cynical perjury, but he was so cunning at finding legal quibbles to justify his conduct that it would be dangerous to reply on any form of words, no matter how carefully composed, to safequard the rights of the Church. But if Henry would exchange the Kiss of Peace, Thomas might rely on an honest and friendly interpretation of even a vague formula.

Suddenly he was face to face with King Henry, his old comrade and commander in the exciting business of bringing peace to England, his companion in the hunt, his friend who had roistered with him in the taverns of Cheapside when the world was young. Of course King Louis had been right! Two such gallant knights had only to meet in a meadow and discuss their grievances, and they must ride away together, firm friends once again. In a transport of affection he slid from his high war saddle, to kneel before the King as a vassal kneels before his lord.

King Henry was equally affected. The Archbishop was after all good old Thomas of Cheapside, the gay companion who made fun of his shabby mantle and handled so efficiently the complicated affairs of the Chancery. Poor Thomas, exile did not suit him. He was blue with cold, as one might expect in a meadow in January; but he was also careworn, tired, and very thin under his usual mountain of thick clothes. He remembered his old friend's stubborn Norman pride, and knew that to kneel thus humbly in the mud was a remarkable demonstration of loyalty. He in turn jumped from his charger; he assisted the Archbishop to rise, and held his stirrup while he mounted. Only then did he mount his own horse, to ride beside him at a slow walk; until they were far enough from King Louis and the group of advisers to begin their private discussion.

"My dear Thomas," he began, "I am very sorry we have drifted into this foolish state of enmity. I am sure it was my fault, but you know how my rage overcomes me when once it is roused. Let us make a fresh start. You must come back to England as soon as you can. I shall chase out those rascally Brocs and restore to you the lands of Canterbury as they ought to be. You shall have the chief place in my Council, as is your right; and between us we'll shake up that pompous ass sitting under his lily banner. Really, that Louis! I don't know whether he is just tactless or deliberately malicious, but every time we meet he inquires after the welfare of my queen."

Thomas suppressed the smile that struggled to his lips. There was more wit in the gallant Louis than one might suppose.

"However, let's forget Louis for the moment," Henry continued. "The important thing is to get you back to England. There will always be disputes about the jurisdiction of Church and King. Even in my great-grandfather's time they occurred. But the Conqueror and Archbishop Lanfranc worked together, and because they were personal friends they got along without quarreling. You and I can do the same."

"Well, sheriffs and archdeacons are sure to squabble, because no one can prevent an occasional clash of jurisdictions," answered Thomas with a friendly smile. "But so long as we, their masters, remain on good terms the squabbles can easily be patched up. There are men all over England who claim to be clerks, though when they get into trouble they can produce no records of their ordination. How would it be if we drew up a comprehensive list, and tried to keep it up to date? Then each sheriff would have the names of all the clerks in his county, and he would know exactly who was to be handed over to the bishop's court. It sounds a big undertaking, but Domesday Book was a bigger. When I was at the Chancery we could have got out the lists in six months."

A frown gathered on Henry's forehead. But in a moment he smiled again, as he answered with forced friendliness. "My dear Thomas, surely you don't intend to go back on your solemn promise? At Clarendon you swore to observe the ancient customs of the realm. I am only guessing, but I believe you had direct orders to swear, orders from the Holy Father himself. Are you trying to be more papalist than the Pope?"

"Of course not. That would indeed be absurd," said Thomas, also stretching his mouth into a smile no deeper than his lips; already the first shock of pleasure, the delight of two old friends in meeting after long separation, was giving way in both of them to the wary fencing of the politician. "I still think it wrong and unchristian that clerks who have received the Sacrament of Holy Order should suffer the same punishment as ordinary criminals; though I admit some of them behave very wickedly, deserving stern punishment. But on that point I stand alone. As you say, the Pope disagrees with me, and I must bow to his decision. If in any particular case you think a clerk merits further punishment after I have done with him, I won't stand in your way, or even make a protest. I hope you won't do it too often, but that must be a matter of give and take. Far more serious is the privilege of free appeal to the Curia. You must see, my dear Henry, that if the Church is one, then all her members must be free to communicate with her Head."

"H'm, are they so free, even when kings don't interfere? Could a layman appeal to Rome over your head? If you can stop appeals because you consider them frivolous or scandalous, why shouldn't I prohibit them if I consider them a danger to my realm?"

"I don't stop them, I assure you, my dear Henry. Do you think Bishop Gilbert of London would appeal so often if he had to seek my permission first?"

"Oh, Gilbert! There's never any holding him, in questions of politics or questions of law. He knows better than anyone else, as he will tell you if you ask him. All the revenue of his see must go to the Roman lawyers, except the part you compel him to spend on traveling."

They both laughed happily, beginning to feel the ties of old association creeping back to bind them together. Bishop Gilbert was notorious for his tactics of appealing to Rome whenever a case was given against him; which delayed proceedings as only the Curia understood delay. In the end, when the case came to trial, he would submit to judgment without argument, having avoided for some years the enforcement of the original verdict. Last year Thomas, anxious to rebuke him for disloyalty to his metropolitan, had ordered him to report in person at Sens. Gilbert appealed against the order; though in the meantime he began his journey, as by canon law he was bound to do; for his well-trained conscience would not permit him openly to defy his superior. Then the Pope intervened by suspending Thomas's powers until Easter 1169; and Gilbert gladly returned to London, an adversary of the Archbishop whom he had sworn to obey; but not technically guilty of the sin of disobedience.

"Certainly, if Gilbert can remain your faithful subject, you and I can get along without quarreling," said Henry, completely friendly and at his ease. "Why don't we settle this matter here and now, with the King of France for witness? You have already sworn to keep the customs of the realm, so there is no need for you to swear again. That would look like an admission of defeat, when nobody has been defeated. If you just repeat the ordinary ceremony of homage, which you owe to me as lord of the lands of Canterbury, you may come home as soon as you are ready. You will receive your endowments in time for the spring plowing."

"And you won't enforce the letter of your customs, which are not the old customs I remember from my childhood?" asked Thomas, anxiously.

That was a mistake. In the last four years Henry's bad temper had come nearer the surface. He frowned, and made an effort to speak gently.

"Just do homage, that's all I ask. In other matters you have already sworn all that I require of you."

They rode back to the little group by the standards of France and England and the metropolitan cross of Canterbury. Thomas felt his mind in a turmoil. In legal affairs Henry was given to sharp practice, and there might be more in this oath of homage than appeared on the surface. Evidently Henry considered that when he had got his Archbishop back across the Channel he would be able to bend the Church to his will. It was better to play for safety. Luckily there were plenty of saving clauses to choose from; this question of the full implication of an oath demanded on the spur of the moment was one that arose frequently, since important negotiations were more often settled by an oath before witnesses than by a sealed agreement.

When the time came for Thomas to dismount and, kneeling, renew his homage to King Henry, his mind was made up. All the witnesses were intensely thrilled to see this famous quarrel composed before their eyes, and the Archbishop's clerks in particular were wild with excitement. In a few minutes their long exile would be ended; they could ride straight from Montmirail to their waiting benefices in England. Peace had come

after more than four years of struggle in which they had borne
an honorable part. At home they would be famous and revered,
the faithful companions who had shared the trials of a persecuted confessor. Thomas was not surprised to hear a groan of
dismay as he completed his homage by the addition of his saving clause.

". . . saving the Honor of God, and the rights of Holy
Church, and the rights of my order," he wound up defiantly,
his voice raised.

Startled by the sudden excitement of their riders, the horses
set up a jangle of bridles and a stirring of restless hoofs.
Through the confusion sounded a few brief swearwords, but
the first intelligible answer came from King Henry, shouting
in rage.

He was utterly without dignity, yelling at the King of France
as an angry child yells at his nurse. He rocked in the saddle,
his eyes bursting from his head and the veins on his neck standing out like ropes.

"Thomas the proud, Thomas the fool, Thomas the recreant,"
he shouted. "See here, King Louis. For no reason at all, in the
middle of the night, this man ran away from his church and the
responsibilites laid on him by God. *I* did not pursue him,
none of my vassals pursued him. He just ran away, from mere
spite, to make foreigners think me a tyrant. He pretends he is
suffering for the Church, but that's a damned lie. I have never
persecuted the Church. All I asked of him was to keep the old
customs, customs his predecessors always kept. What about
Anselm? He is famous for miracles, a very holy canonized Saint.
He was Archbishop of Canterbury, and *he* never complained
of the old customs. They were good enough for a great Saint,
but not good enough for Thomas of Cheapside, risen from the
gutter only by my favor. Damn it all, years ago he swore to
observe those customs. Why can't he swear to them again,
honestly, without those confounded trick phrases at the end?

Yes, I tell you, King Louis, he swore to observe them; and if he had the honesty to abide by his oath there would be no quarrel between us. Instead of which he went to Vezelay of all places, the most famous shrine in France, where he could be sure of finding a crowd of my enemies. There, as publicly as he could, he denounced my customs as evil, and excommunicated my faithful vassals who observe them."

It was all true, thought Thomas, that was the worst of it. What use was it to explain to these resentful politicians that you could not trust King Henry to keep an agreement honestly; that even his mother, whom he had cheated of the crown, thought his new customs a disgusting piece of tyranny; that if Henry were allowed any power at all over the Church he would bend it completely to his will, until it permitted him to put away his wife in favor of a prettier face, to steal the endowments of the monasteries for his pleasures, to use the benefices given by the piety of past ages as rewards for dubious political services? The King of France did not know Henry. Thomas did. But that was not a reason he could give publicly on this occasion.

King Louis was speaking, addressing the assembly with all the dignity of a crowned king who was also a good knight and an eminent Crusader.

"My lord Archbishop, it seems to me that the King of England has just cause to complain. I know you for a gallant knight and a man of honor. Will you not once more repeat the oath of homage you owe to your sovereign, omitting the final clause which, justly, displeases him?"

The clerks of his household gazed beseechingly at Thomas, mutely begging him to make peace with the King and permit them to go home; the whole assembly hung on his words, expecting him to give way gracefully. All the world knew King Louis as the pattern of chivalry, the chosen arbiter in difficult questions of honor; he had advised the Archbishop to swear as King Henry demanded, and he was not accustomed to see his advice disregarded.

But Thomas remained stubborn. He could give no convincing reason for his refusal; convincing, that is, to men who did not know King Henry as he did. He took refuge in an evasion which sprang naturally to the mind of a scholar trained in debate.

"If King Henry wishes me to obey him when he dishonors God, or invades the right of Holy Church or of the episcopal order, I am amazed at his shamelessness in demanding public agreement from me beforehand. Let him find another clerk to be his accomplice in such wickedness. I have already sworn that I will obey him in all things lawful. He shall get no further oath from me."

King Louis regarded him with a disdainful stare. He was too sensible to argue with a trained rhetorician, but he did not pretend to be convinced. "Is that your last word, my lord Archbishop? I am sorry to hear it," he said quietly. Then he wheeled his horse, with a glance at King Henry. In a moment, without a word of farewell, the two kings and their followers were riding toward the town of Montmirail; the Archbishop and his clerks were left alone.

Herbert of Bosham was the first to speak. "Well, my lord, I suppose we ride east, to St. Colombe, where we left our baggage. We won't be staying there, of course. After today's colloquy King Louis will not press us to be guests in his royal abbey. It's a pity you had to add that clause to the homage every English bishop has sworn since we Normans taught the English to live as civilized Christians; no earlier bishop felt the need for it. But there it is; what's done is done and there's no use complaining. Where shall we go when we leave Sens? In Italy or the Empire the Ghibellines would compel us to serve their schismatic anti-Pope, and the Count of Flanders tried to catch us when we traversed his dominions. That seems to leave only Spain. Aragon and Navarre are allied with England, but we shall be safe in Castile until you quarrel with their king also."

Even his most intimate companion had never before used that tone to Thomas; the shock stirred him more strongly than had the disapproval of King Louis, which he had expected. He was tempted to answer in anger, but he remembered the rages of King Henry. A man who lost his temper might commit any crime; that was a warning ever in his mind. He replied in a neutral, expressionless voice: "I am answerable only to my conscience for the form of the oath I swear. Learned theologians may dispute over which oaths are licit, but an archbishop is not bound to any particular version. If King Louis expels us from France I don't know where I shall go. It doesn't matter, anywhere will do. But I shall not be able to provide for my followers. You, my faithful brethren, may swear whatever oath King Henry demands, to get back the benefices he has stolen from you. If you prove obedient there is no reason why you should not live happily in England. I may visit Ireland, where the great abbots like to have a consecrated bishop about them to ordain priests and bless the oils. The Pope may translate me to a titular see and give me work in the Curia. Or I can lecture in the schools for a living."

In truth Thomas did not greatly care what became of him. He knew he was right; but everyone else thought he was wrong, and he felt too weary and discouraged to set about the task of persuading even the faithful Herbert. He had to keep on repeating to himself that he was right, for half his mind told him that Pope Alexander would think he had mishandled this long-awaited interview, from which such great results had been expected. He had now sentenced himself to penury as well as exile; and all for nothing. Some other bishop would be translated to Canterbury, and the Pope would barter the liberties of the Church in England for King Henry's financial and political support. He was quite alone in the world, the last upholder of a defeated cause.

Even the unimportant Henry of Houghton, a minor member of his train, thought it appropriate to make his sentiments clear. His horse stumbled over a stone; as he jerked at the reins he muttered, so loud that the Archbishop must hear: "Will you pick up your feet? But of course you need not obey my command if it is against the honor of God or the rights of Holy Church or the rights of your order."

There was a snigger from the other clerks. Thomas had to admit that it was a moderately funny joke; but it was not the first time he had been in at the birth of a popular catchword, and he groaned to think how often he would hear it in the future. Everyone who sought a reputation as a wit would tack the famous saving clause to every order, whether he called for wine or told a servant to shut the door. All the same, he *had* been right, even if no one agreed with him.

The early dusk of January drained all color from the woods as they crossed the border of Henry's County of Maine and entered the dominions of King Louis. It was the time when peasants led their beasts to stable, when travelers should be unsaddling in monastic guest houses or roadside inns, a time when the open country should be emptying. But to the east the great road seemed unusually crowded. With the caution of a veteran warrior, Thomas checked his horse and peered into the dusk. These men waiting on the road were all on foot, so they could not be hostile raiders; and the swift chargers of his clerks could gallop safely through mere footpads.

As he drew level with the group who stood in silence awaiting his approach he saw they were all peasants, the miserable harried plowmen who scratched a living from these war-torn borderlands. The peasants shuffled to the side of the road, kneeling to leave him a clear passage. Pleased at their devotion, he raised his hand in the usual gesture of blessing. To his surprise, the crowd broke into frenzied cheering as he passed.

At the wave of sound the tired horses danced and sidled, and the clerks looked round in astonishment. The crowd shouted phrases in unison, as men shout a war cry; Thomas drew rein, to hear what they said.

"Hail to the holy Archbishop," they shouted. "Hail to the Archbishop who would not deny God even though two great kings so commanded!"

Thomas knew he was not alone in his stand against King Henry, though every magnate from the King of France to the meanest knight and every bishop from the Pope to the most junior suffragan thought him in the wrong. The poor, who saw in an independent Church the only check on their greedy and capricious lords, hailed him as their champion.

They rode from Montmirail to the Abbey of St. Colombe at Sens by roads lined with cheering peasants.

Two days after their return to the abbey, the King of France summoned the Archbishop to wait on him. When Thomas entered the hall of Sens castle, in the full state of cope, pallium, and miter which was fitting for a call on such a great lord, King Louis fell on his knees before him.

"Bless me, Father, for I have sinned," he cried for all his counselors to hear. "Last week at Montmirail my heart was angry at your stubbornness, and I left the field determined to expel you from my dominions. Since then I have been much in the company of King Henry, and I recognize that you have good reason to mistrust him. My determination to expel you was sinful, even though I repented before I could put it into effect. For that sin I ask absolution from you, and pardon from God."

"*Ego absolvo te,*" said Thomas hastily, unsure whether this most public declaration should be treated as a sacramental confession. When he had raised the King from his knees and blessed him he asked, proudly, "Do you still wish me to leave St. Colombe? I can be ready to move at a day's notice, and beyond the Pyrenees I shall find another refuge."

"Good gracious, no, my lord," answered the King; and then continued, with the devastating candor that made him the darling of every gallant knight and the despair of every politician: "What really changed my mind was seeing the common people flock to you. I am surrounded by greedy magnates, whose cortèges are more powerful than those which follow the oriflamme. My only chance of making myself truly King of France is to win the support of the common people. With the people behind me I can rule as well as reign, and the people are behind your lordship."

"That's true, though not everyone would say it," said Thomas, falling into the easy tone of a diplomatist in a confidential discussion. "I think that if I went back to England the common people over there would support me also. But I must go back with King Henry's permission and good will. If I cross the Channel uninvited I can only throw myself into the arms of his enemies; that would be to begin a civil war, and I have seen civil war."

There was another strong reason, though he did not copy the frankness of King Louis by mentioning it openly. The Pope would be very angry if he drove King Henry into the Ghibelline camp.

"I am sorry the colloquy arranged by your lordship came to nothing," he continued. "Perhaps I was too obstinate. If you, my lord, can arrange another meeting with King Henry, I shall come to it as fast as horse can carry me. I shall do all in my power to win his friendship, and to deserve it."

That delighted King Louis. He was never happier than when acting as peacemaker; though his efforts in that field were rarely successful, for he could never understand that serious differences of principle could not be resolved by an embrace and a few gracious words.

Nevertheless, though not only King Louis but the Pope himself, and every politician and clerk in Christendom who fancied his skill in diplomacy, tried to heal the breach between the faithfully papalist King of England and his too-papalist Archbishop, from January to November no meeting could be arranged. There were incessant negotiations at long range through third parties, and endless redraftings of complicated saving clauses. For Henry now answered his antagonist with his own weapons; he announced that he would accept Thomas's addition to the oath of homage if he in his turn might add that he accepted it "saving the dignity of the realm of England." Thomas replied that this exception was too wide, and both sides were back where they had started.

The long dispute had reached a stage where innocent bystanders might be hurt by flying missiles. In England the Church was drifting toward chaos, since there was no supreme authority to resolve disputes between diocesan bishops; in so far as it was ruled at all it was administered by the Bishop of London. From his intervention he gained neither honor nor profit.

Bishop Gilbert had been studying the new, fashionable romances about King Arthur, a frivolous diversion for a holy monk of Cluny. Geoffrey of Monmouth described a state of affairs, in the fifth century, when the Church in Britain was ruled by an archbishop of London. At this, Gilbert's imagination took fire, and he began to claim that his see should be raised to metropolitan status; at the same time King Henry relied on him to administer all benefices left vacant by the exile of the Archbishop's supporters. At last Thomas lost patience with the holy and ambitious prelate. On Palm Sunday in 1169, at the great Abbey of Clairvaux, the abbey which St. Bernard had made so famous that anything done there was speedily known all over Christendom, he pronounced public sentence of excommunication against the Bishop of London.

Bishop Gilbert could not deny the Archbishop of Canterbury's authority to excommunicate him. He took refuge in the quibble that this talk of excommunication might be only a rumor; he would submit to the ban when he received a formal document bearing the seal of his Archbishop. Since the King forbade anyone to bring such a document into England, and the ports were watched against it, the stalemate might have endured indefinitely.

But for the first time since his exile Thomas intervened directly in the affairs of England. When a layman, a knight of Champagne named Odo, volunteered to serve the writ at risk of his life, the Archbishop gave him the precious parchment and allowed him to try the dangerous enterprise. Since Sir Odo was a vassal of the King of France he could not be accused of treason against King Henry; the worst punishment he might face would be unpleasant confinement until he was deported across the Channel.

Sir Odo was completely successful. In July he returned to Sens triumphant. For once the little study where the exiles penned their interminable manifestos was lit by an air of accomplishment; as Sir Odo stood by the door, telling his carefully prepared story to the Archbishop and his companions, he might have been a troubadour reciting the gallant deeds of a Crusader. He was very pleased with himself, and rightly; Thomas felt his flagging energy revived by the fresh breeze of knightly prowess.

"When we got to London, my squire and I," said Odo, hand on hip and right foot advanced in proud flamboyance, "we learned that Bishop Gilbert had gone into hiding. He feared that a stranger might hand him the notice of his excommunication, in spite of all King Henry's precautions. So he traveled about his diocese, alone and meanly dressed; even the canons of St. Paul's Cathedral did not know where he was. We made a few inquiries, but evidently we would never reach him; so we decided to use our second plan. We had been told that if we could not serve the document on the Bishop in person, the next best thing was to have it read from the altar of his cathedral. I believe that is binding in law."

"Legally it is as binding as if you handed it to Gilbert," said Herbert of Bosham. "But of course he thought it could never happen. How did you persuade a priest to read it from the altar, and how did you get away afterward?"

"We thought it out carefully. Peter, my squire, who has a very strong head, drank with the Londoners in their taverns until he knew the habits of the congregation in St. Paul's. It seems that on great feasts most Londoners go early to Mass in the parish church, to fulfill the obligation; then at midday those of them who appreciate good music and eloquent preaching drop in at St. Paul's to hear some of the High Mass. On Ascension Day we went early to the cathedral, and found good places near the altar rails. I had the writ of excommunication all ready in my pouch, folded with the seal outside so that it might have been any kind of legal deed."

"How had you got it into England in the first place? I heard that they were searching the baggage of all travelers from France," asked Thomas.

"We were never searched. We chose to travel on a crowded boat, and though a sergeant of the Dover garrison stood on the quay, reminding us that it was forbidden to introduce papal writs into England, he searched only the baggage of clerks, and left us alone."

"I see. Nowadays King Henry is not well served. When I was Chancellor there would have been a knight on the quay to see that the sergeant carried out his orders in full."

"Anyway, I had the writ safe, and I waited through the long Mass until the priest came to the Offertory. Then we went up to the altar rails and knelt, displaying the sealed writ. I suppose the priest thought we were offering the deeds of a manor for his cathedral, and had chosen this public way of displaying our generosity. He came down to the rails, took the parchment from my hands, and began to read it aloud. As soon as we heard him pronounce the opening words my squire and I stepped back into the crowd. There was a great stir as the congregation began to take in what he was reading. Someone shouted that the citizens must arrest these impudent messengers. We were trying to push our way to the west door, while the rest of the crowd surged toward the altar to hear better. I thought we were stuck; but an elderly burgess caught me by the shoulder. 'I worked with Tom Becket in the counting house of Osbert Huitdeniers,' he whispered. 'Follow me.' He struggled toward the west door, while his servant went in front crying: 'Way for Goodman Robert, who is sick and must get into the fresh air.' The crowd let us through, and Goodman Robert took us at once to his own house. At dawn next day we passed through the city gate, mounted on the Goodman's horses, disguised as his serving men. He had a train of pack horses leaving for Southampton and we journeyed with it to the coast, unmolested. That is all. But you may be sure that Bishop Gilbert now knows he is excommunicate."

"You understand, my lord," said Herbert of Bosham eagerly. "Sir Odo was brave and fortunate; but he succeeded because the common people of England support the Church against the King. Sir Odo was hidden by a rich burgess; that in itself is comforting. But the burgess could not have hidden him, in fact he would never have reached London, if the King's sergeants had done their work zealously. King Henry no longer gets loyal service, even from his paid followers."

"Yes," said Sir Odo, "at Montmirail the peasants of France

showed that they loved you. Now you can count on the people of England. If you wish, you may dethrone King Henry."

"King Henry was once a good friend to me," answered the Archbishop. "I do not seek to dethrone him. When he admits that the Church is ruled by God, not by kings, we shall be good friends again."

When he learned that Gilbert, his most useful adherent among the bishops, had been openly excommunicated in his own cathedral, with the connivance of his flock, King Henry fell into one of his worst rages. He recognized as clearly as Thomas that this was a symptom of widespread disaffection. Then news reached him that on the Feast of Candlemas next, the 2nd of February 1170, Thomas intended to place all England under interdict. He saw he must patch up a peace, or be overthrown by rebellion.

Unfortunately the King of France no longer offered to mediate; if Henry wanted peace he must make the first move himself. But when he invited his Archbishop to confer with him in Normandy, Thomas answered that he would only negotiate under the protection of King Louis, for he feared assassination if he entered the dominions of King Henry. Henry therefore let it be known, unofficially, that an invitation to negotiate on French soil would be accepted. But King Louis, who disliked Henry's bad temper and foul language, did not issue the invitation.

By November Henry was desperate. He must make peace by February, or lose his throne. He also knew, or could guess from his experience of foreign affairs, that the Pope had ordered Thomas to accept peace if it was offered; for the cities of Lombardy were fighting gallantly against the Emperor, and at this time of crisis the Guelph cause must not lose the support of the wealthy King of England. If only he could get Thomas to a conference the trouble would be quickly ended.

It was a most humiliating position, as humiliating as that awful summer more than twenty years ago when King Stephen had contemptuously paid the traveling expenses of his defeated rival. The only solution was to visit the Ile de France uninvited. If he made an excuse to come to Paris he was sure to run into Thomas.

In November 1169 Thomas was staying in Paris, on the invitation of King Louis; he had been given a little house in the Cité, among the lodgings of the canons of Notre-Dame, and there in a snug chamber he talked over his plans with Herbert of Bosham.

"Tomorrow King Henry rides on pilgrimage to the shrine of St. Denys on the hill of Montmartre," he said. "I shall meet him there, with the King of France present to guarantee my personal safety. You may pass word to all my clerks that by Christmas we shall be in England. For I shall swear the oath Henry demands, and end the quarrel."

"On what terms?" asked Herbert sharply.

"On any terms, or on no terms at all. What does it matter? I may get all sorts of promises from Henry, but when he loses his temper he will disregard them. The Pope forbids me to put England under interdict, though I have promised publicly to do so by Candlemas. I can't back down without utter disgrace, so the quarrel must be settled before February. It's peace at any price, but that's what the Curia requires of me."

Herbert stared at the Archbishop. Thomas was nearly fifty-one, and he looked seventy; he was bent and haggard, and curiously ungainly, a thin wrinkled neck emerging from a bunchy bundle of warm clothing. As usual he shivered with cold; and his face, save for its purple nose, was yellow and roughened. He seemed utterly worn out, so crushed with disappointment that he had scarcely the strength to speak.

"But you must agree on some of the questions in dispute,"

Herbert persisted. "What about freedom to appeal to Rome, and the enforcement of those customs King Henry invented at Clarendon? You can't just leave all that in the air."

"We shall, all the same. I won't promise publicly to obey them, and Henry won't promise publicly to withdraw them. We just shan't mention them at all. One of the royal clerks wrote to me unofficially. If I do homage I get back the property of the See of Canterbury; then I return to England and we make a fresh start. I know it's ridiculous. We are sure to quarrel again within the year. But so the Curia orders."

"At least it will be pleasant to be home again," said Herbert with all the cheerfulness he could muster. "For five years we have held our ground against a mighty king, and it's no disgrace to yield after such a resistance. Besides, when we get to England Henry may not have it all his own way. Even with you out of the country he could not make the clergy swear to follow him against their true lord."

"No, they behaved very well," Thomas answered with the flicker of a smile; the well-chosen reminder was sure to bring him comfort. "Even Roger of York refused to swear, though he still thinks of me as Bailhache. But half of them tried to dodge the issue, by neglecting to take the oath without a definite refusal. No one can say which lord Salisbury and Norwich would support, if there were no monastery where they could hide until the topic was forgotten."

"You have the support of the common people, and of the clergy. In fact you have the support of every good Christian except the Pope. When we are back in England Henry must behave with caution."

"He expects me to die soon, and I hope he is right," Thomas answered mournfully. "He gambles that his next Archbishop will be easier to manage. As you say, five years is a long time to maintain a hopeless fight. But I am sorry that at the end we must surrender unconditionally. It would have been better for the quiet simple Christians of England if I had yielded at Northampton. Then there would have been no excommunications, no sending into exile."

"It was exciting while it lasted, but I look forward to Christ Church. Five years' absence from my cloister makes a serious dent in my vow of stability." Herbert could stomach even surrender, if it brought peace.

King Henry rode to the hill of Montmartre feeling on the whole more pleased than angry. King Louis had behaved most discourteously to a brother sovereign. Since he had not been invited to visit Paris he had ridden thirty-six miles from Mantes, the nearest castle which flew his banner; that was not a long ride, as Angevins reckoned riding, but of course he must appear splendid and unruffled at this famous colloquy. He had managed rather well, he considered, by sending on ahead his fiercest and most imposing war horse and his robes of state, while he himself cantered up on a smooth hackney; after praying at the shrine of St. Denys he had changed clothes and mount, and now he felt ready for anything. But there had been a muddle over his dinner, and it was unfortunate that etiquette would not allow him to enter Paris to eat at an inn. Still, he knew that all the best cooks in France had been assembled to prepare a magnificent feast in honor of the reconciliation; after he had finished this business with Thomas he was sure of a good supper.

Apart from that little snub from King Louis he had every reason to be pleased with himself. He had been firm, but patient; he had maintained the letter of his legal rights, but he had restrained himself from the kind of atrocity that would have soothed his sore-tried temper; no one could accuse him of an outrage like his father's gelding of the Bishop-elect of Seez. He had been sure that time was on his side, and now his patience was to be rewarded. Thomas was going to swear homage, not because he had been driven to it by persecution, but because his own superior, the Pope, commanded it. That ought to settle the question once and for all.

He was first at the rendezvous, but King Louis and the Archbishop were punctual. As they arrived he felt a surge of self-confidence, knowing what a fine figure he made on Golden Leopard, the handsome chestnut that was his most showy charger. The stallion was too restless and hot-tempered to be comfortable for a long ride, but he was just the mount to make an impression at a stately conference. King Louis was muffled in woolens against the November weather, and Thomas, who used to dress so splendidly, looked almost insignificant in his bulky Cistercian cowl; the King of England, prancing in purple mantle and golden crown, was the most distinguished personage on the hilltop.

First Thomas raised the question of the restoration of English benefices unlawfully escheated from his exiled companions. Henry could not look dignified while he haggled over money, yet haggle he must, since there was money at stake. Thomas had a good memory for figures. The discussion continued for some time, while the King of France yawned.

At last all these tedious matters of business were arranged. Nothing had been said about the customs of England or the right of appeal to Rome. These disputes would remain unresolved; what mattered was a display of reconciliation before the eyes of the world.

Thomas dismounted, and kneeling before his King swore to serve him as a loyal vassal and faithful friend. It was a complete surrender.

King Henry, hand on hip, swayed to the curvets of his war horse, savoring this moment of triumph. Now they had only to ride down the hill and begin drinking the good French wine. But it seemed there was more to be done. King Louis was prompting anxiously from the background.

"Now you in your turn dismount, my lord King, to embrace the holy Archbishop with the Kiss of Peace. Such was the ceremonial agreed by our heralds."

King Henry stiffened. Thomas had once been his friend, but he was his friend no longer; he was a pardoned rebel, lucky to get back his forfeited estates. The Kiss of Peace was given by brave knights to trusted comrades; this man did not deserve it.

But he could not refuse it without explanation. He snatched at the first excuse that came to mind. "My lord King, I cannot grant the Kiss of Peace, because of a great oath I swore in my rage, that never would I embrace this defiant clerk. Surely you would not have me perjured? It was a very terrible oath, though I forget the exact terms. Of course I shall treat my Archbishop as a friend, but the Kiss of Peace is not lightly given."

"If an oath that you swore in blind rage is all that holds you back," said Thomas sardonically, straightening his shoulders as he stood before the restless charger, "the impediment is easily removed. I have power to loose and bind the Christians of the Province of Canterbury. Recently I absolved a great multitude of Englishmen from an illegal oath they swore against their metropolitan. I can absolve you here and now."

That was not the answer of a man anxious for peace. Henry recalled all the trouble he had taken to make his vassals swear before the sheriffs that they would support the King in his quarrel with Canterbury; it had been a more difficult business even than the compiling of Domesday Book ninety years ago. When at last it had been done, after enormous expense and tedious delay, Thomas made nonsense of the whole enterprise by releasing the entire population from an illegal oath extorted by fear. Such an artful and self-willed politician would never deserve the Kiss.

"The Archbishop shall have my friendship, but I will not

embrace him. Do not press me further, my lord King. My decision is firm," he said curtly.

"In that case I withdraw the oath I have just sworn," said Thomas. "I am within my rights. That oath was part of a mutual compact; unless I get the counterpart it does not bind me. The King of France is the best knight in the world, the greatest authority on all that concerns homage. If King Louis says I am wrong I shall reconsider my position, but if he upholds me my submission is void."

King Louis nodded assent. "The Archbishop is right. If he receives no counterpart his promise may be withdrawn. Do you still withhold the Kiss, my lord King?"

"I withhold it," Henry said fiercely, "and that is my last word."

"Then the conference is concluded," King Louis replied stiffly. "Come, my lord Archbishop, I desire you to sup with me in my good town of Paris."

Thomas climbed clumsily to the saddle (he had aged greatly since he rode with the knight-service of England against Toulouse). Without looking back he cantered to overtake the King of France, who was already riding down the hill to Paris.

King Henry, alone on the hill of Montmartre, belched from sheer hunger. "They never invited me to supper," he exclaimed in dismay, as Golden Leopard reared to follow the other horses. Then the full horror of his situation came home to him. He was thirty-six miles from a meal and a bed, and he must ride every yard of that weary way on this confounded peacocking charger, the last mount he would have chosen for a long journey over rough roads in the dark.

Thomas was a dangerous enemy, richly deserving the worst punishment that could befall him.

CHAPTER XI

The Last Joust

EIGHT months later, in July 1170, King Henry rode through the little Norman village of Freteval, returning from hawking; he was in an amazingly good temper, so friendly with all the world that his courtiers surmised good news must have reached him secretly. In fact there was no particular incident to account for his feeling of contentment; it was just that things in general were going very well for him. Five weeks ago he had assisted at the Coronation of young Henry fitzHenry; his dominions were at peace, from Northumbria to the Pyrenees, and in Ireland he had opened up a new field of conquest and plunder where his restless vassals might wage war without disturbing the orderly administration of his fiefs; Queen Eleanor was in England and he was in Normandy; a gay un-married damsel, the lady Rosamund Clifford, no longer in her first youth but an astonishing fine woman, evaded his dis-honorable advances in a spirit that showed she expected to be caught quite soon; his new gyrfalcon had flown gallantly, returning at the first whirl of the lure, a credit to his taming of her; he had eaten a good dinner, sitting in the sun by the river bank, and he looked forward to a good supper in his own hall. The world was treating him kindly.

There was one nagging little worry, his feud with the Archbishop of Canterbury; but that had gone on for so long, more than five years, that he had grown used to it. Besides, the Pope was now definitely on his side, and probably poor old Thomas would find himself translated in the near future to some titular see where he could not be a nuisance. He was not sure he relished such a tame end to a stirring quarrel. It was a pleasure to strive against Thomas and his little band of exiled clerks. They were brave, and yet so weak that they could not hurt him. One could admire their courage, standing back to look at the dispute as a spectator.

He lifted his red freckled face to the sky, smiling inanely, out of pure content, at the declining sun.

There was suddenly a tension in the movements of his horse, and he knew that the well-trained beast winded strange horses. He was unarmed, but there were courtiers round him and a strong escort within call; unafraid, he gathered the reins, gripped the saddle with his knees, and peered down the village street.

Toward him rode a knot of horsemen, foremost among them a tall rider in a Cistercian cowl, mounted on a warlike charger. The challenge was unexpected, but in his mood of gay content he accepted it without hesitation. He cantered forward alone, calling cheerfully: "Ah, Thomas, do you come to joust with me, or to call me to repentance?"

The Archbishop slid from the saddle as he answered: "Neither, my lord. I come to make peace between us. I am your vassal for the fiefs of Canterbury, and as ruler of the Church in England your chief counselor. Accept my homage. Wipe out the five years of contention between us."

Thomas knelt in the dust, his hands stretched forth in the gesture of homage. But the King, seeing suddenly that all was won, received him courteously. He also dismounted, and touched the other's shoulders in a formal embrace. Then he stood by the Archbishop's horse, holding the stirrup, and insisted that he should be the first to mount. Ten minutes later they were riding side by side, chatting excitedly of old days in London and Toulouse.

While half his mind had fallen into the old groove of bantering talk with his dear friend Henry, Thomas felt below the surface a nagging warning. "That embrace was not the Kiss of Peace," it said. "It was something very like it, and this is an occasion when the Kiss might have been expected. But Henry did not grant it. He is not truly your friend."

This was disappointing, for he had yielded without haggling, thinking only of friendship. He was still surprised at his own sudden change of front, but common sense told him it had been the only course left. He had never expected to gain every point in dispute; in no Christian realm were clerks completely beyond the jurisdiction of lay courts, and there must always be some check on appeals from Canterbury to Rome. He had struggled for five years to make Henry see that the Church was not a mere department of the realm, and to save the soul of his old friend from the deadly sin of pride. If he could have forced him to yield he would have been assured of his salvation. But since the Pope no longer supported his Archbishop he could never make Henry yield; so he himself must surrender. For peace on any terms was better than unending strife which tempted great men to sin and left the Church in England leaderless. In the cause of friendship someone's pride must be sacrificed; it would have to be his own.

Henry was making things easy for him, seeming genuinely anxious that between them they should rule England as it ought to be ruled. He had hardly mentioned the Coronation of young fitzHenry when the King began eagerly to explain it away. "I know that you, and you alone, have the right to crown a King of England. My dear Thomas, if I had known you were about to return to your allegiance I would have waited for you. But I was in a hurry. My son is fifteen, and unless he is crowned there would be another civil war if I dropped dead tomorrow. On the worst construction, I took only what was offered to me unasked. The real culprit is the Archbishop of York."

"Who still remembers me as the gawky and undignified Bailhache."

"Exactly. He offered to crown the lad, and it seemed absurd that I should refuse my heart's desire on a minor point of religious etiquette. I was guided by the counsel of an archbishop, as in future I shall be guided by your counsel. There's nothing wrong in that, is there? As a matter of fact we can put all to rights, and quite soon too. My daughter-in-law was not crowned with her husband, and King Louis threatens to ravage the Vexin in revenge for the slight on her dignity. I must make amends, and the simplest way is to hold the Coronation all over again. Next spring both children can be crowned together, by you, the Archbishop whose right it is to crown the Kings of England. It will make a good excuse for another great feast in Westminster Hall."

"Of course I will be glad to crown them, unless the Pope forbids it. There is no reason why he should, but you may remember that Archbishop Theobald was forbidden to crown Eustace fitzStephen."

"He was the son of a usurper. I already have the Pope's permission for the Coronation of my son."

Henry answered sharply. Of course there could be no doubt that his son had been crowned with papal approval; Thomas was going out of his way to remind him that if a conflict should arise on any other question Canterbury would support Rome.

He envied the Emperor his jewel of an Archbishop of Cologne; how useful to have a primate who followed his sovereign into schism with uncomplaining loyalty! But Thomas was looking very old and worn. He would not last long. Yet before he died the quarrel must be ended; so that a peaceful election, with every opportunity for royal pressure, should provide an amenable successor to lead the English Church.

"I do not blame you in the slightest, my dear lord," Thomas continued with an irritating plodding forbearance which carried a hint of patronage; as though to say one should not expect anything better from a king. "As you say, you took what York offered, thankfully and without inquiry. But I blame Archbishop Roger, and the bishops who assisted him. They knew they were doing wrong."

"I expect they will apologize, when they see you restored to power. Can't you overlook their fault, at least for the present? This is supposed to be a joyful reconciliation. Threats of punishment are ill timed."

"Then complete the reconciliation with the Kiss of Peace. Come on, Henry. I suppose you fear your courtiers will despise you for changing your mind after you vowed you would never grant me the Kiss. But I have surrendered all the principles for which I endured a long exile. Won't you give your dignity just the slightest bruise?"

"Perhaps, one of these days. I can't bring myself to do it here and now. Let's talk of other things. What do you think of my new gyrfalcon?"

They rode side by side, talking as they had talked when Henry was a young untried ruler and Thomas his Chancellor and tutor in the art of government. But Henry was now a grown man, who for six years had ruled his realm singlehanded; Thomas's patronizing manner began to ruffle his nerves. And each had in his mind one overmastering thought which might not be uttered. Henry felt singing through his brain that unworthy hope: "Thomas is a sick man, Canterbury will soon be vacant." Thomas heard an interior voice repeating: "Henry will not grant me the Kiss, he is not really my friend."

On the 26th of November 1170 the Archbishop of Canterbury took counsel with his clerks in the little Norman seaport of Wissant. He was lodged in a decent stone house, the requisitioned property of a rich burgess, where there was a study, snug and dry, with windows of oiled silk, an excellent place for such a meeting. He was once more living in comfort, now that he had the resources of King Henry at his back; though it was unfortunate that the clerk in charge of his traveling arrangements should be John of Oxford, who had incurred his special excommunication by swearing obedience to the anti-Pope at Wurzburg. However, John steadfastly denied that he had in fact sworn obedience, and the choice of such an unsuitable courier might be evidence only of Henry's carelessness, not of his spite.

The Archbishop's household were madly excited at the prospect of returning to their homes and benefices, and anxious to return in a friendly manner. It was impossible to disguise that they were returning in defeat, defeated because the Pope was tired of their leader's obstinacy; in England they would be at King Henry's mercy, and it seemed only common sense to give as little trouble as possible. If they wanted to stand up for their rights, reckless of consequences, then they had no business to be waiting here for a passage home.

But Thomas saw matters differently. Foremost in his mind, as he sat in his chair at the head of the table, was the knowledge that he had never received from King Henry the Kiss of Peace, though he had delayed from July to October to obtain it.

In itself the ceremony meant very little; Henry had sworn

to be his friend, and an oath on the True Cross could not bind him more firmly than his word of honor. But it was obvious that Henry had a superstitious regard for the actual physical Kiss. If only he could be induced to grant it he would in future bear himself as a loyal son of the Church.

But Thomas could not extract the Kiss from him, even by sharp practice. Six weeks ago he had appeared uninvited in the chapel of the King's castle at Amboise just before Henry was due to hear his morning Mass. That should have done the trick; for ritual demanded that the celebrant, at the words *"Pax Domini sit semper vobiscum,"* should bestow the Kiss of God's Peace on the most eminent member of the congregation, who on this occasion would be Henry himself; then Henry must pass on the Kiss to the second in dignity, who in this company would be the Archbishop of Canterbury. The Kiss was what mattered, not the intention behind it; and Henry would be trapped into friendship.

The King had been warned before the Mass started, and the quick brain of a royal chaplain found a way out, at the cost of doing violence to the *Ordo* for the day. It was the 12th of October, the Feast of St. Wilfred of York, a famous English Saint; but the chaplain ignored him, and sang instead a Mass of Requiem, at which the blessing takes a different form and no Kiss is given. When Mass was over Thomas rode away without seeking a private interview. He saw that the refusal was final, and that he would never receive the Kiss.

His mind was made up. The King was still his enemy, but he asked his Archbishop to return to England. The Pope also desired it, and in fact it held out the only hope of peace for the Church. So he would return. He would take no steps until everything had been discussed with his advisers, and he would not be the first to renew the quarrel; for if he lost his temper he might put himself in the wrong.

Now he spoke temperately, relating the damning facts without eloquence or emphasis. "Brethren," he said calmly, glancing down at his notes on the table, "the first problem is the return of our endowments. It would be completely wrong, and an act of dishonesty to our successors, if we returned to England in peace while the King still detains the property of the Church. Last July we were assured that our lands would be returned to us. Yet the Michaelmas rents of Canterbury have been received by Ranulf de Broc on behalf of the King. Most of my lands pay rent once a year, at Michaelmas. If I submit to this injustice I shall be penniless until next September."

"A dirty trick, certainly," said Henry of Houghton, "but no dirty trick is too low for King Henry when there is money at stake. We shall be cheated by the King's officers; but our brethren who never left England are cheated by them. We must bear it as patiently as we can. What would Christendom think of us if we broke this peace, which we have sought for six years, over the question of one year's rent?"

Henry of Houghton was the most eager of all the company to return to England. He was a learned lawyer and a skilful advocate, whose career had stood still for six years while he followed his lord from one foreign monastery to another; he was impatient to get back to his practice in the Church courts before his reputation was entirely forgotten. But he was too honorable to desert after he had once taken his stand, and he knew that if he deserted prospective clients would despise him; he could not return without his leader.

"Yes, well, King Henry is not very honest over money; as I recall from the days of my chancellorship, when I used to help him rob his vassals. Perhaps it is only justice that now he will keep me very poor for a year. As you say, Henry, it is not an issue on which we can appeal to public opinion. I shall endure in silence anything the *King* does to me."

He emphasized the word "King," and Herbert of Bosham looked up sharply, guessing what would come next.

"But I am charged, by God Himself through His deputy the Pope, with the rule of the Christian people of my province," Thomas continued. "It is my duty, which I may not avoid, to protect them from false shepherds who would lead them into sin. The bishops who defied me must be punished for the part they took in the Coronation of the Young King."

"They were in the wrong, but surely you will overlook it. Your reconciliation with the King should wipe out also any wrongful acts done by his supporters in his name." That was Houghton again, still pleading for peace.

"I am prepared to overlook it," said Thomas with a gathering frown, "for according to their lights they were justified in disobeying me. The King's party held that my authority as Archbishop was suspended during my exile. But now I am once more the first magnate of England, a loyal vassal of the King, who should protect me as he protects his other vassals. Our reconciliation is known throughout England, and all the bishops of the Province of Canterbury should know that they must obey my commands. Yet I have just heard news of a very grave nature. The message came to you, Herbert, and you will explain it. I might be carried away by my feelings."

Herbert of Bosham coughed and looked solemn. He was wholly faithful to the Archbishop, and though he would be glad to see England at peace he did not look forward to the finish of his intimacy with his adored leader; as a monk of Canterbury he would miss the close contact with great events which had lightened his exile. The others knew that if he thought Thomas justified in continuing the struggle he would advise it without flinching.

"Since we left England," he began formally, "five sees have fallen vacant by the death of their bishops. The King wished to avoid answering the awkward question whether Canterbury also stood vacant; for if there is a metropolitan, the metropolitan presides over the consecration of a new bishop. So these sees remain vacant to this day. I have just learned that the King intends to fill them before we reach England. Our leader, when he resumes his duties, will be faced by five young suffragans of the King's party, who will of course oppose him in all he does. I learned this news from a sailor, who did not understand the import of what he said. It is still most secret."

The others craned forward. That they should have got so far as Wissant, honored guests of King Henry, only to break off negotiations and return to exile, was more than most of them could bear.

"Elections to the vacant sees of Lincoln, Hereford, Chichester, Ely, and Bath are to be held in Normandy, in the presence of the King. Delegations from the chapters of these cathedrals are now at his court. After election must come Consecration, and the King fears that Norman bishops will heed the canons, and decline to consecrate bishops for a foreign province. So the Archbishop of York, and the Bishops of London and Salisbury, are waiting at Dover for a favorable wind. As soon as may be they will cross to Normandy, and consecrate the new bishops before our master can reach Canterbury. It was planned that we should know nothing until all was done; and the plan would have succeeded if a sailor had not gossiped to me about the distinguished company he had left waiting in Dover castle."

There were murmurs of shocked indignation, but Henry of Houghton was still anxious for peace. "These bishops do wrong, as they must know themselves. But can you, my lord, force them to their rightful obedience? Has not the Pope forbidden you to inflict any ecclesiastical punishment on your own responsibility?"

Thomas swept the clerk with frowning eyes until he blushed and wriggled. "Blessed are the peacemakers, my dear Henry," he said quietly, but with a note of triumph. "I am glad to see you so earnest for peace, under all provocation. As you remind me, the Holy Father has suspended my disciplinary powers, I suppose because he fears my notorious lack of self-control. But he has not left me entirely helpless, for though peace is good, justice is better. I have bulls from the Pope himself, excommunicating London and Salisbury for their disobedience to me. I have also a letter which suspends Roger of York, who cannot disobey me since he is not my subject. But he is subject to Rome, like every other Christian, and in opposing me he opposed the Pope. The Holy Father gave me these sentences to publish or suppress as I thought fit, and as soon as this news is confirmed I shall publish them. On that I am decided. I seek your advice only on the question of whether after publishing them I should return to England."

That was a desperate question, on which opinion was divided. But Thomas did not really seek the advice of his council, for he was determined to return; he had only informed them of this new development in case they themselves feared the vengeance of the King, and would prefer to remain in France. Some, if allowed to decide in private, might have chosen the course of prudence; but Herbert of Bosham took it for granted that no clerk could desert such a leader, and in the publicity of the council chamber no one had the hardihood to disagree.

In Advent the Archbishop of Canterbury excommunicated the Bishops of London and Salisbury. In the name of the Pope he also suspended the Archbishop of York. On the same afternoon he and his clerks sailed over a calm sea to England. In midchannel they passed the ship which bore the sentenced bishops to the elections in Normandy.

CHAPTER XII

Defeat and Victory

THE bells of Canterbury were ringing for joy, as they had rung without stopping for the last three days. But the gates were closed and the wall manned, for the sheriff of Kent had mustered the King's vassals and at any moment civil war might begin. The vassals of Canterbury were fulfilling their elementary duty of guarding the person of their lord.

Thomas sat in his chamber, not heeding the turmoil of warlike preparations round him. After his long absence he was taking over the neglected affairs of his diocese with the ability and concentration of a veteran who had been both Archdeacon and Chancellor.

As he tried to sum up the finances of his Church, after its long and dishonest administration by Ranulf de Broc, he was constantly interrupted. Every new vassal of Canterbury, who had inherited his fief in the last six years, sought the earliest opportunity to confirm his tenure by doing homage to his lord; messengers were riding in from every English diocese, bearing messages of congratulation; and a deputation of the commons of London came to beg the most distinguished living Londoner to visit his native city as soon as possible. He dealt with these callers absently, for the most urgent need was to suppress Ranulf de Broc. The ex-receiver of the Honor of Canterbury still held the Archbishop's castle of Saltwood, where he had reinforced his garrison with a band of brigands led by Hugh of Horsea, the renegade clerk famous in Kent as the Evil Deacon; already his men had plundered a ship carrying the Archbishop's baggage, and it was expected that soon they would ride out to ravage his lands.

But all business must be interrupted to receive a messenger from the King himself. Luckily the man was only a letter carrier from the Wardrobe, not a gentleman who must be entertained and invited to a conference. Thomas answered him shortly.

"Since the King particularly desires it, I shall release from excommunication the Bishops of London and Salisbury, who are my subjects. They must of course come before me in person, to ask pardon for their disobedience. But you may tell them that when they come they will be pardoned. The case of the Archbishop of York is different. He is not suspended by me, but by the Pope. I cannot pardon him. If he seeks pardon from Rome you may tell him that I shall beg the Pope to be merciful. That is all. My clerks will put it into writing, but you may find it quicker to inform your lord by word of mouth."

Thomas had composed his answer as the King's letter was read to him. There was no need for hard thinking about what to do next. Henry and his adherents would receive justice until they begged for mercy.

He dismissed the messenger, and turned to the tangled

business of persuading the Abbot of St. Augustine's that the Archbishop of Canterbury was entitled to visit his abbey. Long absence had undoubtedly impaired the rights of his see, which he must hand on undiminished to his successors.

At Henry's court in Normandy the magnates were assembled for the Christmas crown-wearing, though it was yet late in Advent. The King was feasting in a crowded hall when the messenger from the Wardrobe brought him Thomas's answer. The courier read the letter aloud for all to hear, and at first the magnates thought it fair enough, perhaps better than it might have been; for all knew that Thomas would stand on his rights against the Crown.

But to one man it brought deep disappointment. Roger, Archbishop of York, sat at the high table, as was his due in right of his great position in the Church; but he wore none of the insignia of his episcopal rank, for he was suspended from all spiritual functions, unable even to offer Mass as a simple priest. Now he heard it confirmed that his suspension would hold over Christmas, in fact until he had accomplished the long and expensive journey to Rome to seek absolution at the hands of the Pope. He had taken it for granted that Thomas would grant the first friendly request he received from the King after his reconciliation, and the shock of refusal was more than he could bear.

"My lord," he said with a sob in his voice, while tears started from his eyes, "you must order my brother of Canterbury to lift my suspension. Can I sit through the Christmas feasting, the three Masses of the Nativity and all the splendor of Epiphany, as a mere tonsured clerk, unable to participate in these great actions? Bailhache oppresses me because I remember his vile origin. Command him to be merciful."

"I have commanded him, and he will not obey. You must approach the Holy Father," the King answered shortly. He felt indifferent to the distress of any archbishop, even an archbishop who supported him.

Then he realized that Thomas was defying him openly.

"What sluggards, what cowards, have I reared in my court?" he screamed. "Recreants, men who care nothing for the welfare of their lord. Not one will deliver me from this turbulent priest!"

Now the glorious intoxication of rage possessed him utterly. He wallowed on the floor, cramming rushes in his mouth as his heels drummed on the paving stones. Men came running from every side, and he knew himself the center of attention.

When the screaming was over, and he sat once more in his high seat before the wine cup, the Justiciar broke one of the most stringent rules of etiquette by referring to what he had said in his paroxysm.

"My lord," he urged anxiously, "it might be wise if you proclaimed once more that the Archbishop of Canterbury is within your peace and friendship. There are knights in this hall who may have taken your threats seriously. I saw a group of them go out immediately you had spoken."

"I don't know what you are talking about," the King answered crossly. "Perhaps I threatened the Archbishop, though I can't remember exactly what I said. Everyone knows I am not myself when the Devil my grandfather takes possession of me. I am a great king, not to be judged as ordinary men are judged. Why, you must remember: I have threatened to kill my dear son Henry, and my gracious queen, and all sorts of other people. Once I said I would tear the guts from the body of King Louis, to use as my girdle. The French envoy heard me say it, but he only laughed and proposed to adjourn negotiations until I was restored to health. Nobody takes my threats seriously, or would dream of acting on them."

"A bit of a fright would do Bailhache no harm," put in the Archbishop of York. "He has given me a thousand-mile journey to get my suspension lifted. Perhaps when he punished me for serving my lord the King he also was chewing the rushes from the floor."

"That's nonsense, Roger," said the King with a petulant frown. "You can't frighten Thomas. If you could, I would have frightened him at Northampton, and all these bothers would have been avoided. As for his chewing rushes from the floor, he is as famous for self-control as I am for a noble and kingly rage."

"I believe you still love the sanctimonious old troublemaker," answered Archbishop Roger. "Well, he is more your enemy than mine. He cannot harm me, for I am his peer, and I can remember him as the uncouth hatchet carrier who joined Theobald's household. I am not impressed by his metropolitan cross, for I have one of my own, just as good."

"Then let us forget the whole thing," said the Justiciar. "In that case you, my lord Archbishop, must face a long journey before you say your next Mass. I suppose the King will not seek favors from Archbishop Thomas."

"I shall never ask him for a favor. But neither do I wish him harm. As the Justiciar says, let us forget the unimportant episode. Now I would like to hear more of that new song about my predecessor, King Arthur."

The court settled down to drink wine and listen to poetry.

On the 29th of December 1170 the Archbishop feasted in the hall of his palace in Canterbury, as was fitting during every one of the Twelve Days of Christmas. Crowded tables filled the spacious room, and the high table on the dais was also crowded. Outside the open doors waited the poorer inhabitants of the city of Canterbury; some were in truth hungry beggars, and the rest wore their shabbiest clothes; for even the leavings from the Archbishop's table were better than the feasts of many a prosperous burgess.

Thomas was sipping that queer drink made from boiled hay with which he soothed his stomach at the end of a long meal. Most of the clerks at his table were still drinking their wine, though a few, influenced by their environment, had changed to English beer. The talk was gloomy, chiefly about the unexpected hostility of young Henry fitzHenry, who nominally ruled England as deputy for his father.

William fitzStephen, a veteran clerk of the Archbishop's household, was expounding Norman usage to Grim of Cambridge, a new comer and the only Englishman in the company. "Perhaps you don't understand the bond that should persist between a young knight and the lord who nourished him. It should be as strong as fosterage, or the spiritual relationship of a godparent. That makes young Henry's behavior quite unpardonable, for he was reared in the Archbishop's household. Yet he returned the Christmas present we sent him, three magnificent chargers. In a way that's not a bad thing, for I don't know how we could have paid for them; we shall have no money until next Michaelmas. Furthermore, he spoke openly of the Archbishop as his father's enemy. That's no way to keep the peace. You should not call anyone the King's enemy until swords have been drawn."

"Even I can see that, though I can't follow all your distinctions about homage, and the occasions when rebellion may be honorable and blameless. To call a man the King's enemy is to put him out of the King's Peace. All the same, our lord the Archbishop seems to have gone rather far in his Christmas sermon. I was on my way here at the time, and I didn't hear it; but it sounds seditious to compare our lawful King Henry with the drunken and heathen invaders who martyred St. Alphege. They tell me he said as much."

"Not quite, though his hearers were encouraged to make the comparison. What he actually said was that the Cathedral contains the tombs of several holy archbishops, one of them a

Martyr. That was going far enough, and I wish he hadn't said it. But our lord is apt to see himself from the outside, as it were, and then act as a man would be expected to act in that position. They tell me he was once a caricature of a money grubbing archdeacon; certainly as Chancellor, when I first knew him, he was the quintessence of a chivalrous knight; since his consecration he has been an archbishop from a book of homilies. I've heard men say that proves him insincere, but I don't see it myself. He *is* a holy archbishop, even if he has to stop and think how to behave like one; instead of his good deeds coming to him naturally."

"Oh, everyone agrees he is a holy man. We know that even in Cambridge. But the omens are against him. Did you hear that in Eastry was born a two-headed calf, which shouted 'Woe to the Archbishop' as it expired?"

"You had better not mention that here, unless you saw the calf and heard it speak. The Archbishop does not hold with omens."

"Oh, I am a simple rustic, and I know it. But in the lives of all holy men, as you hear them read at Collation, the omens come thick. The Archbishop is a holy man, and twice his life has been preserved by miracle: once when he fell into a mill-race, once when the gate of Northampton castle was opened for him by an angel as he fled from the wrath of the King."

"The angel was Herbert of Bosham, across the table. There was nothing extraordinary except that he had very good luck in picking the right key at once out of a large bunch. Of course, if the Archbishop is under the protection of Heaven we have nothing to fear. But I lack your faith. . . . Hallo, who are those strangers who thrust themselves on the Archbishop?"

Thomas was talking earnestly to his old confessor, Prior Robert, about the state of his soul and his plans for the government of the diocese.

"I don't think I am unduly influenced by anger. When you

consider how the King speaks of me, I haven't said anything about him to match it. But I shall have to do something about those Brocs in my castle of Saltwood. They hold it by force, against the King's Peace. By rights the sheriff ought to expel them for me."

"He won't, of course," said Prior Robert grimly. "The King's friends are above the law, though his opponents must obey it. If you send your forces against Saltwood *you* will be amerced for breaking the peace."

"Then I suppose I must bear it in silence, as I bear many other injuries. I have excommunicated Ranulf, the head of the family, which is the most I can do in my spiritual capacity. But the only argument a man like that understands is the point of a lance. I wish I could ride against him, as in the old days I rode against the men of Toulouse. Yet I suppose an archbishop who takes the field in his own cause would give scandal to the faithful."

"Yes, it would be sinful for you to fight for a castle, even your own castle. I say that as your confessor. Heaven help us, what a mess we are in! I hoped that when we came home, reconciled to the King, we could make a fresh start."

"That's what I thought, also. I have never quarreled with young Henry fitzHenry. If he had received me at court I might have persuaded him to be friendly. But he follows his father blindly."

"By the way, my lord," said Prior Robert, almost interrupting in his anxiety, "have you noticed the knights sitting near you? They have been here some time, and they are trying to catch your attention."

"I noticed them, but it will do them no harm to wait until we have finished our wine. I recognize one, at least, as a household knight of King Henry. If he bore a message from the King he would have informed my steward. This must be a private visit, either mere curiosity or a plan to insult me under my own roof. I shall attend to them later. . . . Now the thing that really makes my blood boil is the latest exploit of the Brocs. Young John, Ranulf's nephew, captured a horse of mine on the high road. It's a valuable beast, but to give him his due he's no thief. He cut off its tail and let it go. That's an insult which should be wiped out in blood. Could I ask the Pope to make me a layman, just for a week? When I had killed all the Brocs in fair fight I could go back to being an archbishop."

Though he smiled at the extravagance, Robert of Merton was worried by this return of chivalrous feeling in his lord and penitent. Six years ago Thomas had still hankered after the free life of a warrior, as his confessor knew better than anyone else. Long exile had buried the sentiment; but here in Canterbury, where vassals crowded to do homage, it seemed to be reviving. He did his best to change the topic.

"Curious how obsessed they are with tails, here in Kent," he said casually. "There is a story that they are born with tails themselves; or at least that is what they tell you in Sussex."

"In Paris they say it of all Englishmen," Thomas interrupted with a chuckle.

"Well, why don't you lay a curse on them, so that they are all born with tails in future? In Ireland holy men do that sort of thing, and it seems the only good custom in that queer country. My lord, if you keep those knights waiting much longer they will say in Normandy that courtesy has been forgotten at Canterbury."

Thomas turned to the newcomers. At the moment he saw himself as a knight, sitting once more in his hall surrounded by all the state of a great magnate; with dignified politeness he beckoned them to approach.

The four knights had entered the hall an hour ago, wearing everyday tunics and shabby traveling mantles. Without speaking to the steward they had wandered round the high table, searching for empty seats; since they carried no arms, and wore the gilded spurs of their rank, no one hindered them. At the high table there were no empty seats, so the strangers did what was often done in a crowded hall; they heaped up rushes from the floor and squatted on the bundles. However, they had taken neither food nor wine, which was rather ominous; it seemed they would not accept the Archbishop's hospitality. And since they sat down they had been trying to catch his attention.

As soon as they were summoned they clustered round his high chair, all shouting together. For a moment Thomas was taken aback by this display of bad manners in a place where his authority was usually unquestioned—so taken aback that he could not catch what they shouted. Then he understood they were merely demanding, more peremptorily and in coarser language than was usual in addressing an Archbishop, that he should lift the suspension of Roger of York.

Everyone in the hall listened to the unexampled disturbance. Thomas was tempted to answer them as roughly as they had spoken; but he remembered that he must not give scandal to the crowd at the lower tables, and he replied with courteous moderation.

"I could not lift the Archbishop's suspension even if I desired it; which I do not, for his punishment is deserved. You must understand that the Pope suspended him, and therefore only the Pope can absolve him. If you give him that message he will understand it, for it is clear canon law."

The strangers went on to demand that he should absolve the Bishops of London and Salisbury; they shouted very rudely, but since now they knew they would get an answer they presently fell silent to hear it.

"Those bishops are my subjects, and I can absolve them," said Thomas with a frowning countenance. "I have already promised to absolve them, when they have fallen at my feet and admitted their fault. But to absolve them now, before they have expressed repentance, would be to imply that my sentence was unjust. On the contrary, it was completely righteous and justified, for they had disobeyed their metropolitan. You gentlemen know the obligation of a vassal to his lord. You will understand that disobedience is always a serious fault. Again, if you think I am exceeding my powers, ask the bishops themselves. They will admit the justice of my stand."

"Never mind that," shouted the leader of the strangers. "This is England, where King Henry rules, and we are his men. We demand that you absolve the loyal bishops, because the King wills it and for no other reason."

"King Henry rules the knights of England, but I rule the bishops. In this matter I cannot please the King; though I am his friend, and anxious to serve him."

"Absolve the bishops!" they all shouted together. The leader added: "If you refuse, it will be the worse for you," and another called: "Remember the Bishop of Seez. King Henry is as good a man as his father."

"Even if I had been open to persuasion, you must see that I cannot yield to threats," answered Thomas. "If you bear a letter from King Henry I will examine it tomorrow, in my chamber. But if you have come without credentials I must ask you to leave at once. I do not turn away travelers. If you seek hospitality my steward will supply your wants. But you have not behaved as guests in my hall should behave."

"We are not your guests, and we will not taste your food. You have half an hour to change your mind. Then the King will be served, no matter what the cost."

The leader was as stern and dignified as Thomas, speaking formally as though summoning a castle to surrender; but one of his followers, as they strode out, drew his hand across his throat with an unseemly noise.

Within the hall there was a moment of awed silence, and

then a clamor as every clerk spoke at once. With an anxious frown Prior Robert turned on his lord. "Those ruffians mean what they say. You must leave immediately. I suspect they plan to bind you, and carry you before King Henry like a pig tied up for market."

"I know knights, for I was one myself not so long ago," answered Thomas. "King Henry is too careful of the law to have ordered them to murder me unjudged. If they try to take me captive I shall resist, though without shedding blood. More likely they are only drunk and a little excited. Let us send out some sensible layman to see what they are doing. A layman, because they are in the mood to insult any clerk. Ah, there is my steward. Sir William, will you go into the courtyard and see what our visitors are up to? Come back and tell me, here."

"I still think you should leave," said Prior Robert, while William fitzStephen called in terror: "My lord, get away at once!"

Grim of Cambridge stood up with a puzzled frown on his face. "Will someone explain what is going on?" he asked in careful Latin. "I can't understand Frenchmen when they talk so rapidly. If these men are threatening our Archbishop we must tell the sheriff. The law will protect him."

No one had leisure to explain. Thomas still sat in his high seat, his face expressionless and his hands on his knees, as a bishop sits on his throne in his cathedral. He was too angry to be afraid. Once heathen Danes had martyred an Archbishop of Canterbury, but it was unthinkable that baptized Christians, knights bound by the obligations of chivalry, should offer violence to the Primate of All England, here in his own hall.

He was the only unmoved member of the company. The servants gathered in an anxious group by the door leading to the cloister; the clerks moved from table to table, talking in whispers and glancing nervously at the main door, bound with iron straps and studded with iron nails, which was the only opening from the hall to the outer world. That door was wide open, for the convenience of the poor of Canterbury; a monk stood ready to close it at a signal from the Archbishop; but the Archbishop sat in dignified calm.

Sir William fitzNigel hurried in, running the length of the hall to throw himself on his knees before the high seat. "My lord," he gasped, "the knights are arming in the courtyard. They have with them a rabble from the brigands of Saltwood; I saw Robert de Broc and Hugh of Horsea. You must escape, this very minute, before they murder you."

"If King Henry wants to murder me he will do it wherever I may be. I shall wait here, so that the crime is done openly, before witnesses."

"Then, my lord"—the words came tumbling out of the steward's mouth in a frenzy of panic, yet he kept to the legal forms engraved in the mind of every Norman official— "I take these clerks to witness that I hereby resign from your service. I am your vassal no longer. In England no man is bound to follow his lord against the King. I shall serve King Henry, who is the lord of this world."

"Your oath was not lent, Sir William, it was given. But I release you. Go in peace."

Sir William stumbled through the open door, and Grim called after him: "There goes the only coward in Canterbury. I am glad he is a Norman."

FitzStephen and Prior Robert laid hold of the Archbishop's mantle, tugging at him to get up. "They mean to kill you," they shouted together. "You will be guilty of suicide if you go on sitting there. If you won't think of yourself remember King Henry, who was once your friend! Will you let him stain his soul with murder? It's too late to fly to the Young King, or to the Sheriff at Dover. Tonight these men can do what they like. Hide in the Abbey till help comes!"

There was sense in the proposal, as Thomas admitted in the

privacy of his own mind. Evidently these strangers were not acting on the express orders of King Henry; or they would have produced a sealed document, or some token, as a warrant of authority. Within a few hours the Sheriff of Kent could bring his *posse comitatus* to enforce the peace, or if he neglected his duty the Young King could reach Canterbury from London in a long day. It should be easy to hide in the great rambling buildings of Christ Church, where every inhabitant was a clerk who would help to conceal him.

But danger had filled Thomas's mind with icy calm. He saw everyone—himself, the frantic fitzStephen, Prior Robert, the knights—as so many pieces on a chessboard. It was not yet his turn to move, though he knew what his next move should be.

He refused to fly. An Archbishop should not leave his flock in time of danger; his flight from Northampton had given England six years of turmoil, without bringing nearer a resolution of the quarrel. Besides, the Archbishop of Canterbury was too well known to remain hidden; someone would recognize him, by his great height if for no other reason, and then he would be killed meanly, cowering in a corner, his end stained by cowardice. But these arguments were only rationalisations. He would not fly because he was a knight, attacked by his enemies in the open field. He had heard what Grim called after William fitzNigel, and he must show the Englishman that it was the Norman custom to stand fast.

Meanwhile each man in the crowded hall took his own measures in face of this deadly danger. The servants pushed through the little door opening on the cloister; across the square loomed the north wall of the great Cathedral, and once within it they might escape unnoticed through its wide west porch. A few monks gathered by the main door of the hall; they pushed shut the great oak timbers, and bolted it with stout iron bars. Some clerks, visitors unfamiliar with the Archbishop's palace, huddled at the far end of the room, as though they would be safer at a few yards' distance from the intended victim. Most of the monks were forming in twos, as if for a procession.

The same thought was in every mind. Once the desire to kill has been gratified, a man with a bloody sword will slay and slay so long as there is a living creature within reach; it had happened in many towns and castles taken by assault, when women and children were cut down after the last warrior had been slaughtered. Every Norman and Englishman more than thirty years old could remember the terrible massacres of the civil war. If those assassins murdered the Archbishop in his high seat they would then exterminate every clerk in the building.

A bell sounded from the Cathedral. Prior Robert turned in triumph to his lord. "That is the summons to Vespers. See, the monks form in procession; as they should, for the divine office is the highest duty in the world, to be carried out even in the midst of catastrophe. I shall join them, since I am absent from my own community. You, my lord, should come also. You are Abbot of Christ Church, and you should attend the regular office."

Thomas permitted himself to be led to the cloister door, half pushed by the eager throng. He had a new plan, but he must keep it a secret.

Henry's knights would kill him; there was no sure way of escape, and the bare chance of hurried flight was too ignominious to be risked. But his duty to the flock in his care demanded that the murderers should find him and kill him alone; otherwise they would go on to kill all his companions. Therefore he must leave this crowded hall and meet death in the cloisters. It was as simple as the answer to a problem of logic in the schools.

Though he would appear to be seeking the Cathedral, he must take care not to reach it. Shed blood pollutes a church; if he were killed on its pavement the great shrine would be desecrated, a place unfit for the Sacrifice of the Mass. He would delay in the cloister until he was overtaken, alone.

The early dark of December had already fallen. At the black entrance to the cloister he halted, leaning back until his companions ceased to push him. "I will attend Vespers," he said in a level voice, "but in the proper state of my rank. Where is my cross? It must be carried before me."

"But you sent Herbert of Bosham off with a letter, only this morning," expostulated Prior Robert. "Ah, there's the cross. Henry of Auxerre has it. Let him bear it, since your crossbearer is away."

"Yes, that will do. There is no hurry. These monks are too timid, like all monks. But remember: it is not fitting that a church should be polluted with the blood of a sinner. Whatever comes must be borne with patience."

The great iron-bound outer door shuddered under heavy blows. A moan of terror rose from the far end of the hall as the lath-and-plaster partition fell in and an armed figure appeared in the breach. He wore complete mail, so that his face was entirely hidden by the great helm resting on his shoulders; he still carried the hatchet with which he had hewn down the party wall, and behind him another armed figure pressed forward.

While the company shuddered at this first sight of naked steel Thomas was chiefly interested to identify his assailants. At dinner he had noted their faces as vaguely familiar, seen before among the knights of the King's household; but he could recognize every blazon of Normandy and England. To him men in great helms, with painted shields before them, were more clearly labeled than if they had been bareheaded.

"Gules, a bear argent, muzzled sable," he muttered to himself. "That is Reginald fitzUrse. The man behind him bears

Broc with a label of cadency; he must be the Robert de Broc who cut off the tail of my horse."

There was something familiar about fitzUrse, or why did he at once remember his Christian name? Of course, he was one of the vassals of Canterbury. That was too much. Thomas felt the blood hammering in his temples, and his hand groped for the sword-hilt which once had rested on his hip. Here was a vassal come in arms to murder the lord to whom he had sworn homage! FitzUrse was recreant! He must be told so, to his face, in the hearing of as many witnesses as possible.

Meanwhile there was no excuse for further delay. He stepped into the cloister, and at once saw that chance had intervened to keep him from the consecrated sanctuary of the Cathedral. That was all for the best. Now he would certainly die in the open, under the unconsecrated sky.

For the usual passage to the Cathedral, left-handed round the cloister, was filled with armed men, the brigands of Saltwood who had ridden in with the knights. The right-hand passage appeared to offer another way, but Thomas remembered that a disused door of the servants' dormitory lay round the corner, a door that was always locked. The procession must halt when they reached it.

Within the Cathedral it was already dark, save where candles glowed on the choir stalls; the great west door stood open, and the fifty or so choir-monks standing in their places glanced anxiously into the gloom outside. The chant rose and fell raggedly as nervous men questioned their neighbors in whispers. Most of these choir-monks had dined as usual in the Abbey refectory, and walked in procession to their accustomed places; but, as was customary, a few had dined in the palace as guests of the Archbishop, and when they hurried in they brought with them a spate of disturbing rumors.

The King had sent an army to kill his Archbishop, sack the Cathedral, and cut the throats of all the monks in England. That was the least alarming version. Others spoke of having left the Archbishop weltering in gore at his own table. Even the level-headed, who kept their eyes on their psalters and their ears alert to the cadence of the chant, knew that armed men were mustering outside; for they could hear the trampling of horses and see the gleam of torches reflected from mail. Good monks should be ever prepared for martyrdom, and the Prior kept them to their task; but they looked imploringly into the friendly darkness of clerestory and aisle.

Into this ordered ritual, which had continued in Canterbury for more than four hundred years, suddenly burst a shattering interruption. Two scullions, laymen who worked in the monastic kitchen and lodged in the loft above the cloister, dashed through the disused servants' entrance to shout that the King's men were killing the Archbishop just behind them. They had unbarred the outer door of their quarters, to offer a chance of escape to any fugitives. The chant ceased, and the monks left their stalls to peer through the narrow door by which the scullions had entered.

Through this mean little door came the metropolitan cross of Canterbury, still borne by Henry of Auxerre. Then two by two the clerks of the Archbishop's household, walking hurriedly but not actually in flight. Last of all, with Grim and Prior Robert pulling at his arms, the Archbishop himself stood on the threshold, glancing behind him and clearly reluctant to come further. Beyond, in the gloom of the open cloister, which was not quite so dark as the nave of the Cathedral, the watchers could see a group of armed men, hesitating by the door of the palace.

As the Archbishop was hustled into the Cathedral the Prior of Christ Church ordered the doors to be closed and barred. The same thought was in every mind: if King Henry had sent his household knights to murder the Archbishop, they might hesitate to carry out their orders if it meant the desecration of the Mother Church of England; and if, as was more likely, this was an unauthorized act of private revenge, the Sheriff of Kent or the sergeants of the Young King might arrive before the doors were battered in.

But the Archbishop countermanded the order of his Prior. "The House of God should not be made a castle," he protested. "I command you, under holy obedience, to open those doors."

Hearing that invocation, no son of St. Benedict could disobey his abbot. The doors were flung open to the night.

Dazzled by the lighted hall, Sir Reginald fitzUrse gazed uncertainly into the blackness of the cloister. The Archbishop had gone that way, but there was no telling whether he would hide in the Cathedral or take horse to seek refuge with the Young King. It was all very difficult, and he wished he had never undertaken this adventure. When he left Normandy with his three companions they had made a plan, a good plan, with everything cut and dried and no loopholes for mistakes. They would march up to the Archbishop, give him one last chance to absolve the King's loyal bishops, and when he refused, as he was sure to refuse, they would bind him, sling him over a horse, and take him ignominiously before the judgment seat of the master they served. No one would suffer greater injury than a whack from the flat of a sword, no blood would be shed, and no law would be broken. For the King's outburst over his wine surely empowered any loyal vassal to arrest the Archbishop.

The plan had worked perfectly, right up to the moment when they made their final appeal to the Archbishop in his hall. He had refused, of course, and they should have seized him then and there. But there were too many people in the room, and knights accustomed to fighting in mail always felt naked and helpless when unarmed. They had retired to put on their armor, a sensible precaution, fully warranted in the circumstances; and then everything had begun to go wrong.

That impetuous lawbreaker Robert de Broc egged them on. Reginald recalled that he himself had found the hatchet he was still carrying, in a pile of carpenter's tools lying untidily on a half-finished outside staircase. When Broc discovered the unbarred door near the palace kitchen he, Reginald, had used the hatchet to hew down the partition between kitchen and hall. That was house-breach, burglary, and invasion of the Archbishop's peace; three felonies, each carrying the death penalty. He had put himself hopelessly in the wrong; if he went home quietly, admitting that the Archbishop had escaped him, he would hang within the month.

His only chance was to do the King such a service that any breach of the everyday law would be forgiven. They must secure the Archbishop, if they had to knock him down on the steps of the High Altar and bind him with his pallium. There was nothing left but to plunge onward.

He surveyed his companions. The Brocs and their followers would be happy to sack Canterbury and go home to Saltwood; they were not afraid, but it would be difficult to keep their attention to the matter in hand. But Tracy and Morville stared vacantly about them, and Richard le Breton was already edging to the rear. Reginald had led more than one storming party into a breach bristling with sword points; he recognized the moment when the balance hangs even between charge and retreat, the moment when doubtful men will still follow their leader, though already they wish to flee. He shifted the hatchet to his left hand, holding it awkwardly inside his shield. He drew his sword, to wave it aloft in a gesture of encouragement while he shouted the war cry of the King's household, *"Realz!"* (King's men).

As he set off steadily plodding round the cloister to the dark yawning door of the Cathedral he dared not look behind, for the slightest sign of hesitation would have brought his comrades to a halt; but he heard footsteps following, and knew that the war cry and the brandished sword had done their work.

Within the Cathedral the monks were scattering, seeking dark corners in crypt or clerestory where they might escape the massacre. Henry of Auxerre, leaning on the great metropolitan cross which he had been commanded to carry, tried to discern the bearing of the leader who stood beside him. In the murk he could see nothing of his face; but his figure had stiffened, so that his great height would make him unmistakable in any crowd. What was worse, the Archbishop was not attempting to hide; instead he made a stately and unhurried genuflexion, and began to walk eastward toward the High Altar.

With a sob of sheer misery Henry of Auxerre pushed the cross from him and took to his heels. As it swayed, the silver pole flashed in the candlelight, and Grim of Cambridge caught it before it could touch the ground.

Holding the cross erect in both hands, Grim marched with dignity toward the High Altar, the first in a little procession of four: behind came William fitzStephen and Prior Robert of Merton, and last of all the Archbishop. They had reached the steps leading from the north transept to the choir when the doorway behind them was suddenly filled with armed men.

"Where is Tom Becket?" called a mocking voice. "Where is Tom the Londoner? Where is Tom of Cheapside? Where is Tom the son of the drysalter?" The gloating voice continued its insults. Then someone shouted, more seriously: "Where is the traitor, the Archbishop of Canterbury?"

Thomas recognized that voice. It came from Reginald fitz-Urse, his sworn vassal. The indignity that such a felon should shout after him, a felon who drew his sword on his own lord, was more than he could endure. He turned to shout back: "Here am I, no traitor, but priest and Archbishop."

His heart was pounding as it had pounded when he rode out to joust with Engelram de Trie. The time for flight was past. He was a knight, a Norman, and a warrior. He would face these recreant murderers, to answer them as they should be answered. He turned to walk westward, that he might meet his fate standing. His three companions turned also, and walked behind him.

"What do you seek of your lord, Reginald my vassal?" he called contemptuously. The answer came from several throats: "Absolve the bishops, or you die."

"I choose death," said Thomas readily; then his long training in the schools asserted itself, and a little speech followed, composed without conscious thought in his excited mind.

"I accept death in the name of the Lord, and I commend my soul and the cause of the Church to God and Blessed Mary and the Patron Saints of Canterbury. But by the authority God has given me I forbid you to harm my followers."

As he spoke he turned aside to stand before a little altar of Our Lady, cut off from the nave of the long church by a low party wall.

Four knights, faceless in their great helms, loomed over him in the dark; they held their shields high, and their swords were raised. Before the terrible menace of those anonymous figures William fitzStephen and Prior Robert flinched away, to melt into the gloom. Only Grim of Cambridge remained by his lord, holding aloft the metropolitan cross as though it were a standard on a hard-fought field.

The very air of the Cathedral reeked with the scent of fear, for the great building was full of frightened men. Only Thomas, and Grim his squire, confronted death with unmoved hearts. The attacking knights were as frightened as any monk;

they had blundered into a position where the King's law would hang them, and at the same time they imperiled their immortal souls. Reginald fitzUrse, snatching at a last chance of pardon, still sought to win the King's favor by capturing the Archbishop alive, even at this eleventh hour. He threw down the hatchet which hampered his shield arm, and as he came within reach launched a swinging blow with the flat of his sword.

The Archbishop's skull cap fluttered to the ground, but the blow had missed its mark. Thomas still stood erect and defiant.

Three knights closed round him, tugging at his cowl to lift him bodily onto the shoulders of Tracy, who waited with bent back to carry him from the Cathedral. Grim seized him from behind, and the whole group wrestled together, grunting. Suddenly Thomas, that statue of Christian suffering, came to violent life. With both hands he caught fitzUrse by the skirts of his mail, pushing so strongly that his enemies staggered back.

For a moment he stood alone, save for Grim crouched at his back. "Reginald, you pander," he growled through set teeth, "you have struck the lord to whom you swore service!"

FitzUrse answered doggedly: "I owe you no service against the service I owe to the King my liege lord." It was the excuse that had beaten through his brain since he left Normandy, his only excuse for the supreme crime against knighthood, a crime much worse than the mere murder of an unarmed clerk. Presently the King would forgive and reward him, and after that he would be free of reproach.

"*Realz!*" the attackers shouted again, to hold their courage to the sticking point. "In the Lord's battle I shall fight it out toe to toe!" answered Thomas, in the clarion voice of a knight calling his war cry. "Out, Holy Cross!" added Grim in English, as his grandfather had long ago cried at Hastings.

Reginald heard movement at his back, and stole a hasty glance over his shoulder. There was no time to lose. The great

west porch was filling with townsfolk, unarmed burgesses
who feared to oppose mailed knights, but who might intervene if some brave man gave them a lead. The attackers were
experienced warriors, and Hugh de Morville ran back, unasked, to hold the nave against rescue until the deed was
done.

As swords swung aloft for the kill Thomas raised his hands
to his eyes. His racing brain showed him a little picture of all
this happening a long way off, to little figures who were
knights, clerks, and an archbishop; the mannikin of an archbishop must play his part worthily so long as he, Thomas, could
control his actions. But no warrior trained in swordcraft, as he
had been trained at Pevensey, could watch a sword descend
on his head without dodging or throwing up an arm to parry.
If he was to meet his doom erect he must cover his eyes.

He felt a smarting rap on the crown of his head, right across
his priestly tonsure. It did not seem to be death, though that
could not long be delayed. His brain was still working with
astonishing clarity, and he commended his soul to St. Denys
and St. Alphege, choosing without hesitation from the whole
Calendar two saints who were his peers as Martyrs and Archbishops.

The first blow, struck by fitzUrse, had failed because Grim
interposed the metropolitan cross to parry it; but the English clerk was not a trained swordsman, and he held the cross
aslant; the sword glanced down the staff to bury itself in his
arm. Grim fell to the ground, still grasping the cross with a
hand from which blood spouted.

Then Tracy swung his sword again and again, and at the
third stroke Thomas pitched forward. A last shred of con-
sciousness reminded him that he was an archbishop in the act
of martyrdom. "For the Holy Name of Jesus and the safety of
His Church I offer myself to death," he murmured. His legs

groped as he gathered them under his cowl, that his body might lie decently until men came to carry it to burial.

Reginald leaned on his sword, breathing hard. This was not what he had planned, but perhaps it might please the King. Anyway, they were all in it together. Then he recalled that Richard le Breton had not struck a blow; an eyewitness who bore no guilt for the murder might afford inconvenient evidence. "Strike," he murmured, laying a hand on Richard's shoulder; and Tracy added, "Strike, or lie with the Archbishop."

Richard le Breton heaved up his sword. It was hard to hate that crumpled figure on the stone pavement, but he summoned up again the grievance which had brought him from Normandy. "Take this," he shouted, "for love of the King's brother, who died of grief because you forbade his marriage."

Impelled by hysterical rage, his sword smashed through the skull, striking the pavement with such force that the point snapped from the blade. With an oath, Richard flung the useless weapon to lie by the shattered body.

The murderers lingered by the corpse. It was hard to imagine that this messy bundle of rags and torn flesh was Thomas, the great Chancellor, the gallant knight, the skillful falconer, the holy Archbishop; he might yet get up to denounce them. Then from the shadows of the west porch stepped Hugh of Horsea, the brigand clerk who was known as the Evil Deacon. He had followed the murderers because he delighted in murder. With the point of his sword he scrabbled inside the smashed cup of the skull, scattering white brains on the pavement.

Presently the Cathedral was quite silent; until the sacristan crept out from under a choir stall to remove, as reverently as his shaking hands would permit, the pyx which might not remain in this desecrated House of God.

EPILOGUE

Thomas Forgives

IN June 1174, more than three years after the crime which had shocked Christendom from Iceland to Sicily, King Henry staggered out through the west door of Canterbury Cathedral, bleeding and exhausted. He wore only a shirt, from which blood dripped to his naked feet. But the pain of his lacerated body was nothing to the apprehension and misery which filled his mind; and the greatest anguish of all was the conversation of the Prior of Christ Church, who walked beside him and would not stop talking.

"Of course we did not like to make any structural alter-

ations until last year, when Rome pronounced the formal Can-
onization," he was saying, as he offered his arm to support the
fainting King. "Since then we have moved pretty fast, I consider. By the way, have you heard the story about the first
Mass sung in honor of St. Thomas the Martyr? It's a pleasing
tale, though I'm not sure I believe it. They say that, when he
heard of the murder, the Pope commanded a Requiem Mass
in his cathedral of the Lateran. It was to be a most solemn affair, and all the canons of the Lateran assembled in choir, wearing the black vestments of mourning. But when they began to
sing the opening verse, *Requiem in Aeternum,* the roof
opened to Heaven and the Angelic Choir appeared singing
Laetabitur Justus, the opening proper to a Martyr. The canons
naturally joined in, and looking down saw their black vestments had changed by miracle to Martyr's red. A nice story,
but I have never met an eyewitness. However, I was telling
you about the changes in the Cathedral. Besides the shrine,
and the Altar of the Martyrdom, we have another altar where
Richard le Breton's broken sword is dedicated as a relic; the
hatchet dropped by fitzUrse is kept in the Treasury in a splendid reliquary. Yes, I think we have done all that could be expected. But perhaps you were too occupied to notice these
things."

For the first time in his life King Henry made a serious
effort to keep his temper. What had occupied his mind was a
scourging on his bare back, the strokes laid on by seventy choir-
monks. Was this silly Prior deliberately baiting him?

Outside the Cathedral the Prior turned to him again. "Do
you seek absolution, my son? Your penance has been worthily
performed, and I will absolve you with all my heart."

"No, you blasted fool, I do not seek absolution," the King
answered shortly. "Two years ago, in Normandy, I was absolved
from all guilt in the murder; and anyway I was never guilty."

"Then why, my lord, did you suffer this scourging?" The

Prior was certainly mocking him, but never again would he lose his temper.

"Because St. Thomas, my old friend and Chancellor, still keeps up in Heaven the feud which came between us during his last years on earth. I have done everything demanded of me. Appeals go freely to Rome, and clerks are tried in the Church courts. In addition, as penance for driving the holy man into exile, I have promised to go on Crusade if I can leave my realm in safety, to pay the wages of two hundred knights in Outremer, and to found at least three monasteries. I am paying the knights now, and arranging to found the monasteries; but with my realm so troubled I may never be able to start on Crusade."

"And did you show your abhorrence of the murder by punishing the murderers?"

"Well, no, because they were never in my power. Of course they lost their positions in my household. They fled to Scotland, and finally surrendered to the Church. The Pope sentenced them to go and join the garrison of Jerusalem until they died. Three of them are there now, absolved, and as far as I know happy and prosperous. Reginald fitzUrse must be in Hell, because he died in Naples, still excommunicate; he had sworn to go to Jerusalem, but he thought there was no hurry. The other three have their chance of Heaven like the rest of us."

"Then our St. Thomas has been lenient to the miscreants who struck him down. What makes you think he still wages war on you?"

The King's eyes bulged, and his hands knotted into fists; but he took a deep breath, and answered in a calm though shaking voice: "Do you in Canterbury never get news of the outer world? Three years ago I was the mightiest king in Christendom, and my power stretched from Scotland to Spain. Now my false queen has forsaken me, three of my sons are in rebellion, and all my realm is in peril. As I knelt before your

altar to receive the scourging which I admit I deserve, I recalled that the Castellan of Rouen begs me to hasten oversea
to deliver his city, closely besieged by the King of France; and
the Castellan of Alnwick begs me to hasten north to deliver
his castle, closely besieged by the King of Scots. My rebellious
sons hold all Aquitaine and Anjou. I have not a friend in the
world, and my most dangerous foes are of my own family."

He shook his head to clear it, and forced his mouth to smile.
He must not mar this holy occasion by a display of rage.

"Father Prior," he continued graciously, "is there any favor
you seek for your community, from its secular lord?"

He told himself that he had endured more than his middle-
aged health could stand, for his eyes seemed to be playing tricks
on him. The Prior suddenly shot up to a great height, and grew
the hooked beak and bushy eyebrows of an old friend. A voice
from his youth issued from that changed mouth: "Well done,
Henry. At last you have kept your temper under provocation.
The feud is ended, and I shall help you in Heaven as I helped
you before Toulouse."

The King staggered, and as he recovered was surprised to
notice the onlookers staring past him (for a king is accustomed
to being stared at, everywhere, all the time). A dusty horseman pushed his mount through the throng, waving a letter
and shouting: "The King of Scots is a prisoner, and his army
in full flight. In thick fog he rode into the midst of our army
before Alnwick. The north is safe!"

"Thank you, my dear Thomas," Henry murmured. "In future I shall always keep my temper."

In fact he did not, but at the moment he meant what he
said.

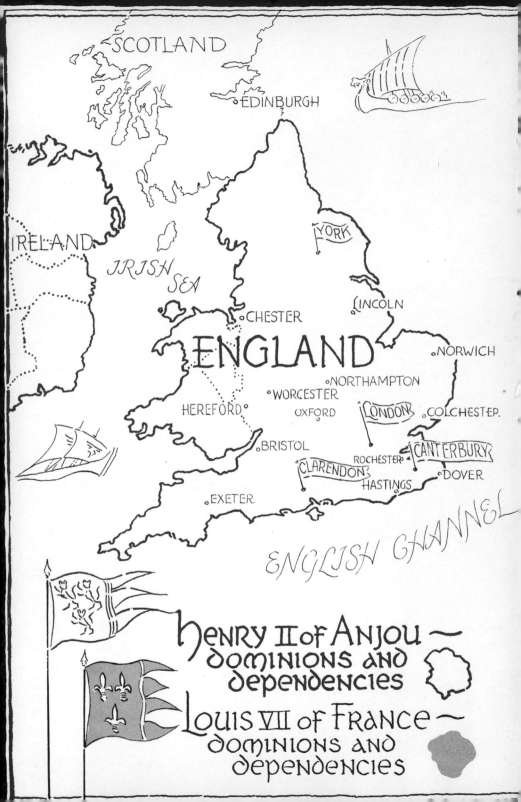

SCOTLAND

EDINBURGH

IRELAND

IRISH SEA

YORK

LINCOLN

CHESTER

ENGLAND

NORWICH

NORTHAMPTON

WORCESTER

OXFORD

HEREFORD

LONDON

COLCHESTER

BRISTOL

ROCHESTER

CANTERBURY

CLARENDON

DOVER

HASTINGS

EXETER

ENGLISH CHANNEL

HENRY II of ANJOU —
DOMINIONS AND
DEPENDENCIES

LOUIS VII of FRANCE —
DOMINIONS AND
DEPENDENCIES